GARDEN *of* SOULS

JOHN WESTON

ISBN: 978-1-0686656-0-8

Thanks Mum and Dad

Prologue

"Somebody help him! I think his heart has stopped!" As the people in the gym circled around Thomas, a man who was in a chaotic haze, he felt his vision begin to fade. "So, this is death then..."

Chapter 1

Thomas was so engrossed in his work that he had forgotten to keep track of time as usual. Mondays were always busy for him. Company work took up most of the day. He glanced at the clock, ten past seven. "Blast!" He should have left forty minutes ago for the gym. He jumped up out of the chair, realising he hadn't prepared his health drink. He rushed to the kitchen, mumbling to himself, "I'm always bloody late." In haste, he tipped beetroot juice, with a tinge of orange and apple juice into a sports bottle and then he was ready to go. Just before leaving, he turned to look at the clock again. Three minutes had passed since he realised he was running late. Screwing the top on the bottle containing his concoction, he continued to talk to himself. "Relax! It's nothing new. You're always late. Let's go." He rushed out of the kitchen into the lounge and grabbed his kit. Out the door, with keys in hand, he headed towards his car.

Parking dealt with, he threw his bedraggled kit bag over his shoulder. Inside the Leisure Centre he ran the membership card through the reader and climbed the stairs to head straight for the changing room. He looked around, hoping to catch a glimpse of Sarah, the Yoga teacher. The attractive Yoga teacher – the lady who instantly brought a smile to his face, which wasn't often these days. He scanned the gym, but Sarah was nowhere to be seen. *No worries*, Thomas thought, *she must be around somewhere...* Seeing her was something to look forward to while he worked his socks off on the spin bike!

Five minutes later, he was sitting on the bike, warming up, knowing full well he'd fall short of the programme set by one of the gym instructors. He had to wind himself up and push. Push, on and off. Another fifteen minutes passed. Then finally he got an urge to push. Push like mad! But that had happened before. He went with it, sweat dripping from his forehead. *Nice*, he thought to himself. *Good job Sarah isn't around!*

His mind began to wander as he suddenly became aware of how lightheaded he was feeling. So lightheaded that he didn't realise he was falling from the bike until he felt his flesh smack the floor. Weirdly though, as his body took the three-foot journey from the bike to the ground, time seemed to suspend in a strange limbo. He felt like concrete, but as light as a balloon all at once. Then he felt fixed to the floor. Stuck to it. Paralysed. But, the paralysis began to subside and now he was light and free. The feeling was unusually satisfying yet disturbing.

Just as he began to notice other people in the gym gathering around him, he was completely unaware of how long he had been suspended like this. He was trapped in this strange, echoey vacuum. He could hear the panic in their voices racing inside his head. Then in the distance, he heard someone scream. "Someone! Call an ambulance! I think his heart has stopped!"

As he stared into nothingness transfixed by the bizarre scene happening around him, unable to do anything, an abstract thought made him silently gasp. *So, this is death!*

Patiently he waited but time had stopped. He was stuck. Waiting. Wondering. Confused. He was struck by the emptiness in his chest. *My heart has stopped!* He felt strangely hollow as the panic began to bubble. If this was death, then he was scared. The fall had caused a cut above his eyebrow that was beginning to bleed. His mind was reaching a very dark place.

A flash of blinding white light exploded in front of him. It struck him wide awake like a splash of cold water would. Now filling the whole space, the light adjusted. Then through the haze he began to see an elderly guy, like a biblical figure, gracefully approaching him. As the man drew closer, Thomas could see his face which was drawn and sallow.

He could see him clearly now and could do nothing but stare at this apparition.

"Hello, Thomas. Sorry about this. I had no option. I'll explain tomorrow." In an instance, the old man was gone. The light had also disappeared leaving Thomas to deal with the panic developing around him.

"He's coming round! He's alive!" Thomas heard someone say.

As Thomas felt his eyes begin to adjust, he noticed people around him. People he knew.

"Are you alright, Thomas?" This voice… he knew.

Sarah!

"Say something, for goodness sake!"

"What would you like me to say, Sarah?" he asked, as he grimaced at the almighty headache that had just began to give him pain.

"Well, it would be helpful to know you're alright! Without you being smart! There's blood streaming down your face, and a huge bruise developing on your forehead right in front of my eyes! You look a mess!"

Tod and Sam, who worked in the gym, came over. The sheepish look Thomas was giving Sarah made them chuckle with amusement, until Sarah pointed out that at first, she thought Thomas was dead. That took the smile off their faces! Gently they helped him sit up and he could see that they were concerned about him.

When he stood up, he was feeling nauseous. His legs felt like jelly.

Sarah turned to Tod and mumbled something about getting the first aid kit. "We need to stop the bleeding before he moves anymore."

Thomas started to get his bearings back. He remembered the light and the old man. "Who was that odd guy? Who was here when I fell?"

Sarah looked at him. "What odd guy?"

"He was here. Standing just by me. All lit up. He looked like a character out of the Bible."

"Thomas, I don't know what you are talking about." She put a plaster dressing over the cut on his forehead. Then she turned to Sam again. "Go down to the canteen and ask for a sweet tea, please."

A few minutes later, Thomas was sitting on a chair sipping tea. "I don't feel sick anymore. Slightly embarrassed, but much better. I just can't believe I fell off the bike and got injured." He was more than embarrassed.

Sarah pulled a face. "Well, you're looking a little better now. What happened?"

"I honestly don't know! I've done that programme before. I know I've missed a couple of sessions, but I felt fine."

"You had me worried."

"Sorry."

"Do you need me to drive you home?"

"Once I have a shower, I'll be fine, thanks."

"Don't get the dressing wet, will you?"

"Don't worry, Dr. Sarah, I won't. Thanks again. You go back to your workout."

Sarah gave Thomas a funny look then went back to her Yoga students.

A shower was exactly what Thomas needed. He started to feel more like himself again. All he really wanted to do now was to go home. He looked around for Sarah. As he did so, he caught a sight of himself in a mirror. His face didn't look good.

He decided that he looked too much of a mess to say goodbye to Sarah.

As he started to walk towards the stairs, he saw Tod and Sam chatting. "Thanks, lads," he mumbled, walking past them. He could feel the heat rising to his face with embarrassment.

"No probs, Thomas," said Sam. "You look a lot brighter, mate."

As if he hadn't had enough bad luck today, now Sarah was coming down the stairs to join them. Thomas was beginning to wish he hadn't stopped to chat! "I'm good now, Sarah" he said, smiling weakly.

"Really? What about your face, then? It looks like you've been run over by a bus!"

Thomas let out a big sigh and hung his head.

Sensing it was time to go, Sam and Tod left Thomas to the mercy of Sarah.

"Don't worry about me, Sarah. I have some cream that will fix that," Thomas said.

"Good. I was thinking I should pop round and check on you tomorrow after the class. About one fifteen?"

"I'll look forward to that." *Wow, perhaps falling off the bike wasn't such a bad thing.*

She gave Thomas a gentle hug and then a kiss on his good cheek.

He smiled at her and headed for the exit. "See you tomorrow."

She waved him goodbye with a smile.

He strode up the ramp to the car park. As he drove towards home, he had Sarah on his mind. She was a real sweetie, intelligent, and very attractive! At that point, he misjudged a bend on a narrow lane. "Sod it," he said firmly, and out loud. "Concentrate on your driving. Otherwise, you'll have more than cuts and bruises."

Chapter 2

The next morning, Thomas woke up feeling bright and back to his normal self. By some miracle, the dressing on his forehead had stayed on. He showered, shaved where he could, cleaned his teeth and headed downstairs to work. This was so much better than driving down the motorway. And quicker! He switched on the computer and made himself a coffee while it was loading. *7 am, nice and early.* The good thing about working from home was he could start when he liked and could take breaks whenever he needed.

Thomas looked out of the window and smiled as the sun gained height over his village Apple Tree End, a quiet, secluded place surrounded by picturesque landscapes supporting an abundance of wildlife. A winding narrow lane lead into the village. There were only eighteen houses, including Thomas's. No. 6 was where he laid his hat.

As he came out of his daydream, he realised that someone was knocking on the door. No one knocked on the door or rang the bell unless there was a delivery. He wasn't expecting a delivery and he didn't have any guests coming over. He wondered who it could be. Thomas got up from his seat. That particular someone knocked again. Louder. *Someone's impatient*; he thought as he headed for the door. "Okay, okay,

I'm coming." He opened the heavy farmhouse door and was staggered for a moment. Standing in front of him was the old guy from the gym. The same odd man he saw when he'd fallen from the bike. *What in the heavens?* Thomas asked himself silently.

"Hello, Mr. Pink. May I call you Thomas?"

"Thomas is fine." He managed to answer, wondering *what the hell is going on?*

"I said I would pop round and see you in the morning, and here I am."

Thomas quickly gathered his wits. "And there's me thinking I had won the lottery," he said cheekily.

"No such luck; it's just me."

"Oh well, perhaps next week."

Thomas looked hard at the old man. He was definitely odd. He still looked like a character from the Bible or from the sixties. He was wearing a peculiar white robe or dress, and sandals, which wrapped themselves around the largest feet Thomas had ever seen. Round the man's neck was a snappy little scarf. He was tall, well over six feet. His skin was white as a sheet and he had enough hair on his head for half a dozen blokes. *Why was he in the gym? Surely, he isn't interested in exercising. Perhaps he works there. Yes, that must be it.*

"Do you work for the Leisure Centre?"

"Oh no, Thomas. I just happened to be there when you overdid it on the training bike."

"I didn't see you when I came round." An eyebrow twitched in confusion as he tried to recall, just to be sure. *Nope, he wasn't there. Until...*

"Oh, I had to go, and now I just needed to check on you."

"Check on me? Why? And why did you say sorry when you spoke to me or did I dream that?"

"No, you didn't dream it. And yes, you are right. I did say sorry because I had to check on your heart."

"What? You did what?" Thomas started to freak out.

The odd guy lifted his hand up slightly, speaking in a calm, soothing voice. "Don't panic. It's no big deal where I come from. It's..." he paused. "I will explain everything very shortly."

Somehow that calmed Thomas down a little. It was strange. He didn't know this weird old man standing on his doorstep at all, and he should have felt uncomfortable being with him. But he didn't.

"The reason I'm here is to discuss some important matters."

Thomas sighed. Of course. "So, what are you selling? Health insurance?" He glanced over to the forecourt over the shoulder of the old man, where his own car was parked. There wasn't another car in the forecourt. *How on earth has this old guy got here to my house?* Thomas started to wonder. His house was in the middle of nowhere; driving a car was the only way to get there.

"I don't need a car when I travel."

"Hang on a sec. How did you know what I was thinking?"

"If I may come in, I will explain."

This odd-looking character had Thomas curious. He thought for a moment. *What harm could it do?* Curiosity won over logic and caution. And he had about fifteen minutes to spare before he really had to get back to work. He ushered him in.

"Fifteen minutes will be more than enough time to hold your attention."

He did it again. That was the second time! His words jangled Thomas's nerves. He became a little anxious about inviting him in, but he wanted to know more.

"Shall we discuss it over a cup of tea?" The man asked, bringing Thomas back to reality.

Thomas indicated an armchair. "Make yourself comfortable while I make the tea." He headed for the kitchen.

"I'll have the same as you have. A little soya milk, no sugar."

That comment made Thomas trip and fall down the kitchen

step onto the floor and thump his knee. "Ahh, sod it!" He stood up, rubbing his knee.

"Are you okay?"

"Yeah, I'm fine," he said, not wanting to sound flustered. "I'll get on with the tea."

"I like what you have done with this lovely oak floor with the red brickwork around the fireplace. It's a terrific room. No doubt the oak came from those people in Cambridge."

Here we go again, thought Thomas.

"Proper nails, too. I bet this cost a fortune. David and Michael did a nice job on the patio doors. As they did with the tiles outside. Let me guess. From Great Hallingbury? What's the chap's name who laid them? Freddie, was it?"

"I am really sorry but I'm trying to make the tea! The noise of the kettle is making it difficult to hear what you are saying. But I have a good idea of what you are implying."

With that, the odd man appeared at the top of the steps. "I have a feeling I've irritated you, Mr. Pink."

Thomas looked at him. "I have a better word than that." He was struggling to manage his anger. The teapot was in his hand, and for a millisecond, he had the urge to throw it but instead he took two steps backwards putting the teapot on the kitchen counter with considerable force.

"Brilliant!" said the odd man.

"What?"

"Brilliant."

Unnerved, Thomas said nothing. Instead, he placed his hand around his chin as if to look like he was thinking, whilst he was trying to calm himself down.

"The vibrations coming from you at the moment and the way your anger peeked were way off the chart. Then you managed to control it. Absolutely brilliant! That's why you're the man for this job."

"What are you talking about? What man?! What job?"

"Please bring the tea over here and I will explain."

"And you'll tell me how you know what I'm thinking?"

The odd man nodded and sat down at the kitchen table. Thomas was still confused but brought both cups in and handed one to the man. He sat down too.

"So, what's your name?"

The man smiled. "Where I come from, we don't communicate that way. We have a recognition. It's not really a name."

"Ha! More strange stuff."

"It's just how we have evolved over the years. What I am called is rather difficult to understand. It isn't pronounced, so what you call me is of no consequence. But I will work your way... Ah, I know." A smile crept across his wise face. "What's your youngest son's name?"

"I think you know that one."

More smiles crossed the odd man's face. "Yes, you're right, it's Dominic. Call me Dominic."

"Okay." Thomas sipped his tea. It was still hot, and so he blew on it like he always did. "Dominic. Your name is sorted. Now, please can you tell me what's going on? You obviously don't need any information from me as you seem to know it all."

"I suppose. Hmm, maybe not all. We're only allowed so much."

There was a question that had been bothering Thomas since he'd met this Dominic. "Am I dead? Is this the phase before afterlife? Did I die at the gym?"

"No."

"Then, are you a magician?"

"Oh, that's definitely not the case!" The old man smiled brightly.

"Are you a spirit? You know, like a ghost?"

"Not in the sense that you know. I'm a light spirit. An evolved soul. No disrespect to you, but if I tried to explain, you wouldn't comprehend and most likely nor would anyone else on your planet. My race has been around a few million years before you lot were even thought of."

"And there's me thinking you're off your trolley," said Thomas with a bit of sarcasm. Dominic didn't look too pleased. Thomas didn't really know what to think. He was at a loss. This was all too farfetched for him. It was hard to take any of it in.

Just as he thought it must be a joke, to his utter amazement, Dominic disappeared from the chair he was sitting on and appeared in the lounge next door! It was the most surreal moment. One second he was there, in front of Thomas, then he was gone. Just like that!

Thomas started to panic. He could feel cold sweat streaming down his forehead. *I must have hit my head harder than I realised.* He felt very nervous. This guy, Dominic, or whoever he was, just didn't make any sense to him. He couldn't believe what he'd just seen with his own eyes. As he was trying to work out how it had happened, Dominic appeared, in the same chair, he'd just vanished from!

"You're freaking me out! Please don't do any more magic stuff!

"Oh, it's not magic."

"Okay. Whatever it is. It's unsettling!

"There was a reason I did that," Dominic said.

Now he's trying to calm me down, Thomas thought. "I've figured that one out," he said. "You're proving a point. What I don't get is why you've turned up here? Who are you? What do you want from me?"

Dominic looked straight through Thomas, put his hands together, slowly moving them as if they were cold, he muttered something under his breath.

"Okay, I hope I have just demonstrated to you that I'm not odd. Not off my trolley. Not crazy. Just different from you.

Like I said, I'm an evolved being. I'll use that word because I'm sure you'll be more comfortable with that."

"Right, an evolved being you say. I'm fine with that at the moment. Just no more shocks. No dramatics, please. Just try to be normal for the time being."

"I promise."

Thomas wondered how capable Dominic was of being normal. "Yes, I will. I'll be normal."

Thomas frowned. "That means you need to stop reading my mind!"

A little sigh escaped from Dominic. "Sorry, but where I come from, that's how we communicate. Force of habit. It won't happen again."

"Okay."

"Shall we finally get on with this Thomas?" Dominic sounded a tad impatient. "I'm not reading your mind again. I've realised how I sounded then. It's just that I've taken a year to make contact with you when it should have taken ten minutes. We have been..."

"Who's we?"

"Can I answer questions when I have finished, please?"

"Carry on." Thomas could hear himself sounding anxious. He couldn't help it. Curiosity and nervousness were getting the best of him.

"As I was about to say, we have been monitoring you from the day you were born, from the very moment you came into this world. You and six hundred and ninety-three other new-borns entered your world at exactly the same second. On that day, something momentous happened. You were all breached. There were other births, but not breached. These difficult births activated a chemical reaction within all of you. You were then all exposed to a power surge from the Accline province."

"Where?"

"A province that sits very far north of your universe. The

impact on all of you was unforeseen. Quite incredible! As it stimulated the next evolutionary seed within all of you, it allowed premature development to take place with the help of the old souls. It was very exciting for the observers."

Thomas could see Dominic was still excited, even now, fifty years after the event.

All the time Dominic was explaining why he had made contact, Thomas never took his eyes off him, but he just couldn't keep still. He kept fidgeting. He scratched his head. He frowned. He rested his chin in the cup of his hand. He fiddled with his ear. He was showing the stress he was feeling inside. It was clear Dominic was picking up on this.

"I have a feeling that I'm not doing a good job getting through to you, Thomas. I haven't tuned into your psyche."

"My psyche?"

"I feel I'm losing you."

Thomas shook his head. "You are getting through okay. I think! But what you're saying beggars belief."

Dominic sighed. "I usually have no difficulty breaking down communication barriers. But you have a very strong will and a busy mind too. That's why you have been chosen." He leaned forward. "I have an idea, a different approach," he said, pointing his finger to the ceiling as if something was about to materialise above his head.

Thomas glanced up. Nothing was happening up there. "Well, as long as the new approach doesn't take another year," he quipped, feeling somewhat profound.

Dominic was taken aback. "Goodness me, no! We don't have that kind of time."

"So, what do you suggest?"

"Well, I can calm your thoughts. That will make your mind more receptive to what I'm saying. It will also allow me to tune in."

"What exactly does that mean?"

"Umm".

"Don't pussyfoot around. Just tell me!"

"I'll know how you work. What you think. What you expect. How you rationalise situations. Armed with that information, I'll be able to communicate on your terms on your level. I need your permission, though."

Thomas didn't hesitate. "Okay, okay," he sighed.

"Why don't we go and sit in the lounge?" Dominic suggested.

They sat in comfortable chairs, and within minutes, Thomas felt that Dominic had him all worked out.

"Right, now down to business." Clearing his throat, Dominic began again. "This sort of power surge activity only happens once in a million years. It's so rare. It makes all of you special! The ones that are left anyway."

"What do you mean? Oops, sorry! Questions after."

"That's okay. I'm amazed you stayed quiet so long! Anyway, we have a task for you."

Thomas immediately shifted his weight in his seat and opened his mouth to ask what task. Dominic raised his hand, stopping him from interrupting. Thomas sighed again, this time with some irritation.

"Now, the reason you've been selected is quite simple. You're needed. You have that something special inside you." He leaned back in his chair. "That's the good bit out of the way. Now for the not so good bits. You have a knack... a real knack of knowing how to cock things up. It's never-ending."

"Like what?" Thomas asked defensively, convinced he knew what was coming.

"Well, where do I start? All these marriages. Companies. They've all gone wrong."

Thomas stood up. He needed to walk around. It had been hard enough dealing with those problems when they had happened. Now a perfect stranger was ramming it down his throat. If he could get even more anxious, now was the time. He was losing his patience.

"Shall I continue?"

It was now Thomas's turn to put up his hand. "No! What was all that r-rubbish you came out with about t-tuning into my psyche, so you would know how I worked?" He could hear himself beginning to stutter. It seemed difficult to put his words together. It took a second or two of deep breathing to compose himself. "Well, what's done is done," he said more calmly. "This conversation is all unnecessary rubbish."

"Rubbish or not, I'm just stating the truth. That's how you are. That's how you express yourself. You need to understand yourself if you are to survive. Critical analysis of one's own state of mind is the supreme level of acceptance."

Thomas was now exasperated. He started pacing up and down the room. Then he suddenly stopped. "You said *survive*. What do you mean?"

Dominic ignored the question and continued as if he hadn't heard Thomas. "Of course, it's not for me to judge. That's for when you eventually return. But rubbish or not, mistakes have consequences. If it makes you feel better, it's not just you, it is all of humanity."

Thomas couldn't help but think his answer was evasive. He asked again. "You said IF I'm going to survive?"

"Can I answer that a little later? It will make more sense then, I promise."

Thomas thought for a second, realising he wasn't going to persuade Dominic to do something he didn't want to do. The talk about survival made him worry about dying. Death seemed like a terrifying idea at the moment.

"Okay. But how am I supposed to figure out all this other stuff? I'm not clued up like you."

Dominic looked hard at him. "Where do you think all the wisdom you own is held?" Thomas sighed. He really didn't give a jot about wisdom, his or anyone else's.

Dominic brushed Thomas's reaction aside and continued.

"You must listen to what's inside you. You've managed it before. Now unfortunately, your life moves far too quickly. There's no real thought given to any decision. You must get into the habit of not making mistakes."

"I know that, but you're exaggerating that point. Why?" He hesitated. Then the penny dropped. He began to see where this was going. "You're preparing me for something, aren't you? You mentioned some job earlier."

Dominic looked steadily at Thomas, but he didn't utter a word.

"I'm not going to like it, am I?"

"Hold up. There you go again. Presuming."

"No, I'm not, that's just me."

"Yes, that's just you, and you're who we need. Just... finely tuned."

Thomas gave Dominic a look showing how he felt. He was miffed yet again, being forced to think deeper than he would normally during, well, just a working day. He tried to concentrate on all the cockups he had made, the ones he had worked hard to forget. After all, he couldn't change anything.

Feeling very agitated, he sat down, resting his forehead in his right hand. He realised the consequences of all the problems he had faced and how his decisions had changed the path he had planned. He sighed again, this time out loud.

He sensed Dominic looking at him, but more sympathetically now. "Good, it won't take you long."

For once, Thomas didn't move except to lift his eyes from staring at the floor to giving Dominic a brief cursory glance.

"You're a good chap, I have to say," said Dominic. "Many of the problems you faced weren't of your making. You cope well, and that's what we're looking for. You're respectful and responsible. You know how to lift your spirits when you're down. You are mentally strong, without a doubt."

"Me?" Thomas shook his head. "I don't think you have the right chap. Are you sure about this?"

"Oh yes!" Dominic now sounded confident. "You and the others have been in our sights for a long time. And it's these qualities that have placed you at the top of the list."

"List! You have a list?"

"Yes, of course," said Dominic, nodding his head and beginning to sound impatient. "Now, do let me finish what I have to say."

That annoyed Thomas. He was in no mood to listen to all this fate business. And Dominic should know that.

Dominic knew but carried on regardless. "Right. Now I've forgotten to mention your greatest asset... It's your anger, perfectly demonstrated in your kitchen a few moments ago when you were making tea."

"My anger?" Thomas felt angry, alright. Anger brought on by the stress from listening to Dominic. In fact, he couldn't remember the last time he'd felt so annoyed. He looked angrily at Dominic. But now his breathing was changing, becoming deeper, ending with just an irritated sigh. Was Dominic just adding to his disbelief?

"It comes from the deep reaches of your soul, Thomas Pink. There's no malice with that anger, and that is a rare quality. You're special."

"I wish you would stop saying that. It doesn't sit well." Listening to all that had positively disturbed him. He didn't think he wanted to be any part of it, whatever "it" was.

Dominic ignored him again. "I understand you have issues with what I've been saying, but I need to say even more. Try to relax for another five minutes."

Thomas stayed in silence. He closed his eyes and tried to calm his breathing.

"You must realise that your species are not the only life force in the universe."

"Yes, I am sure of that. My father used to tell me about it."

"Well, then, I'm another life form."

"And is this the shape or look you all have where you live? Or where you come from? I mean, you have huge feet. And your hair, there is so much of it! Are you all like this?" Thomas had so many questions.

Dominic chuckled, "I dressed up for the occasion. I might have got it a little wrong. We're light spirits. No physical body. But don't concern yourself about that now. Given time you will have a better understanding."

"I understand the words you're using. But I can't get my head around what you are saying. Overwhelmed would be an understatement."

"As we continue to discuss this, you will get used to it. I promise you that." There was unwavering confidence in Dominic's tone.

"Okay. Question time. Why were you in the gym last night?"

Dominic looked flustered, all of a sudden. He started to move his weight from one large foot to the other, giving the impression that the question was awkward.

"Easy," he said after a moment. "To make contact."

"Hang on a sec. You said you had been trying for a year. I'm confused."

"I have been, but your mind is so busy, it was impossible. I had to resort to a more dramatic approach."

Thomas didn't like the sound of that. He wished he hadn't started the questioning. But he had, and he needed to know. It was too late now. "What was that?" He focused on Dominic, picking up on his reluctance to continue. "What did you do differently when you and I were in the gym last night?"

Dominic looked uncomfortable and made an odd expression on his white face. Then, clearing his throat, he spluttered. "Okay, don't be alarmed. Take a deep breath or two."

"Why?"

"You're about to find out."

Thomas could tell he wasn't going to like whatever Dominic was struggling to say.

"While you were cycling in the gym, I encouraged you to push yourself over your limit. That enabled me to stop your heart for a few seconds, which helped you to see me."

Thomas couldn't comprehend what Dominic was saying. He thought he was joking. But then he realised he wasn't. "That was you! Me falling off the bike that was all your doing! There's me panicking, thinking that I have a heart problem." Thomas shook his head in disbelief. It felt like a bomb had just exploded in his mind. "You made me look like a complete idiot in front of forty-odd people! Worst of all, Sarah thinks I could drop dead any second. And now you just come out with this revelation as if it's nothing!"

"If you remember, I did apologise. You should look on the bright side. Your heart's in great shape!"

That didn't calm Thomas down. He was too angry. "Apologise!" His anger grew. He placed his hand carefully on his damaged face, reminding Dominic of the incident. "All this sophistication emanating from you and that's all you come up with? What rubbish!"

"Oh dear, you're not happy, are you?"

"You could say that."

"I suppose the method we used appears a little crude. We didn't have a choice. Contact was essential for all of us. We needed a bridge between us and you. Time was becoming critical."

There was a short pause. Neither spoke. Silence slipped in between them like an elephant in the room.

Thomas was thinking again. This download of new information was throwing him. Too much stuff had happened in such a short space of time. Extraordinary stuff.

Dominic broke the silence. "Can I assume you're okay with all this, Thomas? You haven't gone white and fainted. So, I will take it that you are good with all this."

Thomas looked up at Dominic, exasperated.

"I assumed you could cope. Maybe I was wrong? You look seriously miffed."

"Let me get this right. You come from a galaxy all these light-years away. You've been trying to make contact for a year and failed. So, then you decided to kill me! In the gym of all places! In front of all those people! Why there, for God's sake? I fall off the training bike, cut my head open, get a bruise covering half my face and you ask if I'm okay with it all!"

"That's a little harsh. I couldn't avoid the cut. Oh, and the bruise. But what I can do is make both go away if they're bothering you." Dominic stood up and walked over to Thomas, who was full of disbelief. He put his hand across Thomas's face.

"All done," Dominic stated casually.

"All done what?"

"Your face. It's back to normal."

But Thomas didn't believe it was that easy. He just sat there in absolute silence.

"You don't believe me, do you? No one has doubted me before. Look in the mirror. Go and see for yourself."

Jumping up, Thomas headed towards the cloakroom. He stood in front of the mirror and looked at the dressing Sarah had put on. That was there, alright. He got closer to the mirror searching for the angry bruise that he had seen when he had woken up. There was no bruise. He tore the dressing off. *No cut on my face! Nothing*! It had disappeared. All he could do was stand in front of the mirror, trembling, not knowing what to do or say. He was speechless.

Dominic called out to him. "Well, what do you reckon? Cool or what."

That brought Thomas to his senses. This guy was the business. "Yes," he said, coming out of the cloakroom. "But you made it appear in the first place."

Dominic twitched a little, but that was about it. Begrudgingly, he apologised once more. He began to explain. "As you still don't understand how things work, I will point out the parameters we adhere to."

"Hang on a second. How am I supposed to understand what I haven't been told yet?"

"I don't want to overload you with information. I'm in your psyche, but you're not in mine. You communicate through your thought and mouth. I work differently."

"How do you do it?"

"From one soul to another. That's how we communicate. It's pure. But it won't take long to learn your way. Bear with me."

Thomas nodded while trying to understand what he had just been saying. He thought he had it. Or thereabouts.

"May I continue? You might explode any minute, right?"

Thomas nodded again. "I'll be quiet."

"Free will is the key to your existence. It is with every life form ever created. But when the likes of me turn up, the vibration levels increase."

"Sorry? What do you mean? Vibrations."

"Energy levels. Mine are much higher as an evolved soul, so I can be picked up on the darksiders' radar."

"That's not good."

"It's okay in short bursts. But I'm not allowed to overstay on this planet."

"Why not? Who would know?"

"Darksiders."

"Darksiders?"

"The beings you'll come up against!"

"Well, I'm sorry to be a spoilsport, but I still don't understand what you're talking about."

"Darksiders are on the other side of nature. No, you won't understand yet. But you will."

Dominic started to fiddle with one of the buttons on his robe. Thomas hadn't noticed them before. He began to wonder if Dominic was nervous. That didn't look good on him. His imagination went into overdrive; what did the odd man mean by 'being'?

"Here's the thing... The massive thing you need to know. There's a big problem with your world. I'm not talking about recycling, the hole in the ozone, or global warming. The real problem, the stem of all these issues on Earth, is the people in this world. It's all going the way of the dark side. Mankind is leaning towards the abyss, and that's not acceptable. With free will being the substance of your existence, it can only deteriorate further."

Thomas was getting fidgety.

Dominic fixed his gaze on Thomas and made him feel that it was almost as if it was Thomas' fault.

"I have been sent to change this imbalance. With the people we already have here, the Shides, and with your help, we can do it."

Thomas clasped his hands together. His knuckles went white. "Who sent you?" he snapped.

"The Maker." Dominic stated calmly. "I will keep this very simple."

"The M-m-aker?" Thomas stumbled over the words. "Is that who I think it is?"

"Exactly."

"You call that simple?"

"I could make it more complicated if you want."

"My God!" He bit on his knuckles. He felt dazed and completely out of his depth. Dominic was so casual about all this as if he was talking about dinner. "Please, carry on." Thomas needed to hear more now. And know everything.

"As I said earlier, you are top of the list now."

"You said all the children born on the same day have this special ability and you're telling me I'm top of the list?"

"Well, you weren't but you are now."

"How's that then?"

"The others have returned."

"What? Do you mean that they're dead?"

"I suppose. If that's your interpretation of returned. They're now in the Garden of Souls."

"And what's that?"

"All in good time."

"How did they die?"

"We sent them on the same job we want you to do."

"And now they're dead?"

Dominic shifted slightly, almost imperceptibly.

Thomas looked hard at him. "So, how did you manage to lose them?"

"Unfortunately, we underestimated the darksiders, and we overestimated our people. Or should I say your people? Humans. But it was entirely our fault. That will never happen again."

"Well, as you're talking to me, you would say that! And why me? I still don't know why me! I'm nobody."

"Ah, not quite. You're somebody. Somebody that nobody knows. I might add somebody who doesn't lose heart! Very crucial for our mission. And now it seems you've asked a million questions! Your attitude has pushed you to the top of the list."

"I understand you don't want to fail again! I certainly wouldn't want you to! But I can't guarantee you won't. And if it's me you want, well, if I'm up to the job remains to be seen."

"We believe you're our man."

Thomas gave a half-smile. "Hmm... That's a long way from achieving whatever it is you require. I certainly don't fancy dying!" He hesitated; an awkward smile etched on his face. *Surely*, he thought, *Dominic can appreciate my reluctance.*

Dominic continued anyway. "What we have in mind for you is something that's been going on since time began. It will sound shocking to you right now but that will ease when you have evolved."

Thomas stared. "Evolved? So, I'm going to be like you? Big feet and a mop of hair."

There was a glint in Dominic's eyes, and his face cracked a smile. "I'll see what we can do about the hair." He pressed on, "we need you to send back ten of the biggest culprits contributing to the rise of the Dark Force."

It took a few seconds for this idea to fully register in Thomas's head. "You are saying send back? Kill? Get rid of?" Thomas began biting the skin on the knuckle of his index finger. What he had just heard was the last thing he expected, and it shook him to the core. Admittedly he hadn't been sure what to expect, but certainly not what he had just heard. This was all getting too much. He sat down, his hands fidgeting in evident anxiety. Dominic waited in silence.

After a minute or two, Thomas jumped up and started pacing up and down in the room once more. Then he stopped and turned to face Dominic. "Dark Force. You mean the Devil, don't you? When you say Dark Force, that's the Devil you are talking about!"

Dominic nodded. "We don't use that word. Stop pacing, Thomas. You'll wear that fine rug out." There was half a smile on his white face.

"You said you want me to kill ten people? Am I hearing correctly?"

"If that's the word you choose to use. We do, yes."

Thomas sank back into his chair. "That's absurd. I haven't got it in me to kill anyone. Flies or mice in the house, yeah. But that's it. Not people."

"These beings we want you to dispose of aren't people."

"So, what are they?"

"I know I keep on repeating myself, but you will understand in the end. And I say this again – you'll understand if you agree to help."

"Oh, yeah. Really?"

"Yes. Now to answer your question, they are corrupt souls. They need to be sent back."

"Where to?"

"It depends."

"Depends on what?"

"If there is any remorse."

"How could anyone possibly know that?" Thomas started to calm down a little. This was the moment Dominic needed.

"Try to look at it this way, Thomas. You have the endorsement from the highest possible authority. The Maker Himself. You will be his soul remover, collecting souls and moving them on. Consider this. You and everyone on this planet has a right to evolve. The right! At this moment in time, that right is being undermined by the minority, purely for their own gain, or misguided thoughts."

"You really believe I can do this job? Someone who has no idea where or how to start? I don't have a clue. I have no experience. I'm certainly not the bravest of men. So, Dominic, I've been chosen, with the highest endorsement possible? This sounds far-fetched. Now I'm beginning to wonder whether you are really here, or if this is just a dream brought on by a knock to the head."

Dominic nodded. "I am here."

Thomas began to panic; his stomach began to churn over and over. His forehead was hot. His hands were sweaty. Dominic was in front of him. He was real. But this was all so much to take in, and clearly very hard to believe. There was definitely something about Dominic that made everything he was saying believable. Thomas couldn't explain it. It just made sense, like a wave of refreshing clarity washing over him. Like a cold shower. That didn't mean he wasn't nervous though. He was. Terrified, in fact. He needed a hug from someone he loved but there was definitely no chance of that. The longer he thought about what Dominic had said, the worse he began to feel. He knew he was no hero. He could be brave in the face of a normal, regular life, yes, but a dark side of life? Threatening missions? Sending back souls? He sat down, clasping his sweaty hands tight, rocking back and forth. He could feel his body language telling him he needed strength – from somewhere! Dominic just sat there watching him, not saying a word. Thomas was struggling to concentrate now. He had never felt this bad ever in his life. He needed to say something. Anything. He plucked out the first thing that came into his mind. "How did you move from one room to another earlier?"

Dominic gave half a shrug and smiled. "It's part of what I do. As I mentioned, I am a light spirit. As all my kind are. We can engage with the light on your planet and as the light moves, so do we. We focus on where we want to go and we're there."

"Just like that?" Thomas gave it some thought. "How the heck would that work?" It was an interesting idea. He began to feel the grip of terror that had swamped him dissipate.

"Yes, just like that."

"So that's why there was no car parked in the drive?"

"You're getting it! And you're calming down. That's useful."

Thomas did feel calmer. "You spoke of Shides earlier. What's a Shide?"

"One of us. A volunteer who watches over the evolution of your planet. We are all trying to keep a balance. We have found in previous encounters with other new worlds, it's the early stage of development that requires a good deal more attention. Your planet is no different. Pure goodness is lacking. Evil is developing. And I have to be honest with you, we're struggling."

"But if you have your own people here, why are you struggling?"

"Oh, every planet, or new life – call it what you will, is different. We never know until developed life takes a hold."

Thomas sat there wide eyed, feeling like a school child having a lesson. "Do Shides all have powers like you?" *This is taking an interesting turn.*

"Yes, but you wouldn't know it."

"Do they all have big feet? Masses of hair?"

Dominic laughed. That shook Thomas, the best he had seen

was a smile, and he had started to think that Dominic had no sense of humour. *Things must be looking up.*

"Shides look no different from you or anyone else. They have positions of power in every industry. Banking, government, energy, sciences, the forces, the Police, and still we are losing the battle."

"Who to?"

"Drugs."

"I know what drugs are. But you need to explain more."

"Particular drugs in particular countries are produced by just a handful of people. They infect, corrupt, kill, and control so many. These people need removing."

"Why can't you just go and deal with them?"

"It doesn't work that way. Free will. It's all to do with free will."

"So, are you saying you want me to travel halfway around the world to kill ten people who deal in drugs?"

"Not quite. Well maybe to South America. But there are only three there. Your action, if you agree to work with us, will set off a reaction which will take care of a lot more people in the drug business than that. And there will still be seven others not related to that business that have to be sent back."

Thomas laughed.

He couldn't help it. He felt so amazed at what was being said. "Great! It just gets better! I'm flattered to know how you imagine me capable of killing three of the most protected people in the world! How the hell do you expect me to achieve that? Surely, they have their own army!"

"We will give you all the help you'll need."

"Oh yeah?"

"We will not let you down."

Now Thomas was slowly realizing the gravity of what he was dealing with and by the sound of it, it was best that he didn't have anything to do with Dominic's hair brain scheme –

it was far too dangerous, far too dodgy. *I would be crazy to comply. But how am I going to get out of it?* Somehow, he sensed he was no match for Dominic. "You do know I am fifty years old? Of course you do."

"A very minor detail."

"Fifty years old, a minor detail!"

"By the time you have gone through the enhancement process at the Garden of Souls, you will be able to take on the world. Gradually, mind."

"Now you're talking! You have been here now, what, almost two hours? And that's the only bit I like. These Shides you have, how long have they been here?"

"Over different periods of time. They come and go depending on requirement. The Shide who co-ordinates the programme has been here for two hundred years."

Thomas let out a big sigh as he looked at Dominic in disbelief.

Dominic ignored his stare. "His name is Jonas Barley, and he runs the largest energy company in the world."

"How long?" Thomas wasn't going to leave this one. "How old? How old is he?"

Dominic smiled broadly. "We don't age like you do."

Thinking that was more than a little odd, he also wondered if Dominic was beginning to lighten up.

But when he spoke, he was just as serious.

"We have reached such a high state of evolution, we don't really go through the dying cycle anymore. We just embrace the light and submerge. It's complicated, but in short, we are light spirits, always there. Spirits of light. Everything I have told you will be become clearer. And there is more. That's if you decide to join in and help us."

Thomas sat quietly for a moment trying to look as if he understood, but he knew he needed to know much more. None of this was simple, and Dominic was expecting so much of him. "How does the enhancement work you talked about happen with... what is it? The Garden of Souls? Do I get enhanced through drugs of some kind?" He corrected himself. "No. No, of course not. The way you've been talking, it's got to be more sophisticated than that, hasn't it?"

"Enhancement is just a word to describe evolving. The description probably dates back a few thousand years or so. Let me explain. As you know, we have followed your life. So far, we have seen the terrible sadness you have put yourself through. The traumas you have suffered. Life hasn't been too kind, has it? But what we have seen and like is the way you get on with it. What you have inside is unique, so what we can do is condense the essence of who you are. That will exaggerate your existing qualities beyond imagination. This will enhance your strength. We have the ability to control cell growth and reproduction through higher vibrations. A bit of tweaking and your body will be as good as new. More like a thirty-year-old."

"Are you saying I will look thirty again?"

"Well, not quite," Dominic said, chuckling. "You will have a slightly younger appearance. Maybe a little over forty."

That was disappointing. But then Thomas thought about it. "Forty–ish? That's not bad."

"Ego doesn't belong with us. That's the other lot."

Two hours of listening to Dominic reminded Thomas of fairies at the bottom of the garden. A multitude of ideas went through his mind – all the mistakes, the misplaced trust and the foolish errors he had made. The people he knew and loved, and those who had passed on. It all came rushing back. Melancholy seeped into his consciousness. His eyes glassed over. There was so much to think about.

Dominic sat in silence, watching and waiting. Thomas wanted to get rid of all the needless thoughts that blocked his mind. He knew Dominic needed a decision. He was very aware that much was being asked, and offered, but this was a perfect stranger. Someone from another world. Again, he paced. Then stopped. Suddenly knowing, Dominic could see into his mind anyway, so he spoke out. "There's me thinking nothing could be worse than my last divorce. The one I didn't see coming. I worked for forty years, struggled, and juggled the insurmountable stress, and I had managed to accumulate as much as possible. What for? So she could steal twenty of those years?"

"That's life here on your planet," Dominic suggested. "Now, and unfortunately for the foreseeable future."

Thomas wasn't paying attention. "You know, most of the time, she just watched lots of daytime TV. And read. She read so many books. So many I've lost count. And there's me, naively thinking life can't get any harder. Keep your head down and it will all go away." He rounded on Dominic. "Then you turn up!"

Dominic nodded.

Thomas took a deep breath. "But I reckon I've got it wrong. Just a bit. I don't know what to think or what to say about the job you're asking me to do. Worse, I have this awful feeling death is just around the corner. I'm not keen on dying just yet. Not like the other lot. You did say they all died, didn't you?"

Dominic nodded again. "Yes." It was obvious he wasn't comfortable having to agree.

Thomas felt drained of all his energy, utterly deflated. "And I'm not the bravest person in the world, but you must know that. What I'm saying is, I don't know what to do."

Moments slipped by before Dominic spoke. "You won't die on the job we're asking you to do."

"You can't promise that, unless you're allowed to look into the future."

"No, I'm not, nor can anyone else."

"Then all your reassurance translates really to, we hope you don't die."

"Really Thomas, you're becoming dramatic."

Hmm, Thomas thought about that. "It has rubbed off from my ex. She was full of drama!"

Dominic began to smile. "While we were watching you, we did note what she got up to." He stood up. "Look, Thomas, I can't imagine the anxiety you are going through, or what your deeper thoughts are telling you. What you've heard from me is daunting. I do understand. It's very difficult. There is something I'd like to suggest if I may."

"What?"

"Get in touch with your soul. Dig deep. That's where the essence of life lies. Calm your mind. Listen. Your soul will tell you what's right for you. And while you're working on that, I'll leave you in peace." He walked towards the kitchen. "I'll make the tea."

Thomas, without realising he was doing it, nodded his head. He felt anxious. His palms were sweaty as he rubbed them together. His mind was blank, that wasn't unusual! He would often daydream, but this, this was different.

While Dominic rattled around in the kitchen with cups and a teapot, banging cupboard doors and making a racket, Thomas sat quietly realising he had no idea how to get in touch with his soul. *How on earth is that even possible?* After all, it had to be said, his mind was in a dreamlike state. They had talked half the morning. He hardly felt like he understood any of it, but somehow, without realizing it, he had absorbed everything Dominic had told him. He jumped up and started to pace the floor, but then he changed his mind and went anxiously into the kitchen. "Sorry, Dominic, I think I need to go over this again."

Dominic put down the teapot and looked at him for a moment. "I think I'll take you on a little trip. It won't take long, and it might help you decide. Before you say anything, it will only take an hour."

Thomas gave the tiniest smile. "Shall we have our tea first?"

Chapter 3

As Thomas put down his empty cup, he felt Dominic's hand on his shoulder. Then nothing! They were gone. It happened so fast he couldn't work out how or why. Were they somewhere else? Yes they were. He was completely disorientated. He felt as if he was in a horizontal elevator that had suddenly stopped. He stumbled and fell onto the dusty ground.

"What the hell was that? What happened?" He got back onto his feet and brushed himself down.

Dominic smiled. "That was your inaugural light trip."

"Whoa, I don't know about a light trip. Lightheaded, more like. It's... I'm a bit, eh, I can't get the words out. I know I've just got up, but I need to sit down again. Otherwise, I'll fall down."

"You'll get used to light travel."

Thomas took a deep breath. Light travel sounded good. No, it sounded brilliant. And the thought of travelling as fast as the speed of light was mind-blowing.

"So, where do you think you are?"

Thomas had no idea. He wasn't ready for questions yet. He was trying to rationalise in his head what had just happened.

"Thomas, are you with us?" Dominic felt rather chuffed. "This is the exact spot I was aiming for. And here you are, daydreaming! But do have a moment or two!"

"Are we...?" Thomas thought back across their earlier conversation. "Are we in South America? In Columbia."

"Well done, Thomas! You're right."

"That's amazing. A second ago, we were in my kitchen!" He looked around, dazed and fascinated. He wanted to see more. "Come on then!"

"Are you sure you're okay?"

"Yes! I think so."

"This is an isolated part of Columbia. The area produces more opium than any other. Rich pickings for the cartel running the district."

Thomas took a step, but his foot didn't land properly. "Hold up. I'm not right yet. I'm wobbly."

"That'll pass, sit down again. When you're ready, we'll take a good look around. Don't worry. No one can see you."

Thomas thought about it for a moment. *Wow, we can't be seen!* The possibilities of what he could do with that sort of power began to circulate in his mind. "Awesome." Thomas stood up and he looked out across the sea of colour. "Poppies?"

Dominic nodded his head.

As they walked into the field, they could see hundreds of workers toiling hard, while men with powerful weapons looked on. The workers were arched over, backs crooked from their daily labour. Sweat dripped from them under the intense sunshine. Although there was no pressure on Thomas, and of course, no one could actually see him, he couldn't help but fidget. He was witnessing evidence of a huge drug trade.

"Is this a typical poppy field?"

"Typical for this district, yes." Dominic replied.

Although he knew he was invisible, he was still uneasy. He was standing so close to these Columbian gunmen supervising the harvest of the poppies. Grown for greed, to supply misery.

Suddenly, one of the workers stumbled to his knees with exhaustion. A guard was immediately beside him butting him with his gun and shouting at the poor soul. He struggled to his feet.

"Poppy fields as far as the eye can see, Thomas."

"I get the message. That's all I see. I feel as if I'm going from one nightmare to another. Problem is, I'm not going to wake up from any of them, am I?"

"This is reality, Thomas." Dominic's tone had changed. There was a sadness to it. As Thomas surveyed the scene around him, he understood why. Hundreds of zombie-like people struggled to harvest the crop. Children were working too and not playing as young children should. It was heart-breaking to witness such cruelty.

"These people are slaves. Skin and bones. Drained. Dressed in rags and surviving in tin huts. Life expectancy is limited."

Thomas looked at the armed guards. They were unnecessary. There was no resistance from the workers. The cartel had them all hungry and addicted. The smell of death around him was real. Overpowering. He did not want to be there.

"Come on, Thomas, let's go." Dominic performed his light travel magic again.

They landed a second time. Thomas didn't have a clue where he was. He didn't fall as he had on his first light flight, but that didn't mean much. He looked around at the new surroundings. They were inside a processing plant, in a complex series of laboratories full of scientific equipment. This was all new to Thomas. It was difficult for him to appreciate the gravity of what he was observing. It began to sink in as he did a head count of the laboratory workers. He counted twenty. It was hard to tell if they were men or women, because their faces were covered as a dentist might be. *Chemists probably. Apparently, the next stage in the drug process*, he thought, but it was not something he particularly wanted to see. He felt sick to the pit of his stomach.

"Have you spotted the other labs?" Dominic pointed ahead.

"Yes, I've seen them."

There were at least four other labs with probably one hundred men working on processing. This was a serious setup.

"Where are we in the world?" he asked.

"We're somewhere in Mexico. This operation with its five laboratories is just the tip of the iceberg."

Thomas turned away from the chemists to better hear what Dominic was telling him.

"The same cartel running this processing plant has many others. Around forty-five percent of the world's production is controlled by these people."

They walked outside to get a better idea of the whole set up. The impression Thomas had was of a well-organised operation. Security was clearly a top priority. The guards were soldiers, very professional, and strategically placed to deal with outside threats. In the grounds behind the laboratories, he noticed a dozen helicopters. He was so relieved that he couldn't be seen right now.

"The helicopters are the escape plan, should it be necessary," explained Dominic. "And over there." He pointed to the right of a helicopter. "Those are the sleeping quarters. These chemists, as you call them, work for a solid month – seven days a week. Then get a break while another team replaces them. The process never stops."

Thomas shook his head in disbelief. "It's run with military precision. Extremely efficient, with security almost impossible to breach. Look! They even have high towers with guards."

"Thomas, listen to me, it has to be breached… and destroyed. Billions of dollars are generated annually. This is big business. The money is dark and fuelling the rise."

"Fuelling the rise of what? No, don't tell me, more power to hell. More control for the Devil."

Dominic looked at him. "Something like that, Thomas. Now I need to show you the last piece of this lucrative pie. The other end of the drug business. The consumer."

A moment flashed by, and they were gone. Gone from that Godforsaken place where the Devil sows seeds for his soul collection, thought Thomas.

They were consumed by the noise and activity of a city, a big city. It was evening and busy. Very busy. Thomas was sure they were in New York, he had been there once, a while ago. He didn't like it then, and nothing had changed now.

He took a deep breath in. All this whizzing from one place to another and experiencing different situations at each location was making him lightheaded. Desperation in Columbia. Greedy professionals developing the product to get their hands on the misery money in Mexico. This all made him angry and utterly contemptuous of the people trapping others with the poison they produced. Pushing people to the edge of life. Now they were in this sprawling city, just another place of greed and despair. He didn't want to see it anymore.

"Come on, Thomas."

He shook his head. "No, I don't think I want to."

"Come on. Not much more, I promise. You'll be back home in five minutes."

"Okay," he said quietly with absolutely no enthusiasm. He had to run to keep up with Dominic, who had a huge stride. As he did so, he spotted two rough young men accosting a woman in her fifties who was just leaving a supermarket laden with shopping bags. They knocked her to the ground and screamed at her, demanding money. The poor soul was so frightened that she pushed her handbag towards them. One of them grabbed the bag while the other snatched the groceries. They disappeared into the darkness. Thomas's stomach wrenched. What a traumatic day. How could Dominic believe he could make a difference, Garden of Souls or not? "Dominic! Surely you can do something."

Dominic turned to look at Thomas, who was shaking with anger. "I wish I could."

"So, what's the bloody point of showing me this?"

Dominic bowed his head. "It will be you who can make a difference, Thomas."

Just as he was about to demand an explanation, he saw something further down the street. He moved closer. Yet another shocking sight; dealers selling drugs. One was taking money, he was the big one, and no one would argue with him. The others were dishing out small packets. Five people conducted business with them in a matter of moments. Completely in the open. He turned back to Dominic. "Where are the police?"

"You thought a moment ago the Devil sows seeds for his soul collection. This is the place he harvests them." He frowned, "I have used your word, Devil, to emphasise the gravity of the dilemma. You won't hear that word from me again. As for your question, the police can't be in a hundred places at once."

Thomas threw his hands up. *How cynical!* "Is there no control? How do they expect to eradicate drug use?"

"That's where you come in. They do it with your help."

For a moment, Thomas thought Dominic was joking. *You are not joking, are you.*

"One more place to see. Come on. Hurry up. Otherwise, we'll overstay."

Thomas groaned. "More grief, no doubt." He followed Dominic into what looked like a rundown clinic.

"This is a free hospital, Thomas, run on donations. Don't judge it by its looks, it functions, and the staff are angels."

"Proper angels?"

"No, not quite Thomas, but they do qualify."

As they walked to the front hall, there was a security guard on duty. Looking around, it was obvious that conditions here were awful. No wonder it was free. The building reminded him of mansion houses from the eighteen-hundreds where the occupiers, aristocratic of course, would have had servants, and a cook, no doubt. But those days were gone. He didn't think this place had been painted since!

"Joseph Ward is up the winding staircase and round to the left, Thomas. That's where we need to go."

"Okay, come on then," Thomas hurried up the stairs. He knew what he was going to see was going to be bad and he didn't want to dwell on wasting time. As they reached the ward, the only nurse on duty was in the baby unit. Another wave of anxiety smothered Thomas, giving him an ache in his stomach worse than before.

"Here we have twenty-five babies," Dominic whispered, "born to mothers who are addicted to the drugs we've seen. Grown, harvested, processed, and ready to be sold on the streets."

"No more! Don't show me any more!" croaked Thomas, looking at the helpless children, pale and wan. Their little lives hadn't even begun. Yet they were all doomed. It was just a matter of time. Tears streamed down his face.

Dominic had no words of comfort. Instead, he looked straight at Thomas. "Maybe these children do have a chance in life."

"So, how can I possibly make a difference? How am I supposed to help these children?"

A second later, Thomas ended up flat on the floor of his own house. He sat up, feeling like the wind had been completely knocked out of him. Dominic was seated in a chair, looking rather subdued. Neither of them had anything to say.

Noticing the clock on the wall, Thomas jumped to his feet. "Bloody hell! Thirty minutes. I feel I've aged thirty years, not thirty minutes." He'd had no notion of time while he had been travelling thousands of miles. He sank back into a chair. He needed to calm his mind and let everything sink in. Tears found their way back, filling his eyes. "I've seen enough troubled souls in just this one morning to last me ten lifetimes."

Dominic suggested a cup of tea was in order, Thomas was happy to agree.

Thomas stood up. "That's my job," he said.

Five minutes later, sipping tea, Thomas felt his mind beginning to settle. Dominic began telling him about the Garden of Souls, and its purpose, explaining how every soul in existence, including his, had been through the process it had been created for.

Thomas's imagination fired up. What he heard was beyond dreams, beyond the realms of reality he has known all his life. He leaned forward enthusiastically.

Dominic held up his hand. "No questions, Thomas. There is an order of preference we must adhere to. The plan is to get you into the Garden of Souls. Then like magic, any questions, or any thoughts that are in your mind will be satisfied. In an order that will complement the process."

"Process?"

"It can't be explained. It must be experienced. How long would you need to organise a week off work?" Dominic asked.

"A week off? I need that long, do I?"

"If you want to deal with the evil you have seen and come out unscathed, then yes, you have to prepare."

"Monday," said Thomas eagerly. "I can be ready Monday."

"Good. And you are going to keep this to yourself."

"Yes, I understand that."

"That means you will have to tell lies."

Thomas hadn't thought of that! It made him uneasy, but he appreciated he couldn't tell anyone. He drank the last mouthful of tea, stood up, then began to pace the room again. "I prefer fibs."

Dominic smiled. "Of course. Use what you must. Now what I'm going to say, I will repeat again and again, and it is critical that you understand."

Thomas looked at him nervously.

"When you return from the Garden of Souls, you will be different. Your vibrations will be a lot higher."

"What do you mean? What do you mean?"

"Just a second. Listen! I'm telling you."

"If I don't ask what you mean, I won't understand."

"Sorry I keep on forgetting. It's difficult for you. But when you come back from the Garden of Souls, you won't forget."

"Why did you forget then?" asked Thomas.

"I thought you'd ask. As I've tuned into your psyche, I must accept all of your ways. Not remembering is one of them."

Thomas stood with his mouth open. "So, you're on my level now?"

Dominic chuckled. "That's another reason why you were chosen. You never miss a trick. But I can switch between the two of us, so we can be on either level."

"Oh," said Thomas, looking uncomfortable.

"As to your question, when you have been through the process of enhancement and start locating darksiders, you'll be noticed within a five-meter radius, depending on the sophistication of the darksider. When you start to succeed, you'll attract even more attention." He looked at Thomas seriously. "With all your activity, you'll no doubt be light travelling, so you need to be aware that disguising your trail is imperative. Otherwise, it will shine like a beacon in the darkness of history."

"Seriously? Dominic, that's pretty heavy. How does that work?"

"What's done stays done for anyone to view. It becomes written in history."

"How can anyone see how I've travelled?"

"We won't go into too much detail today. You'd probably struggle to take it in, especially in your frame of mind at the moment."

Thomas disagreed. He wanted to know now and showed that by mumbling to himself, throwing his hands dramatically into the air.

Dominic paid no heed and continued. "You'll feel better soon, as the sadness leaves. You'll become stronger mentally from those experiences. Now drink your tea."

"I already have."

"Well, then, you better get back to your work! You're going to be off for a week, remember! I'll give it a couple of days, then I'll contact you to go into more detail about the best bit of the job regarding the Garden of Souls."

"What's that then?"

"Something to look forward to." A smile crept across Dominic's face. "Relax. Try to work out what you are going to say to Sarah when she comes round. That's her name, isn't it?"

"I'll say hello, I suppose. Anyway, how do you know she's coming round?"

"Just a lucky guess. I am curious to know what you are going to say when Sarah asks about your face."

"Oh, sod it. That's a point. What do I say?"

"One more thing, I nearly forgot. If you need to contact me, just clear your mind, and concentrate on what I've told you this morning. I'll leave a channel open. That way, I can pick up on your thoughts."

Thomas stared at him. "What?"

"Bye, Thomas!" Within a second Dominic was gone.

Thomas looked around him, but he had not rematerialised. He was just thinking about work when Dominic suddenly reappeared. "Heck! I wish you wouldn't do that! You almost gave me another heart attack. Can't you warn me when you're about to turn up? Ring a bell or something?"

"Sorry, Thomas. I didn't think, okay, yes, I can. Anyway, all this is very hush hush."

The look Thomas gave him said it all, but he still blurted out what came into his mind. "Firstly, we've already discussed this. Secondly, do you think I could tell people how you stopped my heart? Made me fall? Smashed my face open? Then while lying on the floor dead with blood oozing from the cut, you have a chat? Then you bring me back from the dead? Without forgetting the best bit, you pop round the following morning to work magic on my face as if nothing had happened, all while you are drinking a cup of tea. No, wait! I was wrong! This is the best bit! You transport me halfway round the world in about thirty minutes."

"You're making me wish I hadn't popped back."

"Now, even I would wonder what people would say if I mentioned all of that."

"So dramatic, Thomas!"

"Bye!"

"Bye!" And demonstrating his gentle air of superior knowledge, Dominic was gone.

Thomas laughed. He walked past the kitchen to the little work area he used when he worked from home. He had so much on his mind that he started talking to himself, which always happened when he was overworked or stressed. Now he was speaking out loud which was unsurprising after the morning he had endured. "I must finish my work before Sarah turns up," he heard himself say. "And get myself comfortable."

Chapter 4

He sat at his desk and tried to absorb the contents of his work timetable. There had been no time to plan, but with work on top of his agenda, planning had to come first. He sat staring at the blank computer screen. Concentration was lost to him. The morning's events weighed heavy on his mind. His mind began to wander. He considered the wretches in the fields, then those very young babies, and realised Dominic was right. Ideas whizzed through his mind. *Changes!* "I'll show them changes," he said out loud. His sadness eased as his determination grew. Then without thinking, his hand touched his face. The cut and bruise had vanished, thanks to Dominic. *Impressive!* He stood up and headed for the mirror to take another look. He shook his head in amazement. *No sign of any damage. Nothing.* "Now what do I tell Sarah?" *This is going to take some explaining.*

He was trying to think of a plausible explanation when the doorbell rang. He panicked. *Surely that couldn't be her. Her class hasn't finished yet. Is my brain working?* He walked to the door mumbling to himself. "Best open it and I'll find out!" As he turned the handle, he had an inspired thought. He suddenly remembered things his Dad had told him when he was a lad about spiritual activities, healing and phenomena that he really did not understand at the time. His stories had fascinated him when he was young. Now he could use that information to get him out of this sticky situation. He opened the door and Sarah stood there smiling. Her smile soon faded.

"Your face! I can't believe it! What happened? What have you done? How did you do it?"

"You're early." Thomas put his hand to his face. "What's wrong with my face?" he said, knowing full well what she meant.

She stared at him. "Nothing! Absolutely nothing. That's impossible," she said incredulously.

"Cor! Do I look that good?"

She gave him such a look. She loved it when he teased. But right now, it wasn't going down well. He knew he had just seconds to explain something not far short of a miracle. "My father."

"What about your father?"

He didn't like telling fibs, it didn't feel right. He said the first thing that came into his head, making a weak attempt to explain. "What happened to your class?"

It didn't distract her for a second. "Jane's taking the class. I was concerned about you, so I visited you a little earlier." She stepped closer to him so that she was just a centimetre from his face. Her jaw dropped as she stared at his skin. "What do you mean your father? What did he do? There's nothing there."

He could feel her hot breath on his cheek.

"How on earth have you… The cut. All the bruising. Where have they gone? How did you do it? What did you do?"

Thomas struggled to think what to say. "I'm as impressed as you are. I got up this morning, looked in the mirror. I couldn't believe it; it must have been my dad's work. I talk to him every night and ask for his help. And, of course, my mum. You know I'm bad at communicating. But I talk to them and last night was no different. I thought about my dad and then started chatting, as if he was still with me on this plain. But I must be honest, most of the time it's like I'm talking to myself. Because of yesterday's events, I was not myself. Spirits pick up on that, you know." He didn't know whether she has accepted his explanation or not, but he continued anyway, half believing his story himself. "Apart from asking for the usual information, I asked him to mend my injured face and reassure me that my heart was healthy and isn't going to fail me."

Sarah nodded. "Go on."

"Well, I had already applied a little concoction of creams on the cut and arnica on the bruise, so I jokingly suggested to Dad, he change it to magic cream." He smiled and looked sheepish, but Sarah wasn't convinced. What's more, she hadn't taken her eyes off his face. "Then, during the night," he continued uneasily, "something must have changed. I really felt my dad around! I'm sure he was sending me spiritual healing."

Now Sarah looked surprised. She stepped back. "I had no idea you believed in spirits."

"I did mention it to you. You didn't seem too keen."

"Yes, I remember. It wasn't that I was not keen. It just brought back poignant memories."

"Mm." For a moment, he stood there dreaming. His eyes watered a little. He thought of the past at his parents' house. Discussions regarding spirits and healing powers consumed their evening. Those conversations continued until his father's death.

"You look so sad, Thomas. Are you alright?"

Thomas relaxed a little. He had managed to get out of a tight corner by telling a big fib.

"Anyway, there's not even a scar! How does spiritual healing work?"

"Haven't a clue about that bit! Come on in. We can't stand in the porch all day. Let's go and make a cup of tea."

"In the absence of something stronger, tea will suffice," smiled Sarah.

Thomas glanced at her. The doubting expression on her face had eased. Whether she believed him, or understood, remained to be seen. He assumed he was in the clear for now. He didn't say another word, but as Sarah walked into the house ahead of him, he saw a little shiver run through her. Maybe she sensed her mother or some other spiritual presence.

How Thomas wished Dominic hadn't needed all that information to be kept secret! As he analysed what he'd told Sarah, he concluded as fibs went, it was not too serious. He had thought of his Dad last night and his face was completely healed in a spiritual way, even if it was just a couple of hours ago. He just hadn't mentioned Dominic.

Sarah followed him into the kitchen, "It's amazing. I still can't believe it." She was still confused about his face. "I must tell Alisha."

That grabbed Thomas's attention immediately. That was all he needed! If she confided in her cousin, then half of Essex would know before the day was done.

"I'd rather you didn't tell anyone. They'll think I'm loopy."

Sarah smiled. "Yes, but Alisha has a keen interest in healing and spiritual things, though she never discusses anything with me."

"I wasn't aware of that."

"As far as I can remember, she used to go out with some chap years ago. He got her interested in that stuff. I've no idea what his name was."

"In that 'stuff'. The most fascinating subject ever, and you call it stuff."

She looked at him realising she had touched a nerve. "Yes, you're right. I'm sorry. It's more than just stuff. After all, look what you've achieved." She gave him a shy smile. "Now, where's my tea?"

"Coming up." He switched on the kettle. "By the way, how's your cousin, Alisha doing?"

"Not too good. Thomas, I'm concerned. She's having more tests in the next day or two." Sarah looked worried.

"More? That's dragging on. Which hospital?"

"Oh, the local one in Epping. But apparently, the tests are done in town somewhere."

"Where? Do you know?"

"I think, she said Chelsea."

Thomas knew that hospital. It was the cancer treatment hospital. That didn't sound good. He kept it to himself. There was no point in upsetting Sarah.

"When I mention you and your newly acquired knowledge, she will ask for all the details. Will it be alright with you if I tell her about your – shall I say incident – in the gym?"

Thomas laughed, "Incident? Sure. You can also tell her that my dad has assured me that my ticker is as good as the day I was born."

Sarah laughed. "I bet she'll call you. Will that be okay?"

"No problem. It will be good to talk to her."

Isn't it bloody amazing, he thought. *Where one little fib leads? It'll get me into trouble for sure! Sod it! It's all Dominic's fault. I suppose I could ask him to help me sort this one. See how good he is.* He couldn't quite remember what was wrong with Alisha. She had said something about headaches, but he wasn't sure. It certainly wasn't the time to ask.

Sarah stayed a while, just chatting. That pleased Thomas considering the morning he had been through. Sarah, now in a better mood, seemed less sceptical regarding the miracle cure too. In fact, she seemed to have a plan that involved her poorly cousin. Thomas had a pretty good idea of what was going on. It was written all over Sarah's face. She'd witnessed a miracle. Now she was expecting some help for Alisha. Unfortunately, he didn't know how to help her without Dominic. After all, the miracle cure was Dominic's doing. Sarah's expectations and all their implications dawned on him. He shuddered as he remembered what Dominic had said earlier. "Thomas, it's down to free will, sorry. It's out of my hands."

"Why did you jump?"

Blooming heck, nothing escapes her. "Someone must have walked on my grave."

But Sarah was looking straight into Thomas's eyes. He could see the anguish on her face. *She's counting on me*, he thought. *Hoping for another miracle. Dominic has just left, and already I need to contact him*, he thought. *I'll try when Sarah leaves.* A sudden wave of guilt came over him. Now with her relying on him, he realised that he had forgotten all the bad things he had seen earlier, all the sadness, all those babies dying. But if he were expected to help, how could he cope with everything? He realised suddenly that Sarah was almost sitting on his lap.

"Are you okay Thomas? You seem miles away."

"I was just thinking about Alisha." *Another little fib.* He had no choice. "You must let me know the outcome of the tests."

Sarah gave him a warm, tender smile, showing him trust.

"Are you going to the class tonight?"

"Wouldn't miss it, six thirty, isn't it?"

"Yes, don't be late."

"No, I'll be early. I want to get my spot in the hall."

Sarah gave him a little hug and a kiss on the cheek and was on her way. Thomas tenderly touched the spot where her lips had touched his cheek. *There is no denying it, we have chemistry.*

It was one o'clock, and he had done precious little work. If he was going to manage time off next week, he would need to get his head down and finish what needed to be done, and some extra, probably. He hurried to his work area. *Oh, blast! Dominic*! He had to speak to him about Alisha somehow.

No sooner had he thought of it, Dominic was in his head. *What do you want?*

The sudden voice made Thomas jump.

You need to be more focused to do mind to mind! And just think what you want to say.

What do you mean more focused? I only just thought about it when you came into my head!

Unfortunately, there isn't a lot of time for you to learn, but we'll work on that. Not now of course. We need to sort out your small dilemma. I knew you'd call. I assumed you'd have difficulties, so I kept in touch. I left an open channel.

Whoa, going without going, that's cool! Will I ever learn that?

Probably. That's another thing we'll talk about later. Let's resolve the issues you have with Sarah. I know I left you in an awkward position. But you have handled it well, although you've dug a hole for yourself. After your visit to the Garden of Souls, you will have the ability to deal with the problem.

Thomas felt his anxiety drifting away. *Great!*

Dominic nodded, then smiled, although Thomas couldn't see that. *You'll be okay now to get on with the workload. Next week will be hectic.*

Are you going now? I mean...

Dominic chuckled. *Yes, I'm going, no need to stay. You're quite capable of dealing with any problems that might occur between now and Monday*. Then he was gone.

Thomas was feeling pleased with himself. *No worries about Alisha then, although I have to stay quiet.* Now he had to plan for his time off next week and work out a way to tell Sarah. *Something will turn up.*

It suddenly dawned on him that he hadn't been in touch with the office. What was worse, he couldn't remember where his mobile phone was, or when he last used it. It was obvious the last twelve hours had taken their toll. *Is it in my kit bag?*

Where did I leave my kit bag? There is so much whizzing around in my head! Eventually, he realised he had seen it in the porch when he had opened the door for Sarah. He grabbed the bag and unzipped it. Festering inside was his blood-stained top, but no phone. With all the mayhem of last night, with Dominic turning up, and then Sarah, he had forgotten to take his top out and wash it.

"I can't be without it," he groaned. Then it dawned on him; the phone must be in the car. He found it hidden behind the driver's seat. He sighed as he noticed that he had three missed calls from the office. *What a crazy morning it has been. Right, first things first.* "Let's call work." He dialled and waited. "What's what?" he asked.

"Everything is just fine." John said laughing. "I've dealt with it."

"Thanks, that's great. I'll be out of contact for the best part of next week, so I'll call in daily, mate, okay?"

"No problem," said John. "All under control."

Thomas put the phone down. How he was going to phone in daily was beyond him at the moment. *Well, just another small problem for Dominic.*

The remainder of the day flew by; his head was busy with work and thoughts of the morning's happenings. He glanced at his watch. It was 6:15 pm. "Yoga! Blast! I'm late!" He was talking out loud again! "Sarah will think I'm dead." He pulled on a fresh kit, and with car keys in his hand, he set off.

Chapter 5

Thomas went straight into the class, choosing a spot at the back. He wasn't great at yoga, but it did serve a purpose and kept him fit. The class was full of women. They managed the yoga positions far better than the men could. They made it look so easy.

The hall was beginning to fill, but there was no sign of Sarah. He felt impatient. He needed to get on with the class. He had so much to do. When Sarah walked in with a big smile for the class, she came straight over to him.

"Thomas, you made it."

He nodded. She focused on his face. He had forgotten about that.

"I still can't believe your face. It's amazing," she whispered.

Thomas put his hand across his face. "I'm as impressed as you are."

"It has been discussed at great lengths this past hour."

"So that's why you're late," he said quietly.

She smiled.

"You've seen Alisha then?"

"Yes, you knew I would."

He smiled to himself.

Sarah glanced at her watch. "Class time! Tea in the cafeteria after?"

"Love to," as much as he wanted that, he had very little time. But what could he do?

Sarah scurried away to the front of the class. As he settled into the warmup movements, he looked around at the class again. The only other man there was William. He was a little older than Thomas but looked the worse for wear. His attention drifted from William to Saffron. She nodded at him. He squeezed half a smile at her. She was easy on the eye with a figure to match apart from a generous bottom but there was something about her that bothered him.

"Right, let's get moving. That means you as well, Thomas Pink! Daydreaming is for after class." Sarah kicked off with harder warmups then moved into full swing. The hour soon slipped by. Sarah switched off the soothing music. "That's it! Well done, everyone. Thanks for coming. See you all on Wednesday."

The hall started to empty. Sarah was caught up chatting with a few of the women, one being Saffron. Thomas stacked away the mats for her and then began pacing up and down, in and out of the storage room, fiddling with the mats, waiting for her to finish chatting. "Come on, Sarah," he mumbled to himself.

Eventually, he had no option but to go over to her, something he'd been avoiding. He beckoned her with a little flick of his head. She saw what he wanted and cut the conversation short. "Let's all go for tea," she said.

In the cafeteria, they squeezed around one table, pulling over three more seats to accommodate all of them. Thomas had hoped it would be just the two of them sharing the time. Instead, half the class had come, which disappointed him immensely. Still, he was happy to be there. He checked on who was having what, then went to place the order and with help from Sarah, he collected the teas.

The ladies chatted about subjects Thomas wasn't really interested in, but he gave the occasional smile of participation and started to relax. After his eventful morning, almost anything would bore him. *This is a pleasant way of spending a little time watching the world go by.* That thought lasted all of five minutes.

He began watching a variety of people coming through the turnstile, coming to swimming lessons, classes, and to the gym. It struck him how many older people used the centre. Then he thought of Dominic and how old he was. *Three thousand years, was it?* He had to think about that for a minute or two. He couldn't remember. And what Dominic called the others on this planet? *Got it. Shides. I bet they don't go to the gym.*

Dave, one of the lads Thomas trained with, came over.

"How are you doing?"

"Good, now." They spoke for a bit, although Thomas was still tuned in to the conversation at the table, which had now moved to divorce. Dave grinned and knowing that Thomas and his three divorces were a sore subject decided to go. "I think I'll leave you to it."

Thomas focused on the conversation two of the women were having. He hadn't really paid attention to them properly until now. They were discussing ex-husbands while the others listened. He soon picked up the gist of their stories. One was already divorced, while the other had just started her divorce. She was giving tips on how to infuriate her future ex-husband. That riled him and he set his mood up for an argument. He turned his chair in towards the table, had the last slurp of his tea, moved the cup to one side, put his elbows on the table and then focused completely on the two women.

Time hadn't been kind to them, they were under fifty, and had no sparkle. *Definitely past their sell by date.* The way they spoke and the things they said told him that they were two hard hearted women. He glanced over at Sarah, trying to read her face. She looked embarrassed and shocked at the things they were saying. Her discomfort fired him up even more. She seemed to be the only one at the table who had a glow. He looked at Saffron again. She was pretty, but there was something about her that made him shudder. There was aggression in her voice when she gave advice to Timmidy, the woman who was about to be divorced. It was the usual rubbish, hiding the children from her ex, and other underhand acts. No one sitting around the table knew the ins and outs of a divorce. But listening to Timmidy, Thomas knew that she was bitter about something. The house had to be sold, and she was miffed about that.

"I'd use any excuse for him not to see the children," she growled.

Sarah looked over at Thomas. "Are you going to the gym?"

"I might."

She threw an energy bar across for him.

"Thank you," he smiled as he unwrapped it. Sarah went on talking to Abigale.

Thomas continued listening, thinking what he wanted to say. He didn't want to upset Sarah. The other woman, Ellie, who was already divorced, suddenly became very vocal, "You want to keep changing the days he sees the children."

That kicked Thomas into action. He started on the three of them – Saffron, Ellie and Timmidy. Staying very cool to keep Sarah happy, he explained the consequences of that action, and in the same breath, told the women they were spiteful! His biggest gripe was any of them taking advice from Saffron, who hadn't even had children. He looked over at her and went on giving further examples of why they should not do what Saffron suggested. The other two looked embarrassed, but he was not prepared to be contradicted. When he had finished his piece, the other two stayed quiet. Saffron had other ideas. She didn't get embarrassed. She got angry.

"Ellie and Timmidy can be as nasty and spiteful as they want. It's their choice, not yours."

"Exactly. But not yours either," Thomas replied.

Saffron fumed. Her eyes blazed. Her cheeks were bright red like a dragon's. Thomas half expected her to breathe fire.

"Why don't you go to the gym, Thomas? See if you can fall off the bike again!" she spat.

Thomas smiled, "Yes, that's a good idea. At least I can get on a bike. How about you? Would you fit with your oversized?" He pointed to her bottom. "Is there a saddle big enough for you?" *That did it!* For a moment, he thought Saffron was going to attack him. She stood up and walked out. Ellie and Timmidy followed.

"See you next week then." Thomas turned to Sarah. "That was a lovely energy bar you made, Sarah."

Sarah didn't know what to say. She appeared to be flabbergasted.

Abigale grinned. "Good on you, Thomas. I can't stand that Saffron."

Sarah reached over and put her hand on his. "I know that you've had three divorces, please don't let them get to you. They are wrong, but you can't do anything about it."

Thomas sighed. "I couldn't just sit there without saying something."

After a minute or two, Abigale's friend Winnie, came in.

Abigale waved at her. "Come and sit with us."

Winnie took one of the empty seats. "Had company, have we?" she said looking at the cups on the table.

"You just missed the fireworks," Abigale said.

"Don't tell me that someone has put a flea in Saffron's ear?" Winnie said with a huge smile. She looked at Thomas. "And I think I can guess who."

"Right first time!" said Abigale.

Thomas was baffled. Why would this lady he hardly knew assume that it was he that had confronted Saffron? He sat there, his head resting in his hand. "Actually, she deserved more. I held back."

Sarah gave him a look.

"Only joking," he said.

"You must have hit a nerve. Saffron had a face like thunder. What a nasty piece of work she is. She lives just up the road from me. No one in the village likes her."

"Where?" Abigale asked.

"If you leave my house, turn right. It's about four hundred metres up. The one set back off the lane."

"That horrid green one?"

"That's it. She lives on her own. That's if you don't count the cats."

"How many cats?" asked Thomas.

"At least half a dozen."

Thomas smiled. "That might explain the scars on her arms, and on her chin. She must have really annoyed them."

"What did you argue about?" Winnie asked.

"The other two girls are divorced," Sarah explained. "Well, not quite. Timmidy is still going through hers. Anyway, they all seemed to think that it's okay to use the children as a weapon against the dads by restricting access. Thomas has first-hand experience with that, so it riled him. He let them know what he thought well and truly."

Winnie grinned. "Good for you, Thomas."

"My words precisely," said Abigale.

Thomas nodded, appreciating their approval.

Sarah smiled. "Now you have been vindicated, why don't you go up to the gym and do some running?"

Thomas jumped up. He knew he had no time for the gym, but he couldn't say anything. He gave Sarah a little peck on the cheek. She looked straight into his eyes. "Don't worry. I'll call you in the morning to let you know I didn't fall, and that I'm still alive."

She smiled. "Go on. Be off with you."

Thomas saw the two friends who had helped him the day

before. He gave them a wave. Then he realised that they would remember the cut on his face, so he found a quiet corner. He kept the session short. Just thirty minutes. Then he quietly slipped out, not bothering to shower. A strange mix of anxiety and excitement coursed through his veins as he headed home. *Get a grip Thomas, for Heaven's sake.*

Chapter 6

The following morning, Thomas was up early. Today would be a struggle to get ahead with work so he could take a week off, but he still had to earn a living. He made a mug of strong coffee and retreated to his small office. An hour passed with very little work accomplished. It was so hard to concentrate, just looking at the figures. His mind kept wandering. Dominic had fuelled his imagination. *I've been staring at the same page on the screen for ten minutes*, he thought. *I'll call the office, see what's happening. I don't know why I got up so early. I haven't done a thing yet.*

"Everything's fine," John said, reassuring himself.

As the morning progressed, Thomas managed to do a little work. Then he remembered, he had to call Sarah.

"Thomas!"

"That was quick. It only rang once,"

"I've been expecting your call! How did you do on the running machine?

"No problem. I did some interval running at a good pace."

"What is a good pace?"

"A seven-minute pace."

"Isn't that a bit fast?"

"I'd like to think so, but not really. I used to run at that pace for miles. All I did last night was two minutes on and two minutes off, at a slower pace. But I managed to keep going for thirty minutes."

"Just be careful after what happened Monday night."

Thomas chuckled.

"You might laugh, Thomas Pink, but I'd rather not pick you up from the floor again."

"Okay." He thought back to Monday night. And the culprit. *Dominic has a lot to answer for.*

"I thought I might pop over for a cup of your special tea. Unless you're busy of course."

"Never too busy for you, Sarah."

"See you in half an hour."

In the kitchen, Thomas emptied the teapot in preparation. As he walked over to the cupboard to get some more tea, he realised that he was running low. He couldn't buy it in the supermarket as it wasn't available. Organic black tea, the best tea ever, was only available online. *Oh well, I'll order some more later.* Back in his office, he got on with his work. Then Sarah crept into his mind. He knew the feelings between them were warming up and it was making him nervous. He had to be so careful with relationships. Then there was this thing with Dominic. He sat there for a full five minutes, unable to focus on anything. Angry for procrastinating, he made himself concentrate on his work.

Hello, Thomas.

Thomas jumped. "Dominic!"

Who else could it be? Think not speak, Thomas.

Thomas swung round. "Where are you?" He sighed and cast his eyes up at the ceiling. *I must get used to your phone system, or I'll be on the floor again. Tell you what, why can't you give me a little ring in my head before you speak? That would stop me from jumping out of my skin.*

Dominic laughed. *I'll try to remember that.*

All this supernatural stuff you do and you say you'll try to remember!

I know what you're saying, Thomas. But as you struggle to get used to our ways, I struggle with yours. After your visit to the Garden of Souls, the problem will disappear. Our communication issue will go away for both of us.

That filled Thomas with even more wonder, if that was possible. *I can't wait*, he thought.

You sound keen.

So, this is a phone conversation but without a phone, as you put it, Thomas.

Yes, I suppose it must be.

Well, we have been talking for five minutes and you haven't messed up, so you're on your way.

Hopefully. But you didn't turn up for that reason. No doubt you have a little gem of wisdom up your sleeve?

You're right, Thomas. But before I tell you, there's something I would like to explain. It will help you appreciate where we are coming from.

Go on.

I will put this very simply. Of course, that doesn't reflect on you. It's just so complicated!

Thomas was dying to know. *Go on then.*

So, this is how it works. Every soul on your planet projects an aura. The best way to describe it is an open book on that particular soul.

I already know that, said Thomas.

Of course you do. Now tell me what else you know.

Well, I know certain people, who are gifted, and they can read the aura being projected. Their ability controls the depth they can go to, therefore, they know what a person or soul is made of. Weaknesses and strengths. That kind of gifted person's insight can be used to guide.

Brilliant!

So now, we feel you are getting closer to a relationship with Sarah. Do you agree?

Blimey, I wasn't expecting that! And who's we?

The old souls and don't take it the wrong...

Thomas interrupted, *no, I'm fine with it. Yes, things are warming up. But I am aware of my past mistakes.*

And we're aware of possible future mistakes. What you do is up to you. But the Maker's Department can read your aura, and everyone's on the planet. Absolutely nothing is missed. So, we would like to suggest you create some rules.

Do you mean Heaven when you said the Maker's department?

More like the factory floor.

That made his head spin. It was all too much.

Your understanding will grow with time, Dominic said, sounding sympathetic. *Don't worry about it now. All you need to concern yourself with is a carefully constructed approach to any future relationships. Unfortunately, the timing for your involvement combined with our task isn't good. I mentioned previously that I did try making contact a year ago. It's my fault. I should have persisted and killed you earlier.*

Lovely, thought Thomas.

But what's done is done, thought Thomas, in a very matter of fact manner, and he hoped Dominic might suggest something helpful. *Come on then, talk to me. I can't guess what you're thinking – not yet! You do know that Sarah is about to walk through the door any minute now?*

Unless she can travel through light, you won't see her for another twenty minutes or so. We have time.

How do you know?

Dominic laughed, *Once you return from the Garden of Souls, you will have powers you can't even dream of.*

And it's that we have to discuss? Thomas sighed. *I do know where you're coming from. I also appreciate the importance of what you expect of me. But the three marriages I've been through must tell you that I've been round the block a few times.*

Dominic seemed confused for a second. He didn't answer.

Then there's my trip to the Garden of Souls coming up. You say the knowledge I am going to gain will add to my experience. Surely that will help me handle a situation... if and when it occurs with Sarah.

Yes that is possible, it is good that you're thinking ahead! Unlike in the past when you were gung-ho! But it's that past we're basing our concerns on. And there are going to be problems you could face purely because of the job we need you to do. It's inevitable that barriers between you and Sarah will occur. Nothing that can't be handled, though. Nevertheless, those problems will be magnified. This will be apparent after your visit to the Garden of Souls.

Thomas stopped him there, *I understand the words you're using, but really, you're telling me nothing!*

There was a moment's silence before Dominic said, *Imagine a situation where you are confronted with one of the bad people like the ones we saw on our little trip.*

Okay.

At close quarters, he or she will have a good idea of who you are, because of your higher vibrations. That will be due to the elevated state granted to you by the process at the Garden of Souls.

I know what I have to do, Dominic, in a situation like that. In your words, the soul has to be returned. I have to dispose of whoever, before I'm disposed of. Right? And then... Thomas ran his hand along the edge of his desk, *if I see Sarah later that evening... and she asks me what I did today? I have to fib! I do, don't I?* Dominic didn't answer, but Thomas knew he was right. *Dominic?* he hesitated. *There's one more thing.*

What's that?

I do hope that I'm equipped for the job.

You will be. And I can see you're well adjusted to what's going on in your life. I admire that. I don't think I need to say anymore. Apart from...

What now?

You must follow your feelings, of course... Just put a little caution in front of them.

Thomas sighed. *I don't need any reminding on that. Pain has a long memory.*

Practice disconnecting your mind from your thoughts whenever you can.

Thomas nodded.

I'll see you tomorrow with a little more information to help with your enhancement. Oh, I forgot to mention that you'll be able to do this very soon.

What, the mind phone communication thing?

Yes, exactly.

With that, Dominic left Thomas's mind. He shook his head. The connection was definitely gone. His departure was perfect timing too, as Thomas could hear the doorbell ringing. The door was never locked during the day and Sarah was calling out as she walked in. He only had seconds to clear his head. "I've got to get used to all this," he whispered to himself. "Something tells me I'm going to need to learn fast."

"Talking to yourself again?" Sarah was standing in the kitchen doorway, arms open and smiling her wonderful smile.

"Talking to myself? Ah yes, as always!" he laughed as he gave Sarah a gentle hug.

"So, what do you have to get used to?"

She overheard me! "Oh, nothing much," he lied. "Just work. Difficult clients. They all want something different, so we pander to them. We have no choice."

"There's nothing wrong with that! Now you can pander to me. Cup of tea, please?"

Thomas relaxed. He grinned. "Of course, but not before I

put that wonderful smile you just gave me in my box for later with some of the others."

That put another smile on Sarah's face. "Only some of the others?" she continued to smile.

"I used the others up! They are gone now."

"Oh, Thomas, you are so sweet." She moved a little closer to him and put her hand on his face. Her fingers sent shivers from his toes to the tip of his head. For a second or two, they looked at each other. Then nervously, he moved away. "I'll get the tea."

Sarah seemed nervous too. "How're your legs after your running?"

The kettle boiled and Thomas poured water into the teapot. "They're beginning to ache. They will be worse tomorrow, I reckon." Sarah leaned against the kitchen doorway. "Stretching helps."

"Before I drink my tea or..."

"Why not while you're drinking it?!"

"Yeah, right." He shut up and concentrated on pouring the tea.

Sarah sat down at the kitchen table. "I called a couple of friends up last night. I don't think you've met them, Janie and her sister Sam?"

"Oh, those two. No, I haven't." He was teasing.

She smiled. "Yes, you have! Anyway, I wanted to find out about Saffron."

"Do they know her then?"

"Well, they know of her. The family name is Shortstaff. The family is all a bit odd, but apparently, she takes the biscuit."

"What did they tell you?" Thomas slurped his tea then had to reach for a tissue. "Oops! Sorry I'm not concentrating. Too busy listening to you!" He dabbed up the spillage.

"Right, are you ready?"

"Yes, sorry." He leaned forward, interested.

"Apparently, Saffron had issues with her neighbour a few years ago. Something to do with the garden fence. It went to court, and she lost. Now listen to this. The following day Mr. Cartwright, the neighbour..." Sarah took a sip of her tea.

"Go on."

She smiled. "It's not often I get your complete attention! So the car that Mr. Cartwright, the neighbour had just bought a week earlier caught alight in the middle of the night on his driveway."

"That's not good. Perhaps there was an electrical short in the engine compartment. Was it an old car he bought?"

"Nope! A brand-new BMW. By the time the fire brigade turned up, the car was completely burnt out."

"Wow, that's odd, but I suppose it's not impossible."

"That's what I said, but Janie was adamant something was going on. And what about the builder? The one who fixed her roof."

"What builder?" Thomas frowned. He didn't have a clue what Sarah was talking about.

"I'll tell you. Janie then went on to say that a builder she asked to repair her roof apparently overcharged her, so they had a bit of a to-do. The next thing we hear is that the builder had an accident and fell off his ladder. No, not his ladder, the scaffolding."

"What! While he was working on her roof?"

"No, somewhere else. I can't remember what Janie said exactly, but the people living in the area think that she's a witch."

"Well, I've said she's an old witch before, but they are just words to describe what you think of someone. One thing we both know is that she's a bit of a scumbag, but that's a long way from being a witch."

"Well, Thomas, there's more."

"More?" he smiled.

"You may laugh, but there is more. The postman is a bit of a gossip. If you want to know what's going on, then ask him! Anyway, one morning he was poorly, so he couldn't get to work."

Thomas stayed very quiet now, listening, and wondering why he found it all so fascinating.

Sarah leaned forward. "His round was split up between three other postmen. The long and the short of this story is that a package addressed to Saffron was incorrectly delivered. The person who received it, a woman a few doors up, was also expecting a package, so she just opened it without looking at the label. And what do you think she found in the package?"

Thomas looked at her, bewildered by what he was thinking. "Give me a minute."

"Go on, guess."

"If I were a witch making concoctions and casting spells and wanting to set fire to cars and change the density of gravity to get my own back on a builder, what would I need?" he mumbled to himself. "Bat wings, spiders, frogs, toads, hair from a hog. Perhaps just frogs, or toads. And hog hair."

Sarah gasped. "Thomas, I'll tell you."

He put his hand up to stop her. "Another minute, please. Am I on the right track?"

Sarah nodded, amazed that he knew so much. "Dried frogs, yes, and hair from a hog. There must have been more than that surely. Some kind of mixture."

"I think Janie said the other bits in the box were glass files with code references on them, filled with different coloured powder."

"Crikey, Sarah! I was very close; I must get a few points for that."

"I'm impressed. How did you know?"

"It was the car that caught fire that gave it away."

Sarah laughed and scrunched up her nose. "What do you mean?"

He gave her a smug look.

"Come on, stop messing about. Tell me more."

Thomas giggled a little. He was so chuffed with himself, but he had no clue how he knew. He was beginning to get the measure of Saffron. "I'm not sure where it came from, but I seem to recall something about water and fire. Toads and frogs are water creatures. Saffron's plan was fire, so she needed a frog or a toad. Water and Fire have an affinity, plus whatever else she needed to create the desired spell. She went too far and wrecked a car just to get her own back. She is one crazy woman."

Sarah was spellbound. "How do you know all that? And! What about the builder? How did Saffron do that?"

"That's a lot more complicated. She would have had to be close to the builder to do what she did."

"What did she do?"

Thomas sat like a statue, perfectly still, looking directly at Sarah, but his mind was somewhere else. Things kept popping into his head, and he was having trouble making sense of his thoughts. He wondered to himself where the ideas were coming from. Sarah began to fidget, and her body language suggested for him to get on with his explanation.

Much to his relief the answer dawned on him. "The builder – yes, I think I have it now. In the package, you told me there was hog hair. That's a main ingredient to..." He paused for a second, a smile slowly appearing on his face. "You're not going to believe this."

Sarah's eyes popped wide open. "I will! Go on."

"It's the main ingredient for a spell if she wanted to thin out oxygen. It messes with gravity. So, if the builder was high up on scaffolding, as you mentioned, then he could become disorientated and fall."

Sarah sat in silence, staring at him.

"And" he added. "It would be very local. That's why Saffron

would have to get in close proximity to the builder. Something along those lines. I don't know how the science works exactly, but then witchcraft isn't science, is it?"

"How on earth could she do that? But more to the point, why?"

"Hm..." he murmured. He leaned his elbows on the table and cupped his hands around his chin. He was away with the fairies! Thoughts were trickling into his head, he said them out loud. The information wasn't flowing, though. He had to keep pausing. It was as if he was listening to someone, then repeating what he had just heard. A sudden surge of answers filled his mind. "If she's a dark witch, and the indications are pointing that way, then almost anything is possible."

"What other kind of witch could she be then?"

Thomas knew this one immediately. "There are white witches out there, the good ones."

"Sorry, Thomas. I feel I'm a bit dozy. All I'm doing is asking you questions."

"You're not dozy. Far from it."

"What's the difference between the two, then?"

"I believe the dark ones work with the Devil. The whites work whichever way they wish, but there is nothing sinister going on."

"It shows you that Saffron is a vindictive person. The fence and the builder. She had a disagreement, so she wanted revenge." She shuddered. "But how do you know all this dark stuff, Thomas?"

"I'm not sure, but I have a good idea where it's coming from."

Sarah was in like a flash. "Where?"

"The same place my healing came from."

She stared at him with a look of surprise on her face.

He realised that she wasn't comfortable. *How can she understand?* He wasn't completely sure he did. She fiddled with the empty mug. He tried to change the subject, but she still fiddled with it. Her fingers were trembling. He stood up and reached out for the mug. "Another cup?"

She nodded. "I'll make it," she said, going over to the kettle, "after you explain what you just said about the same place."

How can I explain? He wondered if Dominic's team was already working on his mind, opening it up and making it ready for when he entered the Garden of Souls. He knew his intuition had started to grow stronger and he was sure that was how he had managed to work out what Saffron had been up to. What he had said to Sarah wasn't exactly correct, but he was thinking more carefully now. More had to be done before he would be ready for his mission.

One week to create an evolved soul was a bit of a stretch, even for Dominic. There was a risk Thomas would be overloaded. It was important to prepare him. There had to be a balance.

Thomas turned into his mind again and listened. "I'll explain," said Thomas, "an energy source comes from the other side. How you choose to use it is up to the individual, dark or light. Saffron is using the dark side."

"That means she's a dark witch. What shall we do about her, Thomas?" Sarah sounded anxious.

"There's not much we can do, apart from keep our distance."

That didn't work for Sarah. She stopped making the tea and turned around to face him. "But how can we do that? She does three, sometimes four classes a week. What if someone upsets her! Like you did. She was fuming and walked out."

He grinned.

"She didn't appreciate being insulted. How come you're not showing any concern?"

This was true, he didn't care about Saffron, and he wasn't going to be intimidated by her. *Perhaps it is because Dominic is going to prepare me for almost anything. That includes the likes of Saffron.* He knew that he was forbidden to divulge any information that might ease Sarah's mind. He walked over to her and gave her a gentle hug. "We have an advantage over her victims."

"What's that?"

"We know she's a witch."

"You call that an advantage! I'm not so sure."

"I think it's pretty good. Stop worrying. Let's just forget about her. Come on, sit down with me. We'll chat about something more agreeable. What's that bundle you brought with you?"

Sarah sighed. "I guess you are right. I've been rummaging through my mother's things."

"You miss her, don't you?"

Sarah nodded. "Anyway, I've found this recipe that will suit you perfectly, Thomas."

"Now that's better than talking about Saffron, isn't it?"

"It's a high-energy meal, scientifically balanced, that will benefit your fitness programme. I don't want you damaging yourself in that gym anymore."

"That makes two of us. Why would your mother have come across that?"

"She created it. It was all to do with her job."

Thomas wasn't sure whether he should ask questions about her mum, but he decided to try. "What did your mother do?" he asked, in a soft voice.

"She was a research scientist. She was working with a small team within a large pharmaceutical company. I think she said there were three of them involved on a drug addiction cure programme."

"Wow, that sounds heavy. How does the recipe come into it? Do you mind me asking?"

"No, I don't mind. It will do me good. It might clear my head a bit. As far as I can remember, they had a handful of drug addicts who were their guinea pigs. The scientists explored ways to suppress the desire by using non-addictive drugs.

Apparently, for that to work, the patient had to be in good shape and drug addicts, in general, almost always gave up food for drugs, so most of them were in a bad way. The idea began to work and food played a major part in the process."

"Sounds like you had a clever mum."

"Not for long enough, though," she said sadly.

Thomas looked down at the floor. He didn't know what to say.

"She was clever, but so were the others. She was on the project for a year."

"What happened?"

"She became ill and died."

"Oh, dear. I am sorry."

"Before she died, I remember her telling me about one of the others in the team becoming poorly. But I don't know what happened to them. All I know is that the programme was closed down. This is all that's left. This bundle of recipes and my mum's work notes. I have those at home."

"Her ideas worked. That's what is important."

Tears welled up in Sarah's eyes. "My mum dying was important too."

Thomas didn't know whether to carry on or not. Then Sarah gave a sad smile, so he continued. "So, this recipe will prevent me from falling off the bike?"

"Well, of course, it won't, Thomas!" she said half laughing.

"How about I get the ingredients and you put it together here?"

"It's a deal. Watch and learn," she smiled, "it's a little complicated, but you'll get it."

Thomas felt good inside. It had been a long time since a woman had smiled at him so sweetly. He realised that Sarah had a caring agenda and it involved him. He was in two minds now after all that he had been through and the promises he had made to himself. Thoughts whizzed around his head about things that had happened in the past, and his difficulty with relationships. At this moment in time, he felt that giving in to his feelings wasn't a good option. Meanwhile, Sarah was standing there as if she was appreciating the simple pleasure of being in the company of someone she had strong feelings for.

Feeling a tad uncomfortable, he pretended to glance at the bundle she had brought around and talked to himself as if he understood what he was looking at.

She smiled again. It showed warmth, tenderness, and it seemed to say a million words within an instant. As he continued to look, her smile grew. It was a wonderful moment, and his negative thoughts and doubts began to fade. He had known Sarah for around three years and during that time he knew she had noticed changes within him. At the start of their friendship, he was raw and a little broken. He had been dealing with loads of personal problems. Since then, he had lived for a number of years within a lie, that, until now, he had been oblivious to. His issues had taken their toll. The upshot of that was it clouded his opinion of people, specifically the ones that are supposed to be close. Sarah had waited patiently for him. *Maybe she has played a canny game. She never pushed.* She had been so casual around him but not cold. She had always encouraged him and listened to the rubbish too. All in all, she was the near-perfect partner. However, he was still in a quandary. The timing couldn't have been worse. Now he had to go to the Garden of Souls this coming Monday and he couldn't afford complications. He thought back on what Dominic had told him earlier. "You must follow your heart certainly, but don't forget the secret ingredient. Caution. Emotions always work better with a tad of caution." So that's what he would do. Put things on hold for a while. Now he would have to tell Sarah a fib or two. There was no choice.

"Thomas? Shall I leave the recipes with you for now?"

"Yes, I'll look through them later. It might give me some ideas. Oh, I nearly forgot. My sister called me today."

"You speak to Betty most days, don't you?"

"This time, she sounded fed up."

"Why?"

"You know her partner's poorly. It's getting her down. I said I would go over. She's been talking about selling her house. Now her mind is made up. She is going to move."

"Where is she going?"

"Close to her daughter. South somewhere. I offered to give her a hand."

"What needs doing?"

"The house needs a lick of paint. And all the junk she has stored up over the years needs sorting. I'll probably have to make fifty trips to the dump."

"That'll take a while. What about work?"

"I won't be on my own. Everyone's chipping in. I reckon three, four, maybe five days at the most. I'll call you when I get there. Is that okay?"

"What do you think, silly?"

Thomas thought about what he had said. He had just told Sarah a pack of lies quite easily, and that's only the start of it. He didn't feel comfortable. Then he remembered the conversation with Dominic earlier, and the reasons why he had been chosen. That took away the uncomfortable feeling.

"Have you had any lunch?" asked Sarah.

"No."

Sarah smiled. "So, as you're away next week, I suppose you'll be living in the gym before you go?"

Thomas pulled a face. "Maybe."

"Just teasing. What do you think of this for an idea? That's if you can spare the time."

"What?"

"Let's make the recipe now?"

"Now? But I haven't got the ingredients."

"I thought that! So, I brought the ingredients with me. If

you're going to spend all your energy working out before you go, then you need to eat."

Thomas grinned. "I'm good for time. Now work's all done."

"Come on then. Let's get going."

By three o'clock, they were tucking into the dish they had just made. Sarah was right. It was complicated to make – ground nuts, apricots, bean curd, avocado and ingredients that he had never heard of. The meal was tasty though.

"I like this," he said with his mouth full.

Sarah smiled. "I thought you would. My mother was working on the value of high nutrition for people coming off drugs."

Thomas began to appreciate how clued-up Sarah's mother had been. A clever scientist, way ahead of her time. *Someone with that kind of knowledge should be able to avoid ailments like cancer by being prepared. Shouldn't they?* The work she was doing was clever stuff. His belief was for every ailment, there was a cure, if you only knew where to look. Sarah's mother was interesting. The job she did, how she approached the work, and the techniques she used. Then that programme had suddenly been abandoned and the research discarded. It seemed odd.

This is strange. He was experiencing feelings he had not experienced before. It was like he knew something, but he couldn't put his finger on it. This feeling was beginning to agitate him a little. He wondered if it was the consequence of the work Dominic's team was doing on him. He had to be prepared. There was no room for error.

"What's troubling you, Thomas? What's wrong?"

He hesitated. He couldn't be sure what to say to Sarah for fear of opening up a can of forgotten emotions. "Nothing. I'm just fascinated by your mother's work. I'm looking forward to putting the wonder food to the test tonight in the gym."

"I'll come and watch. I'm not doing classes and I need to keep an eye on you after your fall the other night!"

Chapter 7

When he arrived at the gym, Sarah was already waiting. Thomas walked up to her, smiled, and brushed his lips lightly against her cheek. She squeezed his hand and asked him to take it easy. He listened to her concerns, but was feeling a bit of a fraud, because he was fine. This week was all to do with Dominic!

Before he started training, he thought about his upcoming programme. For what Dominic had in mind for him, he suspected that he would have to be nimble on his feet. *Cardiovascular!* He warmed up on the bike, then headed for the running machine. He hadn't noticed till then how empty the place was. Apart from Sarah, there was no one there. On the running machine, he pushed himself to the limit, making himself feel quite sick. He would rather feel like that now than be dead later, so he felt justified that he was not paying any attention to what Sarah had said.

He was warming down when he noticed Sarah was standing right beside him. "How are you doing, Mr. Pink? No, don't answer. You look like death warmed up. I see that you took notice of what I said then!"

Feeling guilty, Thomas slowed the running machine down even more and grabbed his towel, wiping the sweat off his face. "I did take notice! It must be the recipe working already."

She smiled. "Yeah, yeah!"

"I'll need a few more gym sessions to test your mum's theory."

Sarah nodded. "I'll look through the other papers my mother kept. There should be procedures for a diet plan backing up the cure they created, although that bit doesn't apply to you."

"Great, give me a few minutes to shower."

"Okay," she smiled. "I made another concoction before I came over to yours. It's a drink, supposed to relax the muscles."

"From your mum's recipes?

"Yes."

"That's odd. I wouldn't have thought addicts would need that?"

"Unless they had to work out like you do."

Thomas shook his head. "No, it's not that. I think I have it."

"What?"

"Maybe it's the effect of the drug cure your mum's team created? It took the craving out of the mind but not the body?" He climbed off the running machine, thinking hard. He didn't think Sarah had a clue what he meant. He didn't have a clue where all these notions were coming from himself. "Maybe your mother's team created a substance that worked on the mind, so when the drugs were withdrawn, the addicts coped, but they couldn't relax. Maybe for the process to work permanently, I think you're right. Maybe they had to exercise seriously, and the concoction you've just made solved that problem. Why would a programme as complex as that be dropped?"

"Are you saying there's more to it, Thomas?"

"I think there is."

"But how can you know all this?"

"Well, it just seems logical when you think about it. It would be interesting if you could find your mother's procedures for these people, or patients, or whatever they were referred to. No doubt she would have kept a case file for each patient?"

"Go and have your shower while I think about it."

"Ten minutes. Do you want to go ahead? We can meet at yours. No point in you hanging around here."

"Yes sir, Mr. Pink," she said smiling.

Sarah had left the door open.

"Hi."

"I'll be down in a jiff," she called. "Your drink is on the table. You might want to warm it. I think it has to be at room temperature."

"Right."

The mug containing the magic formula was on the kitchen table. Before Sarah had time to come down the stairs, he had warmed it up and started sipping the drink.

"What do you think of it?" she called.

"It's good stuff. Not sure what's in it, though."

"In the sitting room, you'll find an old leather satchel. Everything my mother wrote is in there. That recipe is on the top inside it."

"Found it." He brought the satchel into the kitchen and sat down at the table with it.

"I'll be down any minute. You rummage through."

He was more interested in the leather satchel than the contents. It looked very old and worn. It fascinated him, but he didn't know why.

Sarah appeared. "Have you found anything interesting?"

"I've been admiring the satchel. It's wonderful. Why don't you treat the leather? That will bring it back to life."

"I hadn't thought of that."

"Tell you what, I think I have some cream at home. I'll do it." He gave her a sweet smile.

"Thank you, that's really kind. What do you think of the drink?"

"It's very substantial, almost a meal. I've only had half and I'm full. I reckon there's everything in it apart from the kitchen sink."

"You're right there. There's a mountain of ingredients! It's difficult to read her notes but I think what she had in mind was to soften the effect of the addictive drugs on those poor souls, trying to reduce the impact so the body could relax."

"That does sound complicated."

She pulled a paper out of the satchel. "Have a look." She handed him the recipe her mother had written twenty-odd years before. He scanned it for a few seconds, then looked over at Sarah shaking his head. "I can't read most of the writing. Pomegranate and the herbs I can, but the rest is like shorthand. But you managed."

"I do still miss her, Thomas, after all this time."

"Of course you do. But I think your mum is still with you, here, at this very moment. I believe she's watching us using her formula. Maybe this was meant to happen."

"What do you mean?"

"How long have you had the satchel?"

The sadness began to leave Sarah's face. She sat down at the table, looking intrigued. "Do you mean me? Or my mum?"

"You."

"Twenty-four years. Since my mother died."

"And how many times have you gone through her notes and recipes before today?"

Sarah seemed agitated. She was rubbing her hands together. He could see she was concentrating. "Once, just once, after my mother died."

"So why did you go through the contents of the satchel today?" He tried to sound gentle, he didn't want to upset her, but he wanted to know.

"Well," she said, staring straight at him, "I don't know. I just had this urge to dig out stuff the day you fell off the bike."

Thomas was starting to put two and two together. He couldn't tell Sarah exactly what he was thinking, but he had to tell her something plausible. He sat there, all ordinary thoughts blanked from his mind waiting for something, anything, to pop into his head.

"I know that look, come on, please tell me!"

Thomas continued to wait. He couldn't work out the connection between Dominic, Sarah, and her mum. *There had to be one.* And he wanted to get it clear in his own mind anyway before telling any more fibs. Suddenly he said, "what if your mum and my dad have been communicating with each other somehow?"

That freaked her out! "Thomas, as far as I'm concerned, my mum is dead, and that's that."

"Yes, I know she is, but something's going on here. I'm not sure what, exactly." He hesitated again. He knew that Sarah needed time. "It just seems strange that you got out your mother's recipes when I fell off the bike."

She stared at him. "Why? Go on, Thomas."

"I feel there's definitely some connection, but I'm struggling with it. I'll think on it for a few days when I'm at Betty's. I remember there was a medium who knew my father."

"That's a bit of a long shot."

"Maybe. But if that doesn't work, I'll go to the spiritual church where both my parents went to. That's where I could find answers."

"I'm not sure what you are talking about, but promise me that you will let me know if you find anything out?"

"I'll tell you whatever happens. Now back to business. What about the recipes? Can you write them down for me?"

Sarah nodded. Then she frowned. "You look shattered, Thomas."

It was true. He was starting to feel the effects of the past three days.

"I'll get the books for you now. Then you'd better get going, otherwise you'll be driving with your eyes shut."

Thomas didn't need telling twice. While she ran upstairs, he managed to ease himself up onto his feet. When she returned, he took the books, gave her a hug, kissed her cheek, thanked her, and walked out the door waving as he went.

"I'll call you in the morning, Thomas."

He turned around and gave her a thumbs-up.

Twenty minutes later, and feeling completely shattered, he was opening his own front door.

Chapter 8

The shrill sound of the alarm clock woke Thomas from a deep sleep. It took him a moment or two to come round. Then, it dawned on him how well he had slept. He remembered the drink Sarah's mum had formulated. "My God, that drink worked well!" *I ought to give it another go! That's if Sarah has more of the ingredients.* He thought about it. And he thought about her mother too. He didn't know what he was working towards, but he just had a gut feeling that something had gone wrong all those years ago. *If the recipe worked so well, why was the programme closed?* He thought it best to keep his thoughts to himself for the time being since he didn't really have a clue.

Thomas sat up and he looked at the clock. *7 am.* Before he could get down the stairs to make some tea, the phone rang. It was Sarah, checking up on him.

"Well, did it work?"

"I slept like a log. Didn't wake up at all during the night."

"I thought it would help. And when you left, I looked around for any other records."

"Why?"

"Because the satchel didn't have individual case files, just formulas and the recipes you saw. So, I went looking."

"And?"

"I went and got the steps from the shed and climbed into the loft. I remembered I put a couple of boxes from Mum's house, up there years ago. I thought they were personal stuff, not work-related, but I was wrong. One of the boxes contained files of six patients my mum's team was working with, and in each case the patient said how well they slept and how well they felt."

"So, the programme was working."

"It seems that way." Sarah paused for a second, "I think I know why you're thinking what you're thinking."

"But I haven't got any further with it yet. I need more time. I'm sure I will figure it out. We will, I should say."

"Well, I'll leave you to get on. I'm going to my eight o'clock class."

"Okay, speak to you later." He put down the phone. Dominic was going to appear this morning and he was going to be given an insight into the Garden of Souls. *Better get on with some work now.* Their last meeting, and the effect it had on him afterwards, meant he couldn't work or couldn't concentrate on a thing. Thomas worked hard and an hour went past quickly. The rest would be done over the weekend. He made a quick call to the office just to let them know he would be busy and not to call.

Thomas went into the kitchen to organise his breakfast, so he could be ready for Dominic when he arrived. Five minutes went by. He had finished his tea and was becoming fidgety. The way Dominic suddenly appeared out of nowhere frightened the life out of him every time. Thomas gasped and swore as it happened again. Dominic was suddenly sitting opposite him. His appearance had made him jump.

Dominic smiled, then made a weird noise as he emitted a laugh.

"I always jump when you show up so suddenly! It's hard to get used to. I'm just glad I finished my tea and didn't throw the cup in the air."

Dominic smiled. "Good morning. I will try to remember our agreed protocol and give you a warning. I'm sorry, but it's been a million years or more since my kind were at your level. I'm afraid that's asking too much from my memory!" he chuckled.

"Well, good morning."

"So, are you in the right frame of mind to start, Thomas? I only have limited time. I am sending out vibrations that can be picked up by the other lot, so time is precious."

"Yes, I'm ready. I think."

"You'll be pleased to know when you return from the Garden of Souls, you will have the ability to sense any life force coming your way, so you won't jump when any of us turn up."

"Well, that's a good start. Let's hope it continues."

"Yes, I'm sure it will. Now, have you organised your week?"

"Yes. People at work are sorted. I told them I would call if I could. Sarah will expect at least one call a day. Oh, blast! How can I call anyone? It's just dawned on me. You don't have phones, do you?" A wave of panic swept over him.

This time Dominic let out a proper laugh. "Are you suggesting we have no communication in one of Heaven's out-posts?"

"I suppose you're going to tell me it's me. I have a problem."

"No, not a problem, Thomas. More like a challenge. This question hasn't cropped up before, so I'll need to give it some thought."

"Well, I would like to as well, but I haven't a clue where to start. Oh, apart from..." Thomas's brain kicked into gear.

"Apart from what, Thomas?" Dominic let him think.

"This is a relatively small problem, I'm sure. When you told me how to contact you through my mind, you said to visualise you and blank everything else out."

"Go on."

"So, I wonder if I did that with my phone, I could somehow make it work and call whoever I want?"

Dominic nodded his head in agreement. “You’re almost there. Good. When you focus on the phone, you will need to concentrate on the number you’re calling. Then with the keypad fixed in your mind you will need to concentrate on one number at a time, just for a second. It has to be in sequence. Then when you have mastered that, stay focussed on the phone you are using. The ringtone will be in your head, bypassing your ears. When you hear a voice, that’s when you really have to concentrate. Speak through your mind. Don’t even think about opening your mouth.”

“What happens if I mess up?”

“Not a lot, you just lose the connection, which isn’t unusual the way you lot communicate.”

“I can’t practice that, can I?”

“Yes, you can. You don’t need to be up there to work the phone.”

Thomas looked puzzled.

“Think about it.”

“Okay, I’m thinking about it.” The idea suddenly gelled. “Got it! Simple!”

“If you know it, yes. Tell me.”

“If the phone is in my house, I can be anywhere?”

Dominic nodded. “All we have to work on now is time.”

“What do you mean?” asked Thomas.

“Time. There’s no time. As you haven’t been to the Garden of Souls, a simple explanation will have to do. When you leave after the week, the more complex one will be in your head.”

“No time? Tell me what you mean. I’m listening.”

“There’s no time structure in the Garden of Souls.”

Thomas felt completely blank. Then he frowned. “No time?” Thomas was feeling confused and a little worried.

Dominic gave him a moment to think about what he had just said, again testing him.

Thomas started biting the inside of his lip, as he thought

deeply. It was almost as if he was drowning in thought. A couple of minutes passed. He stopped trying to think. "What do you mean no time structure?"

"Time doesn't exist."

"How do I work that one out then? How do you know what time it is? How do you know when to eat? Oh, you don't eat!" A big sigh came from Thomas. "So, when I'm there, I won't eat either? Or drink? Do you feel? Do you feel anything? This is doing my head in! How will I know when to call Sarah?"

"Don't worry about it. When you arrive, you'll be aware of a tremendous understanding. It will exhilarate you. Like magic, all your anxieties will fall away."

Thomas was impressed. "I can't wait. Hang on, I'm curious."

"And impatient, Thomas."

"So how will I know when to call Sarah?" Now he was thinking more clearly.

"As I said, you'll have an understanding, and you'll cope with that small problem easily."

Thomas lightened up. "Okay, what else?"

"The soul you'll meet will be Jonas Marley. He is an advanced Shide with superior skills who is based on your planet earth. You remember, don't you?"

"Yes, I remember. That's the Shide you were telling me about? The one that's been on Earth for two hundred years and runs the biggest energy company in the world."

"Yes, good. He will teach you things you'll need to know following your enhancement. But first off, the moment we arrive you will have time – and I have used that word for your benefit; it's easier for now. Anyway, you will have time to absorb, and to be nurtured. That will have a massive effect on you. You'll need to be strong. Your soul will call to you not to leave. It will be powerful. If you're of a weaker nature, it will dominate your thoughts and your will. But I don't see a problem with you. I'm just making you aware."

Thomas took a deep breath.

"Now, on an encouraging note, the team, no, I mean our team, a group of souls I work with and who are working with you, of course, have had good results in programming you for your improvement."

That shook Thomas. He had no idea all this had started already. Then the penny dropped. Thinking about Sarah's mum and the satchel, he suddenly knew why he was bothered. "Why didn't you tell me things were already happening, Dominic?"

"That's how it works. If you had known, it could have interfered with your progress."

Thomas felt miffed. He didn't like surprises.

"It can't be done any other way," Dominic said quietly.

"Okay, it's okay. I don't like surprises. It's my character. I guess you know that better than I do. So, these good results, do they have any benefits?"

"Yes, Thomas, it will reduce the time you need with the souls who will be creating your enhancement."

Improvements. Thomas thought to himself. *Maybe not as long as a week then.* "And what exactly will they be doing? Do you know?"

"I thought you would ask that. Well, I'm not an expert on this, but I have a good idea. Jonas would have worked out an evolutionary strategy before the souls went to work on you."

"Go on."

"Depending on the understanding Jonas has of the tasks ahead, this will dictate the evolving path we need to take for you to be safe and take on the darksiders with success. That's the blueprint for the souls working on you. It's extremely complicated, and as the process moves forward, your body configuration will change a little."

Thomas's thoughts altered from interest to concern. "Change how?"

"As the process has to be natural, we can't just add abilities."

Thomas interrupted. He didn't appreciate Dominic rambling on. He just wanted him to get to the point. "Look, I'm sure I will understand the process afterwards, but that's a little late. I want to know now. Just tell me the changes."

"You're too impatient, Thomas. If we were like you, the probability of you growing another head in the process couldn't be ruled out."

That fired Thomas up. He jumped up, ready to scream out. Dominic put his hands in the air, "I'm joking, just joking," he said, laughing.

Thomas wasn't in a particularly good frame of mind now. He didn't appreciate Dominic's little joke. It was all too much. He was beginning to feel anxious.

Dominic sat back. "Sorry, Thomas, but actually, it's reassuring to see how you react. No thought! In like a shot. That's one of the reasons you've been selected. Look, the reason why I'm rambling on is simple. You need to understand the process, so I have to continue."

Thomas nodded.

"This natural approach is through the skill of the souls in your team. Any other way would throw you out of balance. We have to nudge you gently. Along a more developed path. This will enable you to become a soul that's evolved ahead of your time. And that's where the natural abilities you'll need will come from. The consequences are just small changes to accommodate these new abilities." Dominic thought for a moment. "Think of the advantages. A more powerful heart. Larger lung capacity. Damaged parts in your body regenerated. All in all, a perfect body. The strain of life will leave your face giving an appearance of a younger look too."

"I'm not sure what to say now. This is a lot to take in."

"Say nothing. Wait until the process has been completed, then you can give me your opinion."

Doing as Dominic asked, he sat in silence, thinking about what Dominic had just said.

"Thomas?"

"Yes?"

"When you return from the Garden of Souls, time that has been lost in history will unfold, resurface, forcing you to take a look at it."

Thomas scrunched up his face. He wondered what Dominic was implying. "What do you mean?"

"All I want you to do is remember this moment and what's been said. It will become clear. The past dictates the future. You will have the ability to see that soon."

"I think I understand what you're saying, but I would appreciate a little more clarity. I don't want to mess up."

"When you told Sarah how you managed to get help to heal the cut and remove the severe bruising to your face, you opened the lid, and allowed a glint of light into Pandora's Box. Now you have an obstacle in your path. Which I have to say is critical."

"I've gathered that, it was the only thing I could think of at the time. But I didn't know it was critical."

"The explanation was excellent and well within the realms of possibility. From now on, you'll have the ability to manage any questions. You just have to stay focussed."

"You're not telling me everything, are you? I can only assume as time turns and my awareness crystallises, I'll understand. I do hope you're right."

"Yes, Thomas, I'm not telling you everything because I can't and that's how it is."

Thomas decided that he was okay with that. He was beginning to get used to the thinking behind all this drama. But there were still things he needed to know. "Right, I want to get this time thing sorted before you disappear."

"Go on then."

"I've had a thought."

"That's a start."

That frustrated Thomas and he gave Dominic a seething look.

"What's that then?"

"I'm trying to sort out my life for next week and you're being sarcastic."

"You're a bit sensitive Mr Pink."

"That's because I'm being bombarded with information, and more importantly I know if I don't get it right, then I'm dead! So keep your comments to yourself and listen." Thomas was taking control. He didn't want any loose ends.

"I'm listening," Dominic nodded, and kept quiet.

"I'll start at the beginning again. Firstly, if I leave my mobile on charge, while the clever souls are working with me, will I have the ability to stay in permanent contact with it?"

"Mm," Dominic nodded. "Yes, that will be easy."

"Good. Now tell me how. The rest of the time thing I can deal with myself."

"Excellent, this is how you do it. Look at your phone and memorise the positions of the digits. Once that is in your head, it will stay there. Then as I mentioned, you concentrate on the number you are calling. Look at each number on the phone for a second. That will activate the number as if you pressed it. When you have dialled, use your mind, not your mouth. Simple. Why don't you try it Thomas."

Within a few minutes, Thomas was controlling the mobile with his mind.

"Time is running short now. Anything else you're unsure about?"

"Yes, what's the purpose of the Garden of Souls?"

"The purpose? You want to know why the Garden of Souls exists, don't you?"

"Yes, exactly."

"The answer could go over your head. Even though you had advanced souls working on you, it might be a case of direct communication as before."

"Let's try the old-fashioned way first. Words out of your mouth? That will test my upgrades, wont it?"

"It's a waiting room, a regenerating centre, a preparation space, a war zone, a holiday camp, a holding space."

Thomas interrupted as usual. "A war zone? Why a war zone?"

"You'll know soon enough. Are you sure you want to stick with words?"

"No, I'm not sure now. And I've just realised, you said you were running out of time, didn't you?"

"Yes."

"Best do that odd thing and download from you to me then?"

"Good! In two minutes, you'll know as much as I do about the Garden of Souls. There is just one small issue."

"There always is! Tell me."

"Don't worry. You'll get all the information, but we just need to be careful. I'll need to place the excess."

"What excess?"

"I'll try to explain. Your mind, or call it your brain, has restrictors built in. All perfectly natural. These allow information to be processed. Depending how far up the chain you are, dictates what's allowed in. I'm no different. I will place the excess into a compartment taking up space in your mind,"

Outside, a chorus of birds suddenly sang, breaking the silence.

"That excess will avoid overload and allow you to put into perspective all the new facts whizzing round your head."

"I thought you said the facts were being placed in a compartment?"

"You're right, I did, but they'll trickle out as you progress with your improvements, as you move up the chain of knowledge. Otherwise, you could be overawed."

"I'm beginning to realise how naive I am."

"No, I wouldn't say that. Not at all. You just haven't been around long enough, that's all."

"That's little comfort, but I get what you are saying now. Come on. The two minutes are almost up."

Dominic stood and Thomas felt Dominic's hands close like a vice around his head. He felt like he was lost in space and time.

"All done." Dominic let go. "Just be aware your head and everything in it will go into overdrive."

Thomas grinned. "It does that anyway."

"Not like this, I promise. Whatever you think about, almost anything you think about, then your thoughts will go deeper. It's exhilarating. When the time comes to deal with darksiders, in whatever way, you'll know all there is to know. That will give you comfort."

"How will I feel comforted when I feel I'm about to die?"

"You will feel fear, but you'll know what to do. You won't die."

Thomas sat back in his chair; he was quiet. He didn't move. *I could die!* Reality had hit home finally. Even though Dominic had said, he wouldn't die. He didn't want to talk anymore. He wanted to say goodbye to Dominic right now. Dominic stepped back from him. "You won't be on your own ever, I promise."

Thomas gave a half-hearted smile. "You must go."

Dominic was gone. The last thing he expected two minutes later was Dominic's voice in his head.

Is the mind phone in working order then?

Yes.

You're switched on now. You can call whenever you like.

Cool!

Two reasons why I called. Firstly, I wanted to check the connection. Secondly, I want to elaborate on what's just been discussed.

Really?

Jonas will guide you through the process after your visit. By then, you'll be well aware of your new abilities. He'll suggest ways of using those new abilities to maximise your new powers. When he has finished with you, your vibrations on Earth will be a lot higher. He'll explain the consequences and advantages. You will be shown how to use the anger you have rooted deep down in your soul to your advantage. Your mind, in the new advanced state, will lift your judgement and will be far superior to almost all of the darksiders you make contact with. Those who wish you harm are going to have a nasty shock. At the moment, I know this is just words, but as soon as you have been through the process, these words will have meaning. You are in safe hands Thomas, and you must not worry about being killed in action.

Chapter 9

Thomas stared out of the patio doors directing his gaze at the old yew tree and noticed sunlight trickling through the evergreen foliage. That somehow helped him focus his mind on what Dominic had just said.

It sounds great. It sounds amazing. So now it's up to my imagination to give me inspiration. Trouble is, Dominic, I'm nervous. The thought of someone wanting to kill me is freaking me out right now, and that's restricting my imagination.

It will be there, when you need it.

Thomas nodded, *I suppose once I've been and gone from the Garden of Souls, words will become reality. And I won't need my imagination.*

That's right, and any questions that pop up in the meantime, just clear your mind, and call? Thomas smiled. *How cool is that.* Even though he was probably a thousand light years away, Thomas felt Dominic was smiling too. Then he vanished again.

With Dominic definitely gone this time, Thomas just sat there. Somehow, he couldn't be bothered to move. He knew he needed to empty his mind of all the negative thoughts he had accumulated in the past if he was going to survive. He sat there for twenty minutes before the fidgets got the better of him. *Tea. A cup of tea, that's what I need.* That sounded good.

In the kitchen, he had another thought. He decided to try out his skill on his mobile phone, using it as a point of contact without handling it. After a minute or two, he decided to hide the phone as far away as he could in his village. As the tea brewed, he ran outside, moving along the lane that twisted through the village. He found a suitable spot to place his phone that he would remember then ran back to his pot of tea. With that done, he visualised his phone and went through the motions in his mind. To his amazement, it worked, and he managed to call Sarah.

Thomas! A warm, soft voice echoed around his mind. It was such a strange sensation. He wasn't using his ears either. That threw him and he stumbled over his thoughts for a second. *Hiya*, he thought.

Thomas, are you okay?

Mm, sure.

You don't sound right, a little subdued.

No, I'm alright. He was hesitant. *I just wanted to hear your voice.*

Oh, Thomas. That's a lovely thing to say. It's sweet to hear your voice too.

That lifted his spirit. He felt warm inside. It made him realise that people you care for should be able to do just that. The imaginary relationship door that he had slammed shut from his divorce a couple of years before creaked open a little. *How's the recipe reading going?*

Interesting.

Oh, that's all!

Actually, I'm confused. The problem is there are reams of paper with all these procedures, but I can't follow most of them. Sarah sounded frustrated now. Thomas could tell by the way she faltered over her words.

How do you mean? The procedures to prepare the recipe?

No, not quite. I think how it's supposed to work as a

daily regime, and it's difficult to match the whole day up. For instance, a paper for morning food, as my mother put it – that's breakfast.

Yep, reckon you're right there.

Then there are about seven papers. Hang on, let me check that, Sarah put the phone down. Thomas could hear the old papers rustling in his head as if he were there. Sarah flicked through them and mumbled away to herself. *Ah, here we are*, she shouted. *There's seven for midday and the same for night food. Mother's words again, but in what order? To complement each other? I can't figure that out.*

Thomas stayed quiet; he didn't have a clue how to help her. *The writing at the top of each page must be abbreviated or have a code and it's probably faded.*

You say there's writing at the top of the page? Sarah asked.

Yes, didn't I mention it?

No, I don't think so.

Does that help then?

Yeah, I'm sure I can work that out. Thomas thought of Dominic and what he had said about the past, how history is there forever and can be seen, whereas the future, belongs to someone else.

It will be fascinating to see how you do that, Thomas.

He laughed. *It will be a surprise for me too!*

If you can put them in order, I think these old recipes will interest you more than they do me.

I'm sure they will.

When are you going to see your sister?

Monday. When I'm back we'll make time to sit down and go through them together.

You're on! Are you going to the class tonight?

Is Saffron going?

That little tiff with you wouldn't stop her.

Okay then, I'll just keep my distance.

Yes, keep out of her way! I'll see you tonight.

Thomas was pleased with himself for managing to use his phone like that. This was the ultimate hands-free! Now he had to retrieve the phone from where he had hidden it. After that, he would have time to catch up with work. Thomas wanted to get to class early, and he didn't want to turn up to class after Saffron and her two sidekicks. It could be embarrassing. The time would come soon enough to challenge her. In the meantime, he would concentrate on increasing his flexibility in Sarah's yoga class.

"Thomas! Gosh, you're early."

"I know, I thought I'd help with the mats."

Sarah walked over, not taking her eyes off him. She placed her hand on his face and caressed his cheek. He smiled and allowed himself the pleasure of her touch.

The class filled up very quickly. The usual crowd, including Saffron, but her two sidekicks didn't show. She kept her eyes firmly on the floor. She didn't glance once at Thomas. Things between them were all cool now.

While Sarah got herself sorted for the class, Thomas looked around at the others. *All women and no other men. Only me.* His attention turned towards the door, and he watched as two new ladies walked in. Sarah greeted them and had a little chat. They looked to be in good shape, and half the size of some of the ladies already in the class. Sarah looked quite pleased to have new members. The class was now at maximum capacity.

"Off we go," she said, as the two new ladies found a space to workout.

The hour soon passed. Afterwards, everyone helped with putting the equipment away. As Thomas gathered mats, he saw Saffron leaving. That was his cue to wander over to Sarah and join a few of the others who were milling around her.

"Are you feeling better, Mr. Pink?"

He smiled. "Yes, Miss!"

"Good! Perhaps you might be up for some fun on Saturday?"

Thomas widened his eyes with curiosity. "Why, what's happening?"

"Claribel called earlier."

Thomas didn't react.

"You don't know my best mate, do you?" Sarah asked. "Winnie knows her. I haven't seen her myself since last year when we were at her place in Suffolk."

"Has she got more tickets for Suffolk?" asked Winnie.

"Yes."

Thomas stood there, still waiting to be enlightened.

"I thought I had mentioned Claribel to you." Sarah said.

"No. What are the tickets for?"

"A yoga thingy on Saturday and there will be lots of different fitness classes going on too. Claribel called to ask if we wanted to go."

Thomas was definitely up for it because Sarah wanted him to go. "Sounds great. Where is it being held?"

"Just up the road. In Suffolk."

Winnie jumped in, "Sudbury."

"Yes, that's it, Sudbury. I've been there before. It's held in some rich guy's country house. Very posh. Claribel has about ten tickets."

"Why would your mate buy ten tickets?" asked Thomas.

"She's a hypnotherapist and the tickets seem to find their way to her, with no cost to anyone. We just turn up."

"This is my first time at yoga. Would I be out of place going?" one of the new members asked.

"No," said Winnie, "half the people who turn up haven't done yoga before."

Sarah grinned. "Five tickets gone. Anyone else? What about you, Abigale?"

"And us," came a chorus from the others.

"All done then."

Thomas was keen to know what was on offer apart from yoga. As much as he liked stretching and balancing his mind in class, he didn't fancy a whole day of it. "Do they do anything else?"

Sarah smiled. "Let's grab a tea downstairs. We can go through the details."

Downstairs, Thomas organised the tables while the others bought the drinks. With everyone settled, Thomas was back on the case. "And what else?"

"There are meditation techniques Thomas. Then there's that old misery Rachael who runs Potions and Lotions."

"Lisit. Rachael Lisit, that's her name," Winnie said taking a sip of tea.

"That's her Winnie. And there's a levitation class too," added Sarah.

"I don't think anyone has ever achieved floating around the hall, though," laughed Winnie.

"They have a class on how to nurture your spirit, too," Sarah smiled at all their blank faces. "Precisely what that means, well, Heaven knows."

Thomas knew, immediately. "It increases energy flows."

"Does that interest you, Thomas?" Sarah asked.

The concerns he'd had earlier about the day had vanished. "Sounds great. I'm looking forward to it," he replied.

"I'll ring Claribel and get the address. Does anyone have a pen?" Between them, they came up with a pencil and a small jotting pad. Sarah soon had the address, and she wrote it down and handed it around.

Winnie sat forward. "Sorry I haven't introduced my daughter, Susan." Susan frowned at Winnie. "I'm sorry, she insists on calling herself Susie."

"Hello, Susie," said everyone.

Thomas hadn't paid much attention to her. Susie was about thirty, rather slim, almost skinny, with dark shadows under her eyes and a complexion that lacked spirit. What he did find stunning about her though, was her wonderful red hair. *Why do you look so stressed?*

"She works for the government," said Winnie, proudly.

"No one wants to hear that, Mum."

"Well, just look at you," continued Winnie. "You're always so stressed and grumpy. Your eyes look awful. And you must have lost at least a stone in weight this past year."

Susie just sat there silently while her mother rattled on.

Thomas did the same, though it didn't take a second for Sarah and Abigale to get into the thick of it with Winnie discussing the pressure Susie was under at work.

"It's nothing to do with the job, Mum. I have to work for a scumbag now," she said, bitterly. "Since Nigel Stonely was removed from the office, it's been a nightmare. Nigel was a decent person, doing a top job in renewable energy. My department was getting loads of great ideas. A few of these ideas were mind-blowing. It was his job to help develop those projects. Then out of the blue, he was accused of having an affair with an undersecretary whose name was kept very quiet."

"You didn't mention that to me," said Winnie.

Susie turned to her mum and frowned. Winnie shook her head and looked away.

"So, what happened to him?" Thomas asked.

"He was given a minor job elsewhere. He was shafted!"

"Shouldn't he have been made to resign and the secretary sacked?" Thomas suggested.

"There's more to it than that. On the day the scandal came out, I spoke to him. Something was definitely very wrong."

"With an accusation like that hanging over his head, I'm not surprised."

"It wasn't like that. It's hard to explain. He was in a daze. He was just nodding when I asked him what had happened."

"What did he say?" Thomas was getting drawn into this web of lies.

"He said he didn't do anything wrong."

There was silence for a moment. "You hear about things like this all the time," said Caroline. "Any more drinks, anyone?"

"I'll have a coffee, please."

"Me too."

"And me."

"Abigale, what would you like?"

She wanted tea.

As Thomas organised the drinks, he listened to Sarah talking about meeting in the car park on Saturday. "We can pick the tickets up from Claribel. Will you be travelling up with Winnie, Susie?"

"Oh no, Mum's travelling from London."

"Where do you live?"

"Field Park Lane, in Slipsly."

"That's not far from me. Why don't you travel with us?"

"That'd be great! I haven't a clue where the place is," Susie sighed. "I'm so exhausted from everything that's been going on at work, I don't think I could take in the directions. After tonight's class, my body feels as if I've been run over by a steam roller!"

"It'll be worse tomorrow," said Abigale with a smile on her face.

Sarah beamed. "She's right but keep turning up and you'll soon be in shape."

"What kind of classes shall we go to at the weekend?" asked Winnie.

They started comparing ideas. Thomas was keen to listen. He liked to be prepared. It was in his nature. The one class that took his fancy was levitation. He remembered he had almost signed up for a class in London many years ago. He couldn't remember why he didn't.

"What's the levitation class like, Winnie?"

"No one has floated around the hall yet," chuckled Abigale.

"My friend, Sasha, thought the class was disappointing and she has been going for the past three years. Hey Thomas, if you do the class, I'm sure you'll show them how it's done!"

"That would certainly be something! But I don't think levitation works like that. I think it is more like just hovering. That's what I've read, but I'm going to do the class for sure. I'm dying to know." As Thomas finished talking, a voice popped into his head. *Hiya Thomas!* It was so sudden it made him jump. He could see that they all noticed. Before anyone could say anything, he said,

"I'm not having a heart attack!" He grinned. "Someone just walked over my grave."

"More like jumped on it," remarked Sarah.

Thomas beamed, "very good!" He managed to keep his thoughts together and answer, *Dominic. Give me a sec.* Dominic picked that up and waited.

Sarah gave him a quizzical look. Thomas knew she was remembering him falling off his bike and he could see that she was concerned. Of course, that was all due to Dominic too, but how could he explain that? If only Sarah knew everything! To distract her, he reached out for his coffee. Her gaze was still intense.

Dominic's voice spoke again, echoing around his head. *Come on.*

Now his concentration was being tested to the limit. Expecting someone to speak telepathically was a little freaky and difficult to concentrate on, especially when sitting around a table of women chatting. Thomas couldn't stay cool. It threw him and unfortunately, his coffee too. It splattered on the table and onto everyone sitting around it. He swore under his breath. Embarrassed, he pretended he had sneezed, and with a nervous edge to his voice, he apologised.

That's all I need, he thought, while the others soaked the coffee up from the table and themselves with a collection of tissues from kit bags and pockets. He definitely needed to sort Dominic out. He stood up from the chair, apologising again.

"Does anyone need more paper towels?"

"Come on, Thomas, I'll go with you." Sarah took hold of his arm. He knew she realised he was anxious and was just being kind, but that threw his little plan to talk to Dominic away from everyone. He had to distract her for a few seconds to give him time to focus. And he was certain she was going to quiz him. That meant fibbing again and he didn't want that. Miraculously one of Sarah's friends came into the coffee shop and called over to her. *Perfect timing!*

She looked over, saw who it was, turned to Thomas and whispered in his ear. "Shan't be long."

He breathed a sigh of relief. Now he could concentrate on contacting Dominic. Connecting with him didn't work immediately. He realised he wasn't using his mind correctly. *Of course! I'm talking out loud. It doesn't work that way.* He turned around to check on Sarah. She was still chatting. *Relax, Thomas,* he thought to himself and tuned in. *You called Dominic?*

Yes, bad timing, eh?

You could say that. Still is. I'll contact you later, if that is okay?

No problem, I'll work on the timing thing and let you know what I've come up with.

Wait! Sarah's preoccupied still. What do you want to say?

Oh, right, I was almost gone then!

Sorry, sorry, I'm a bit stressed at the moment. Then he realised he was using his hands as if Dominic were standing in front of him. He cast his eyes up with frustration, infuriated with how he was reacting, and he was worried that everyone would think he was a basket case. *The thing is, it's been a little tricky, Dominic. I must get the hang of this talking through my mind. Otherwise, people will think that I'm losing it. Now, what's on yours?*

Would you like to have a little fun on Saturday?

Thomas sighed. *I would like some fun any time.*

Saturday it is, then.

How do you know about Saturday?

There are a million eyes on you, Mr. Pink, so there's not much I don't know.

Thomas frowned, exaggerating the lines on his forehead. He had to accept the fact that he had virtually no private time now. He glanced over at Sarah. She was on her way over. *I've got to go! Yes, fun on Saturday, that will be great. Bye, Dominic.*

Dominic chuckled. *You're going to like this.*

"Thomas! You didn't get the paper towels."

With all the kerfuffle, the towels had gone completely out of his head. "Oh! I was waiting for you."

"Talking to yourself again, were you?" It was obvious she hadn't taken her eyes off him. He just smiled as she thrust a huge roll of tissue at him. "Here!"

Back at the table, he finished the job wiping up what was left of the coffee spill.

Sarah began organising the journey for Saturday again. "What time should Susie come to mine?" she asked, "I'm not too sure of the way?"

"We should have an early start? Twenty past seven?" suggested Thomas.

"Once we get to the Black Lion pub, I'll know how to get there. What about you, Winnie? Do you remember?"

"I'm sure I do," said Winnie. "If there are any problems, we can keep in touch by mobile. Don't forget registration starts at nine."

Sarah nodded, glancing at Thomas. "Don't worry. Our chauffeur won't be late!"

Chapter 10

Thomas had already packed everything he might need. *Can't be late today*, he thought. *I'll grab tea at Sarah's*. He pulled into Sarah's drive at two minutes to seven. To his surprise, Susie had already arrived. Her cherry red Mini was already in the drive, with her kit bag on the ground by it, waiting to be stowed into Thomas's car.

"Mm, nice car," he said, talking out loud to himself again, reaching for Susie's bag. Sarah greeted him with a warm smile and a big hug. "I've made you tea Mr Driver," she said. "We just have enough time to drink it."

Thomas grinned. "I can't be late for this one."

Susie was sipping her tea when he walked into the kitchen. "Morning Thomas. You seem ready for the day."

"I fancy this might be a special day. And exciting." Seeing Sarah all day would be a first, and his feelings towards her were beginning to grow. But there was a big but. He had felt like this more than once in his life. Up in the clouds one minute and then down in the dumps the next. Divorces were costly pastimes. However today, everything seemed just great, and he was determined it would stay that way.

Sarah had loaded her things into his car.

"Are we ready?"

"Yes," replied Sarah.

"Let's go then." The three of them climbed into the car, and as they pulled off the drive Sarah called out. "Oh no, I've left my main bag!"

Thomas pulled over and backed up. Sarah jumped out and ran back inside to retrieve her bag. She bundled it into the boot and then climbed back in.

Thomas grinned at her. "Are you sure we're ready now?"

Sarah and Susie both laughed. "Off you go, driver."

Saturday. Fun day! As he drove, Thomas wondered what Dominic had in mind for the day.

"What are you thinking about Thomas?" Sarah asked.

"Levitation. I can't wait to see what that's all about."

"Nor can I," said Susie. "Do you think anyone has ever done that? I mean, I don't how a person can just hover in mid-air? I'm definitely going to that class."

"Not according to Abigale. She reckons no one has ever managed hovering." Thomas said, shifting into fourth gear.

"That's right, I have been told no one has got anywhere near hovering." Sarah agreed.

"I don't even think the instructor can, what's his name? Oh yes, Parsley Brown, that's it!" Sarah exclaimed.

"Parsley Brown? Wow, that's a name! He should be able to do anything with a name like that." Thomas laughed.

Sarah smiled. "How long do you think it will take to get there, Thomas?"

"About an hour. We should arrive in good time."

"That's if I can remember the last few miles," she said.

"We have plenty of time, don't worry." Thomas gave Sarah a quick glance.

"Registration is at nine o'clock, isn't it?"

"Yep, then the first class is at ten o'clock."

"What do you do, Thomas?" Susie asked.

"Deliveries."

"So, do you travel to London as well?"

"I work from home mostly. Travelling is half the stress in a job."

"The other half is who you work with." Thomas smiled; he knew what was coming next. *Susie has gone straight from Uni to Westminster and worked her way up in the service.*

"I'm working directly with Ministers now. The last Minister I worked for was moved sideways in what seemed to be a conspiracy," Susie said. She sounded angry.

That is an insight into what she feels about her job, thought Thomas. All the information Susie had told everyone in the cafeteria flashed through his mind, but he was intrigued to find out what had made her so angry. "Who's the new chap you work with?"

Sarah looked over at him as if to ask, what are you doing asking such a confidential question?

Susie sighed. "You don't want to know!"

"I do. It's interesting."

"So, now I'm working for a completely arrogant scumbag who hasn't a clue what he's doing. All the projects we had under Nigel have been shut down."

"Perhaps your new boss is more clued up than your old boss." Thomas looked at Susie in his rear-view mirror as he spoke. This remark did not go down well.

"Actually, he comes from a banking background," she answered furiously. "You know, those greedy bas..." She stopped short of swearing. "What on earth does he know about new sciences? Nothing! The man is clueless."

Thomas nodded.

"Susie, your mother told me your old boss Nigel was an academic, a top man in the science world." said Sarah calmly.

There was silence in the car for a moment. Thomas was eager to know more. "If all the projects have been closed down, what's your department doing all day?"

Susie sighed. "Twiddling our thumbs, mostly. Chasing old projects that have gone too far to be shut down."

"What's your boss's name?"

"George Smithe."

"Why don't you ask him what he's playing at?"

Sarah frowned and turned to Thomas. "You'll get Susie the sack."

Susie answered. "I've already done that! We ended up having a screaming match and I was officially reprimanded. He only came to Westminster twelve months ago from a background of money. Now he is a minister for renewable energy which is ludicrous," said Susie. "He definitely has an agenda. I just want to find out what it is!"

"That doesn't sound easy, Susie," Sarah said. "You need to calm yourself down. Try and relax today. This is the perfect place to wind down. The yoga or meditation classes will do it."

"I suppose you're right, Sarah."

"I know she's right," Thomas agreed.

"There are people out there with great ideas, but Smithe's just not interested. And he's stopped me from working, and I'm not having that!"

Somehow I don't think she will be able to do anything about her situation, Thomas thought. *But there's more to find out.* He knew that.

"Work talk is done now," said Sarah. "Let's enjoy the day."

"I promise not to say another word, unless, of course, you ask me!"

"I think we are almost there," Sarah sounded anxious as she looked for the pub.

"How are we doing for time?" Susie asked.

"Okay, we should see the pub on our right soon."

They found it, much to Sarah's joy. "I know the way from here. And we are early. It's only ten past eight."

They pulled into the very grand driveway. The large house

loomed in the distance beyond all the temporary signs directing traffic. Thomas spotted an empty parking space. "Here we go," he said as he turned off the driveway.

Susie shrieked. Thomas rammed his foot onto the brake. "What's wrong?" He looked around. Susie had her hand covering half her face, and she was turned sideways as if trying to hide herself.

"What on earth's the matter, Susie?" asked Sarah.

"Over there." Susie whispered pointing.

"Who? Who are you pointing at?" Thomas asked.

"Do you see the man wearing a sporty sort of jacket and a flat cap? He is walking past the red van." Susie was struggling to get her words out.

Sarah nodded. Thomas couldn't see him. The guy was on the wrong side of the car.

"That's my boss! That's Smithe. What's he doing here?" Susie was breathing hard.

"Are you sure that's him?" Thomas asked.

"Dead sure! What shall I do?"

Thomas frowned. "That's uncanny."

"Well, don't let him spoil your weekend, Susie," Sarah said.

"I'll go ahead and see what he's up to." Thomas climbed out of the car. "Flat cap and sports jacket, right? Can you park up, Sarah honey?" He headed off towards the main house.

Sarah parked the car, grabbed the bags, and noticed Thomas's old cap on the back of the window ledge. She held it out to Susie, smiling. "Disguise!"

The two women made their way to the registration hall with Susie wearing the cap pulled down, almost covering her eyes. In the hallway door of the enormous house, Sarah spotted Claribel and went over to greet her. Susie followed, trying to look inconspicuous. "Hey, Claribel! This is Susie. It's her first time coming here."

Susie made a face and put her finger to her lips.

"She's just seen her boss," Sarah explained. She looked around at all the faces to see if she recognised anyone else. "Great, all the other girls are here. I can't see Thomas though." She looked around.

"There he is, coming down the stairs," said Susie.

Claribel laughed. "How can you see with that cap over your eyes?"

Thomas had already spotted them and made his way through the crowd as quickly as he could. He had something to report, but when he noticed all the others, he wasn't sure whether to say anything.

"Thank God you're here, Thomas, I thought we'd lost you," said Sarah anxiously. "This is Claribel." Claribel looked at Thomas as if she were sizing him up, but before she could say a word Susie jumped in.

"What happened?"

"Well, you'll be glad to know that Smithe isn't here for any of the classes," Thomas announced. "I found out that he knows the owner of the house."

"So where did he go to, Thomas?" Susie asked.

"He's out in the lobby, I saw him meet up with the owner Tony Barnstable, and he was taken to a room upstairs."

"How do you know that?" demanded Susie, "and how do you know the owner's name?"

"I followed them and just before they got to the room, I asked one of the staff who the short fat guy was."

"Thomas, you didn't! How could you say that?" Sarah couldn't believe it.

"Well, he is short and fat. The person I asked laughed, and she called him a grouchy old, so and so."

Claribel came closer to Thomas, "I've heard a lot about you, Thomas, and it looks like it's all true."

"Don't tell him anymore, Claribel," laughed Sarah. "He'll get the wrong idea."

"So, what have you been saying?" asked Thomas, feeling a little embarrassed.

Claribel turned back to Susie. "You're still hiding under that cap? There is no need."

"Well, I don't want to be seen. Why would a Government Minister be at a convention like this?" Susie looked at all the girls: Caroline, Julia, Sarah, and Claribel. None of them had an answer.

"I think it's just a coincidence. His mate owns the house after all," suggested Sarah.

"No! Susie says he's a scumbag!" said Caroline. "How can we get him to lose his job?"

The girls all huddled together round Susie.

Chapter 11

Thomas watched his classmates chatting. None of them seemed to be making their minds up about classes. Sarah was standing next to him and she was looking at the list of classes. She didn't fancy the potions class. "That teacher is a grumpy old witch. Look, Rachel Lisit, that's her name, I told you that, didn't I? She has history with one of my friends. They had a big argument about the constituents of a plant, and my friend was thrown out of the seminar she was attending!"

Thomas was eager to register. Susie was banging on about George Smithe again and she was getting the other two involved. Her whining was getting on his nerves. He ushered all of them along to the queue, which had now grown substantially. Finally, Thomas knew what class he was attending, so now he relaxed and thought about Dominic's plan. He didn't have a clue what Dominic had in mind. *Maybe just a little fun.*

"I think that Rachel Lisit is an old witch!" declared Claribel. "Maisy works for her and has plans to open an alternative clinic, but she's keen to learn, and Rachel has a vast knowledge of plants and flowers."

"So, Maisy is leaving the clinic in town then?" asked Sarah.

"Yes, only when she feels ready. That's why she's doing that class. I said I would join her. My hypnotherapy class will be available too. We want to make it on our own."

Thomas looked at his watch.

"What time is levitation?" asked Sarah. "You want to go to that, don't you?"

"Yes, it's immediately after lunch."

It didn't take too long before their turn came.

"We're all done. Now we can relax, Thomas," Sarah said smiling.

Susie and Caroline had decided to go and do a little investigating. "We won't be long, Sarah," called Susie as they set off up the stairs wanting to find out what Smithe was up to.

"We have about thirty minutes before the convention starts," shouted Claribel. "Shall we all meet for lunch?"

"Okay," they called back.

"Let's find the room we're in, Thomas," Sarah suggested as they made their way up the main stairs. Halfway up, Sarah nudged Thomas. "Look!" she whispered, pointing down into the hall.

He turned. "Why are we whispering?"

"There he is!"

"Gosh, how can you see with all these people?"

"The one with a cap."

"Yes, I can see him. Talking to a lady with fair hair."

"Hey! I know her. What's going on?"

Susie and Caroline were upstairs on the landing. "We ought to tell Susie." Thomas waved at them and pointed down towards Mr. Smithe. Caroline cottoned on immediately and the two girls ran past them down the stairs as fast as they could. They got as close as they dared using the crowd as cover. By the time they were anywhere near Smithe and the fair–headed lady, they had moved away. Susie and Caroline made their way back to Thomas and Sarah.

"There are so many people here. Let's move to the side of the stairs," Thomas suggested.

"So, who's the lady you said you knew?" asked Sarah.

"I am pretty sure I saw Saffron," said Thomas.

Sarah was surprised.

Thomas looked down into the hall again to confirm.

"Can you still see her?"

"Let's move back across to the banister. It's too difficult to see from here," said Thomas. "Ah, there, I can see her now." Thomas pointed. "She's still with Smithe!"

"I don't think he's attending any of the classes, do you?" asked Susie.

"No, not dressed like that."

"I don't understand Thomas, why would he be with the lady you argued with?" asked Susie.

"I think that might be her sister Sasha," Sarah said.

Susie scrunched up her eyes, trying to see. "Well, I don't know what her sister looks like, but that looks awfully like the lady Thomas argued with."

Sarah looked again. "Actually, Saffron is over there as well."

"How on earth can Saffron and her sister both know Susie's boss?"

What is the connection? Thomas wondered. Why does *Smithe know either of them?* Time was running tight. He checked with Sarah. "We have fifteen minutes, but these things never start on time."

"There's just enough time to follow the three of them." Caroline said. "Right, who's going then?"

"Me!"

"But Susie, if you're spotted, it will mess things up."

"I'll wear the cap," she said.

"Okay."

"We'll save your places," said Sarah. "Wait! Where's the hall, Thomas?"

"Just up at the top of the stairs and to the left, I think. I'll check." He ran up the stairs. A few moments later, he was back. "The hall is just at the end."

"I can still see them," Caroline said enthusiastically. It was evident that she was as keen as Susie to find out what was happening. She put on a deadpan face, beckoned to Susie, who had the cap covering half her face. "See you later."

The hall where the yoga class was held was at least twice the size of the one at the leisure centre, and it was full. If they had left it any longer, there would have been no spaces left.

"Wow, there must be a hundred people in here," Thomas said.

He turned towards Sarah. She was looking worried. "I feel quite bothered about Saffron and the Minister, Thomas. What do you think?"

"I'm not sure what to make of it all. What I am sure of though is Saffron seems to have her secrets. She's a strange girl."

Sarah nodded.

Something is wrong, Thomas thought, *but what?* Dominic had told him things. Then there were the ladies from the yoga class mentioning the odd thing about Saffron, but it didn't amount to much. *Why is she mixing with a Government Minister? An unsavoury character as far as Susie is concerned. Then there is Sarah with her canny intuition sensing something about Saffron. It's all adding up, meaning something is wrong, but what?*

He smiled at Sarah to cheer her up. "We'll forget about it for the moment and concentrate on the class."

Winnie and Abigale waved enthusiastically as he and Sarah made their way over to them. Looking around, he realised there were only three men in the hall, including him, so he was keen to settle down. He unrolled his mat, put the bottle of water on the floor, and sat there, hoping to be invisible. Not so with Sarah. She was far too busy acknowledging half the other women in the hall. *No sign of the teacher yet.*

Susie and Caroline rushed into the hall and made their way over to them. "Guess what? Where do you think Saffron and Sasha went with Mr. Smithe?"

"Where?" asked Thomas.

"Tony Barnstable's private office. Here's your cap back, Thomas."

"How do you know that?" he asked.

"I did what Thomas did and asked one of the staff!" Caroline said, "I made up a story about my mother knowing Tony Barnstable ages ago, and bingo, she told me half his life story in three minutes flat! No one here likes him. Apparently, he's a nasty so-and-so."

Suddenly, Thomas realised half the class in the yoga hall were listening. "We better leave this until lunchtime, I think," he whispered. "We're holding up the class."

The door opened and the yoga teacher came in, followed by his team.

"Are we all ready?" The teacher asked, looking in their direction. Thomas looked down. He was embarrassed. The others didn't care. They just smiled back.

"My name is Parsley Brown," he announced, ushering his three helpers to strategic positions around the class. It was reasonable to think he couldn't manage that size of class on his own. "Well, hello everyone!" he said smiling broadly.

A gentle "Hiya Parsley," came from most people in the hall.

"Great to see you all. As you must have noticed, I do have a little help. There's Sophie behind you all," Parsley pointed to the back of the hall. "Then there's Sash, and Timothy over there. Now, before starting, has everyone done yoga before?" Lots of nods confirmed that everyone had. "Good, let's start by warming up."

People lingered after the class to talk, hoping to catch up with people they knew. Sarah knew at least half the people in the hall. Thomas only wanted to hear the whereabouts of Susie's boss, Saffron and her sister.

"They went into Barnstable's office off that large hallway," whispered Susie.

"What, and he went there with Saffron?"

"Ssh!" the others said.

"Saffron only went in for a minute, then left to go to the potions class. I saw her sister waiting for her there," Susie continued.

"Wait until lunchtime then we can ask Claribel if anything unusual happened in that potions class." Thomas said. "There's a talk on the levitation class, maybe we might find some useful information there."

Forty-five minutes later, no one was any the wiser.

At lunchtime, there were so many people in dining room and Thomas only just managed to find a table to accommodate them all.

Claribel and Maisy had been to the potions class and they had news – and a theory. So, after enjoying the dish of the day, they all listened in disbelief as Claribel described how the class had developed. She told them that Rachel had run through the basics, reminding them of the more established formulas. Then out of the blue, she introduced Saffron, and from then on, Saffron ran the class, bringing Rachel into it occasionally.

"Really?" Sarah was amazed.

"It certainly wasn't what I was expecting. It was all about the creation of new potions, formula, or whatever. I lost my way for a while." Claribel said, as she turned to look at Maisy. "Maisy's miffed as well."

Maisy nodded. "Bloody right! That Saffron is a real piece of work. It was a waste of time going to that class. She had an agenda; it was nothing to do with most of us in the class."

"How do you mean?" Sarah asked.

"It was blatantly obvious she was looking for star pupils," huffed Claribel. "She had no interest in anyone else. That class was like a witches' convention but without the witches. Anyway, there were two ladies in the class who were very clued up! And I mean clued! They were telling Saffron how things worked. As soon as she realised that – well, the rest of us might as well not have even been there!"

Maisy nodded, "What a waste of money."

"Actually, there was a witch there. Saffron!" Thomas announced.

"Thomas don't be daft," Sarah cast her eyes up to heaven. "He had a run-in with Saffron."

"Ssh!" Claribel pointed. "Look! On the table over there," she whispered. "The one with the mass of hair."

"There's something odd looking about her face," whispered Maisy.

Thomas casually glanced across. "Isn't that clever clogs from the class?"

Claribel nodded. "Where's the other one?"

"She went off with Saffron," Maisy whispered.

"Where are they?" They all looked around. "Which way did they go?" whispered Thomas.

Caroline was panicking. "I bet they went to that office. You know, the one we followed them to. I'm going to have a look. Coming, Susie?"

"Give me your cap again please Thomas," asked Susie. "I'm going too."

He rummaged through his backpack. "Don't forget. If you're spotted, it could make life difficult for you."

"Yeah, yeah, and I'll make Smithe's life difficult too."

"Right, we'll leave it to you then." He passed the cap discreetly to her, worried they were attracting attention. "But be careful! Don't forget you only have fifteen minutes before the next class."

"Yes," Susie said, as she almost tripped over her feet in her haste to catch up with Caroline.

Thomas sighed. "I have a feeling this isn't a good idea."

"But she won't rest until she knows what's going on," Winnie said. "My daughter's like that."

"Let's leave them to it," sighed Sarah.

The voices at the other table grew louder. A few minutes earlier, Thomas had noticed someone else sit down next to the smart lady that Claribel had pointed out. An argument was brewing, and he couldn't help tuning in to what was being said between them.

Still cross with the know-it-all, Winnie seemed even keener than he was to hear what was going on. Sarah, Abigale and Maisy, were all listening too.

He couldn't help but watch them as the argument got into full swing. His attention was drawn to the younger lady sitting at the table. She had short hair that exposed her neck. There were marks or maybe scars on her neck, just like Saffron had. He had assumed the marks on Saffron were from her cats. *The exact same marks!* Suddenly he was convinced that she was Saffron's sister Sasha. *Isn't it?* Desperate to see her face, he shifted his chair back.

"Where are you going?" asked Sarah.

"I won't be long; I just need to stretch my legs." He motioned towards the next table. Sarah nodded and positioned herself to get a better look.

She turned back towards him with her eyes wide open. "Sasha?" she whispered.

Thomas stood up, intending to walk in the direction of the exit, which would let him get a better look, but there were people in the way. Going the wrong way round meant he had to turn to look back at her. He moved casually around the tables, looked out at the door as if he were looking for someone, and then walked back. It worked. *Perfect, a clear view.*

Back at the table, he sat next to Sarah. "It's definitely Saffron's sister. She has the same mannerisms and a similar sounding voice. She's aggressive, like Saffron. It looks to me as if she is trying to persuade that clever lady, whatever her name is, to do something she doesn't want to do." As Thomas finished speaking, the argument broke into a screaming match!

"How many times do you need telling, I'm not interested? Now go away and leave me alone," yelled the clever woman.

The younger woman jumped to her feet, pushed the table out of her way, knocked the chair over, and stormed off. The clever lady looked around the room at the people surrounding her. It was clear she was upset.

Sarah hurried over to her. "I'm Sarah. Are you okay?"

"I'm so sorry about that," the woman replied, embarrassed. "Thanks, I will be now that spiteful cow has gone. Sorry dear, I just need a couple of minutes to calm down." She stared down at the table for a second or two. "I can't let that know it all get to me." After a moment or two, she looked up at Sarah and smiled. Thomas, Claribel, and Winnie came over. "I'm okay now."

"Are you sure you're okay?" Winnie asked.

"Oh yes. I am now, sorry. I'm Rosemary."

When Thomas heard Rosemary's name, he joked, saying. "And there I was calling you the clever one. I much prefer Rosemary."

Rosemary gave him a smile.

"This is Thomas," said Sarah, "and this is Claribel and Winnie."

"What did Sasha want with you?" Thomas asked. "It was Sasha, wasn't it?"

Claribel and Winnie cringed at his question, but Sarah didn't.

Rosemary laughed. "Yes, her name is Sasha. You don't mess with your words, do you?"

Thomas grinned.

"Actually, she wanted me to join some sort of organisation or cult."

"Why?" asked Sarah.

"I was in that potions class for one reason only. Eczema. That teacher, Rachel, is highly regarded for curing skin problems. That's why I came. Instead of providing learning, that class was being turned into a recruitment drive. Sasha and that nasty old cow, Saffron Shortstaff, she pushed Rachel to the side-lines and she and her sister ran the class with the intention of getting everyone to join their organisation."

"Heavens," Sarah groaned.

"That's my guess too," agreed Thomas. "They are definitely recruiting."

The others looked at each other. "That's why my dears, the class turned into a who knows what fiasco, not a workshop." Rosemary shook her head sadly.

Sarah, looking thoughtful, asked Rosemary. "Have I seen you before?"

"Not unless you've been to a white witch, dear."

"Ooh," said Sarah, suddenly quite excited. "My mother was a white witch."

That surprised Thomas. He stared at Sarah. *Do such things pass down the generations?*

While the others knew as much as Sarah did about these things, Claribel was very keen to learn more. "Have you ever fancied the idea of being a consultant, Rosemary?" she asked. "Do you ever do appointments? My daughter is setting up a clinic."

Claribel had ignited a spark and animated Rosemary began to share her life story. She mentioned that she was brought up in Surrey and still lived there with her mother.

That put a sparkle on Sarah's face. "Can I ask what your family name is? Is it Plant? Rosemary Plant?"

"How on earth did you know that?"

"I think my mum knew your mum. A long time ago, though. Victoria Overbaund. That was my mother's name."

"Oh, my! That certainly rings a bell."

"Ooh!" Sarah turned to Thomas. "How long do we have before the next class?"

"Five minutes max."

Rosemary dived into her bag and found her mobile. "I'll call my mother. I need to know now!" She dialled and held the phone to her ear. "Mum, didn't you know a Victoria Overbaund?"

"Yes."

"Well, you'll never guess, this is her daughter, Sarah!" She handed the phone to Sarah.

Sarah looked physically shaken to find out that the woman on the other end of the phone knew her mother all those years ago. After a few seconds, she put her hand over the mouthpiece. "She says she has something on her mind that has bothered her for years. She wants to discuss it with me." Rosemary nodded enthusiastically. "Right, shall we meet?" Sarah asked Rosemary's mother. "Yes, I'll organise it with Rosemary. Thank you, I'm looking forward to meeting you."

Rosemary had a quick chat with her mother and then ended the call.

"Are you coming with us, Rosemary?" asked Claribel. "We are going to levitate. Hopefully."

Rosemary wasn't sure about going.

"Look at it this way. We both had a wasted day at the first class. The next one has to be a lot more interesting."

Rosemary nodded. "Yes! Why not! What happened to the other two?"

"I'll explain on the way to class," said Claribel.

Thomas pointed to his watch. "You lot go on. I'll find the other two. Don't forget to save three places," he called over his shoulder.

Typical, thought Thomas. *Everyone has decided to move at the same time.* He pushed his way through the crowd and out of the food hall. In the dimly lit corridor, just a handful of people were going in one direction. He decided to go the other way. "I must find the two girls quickly," he said out loud to himself.

Half walking, half running, he approached a bend in the corridor. *There they are.* He signalled. That didn't work. Susie had her ear to a door. *What does she have in her hand?* He got closer. He realised each of them had a glass to their ear, pressing it against the door. Now he was only about twenty feet away. *Why haven't they noticed me?* He dare not call out. Oddly, it was all making him feel sick. Somehow, he just knew they shouldn't be there. Then to make things worse, Dominic popped into his head.

Thomas, get out now! This isn't a safe place!

"Don't stress me!" Thomas said out loud. "What are you doing, Thomas." He said to himself. "Think it."

Just go. There was an edge to Dominic's voice.

I need to grab these two.

Quickly. Quickly! Be quick!

Susie and Caroline turned. They saw Thomas. "Ssh!"

He beckoned desperately.

They saw the urgent expression on his face and ran toward him. "What's wrong, Thomas?"

He knew he couldn't say what was actually wrong, so he just said, "you've been ages! We're late! That's what's wrong!"

"Oh, is that all?" Caroline said. Susie just pulled a funny face.

"What were you doing?" he asked, as they hurried back towards the food hall.

"We were listening in."

"I've gathered that," he said. Susie passed him her glass. "What's this?"

"For listening!"

"Don't you think that was a bit dodgy? Everyone could see you snooping."

"Yes, but..."

"Now we're late for the class."

He dumped the glass on a ledge, and he pushed Susie in front towards the hall door. He decided that she could take the brunt of the sarcasm they were about to get for being late. Susie opened the door gently and it creaked loudly. The whole class turned around and to make things worse, Mr. Parsley Brown was standing just on the other side of the door. He smiled. "I assume you have been practising. We all expected you to hover into the class."

His comment brought lots of cheers. Thomas bowed his head. He knew something like this would happen. However, Caroline and Susie were not embarrassed.

"Sorry, Mr. Brown," said Caroline. "We made a mistake. We thought we had to hover out of the class, not into it."

That brought a roar of laughter. Even Parsley Brown had a smile. Sarah and the others were sitting over on one side. Thomas and the two girls hurried over to them to take their place.

Don't worry, Dominic whispered into Thomas's mind. *You'll show them how it's done.*

"How?" asked Thomas immediately out loud! He stopped himself fast. *What are you going to do?* He said, using his mind instead.

I'm almost excited for you, being able to easily think your words now.

Thomas didn't have time to continue mind-chatting. *Got to go*. He sat down next to Sarah. She smiled and reached out to squeeze his hand to make sure he was okay.

The class began with a series of gentle, calming exercises. The voice of Parsley Brown changed, into a soft, mellow sound, almost sleepy, as he walked around the huge class. *A hundred and fifty people at least*, thought Thomas. As he circulated, Parsley Brown stopped by his helpers who were making notes. Many minutes passed. Finally, Parsley called in his team. They all chatted for a moment, and then went around selecting potential levitators.

"You! Yes, you young lady!" Parsley announced in a flirtatious manner. The girl giggled and stood up. "Come to the front, please," he said. With her face beaming, she made her way to the front of the class. Meanwhile, the others in his team had made their selection. Two more ladies and one man made their way to the front to join the lady that was still giggling.

"Two more men, and then we can start." Parsley scanned the hall for the other two candidates. The silence was intense. Everyone was holding their breath in anticipation. Calmly, Parsley glided around the hall, knowing exactly who he had chosen but was feeling the need to be dramatic. Everyone lapped it up, waiting for the next two to be selected, even Thomas. "You, sir. Yes, you in the pink top, with no hair."

"Who me?" The hall erupted as the man in the pink top, and no hair happily came to the front.

"Now who should we choose for the last potential expert in effortless travel?" Parsley looked around the hall at his audience all enjoying his theatrics. Head held high, he almost certainly knew the last man he would call but continued to have fun. Suddenly, he swung around and pointed at Thomas.

"You! You, young man! The one sitting next to our pretty Sarah!"

That threw Thomas. Although Thomas had been prepared to be summoned, when it came to the crunch, he didn't feel as prepared as he had hoped to be.

Sarah was shocked too. "I've never met him! How does he know my name?" she whispered. Then she looked across at Parsley Brown's team. "Oh, there's Maggie! That's how. I used to do yoga with her years and years ago."

Maggie saw her looking and waved. "See you after class," she mouthed.

Sarah nodded. Now she was in a very buoyant mood and keen to persuade Thomas to stand up. Dominic popped into his head again, telling him to move his backside and join the other five.

"I've chosen these six recruits because they have a special aura," declared Parsley Brown.

A hush fell over the class. They were keen to witness something they had never seen before. The selected six, as they were now being called, were a mixture of age and size, three men, three women. They were asked to lie on lengths of wood placed on small stalls with their heads on cushions giving the impression of a bridge. Then they were asked to do quite sophisticated breathing exercises. This lasted around five minutes or so.

Thomas was so relaxed he started to fall asleep. Dominic gave him a nudge. *Come on, wake up!*

Another five minutes had passed with Parsley giving out instructions, walking slowly up and down, repeating the same words almost like a mantra. Thomas felt as if he was in another world now and the instructions went over head, but they were academic as he was working to Dominic's agenda, not Parsley Brown's.

Ready, Thomas? Here we go, then. As you start to rise up, the class will erupt. What you need to do is, keep your eyes closed and don't move. I'll do the rest.

Okay. Suddenly Thomas had this feeling of nothingness. It was very odd. He lifted about an inch off the bench and hovered, supported only by air. There was no part of him touching the wood.

Dominic popped into his head again. *Don't move.*

He had no intention of moving.

Thomas, no one can see what's happening yet. As you rise,

just relax. Try not to be tense in any part of your body. It is supported.

How?

This isn't the time for questions! I'll tell you later.

That's what you always say.

Concentrate! Chatting won't get you hovering around the room!

Okay. Do I have to steer?

Even though Thomas hadn't been listening to Parsley, he was still giving out instructions creating an amazing atmosphere in the room, and he could feel the sense of excitement and anticipation building in the hall. Magical was the word that came to mind.

Dominic interrupted his thoughts. *Yes, you can steer, as you put it. All you have to do to move forward, just imagine all your weight is in your feet. If you wish to go back, well, I think you can figure that one out.*

Yep! Let's go then.

He heard Dominic chuckle. That was the signal. Thomas soared six feet up from the bench. They gasped out loud in amazement, and Thomas himself nearly passed out.

So, Thomas, what do you think? asked Dominic.

Flipping hell! Just let me catch my breath. Whoa! It's awesome. Seconds later, he was moving around the hall amazing everyone. *How is this happening, Dominic?*

Just concentrate. I'll tell you another time. Enjoy the experience.

Thomas didn't need to be told that. He was having the time of his life! A few minutes passed and everyone in the hall became silent with astonishment.

When Dominic suggested they shouldn't push the realms of reality too far and they should stop levitating, Thomas agreed.

When I drop you, you will look awkward, we need to make you look ordinary again and take the edge off your achievement.

Come on, then. Immediately, he hit the floor!

Ouch, that really hurt! Why didn't you take me down a couple of feet more?

You said, 'come on then'. I took that as you were ready.

Very logical. I must remember that.

Before Thomas could get up, he was surrounded with what seemed like everyone talking at the same time. He was sitting there rubbing the bruised bits when the class decided to show their appreciation, pulling him up from the floor on to his feet. He was surrounded and being asked all sorts of questions, and as he hadn't given any thought to the class reaction, he didn't have a clue what to say. He just stood there bemused, making gestures with his hands. Feeling a tad panicky, he looked around for Sarah. *There she is.* Sarah was struggling to get to him through the enthusiastic class members.

"Absolutely incredible!" called Parsley, shouting to be heard over the uproar. "How did you do that?"

Me tell Parsley? I don't think so!

Sarah pushed through and wrapped her arms around him. "You're bloody amazing!" she said grinning from ear to ear.

Strangely enough, he suddenly felt guilty, but Dominic was still inside his head.

Don't fuss! You didn't cheat, you just showed everyone how it will be done in five thousand years or so. You've had two minutes of fame. But look what you've done for all these people. It's a memory of a lifetime for them! No doubt you will be talked about for years to come, giving even more pleasure!

Feeling reassured, Thomas could enjoy Sarah hugging him, and everyone's kind comments.

"I can't let you vanish Thomas, without having your contact number," said Parsley. "If I may be in touch sometime in the future, it would be appreciated."

"He can have my number," said Sarah, "can't he Thomas?"

"Yes, of course."

Parsley shook Thomas's hand and left. Thomas was surprised how cold Parsley's hand felt. Icy almost.

Chapter 12

Now the class was over, everyone was making their way towards the food hall. Thomas was keen to find out from Susie what had been heard in the room down the corridor, however, they all still wanted to know how he had managed to rise off the bench and float around the hall. He needed to come up with something better than a shrug of his shoulders. Strangely, all he could do was think back when he was a young lad living with his mum and dad. They were both spiritualists and his dad would tell him about spirits, how they could appear seemingly out of nowhere and drift around the room. And he remembered even further back, when he was convinced, he actually saw a spirit floating down the stairs at the family home.

Sarah took his hand as they all sat down at the table together. "It was the spirits. They helped, didn't they?"

Rosemary couldn't take her eyes off him, "I too am a spiritualist," she said. "You do have an aura around you. I have never seen such a powerful one before. Are you aware of this, Thomas?" She sat down opposite him. "There's something else going on here."

Everyone around the table leaned forward, even the people on the next table wanted to know more! The food hall went quiet, quiet enough to hear a pin drop. He wasn't keen on her continuing. He looked her straight in the eye and shook his head. "Another time."

"What do you mean?" asked Maisy.

Susie wasn't going to let it go either. "Come on, Thomas, you have just done something incredible! How did you do it?!"

Thomas just shrugged his shoulders. The people at the next table looked disappointed and they went off to order food. "Anyway, Susie," he said brightly, trying to distract them all, "I want to hear exactly what happened on your little spying mission."

Sarah nodded in agreement. "That's more important. You can pay Rosemary a visit any time to discuss spiritual things. So come on then, what did you do to get Thomas in a tizzy?"

Susie leaned forward, "It was difficult to hear clearly, but what we thought we heard was that they were recruiting. The lady from the potions class agreed to join. She was offered one thousand pounds a week as a retainer."

"How much?" they all stared at her.

"For what?" Thomas asked.

"Don't know," said Susie. "What we do know for sure is Saffron will be showing her what's what."

Thomas glanced over at Sarah, hoping she might have an idea about what was going on. Her face was blank. However, Rosemary looked as if she knew something. She took her phone out of her bag, called a number, then passed it over to Sarah. "My mother will know."

"Hello Catherine," said Sarah. She listened for a moment and then whispered to Thomas. "She wants to know how you got on."

Thomas smiled.

"Oh, absolutely amazing," She said into the phone. Sarah listened to Catherine speak. "Really? What sort of things?" She listened and then whispered to Thomas. "She doesn't want to say over the phone, and she wants us to meet her."

Thomas nodded. "We could see her tomorrow."

"Okay, we'll be there, mid-morning tomorrow. See you soon." She handed the phone back to Rosemary.

"So, where are we going tomorrow?" asked Thomas.

"Did I hear that you're going tomorrow?" asked Rosemary. "My, that's a bit of a rush. I'll write the address down for you. Did she give you any information on what's going on here?"

It was obvious to all of them that something was going on. *People being offered money, potions, witches arguing and meetings behind closed doors.* Thomas sat back in his chair. Since Dominic had entered his life, his sensitivity was starting to peek. He felt he had an advantage over all of them, except Rosemary. She was very deep. He couldn't read her. Somehow, he knew he would need her before too long. He thought about the day. Susie's boss turning up. Saffron and her sister appearing. Meeting Rosemary. And now actually, even more bizarre, Sarah's connection with Rosemary's mum. His mind was racing. *This can only be a coincidence,* he thought.

"Are you okay?" Sarah squeezed his hand.

He nodded. "Yes," he said quietly. He gave her a warm smile. Rosemary looked over at him. He could see, she recognized there was something special about him.

"Here, Thomas," she said. "I have the address."

He looked at it, "We'll need to leave early. It's a bit of a way."

"Any ideas on where that lady Saffron was speaking to lives?"

"Goodness, Thomas," said Caroline. "That's a strange thing to say."

Sarah laughed. "I think floating around the hall earlier has gone to his head."

"Think about it," Thomas wasn't sure why this was an odd question.

"Why would you want to know that?" asked Sarah.

"Something is up, and if Susie wants to sus out her boss..."

"Good thinking, Thomas! Why didn't I think of that?" Susie said.

Her mum, Winnie, gave her a little hug. "We've had a long day sweetie."

"It's important we stay sharp," suggested Thomas.

"Don't be hard on Susie. It's all new to her," Sarah said.

"But Thomas is right," said Rosemary. "I think we are dealing with evil. One mistake and that's it."

They all stared at her.

"Finding out exactly what these people want with their new recruit is the start to unravelling this mystery," she said. "We don't know her name so we can't track her down that way. She needs to be followed. Unfortunately, we need to do it right now!" She pointed to the edge of the food hall. Their target was walking with Saffron towards a side exit door. "She's leaving, look!"

"We are going to lose her if we're not quick," remarked Thomas.

He was itching to pursue her himself. Winnie jumped up. "I'll follow her. After all, she's the one who messed the class up – admittedly with Saffron's help."

"Be careful, Mum."

"Don't fuss," Winnie said as she looked at Rosemary, "Bye, Rosemary, I'll be in touch."

Rosemary nodded.

Winnie moved like lightning across the hall and disappeared through the side exit, past Saffron and her new recruit, who were still talking there. That gave Winnie extra time to prepare for the chase. Thomas and Sarah watched out of the window as Winnie whizzed between the parked cars, which was no mean feat for her size. She climbed into her car, and before the new recruit came outside, she was waiting in position.

Thomas and his friends decided to wait for five minutes or so, giving time for their targets to exit without being spotted.

Having something to eat had gone out of their minds. They were more interested in talking about what had been discussed. Rosemary gave her contact number out and added everybody else's to her contact list. A sense of urgency was developing, the mood was thoughtful. It was still apparent that Rosemary had information she didn't want to share.

Thomas could feel the frustration of the others, especially Susie, but he wasn't concerned. He knew that when the time was right, Rosemary would supply whatever information she had. "Time to go, we're all done!"

"Yes, okay." Sarah glanced around the hall, just in case she had missed something or someone.

"I need the loo," said Thomas as they all stood up. He handed the key to Sarah.

She smiled, "See you outside, Mister."

He flew up the stairs, two at a time. He didn't what to keep the girls waiting. Loud voices from the landing above caught his attention. It was Susie's boss and the man they thought owned the mansion. He had ten stairs or more to climb so he slowed his pace down in order to hear more of the conversation. When he reached the top, the two men had vanished. The hall was empty. He headed for the loo. At the door of the toilets, he stopped. *Voices again.* He waited outside to hear. *Mm... Something about dark witches?* Suddenly, he was doing the same thing Susie and Caroline had been told off for doing!

Don't go in there, Thomas! Dominic's voice inside his head again was urgent. *This is really dangerous. You have to go now.*

Shh... I'm listening.

"She needs to get us two more if we are going to be able to stick to the time frame, Tony."

Go! Dominic was determined.

Thomas could hear water running. *Definitely, my cue to leave!* He had seconds to get to the stairs, without being seen. He ran down towards the hall, completely forgetting the reason why he'd gone up in the first place. At the bottom of the stairs, he slowed his pace so as not to attract attention when he walked through the hall. And once outside, he calmed down. He repeated to himself what he had heard so he didn't forget.

In the car park, the others were waiting with Sarah and Susie to say goodbye. They hugged one another and set off their separate ways. Thomas jumped in the car with Sarah and Susie ready to head home.

"That was a marvellous day, don't you think, Thomas?" asked Sarah, looking in his direction.

But he was thinking about what he had just heard.

"Don't you think?" she prompted.

"No... Yes! Yes, it was great." He wasn't paying much attention. What he was thinking about was more important, "As I was running up the stairs, I saw Susie's boss and his mate. I couldn't use the loo; they went in there before me." He glanced round at Susie. She hadn't heard, she was so engrossed in her mobile. He turned back to Sarah and said quietly. "I overheard them talking."

Susie leaned forward. "What did they say?"

Thomas smiled, "I heard them mention Saffron's sister."

Susie's eyes widened. "Really, What did they say?"

"They were saying he'd only got two."

"Two what?" asked Sarah.

"Two witches," replied Thomas.

Susie asked, "Who was doing the talking?"

"Your boss but I think the other one's in charge. His words were, 'We still need two more if we are going to stick to your timeframe'."

Susie started to fret. "I knew he was up to something. Come on, Thomas, you know about these things. Any ideas?"

"Yes, Thomas, Susie's right!" Sarah looked into the rear-view mirror and smiled at Susie. "He's thinking! It's obvious to me that they're recruiting people."

"Not just people, Witches! I wonder why?" asked Thomas.

"So, Saffron is one. Her sister is. The new lady also, and they need two more. That's five! I bet there's more to this than we realise. What did you say your boss did before, Susie?"

"Banking, apparently. He was very successful."

"Why would he leave then?"

"Stress, perhaps?"

"How old is he?"

"Mid forty's... ish."

"Okay." Thomas replied looking thoughtful. Since he had agreed to work with Dominic, his intuition had developed beyond recognition. He hadn't realised how much until now, but there had been no reason to test it until today. Now, he felt amazed at how much he seemed to understand. "Check on your boss, Susie. See what he's worth. Dig up all his personal stuff. The same for his friend, Tony. I presume he owns the big house. He must be loaded. Find out where his money came from."

"Hang on, Thomas, I'm writing it down. Okay. Go on."

"Find out who organised the session today? And see if you can find someone who went to the potions class, last year."

"Is that it?"

"For now."

"You seem to have an idea or something, Thomas. What are you thinking?"

"I'm not sure, but I need to speak to Rosemary's mum."

"Why?" Sarah asked.

"I want to ask her what a dark witch is. What do they do? What's their purpose? I have a good idea what they are, but why would Smithe and his mate want them?"

"We do have an advantage," said Sarah.

Susie nodded. "They don't know we're on to them."

They pulled into Sarah's drive. "Keep me in the loop," requested Susie.

Sarah gave her a hug. "See you at yoga, next week."

"Okay, bye."

As she drove away, Sarah turned to Thomas. "Do you want dinner?"

"Yes, please, that will be great."

"Do you like sticky toffee pudding?"

Thomas smiled. "You bet I do." He looked at her as they went inside. Goosebumps ran down his body as she headed for the kitchen. Feelings that he had banished forever had returned and they were going straight for his heart. He couldn't understand why he had no resistance. Why he was being weak. He felt sure he had locked his heart away, somewhere. *Do I want to go back to the way I used to be? No. But...*

Sarah walked back into the room, and she looked at him. "You look melancholy."

He didn't know what to say, "Just thoughtful."

"About what?"

"Lots of stuff. This week. So much has happened. And now, you."

"Me?"

"I can't stop thinking about you."

"Thomas Pink!" she blushed. "I've felt like that for an age too, but I couldn't say anything. You weren't ready." She laughed. "Come on. Come over here. Now, we can have more of each other."

Dinner and sticky toffee pudding didn't happen.

Chapter 13

Thomas ate his breakfast hungrily. Sarah looked across the table at him. "Is everything okay with you?"

He gave Sarah a smile. He felt comfortable. He realised the worries over his heart and his feelings were unnecessary, and the space they had occupied was now filled with joy. "Yes, and you?"

Sarah responded by leaning over the table and kissing him. "What do you think?"

"I think, we're good."

"Much more."

Thomas stood up and took her in his arms.

"We should get a move on Mr Pink; Guildford is a long way."

"Mm... It's a shame we have to go out today. I'll do the dishes while you get sorted."

It was now quarter to eight, the intention was to leave by eight, which they managed.

"Do you think Catherine will drop some kind of bombshell?" asked Sarah as they drove towards Guildford.

"What makes you think that?" Thomas had been trying to work out why an old friend of her mother's wanted to see Sarah in such a dramatic fashion, after twenty years had passed.

"The only thing that stands out in my mind is the nagging feeling I get once in a while when I think about my mother's premature death."

"Does that make you sad?" he asked.

"It's hard to put into words." She was silent for a few moments, then she said, "it affects my mood. It's as if I am suddenly miserable when I think about what happened."

"What do I know? But I do think you've buried something. I think you should try to relax and clear your mind, as if you had just taken a class."

Sarah frowned, but she was intrigued with what he had just said. "Buried something. Catherine will pick up on what's tucked away in my mind, I'm sure." She sighed. "It's so frustrating. Something wasn't right at the time of my mum's death."

He smiled. "Just fifteen minutes and we'll be there then the frustration can go away. But what takes its place might be another matter."

Maybe Sarah is moments away from something that could throw her. Maybe it will change her forever. He sensed bad stuff was coming. Maybe Dominic could help. He was sure that he would have an idea.

Call me any time if you have a problem, Dominic announced in his mind.

So, Thomas did. He was comfortable driving and having a conversation all at the same time. But right now, Sarah was all he was concerned about. With that in mind, he prepared himself. And went at it – carefully.

Yes, Thomas? I'm here and I'm aware that you have Sarah beside you. Well done! And before you ask, Sarah has to tread her own path. No need to worry.

Okay. I'm getting in the swing of this mind-talking. I can't help worrying about her and...

I've been expecting your call.

Okay clever clogs, what's bothering me then?

Things are starting to hot up!

I'm not going to ask how you know that. You didn't see us, did you?

What you need to know, said Dominic ignoring his last question, *is that the vibrations you are generating are raised now. But you knew that was going to happen.*

What I didn't take on board was the consequences.

Be aware, you're attracting attention.

Who am I attracting?

At the moment, only the good guys, but that doesn't mean to say that those that do not serve your higher self cannot see you. When you return from the Garden of Souls, your presence will be much greater. That's when the other lot can most certainly pick up on you. But we can deal with that problem when you're there.

"We're here, honey," Dominic faded out.

Sarah smiled.

Thomas was chuffed, she'd called him honey. It made him feel good.

"We're a tad early. Do you fancy a coffee?" she asked.

"Sure. I'll make for the railway station. There should be a coffee house around there."

Ten minutes later, they were drinking coffee and getting to know each other even better. Sarah took out a map and spread it out on the table. "This was my mother's map. I found it with her recipes."

"This is old. Is that your mother's writing?"

Sarah nodded. "Look, can you see Catherine's road highlighted?"

Thomas moved the map closer to the light. "Yes, I can see the route marked out from the station to her house. Catherine's lived there all that time. I wonder what the other marked roads represent. Curious that."

"We'll ask Catherine."

"Come on then." Thomas rose from his chair and took Sarah's hand. It was a good feeling. All the turmoil that he had experienced twenty-four hours earlier had faded into nothing.

The drive from the station to Catherine's house was under five minutes, but it was enough for Sarah to turn into a bag of nerves. Thomas noticed and pulled over about a hundred metres from Catherine's house.

Sarah looked for the house. "I thought it was number fifty-two?"

"It is, but I thought we could walk the rest of the way."

When she got out of the car, he gave her a reassuring hug, then the pair of them walked towards the house hand in hand.

"I wonder how Winnie got on?" he said as they walked, trying to distract Sarah from her sad thoughts.

"Mm," she said, not paying much attention to what he was saying.

"We should call her later," suggested Thomas.

"Oh, sorry I forgot. My phone rang earlier. I'd better check." She looked at it. "Yes. It was Winnie. She's sent a text. 'Job done. I know where the clever bitch lives now. Let you know on Monday, kisses'. Good!"

Thomas laughed. "Well done, Winnie."

They were now outside number fifty-two. "Let's see if Catherine can add a little more to that story," said Thomas and he knocked on the door.

The door opened and Catherine threw her arms wide and hugged Sarah for an age, but only two seconds when it came to Thomas! "Come in, you two. How was the journey? Would you like tea or something? Sit anywhere you like. You both look very well. You look after yourselves, don't you? Oh! So sorry, I'm rambling on. What must you think of me?"

"Don't be daft, I'm as excited as you are to meet after all these years! Don't worry, we've just had coffee. And yes, we do take care of ourselves."

Catherine was suddenly overcome. Tears trickled down her cheeks.

"You alright?" asked Sarah.

"Oh, it's just me being silly again."

The doorbell rang. "That should be Rosemary," said Catherine.

Rosemary was pleased to see both of them again. "Hello, you two. Have you heard from Winnie yet? Sorry, but her following that woman has been on my mind all night."

Thomas stood back and let Sarah talk.

"She texted this morning, saying 'I know where the clever bitch lives now!'" That tickled Thomas for the second time.

Rosemary punched her fist triumphantly into the air. "Now we can see what they're up to."

With all the excitement of their arrival over, Catherine got down to telling them her story. "It was such a shock, your mother dying within a month of being diagnosed. They said it was over exposure to radiation. At the time, I was so messed up, I didn't take anything on board. The company shut the project down, and then sealed the lab off. The people who worked on the project were dispersed around the company. Your Auntie came for you, and I never knew where you went. It took me ages to get over the shock of it all. I just sat around here in my mother's house, grieving. It took me about a year before I came to my senses. I was ashamed of myself for wasting all that time. Time I should have used looking into what happened."

Catherine sighed. "I did check what happened. A little late, I grant you, but I was in no shape to do anything. Your mother was my best friend ever and she was gone. One thing I'm sure of is that b***** Jeremy Merston had something to do with it."

Sarah sat back in the chair, shocked. "Who is Jeremy Merston? Why do you think he was involved?"

"Victoria had arguments with him on a daily basis. At one stage, she said he was trying to sabotage the project."

"Really? Can you remember how he reacted?"

"I can remember like it was yesterday! He lost it completely! He went for her, shouting at her, saliva spraying from his mouth. Victoria was more than a match for him, scientifically, and that made him worse."

"Why did my mum think he was sabotaging the project?"

"Because of the breakthrough we had made! It was scientifically proven. And it was a procedure that worked. All we needed to move forward was numbers coming through the programme. But he stopped it from happening! It was only one month and a day after that argument that Victoria was gone. A while after her death, I dug deeper."

Catherine began to weep. Sarah moved over to sit next to her and started crying too. Rosemary tried to console them.

"Oh dear, this won't do," said Catherine, wiping away her tears, determined to carry on. "I worked on Jeremy for a couple of years after that and – well, what I'm about to say you will find it difficult to get your head around." She turned to look at Rosemary.

Rosemary nodded. "But now mother, Thomas is here," she said gently.

Catherine paused. Then she glanced over at Thomas, and the look on her face changed as if she was acknowledging something about him. "You're different. You're a powerful man." She reached out and took hold of his hand, held it tightly and looked into his eyes. "I say prayers for Victoria every night but that is no help to her now. I sense that you are capable of great things."

He glanced over at Sarah. He knew what Catherine was saying, but he also knew that Sarah wasn't ready for this yet.

"Jeremy Merston is working with dark powers, those same powers that Saffron is linked to. Of course, that's if Rosemary has read it right, but I don't doubt her. They are so powerful and dangerous; you will need the help of all in the coven."

Thomas could smell a fight coming and this excited him. He was up for it.

"What coven?" Sarah looked nervous.

Catherine looked at Rosemary for reassurance, "Our coven is made up of your mother's friends, white witches from around the country."

"Do you think Jeremy is behind my mother's death?" whispered Sarah.

"Absolutely."

"I don't understand then. Why couldn't you report him to the police?"

Catherine put her arm around Sarah. "Our methods of detection aren't conventional, dear. Plus, the man has strong backing. I went head-to-head with him once."

"Goodness! What happened?"

"That's how I found out how powerful he is. I did inflict some damage. But..." Catherine pulled her cardigan sleeve down. From the shoulder to the elbow were signs of severe burning. Her arm was half its original size. "This is what I got in return!"

Sarah looked urgently at Thomas, remembering how his face had been healed. "Can't you do something?"

Rosemary stared at her. "How?"

"Thomas hurt his face in the gym, and it was fixed by morning. Oh! Now you're going to be mad at me, Thomas! You asked me not to say anything!"

Thomas smiled. He leant towards her and squeezed her hand. "Don't be daft." He turned to the others. "I was spiritually healed." Although, it wasn't quite true, Catherine and Rosemary nodded. He left it at that.

Sarah turned back to Catherine. "So that Merston man killed my mother?"

Rosemary looked at Sarah sympathetically. "I'm going to make tea. You explain Mum."

"I think you'll need to understand how we work, how it's done Sarah dear, if we are going to get into a fight with this lot."

"Educate me!"

"In that particular incidence, I had to call up everyone in the coven for an energy surge that would maximise my abilities. What that meant was I took all their power, so at that moment, they were all vulnerable."

"Was that dangerous?" Sarah asked.

"Yes, I suppose, but it's more, well... inconvenient."

Sarah looked puzzled. Thomas waited for Catherine's explanation.

"A witch in that condition will lock herself down. That's the first safety rule so that nothing can get through to her. The inconvenient bit is they're grounded for three or four days."

"What does that mean?"

"They cannot leave the actual space where they carried out the ritual."

"Do you mean they can't leave the house?"

"Not quite. They can't leave their space."

"What space?"

"Sorry, my dear. I do know what you are saying, but it's hard to explain. They prepare themselves, then shut down the gifted side, so no movement whatsoever can happen from that part of them within their immediate surroundings. A witch will go through a ritual by pacing out an area they call their space. Each witch will have a different area and different size space. But once their power comes back, they can return to normal."

"Are witches normal?"

Catherine smiled. "It's very rare this happens. I, myself, have only had to do it twice in the forty years I've been a member of the coven."

"My life has been so predictable and safe," said Sarah, reaching out nervously for Thomas's hand.

Rosemary entered the room with a large teapot. "Proper tea, for you, Thomas!"

"So," said Catherine, taking her cup, "with that power organised, I checked on Merston's movements. We have to know exactly where the target is at the exact time we make our move. With that established, I set up an attack and timed it for 6am. At that stage, I was aware of his association with the Dark Side, but I didn't dream for one moment how powerful he was."

"But how would you know?" asked Sarah.

"It was my fault, I was angry. I didn't take the precautions needed, and with all that energy in my hands, I released it too late. Because of his power, Jeremy Merston managed to deflect most of the coven's power. Not all, but what didn't hit him hit me." She pointed to her arm. "Big mistake."

"What about him?"

"Drink your tea, dear. It's getting cold."

"Tell us."

"He did get injuries to his pelvis and hip. Now, he needs a walking stick."

"Why didn't you form a coven circle to protect yourself?" asked Thomas.

Catherine looked at him, shocked. "How do you know about that?"

Thomas shrugged. "I probably read it in one of those books I have at home."

Sarah narrowed her eyes at him.

Catherine shook her head. "I was ashamed of myself. You're right, Thomas. I should have formed a coven circle, but I didn't."

Sarah was frustrated. "Can't Merston be caught?" she asked.

"He won't get away with it again," Rosemary assured her. "Anyway, now that Thomas is around, I have a feeling everything's going to change."

"Why Thomas?" asked Sarah.

Catherine changed the subject. "We have a small issue to overcome."

"I knew this would be a challenging day," sighed Thomas. "What's the issue?"

"When I made the attack on that dark soul, I should have followed another rule."

"Another one? I don't think I am ever going to get the hang of how you witches work," said Sarah.

"You will," said Thomas. "Catherine is saying there is a protection plan for the coven."

"I'm impressed, Thomas. Now, tell me how you know that?"

"Probably, the same book," he replied, trying to look innocent.

"I think we may have to talk about your book later, Mr Pink."

Thomas smiled again. "Sorry for interrupting. Please carry on, Catherine."

"When we do that sort of thing, as Thomas said, there are precautions. I ignored them. When there are more witches involved, they are put in place as a matter of course. I know that, but I still stupidly ignored the rules."

"This is great stuff, I'm intrigued," Thomas said. "Are you allowed to tell us more?"

Rosemary answered instead of her mum. "When I read your aura yesterday, Thomas, I knew you were different. I've never seen anything like it before. Although, I didn't feel the need for confirmation, I did ask Mum to give me her opinion."

Catherine leaned forward. "Rosemary's right. You are powerful!"

Thomas sat dumb struck. Suddenly, he was worried that they knew too much.

"Do you have any idea of your power?"

"Yes, I do." He was confident of his answer. "Yes." *Dominic was right, I am stronger and have a higher vibration now.*

"Well, it's the reason Rosemary and I are sharing our ways with you. I have a feeling you will need some assistance before long. So, the more you know how a white witch works, the better."

Thomas glanced over at Sarah, but she didn't say a word. He looked back at Catherine. "So, how did you tie Jeremy?" he asked.

"What?" asked Sarah. "What do you mean tie him?"

"Constrict him to one place," replied Catherine.

"I think, you could tell us, Thomas," said Rosemary.

"Maybe." Dominic entered his mind. Thomas stayed calm and maintained the vacant look on his face, as he listened.

You're doing well, said Dominic. *The people you are with will be an asset on your return.*

I had an idea; this meeting was in your scheme. But how did you know?

I didn't, until now, said Dominic. *You are now linked with your team. Now you're in the fold, nothing is going to happen to you. Your level of importance has gone through the roof. I'm now going to transfer some information then leave.*

Thomas shuddered and Dominic was suddenly gone.

Sarah was nudging him. "Are you with us?"

"What? Oh, yes. Just daydreaming." He leaned forward to Catherine. "You tied Jeremy Merston using his own power. The trouble with exchanging power like that is you can't finish him off. Correct?"

"Yes!" Said Catherine, amazed, "That's how I did it. One witch stays out of the energy exchange and monitors the process. That was my friend, Tara. When she recognised the power surge coming back, she closed it down and used the same energy to tie him. In a nutshell, that means he's wrapped up in his own power. That has neutralised him but, as you say Thomas, he's impregnable to any witches' power." She glanced at Sarah, realising this must be painful. Sarah was in no mood for sympathy. She just wanted a solution on how to deal with the man she was convinced, took her mother's life.

"Is there any way of breaking that tie?" asked Thomas.

"Yes. But before we go any further, I would like to ask you a question."

"Go on."

"The pair of you have been here in the house for about two hours. In that time, have you heard or felt anyone else here, apart from us?"

Rosemary looked at her mum in amazement. "Why on earth did you ask that?"

Catherine put her hand up. "Let Thomas answer."

"What you mean is, am I in contact?"

"Voices in your head?"

"Just the one voice, and yes while we have been here."

"He's your man then, Sarah," said Catherine.

Rosemary realised what her mother was getting at and nodded her head.

Sarah sat back in her chair. "I'm so confused, Thomas, why didn't you tell me about this?"

"You'd think I was doolally."

"I do anyway."

He laughed. "Oh well, suppose that's alright then." He turned back to Catherine, trying to change the direction of the conversation. "So how are we going to get hold of Merston?"

But Sarah wasn't having any of that. "Hang on, Mister! How do Catharine and Rosemary know all this?"

"We're both mediums, sweetheart," said Catharine, "our guides are giving us the same information."

"Am I allowed to ask, what or who?" Sarah was looking confused.

Catherine gave her a warm smile. "You can ask whatever you like, deary."

"We have been informed that a higher being will enter our lives," said Rosemary.

Catherine nodded. "We have been asked to co-operate and help wherever we can. And we believe, Thomas is that person."

Sarah stared at her.

"Mum's right. It is Thomas. I know this all seems extraordinary. If we hadn't met yesterday, this wouldn't be happening."

"But you did meet," said Catherine. "And then, you spoke to me."

"Yes, but how can you be so sure it's Thomas?"

"Right," said Catherine, "Listen, this is exactly what I've been told on more than one occasion. Victoria's daughter will bring salvation from a man with colour."

"Colour?"

"Pink!" said Catherine.

Sarah's jaw dropped. She turned towards Thomas. "What happens now?"

"Confirmation that we are right! That's what we need."

"How on earth can we get that Thomas? Unless you fancy knocking on Merston's door to find out the truth about what happened?"

"If only it were that simple, Sarah." said Catherine. "Unfortunately, we don't know where Merston lives."

"Thomas, can't your guides tell you?"

"I'm sure I can find him. But first things first, Sarah. When I get back, we will hold a circle. And we will need the help of Catherine and Rosemary."

"Why would you want to do that?" she asked.

"Those two reasons, confirmation and possibly finding him."

Sarah looked even more confused. "Who will tell you that?"

"Your mum will tell us."

Sarah went quiet for a moment, then took a deep breath. "Does it involve coming here to Guildford again?" she asked.

"Not necessary. We can hold it at yours or mine. All we need to do is arrange a time that suits everyone."

"Brilliant!" said Rosemary.

"Who do you have in mind to join us?" asked Sarah.

Thomas hadn't thought about the details. "You decide."

Sarah looked at the other two, "Next Sunday?"

"Definitely." Catherine was indescribably excited. "I've waited twenty years for this, and now this great day is just a week away."

Rosemary was just as keen. "But do you think we'll require outside help?"

"What do you have in mind, Rosemary?" asked Thomas.

"Considering what you want to achieve, it's crucial to control the vibration coming from the other side."

Thomas gave it some thought, Rosemary was right. "Yes, the vibration from the other side will be higher. I should have thought of that. I presume, you have people with a solid connection?" This was all very surprising to be thinking and speaking like this. A week ago, he didn't have a clue about any of this. All this could only be Dominic's doing.

Rosemary smiled, "we have a few people. I'll need to work out the geographical position. What I thought was Mum and I will provide a strong segment of the circle here in Guildford and link with your position while the other two, or maybe three, will do the job of establishing the vibrational continuity from your location."

Thomas thought that sounded good. "I'm not sure of the maths enabling those positions to be worked out, but I'm sure you'll have that one covered."

"That's no problem. When you decide where you're going to hold the circle, give me the postcode and I'll look at the shape of the triangle. Then I'll give you the locations of the others and show you how it works. Timing is crucial, so I recommend you co-ordinate the locations."

"I understand."

"I don't, Thomas. And I want to be on this," said Sarah. "Please explain."

Thomas nodded. "We need a shape before we start to create a conduit or pathway to the Spirits."

"That's the triangle, yes?"

"Yes, Rosemary and Catherine have contacts around the country. What Rosemary will do is apply the principles of spiritual mapping for a clean route on the triangle." Then he thought of something important. He looked at Rosemary. "If you have enough people with abilities, it might be an idea to have a closed circle?"

"What's that?" asked Sarah. "And what's spiritual mapping?"

"We have more than enough people," said Rosemary, "and that's a good idea."

"Well, instead of being part of the triangle in north Essex, Sarah, we should be enclosed in it. Then we can link from inside to the circumference of the circle. That will give us more stability. No outside forces can interfere. It will be like being face to face with a spirit, instead of them being a hundred metres away, trying to lip read."

"I've not heard it described that way before, Thomas. Very good. I'm impressed," said Catherine.

Thomas was pretty impressed with himself! It was as if he had a whole new box of knowledge in his head that he could just dip into.

Sarah was still confused, "The mapping thing? What's that about?"

"That's a little darker and more complex," Thomas said. "For instance, can you recollect going somewhere you've never been before, and it's made you shudder because you know something is not right there?"

"Yes."

"Well, that's a dark place we need to avoid. Rosemary can identify those places and show us how to avoid them."

"Are you saying it's to do with the Devil?"

Thomas smiled at her. "Yes, sweetie. That's where Lucifer takes his holidays. Bad places."

They all laughed, and the atmosphere lightened. “The set up will give us the power to go direct to the other side. That’s important. But more so is the information coming back. That’s where Rosemary’s people come in. They have the ability to control the vibration.”

“I’m sure you told me already but tell me again please, about the vibration.”

“Well, spirits work on a higher vibration to us. They have no baggage, no earthly concerns apart from who they have left behind, so they are buzzing. Unlike us lot.”

“I don’t know about that!” said Sarah.

“Anyway, Rosemary’s little team should be able to slow spiritual communication down, bringing it closer to our level. None of us should miss a word.”

“It seems very complicated, Thomas.”

“As you get into the swing of it, it’s like everything else. You’ll wonder what you thought the problem was.”

“I believe you! It’s getting late now. Shouldn’t we start for home?”

“You have a big week ahead, Thomas,” said Catherine.

He nodded. “We’ll let you know the postcode.”

Sarah looked at him, “I know! Why don’t we hold it at my house?”

Thomas was delighted. She had such a cosy home. With that sorted, it allowed Rosemary to arrange her team sooner.

“I might need to call you next week, Thomas, for advice.”

“No problem, Rosemary.”

He needed to think through a plan for answering the phone to Rosemary as next week, he would be in the Garden of Souls and had no idea what to expect!

A few hugs, and they were on the way towards the car.

Sarah took his hand as she turned to kiss him, “Gosh, am I impressed with you!”

“I’m impressed with me, myself. I can’t believe I remembered all that. In fact, I didn’t even know I knew it.”

"It's probably come from the same place as your healing."

"Maybe."

"Right Mister, I'll drive back. That will allow you to concentrate on the questions I'm going to ask."

He smiled, "More questions?"

"I want to know what you know."

She was relentless. Question after question! But it didn't bother him. She was methodical. Her questions designed to extract as much information from him as she could, and all this, she worked out while listening to them all talking in Catherine's house.

"So, what you believe is, anything is possible, Thomas?"

"Well, when I return later in the week, we'll see what can be achieved!"

"I can't wait," she said as they pulled into her drive. "Do you fancy a cup of tea and are you staying the night?"

Thomas was a tad shy, but he was overjoyed at the invitation. "Yes please, to tea. And stay? Yes! I'd love to!"

Sarah walked round the car, flung her arms around his neck, and gave him lots of kisses. *This is how it ought to be. I never thought I would meet the love of my life.*

"Why don't you pop over to your house later and pick up what you need for the week. You can leave for Betty's from here, in the morning."

"Great," he couldn't argue. But then, he gave it some thought. *How is this going to work?* The plan was for Dominic to appear at his house in the morning. He certainly wouldn't be needing his car. *I must remember to turn left out of Sarah's drive in the morning towards the motorway and not right towards my house. Then I'll hide the car somewhere while I'm with Dominic.*

Within thirty minutes, he was driving home, and he had figured out how it could work. Firstly, he must set his mobile phone up, leaving it on charge. Then to test the theory, he called his sons, both calls without physically holding the phone. That worked! While he was speaking to them, he asked each one to call back, explaining he was having problems with incoming calls. They did and that worked perfectly. He managed to answer the phone without touching it. That was almost unbelievable. It set his mind at rest. All he had to do now was chuck a few clothes and other bits into a bag and he was ready to return to Sarah's house.

As he was on the way back, he mulled over all that had been said earlier about holding a circle. He realised he dare not make any mistakes. This was serious stuff that he had not attempted to do before. He was confident Dominic would be hands on if needed, but it was about Sarah's mother and if what had been discussed with Catherine was correct, that concerned him. *There is no reason to doubt them. What I am worried about is Sarah's determination to avenge her mother. I don't want her getting hurt.*

When he arrived back, Sarah was setting the table for a late Sunday lunch. "Where shall I leave my bag, honey?" he asked.

Sarah was too preoccupied to take much notice. "Oh, anywhere. Don't worry. Sit down. Food's ready on the table. Did you get everything you needed?"

"Yep. I also brought a book over for you to glance at, if you fancy."

"Thank you," she said, sitting down too. "You know what? The visit this morning with Catherine has made me realise there's a lot more going on in life apart from yoga! I think, I need to get up to speed, Thomas. Something's telling me that all this will not end with Jeremy Merston."

Thomas was astonished to hear that. "Why?"

"I'm not sure. All I know is something is nagging at me, I never thought for one moment I'd be asking you all these questions about your beliefs. It's the same stuff that Alisha goes on about. Spirits and different levels up there in heaven or whatever up there is. She even mentioned travelling?"

Thomas put down his fork. "Do you mean astral travelling?"

"Mm… yes. That's it, I think."

"My dad told me about that, it makes me nervous, but I would like to think it's in me to do it."

Sarah had stopped eating too. "But travelling where?"

"I think that's the clever bit. I'm not sure."

"What did your dad tell you about it then?"

Thomas let his mind wander. It was a while since he and his father had spoken about spiritual things. Maybe twenty years had passed, but he remembered pretty much everything. "I'm sure my dad mentioned when he was in bed he would visit his dad. He took pains to tell me to be careful, watch out for something like demons. I'm not sure if that was the word he used or not. But I can't remember that bit," Thomas took a very deep breath, "probably because it frightened me."

"But your dad could have dreamt it."

"Yes, I suppose, you're right. But people have reported experiencing travelling under a controlled environment and it's been proven. It depends on the individual."

"You have me thinking and that's an improvement in a week! What are you smiling at, Thomas?"

"You! That look of determination on your face! I'm sure you'll deal with Jeremy what's his name without any help from us lot."

"We'll discuss him after pudding."

Thomas stood up from the table and cleared the dishes while Sarah served up homemade apple pie that had been retrieved from the freezer. They chatted on for an hour or so with Sarah leaning forward, listening intently to Thomas telling her things he had picked up from the books he had read or mediums he had come into contact with. He surprised himself with how much he had heard or read over the years, and how much interest he had taken in it all. Time slipped by.

"What time are you starting out?" asked Sarah.

Thomas was so preoccupied with staying the night he hadn't given that a thought. He hesitated. "I'm not sure." As he wasn't going to his sister's, he wasn't driving. He had to tell a fib. He didn't like doing it. "Around six o'clock, maybe six thirty. I don't want to sit in traffic."

Sarah smiled seductively. "Bedtime, then?"

Chapter 14

The following morning, they were both up early. Thomas was nervous. This was the start of the week he knew would change his life beyond recognition. Sarah was sitting in front of her computer, printing everything she could find on astral travel. "I'll have this cracked, by the time you get back."

He grinned "I would expect nothing less!" He walked over. "Must go now, honey," he gave Sarah a warm hug and kissed her.

She followed him out to the car. "Call me later!"

He nodded. "Of course."

As he went out of the drive, he remembered to turn left, towards the motorway and not towards home. That would have been a silly mistake. He eventually changed direction and headed for home. He knew now where to park his car – the back of the old farm buildings, a few minutes from the house would be perfect.

Once back inside the house, Thomas checked his mobile phone was in place. He checked the time; it was seven fifteen. He remembered Dominic telling him eight o'clock. As he sat waiting for Dominic to appear, he was nervous. His stomach started to churn, not knowing what to expect. He leaned back and closed his eyes. The next thing he realised was that Dominic was suggesting he woke up.

He stood up, "What's the time?"

"Two minutes to eight. I thought I'd give you a moment to come round."

"That's very thoughtful of you, Dominic." It was good to see him in person again.

"Sarcasm, Thomas? I see you have a bag packed for the trip, but you won't need it."

"Yes, I thought as much. But I didn't have any say in the matter."

"You stayed at Sarah's?"

"That's right. Hold up a sec. You told me that your time here was restricted."

"That's right, it is."

"Well, how did you know then?"

Dominic smiled at Thomas's persistence. "It's history now. As you are aware, I can read history."

That threw Thomas completely. He sat back down, just to take that on board. "History? An hour ago is history? Wow! Am I going to be able to do that?"

"Not to the same degree, but yes. There are lots of things that will come out of this week's enhancement course."

"Just a sec." Thomas moved his bag behind the chair. "So, how does it work then?" he paused. "Why won't I need to change my clothes?"

"That's because you won't be in your body."

"I won't what? Hang on a minute, you never mentioned that before!"

"That's right, I didn't. I just assumed you would realise. If you're off to the Garden of Souls, it's the spirit world." Dominic sounded quite nonchalant about it.

Thomas was troubled. "But we didn't do that when you took me halfway round the world."

"That's true as well. You took your body with you, but you just didn't use it."

Thomas was now completely flummoxed. "Well, what did I do with it then?"

Dominic looked as if he was enjoying himself. "Right. Okay, when someone from this planet travels – ah, and I might add you are only the third person to ever do this! I thought I'd tell you that. Anyway, the spirit is in front of your body, in a sense leading, so when you arrive at your destination, the spirit controls the body's state. It places it in parking mode because as we travelled, we didn't want to re-enter it, otherwise we would have been seen."

"I understand what you're saying so why didn't you tell me all this before?"

"You have to ask as you have done now."

Thomas shut up. "Okay, let's go then."

"Just one other small matter. When you return, make sure you change your clothes."

"That's a good point, I didn't think of that. Another question. No, it's not a question. Its confirmation. It's my spirit that's going to be enhanced, not my body. Yes?"

"Almost right. As I told you at the beginning, you will return in better shape than you are now, with more than enough ability to do the job. The key is to learn how to use what you have been given."

"Yes, I remember. Come on then let's go," said Thomas. Now, he was full of confidence.

He took hold of Dominic's robe and they were gone.

Almost immediately, they arrived with Thomas falling again. Their landing spot was on lush fresh grass. He had landed on his feet but then immediately fell to his knees and stayed like that for a moment or two, not wanting to move. *This must be the greenest grass I have ever seen – so short.*

"Are you okay, Thomas?" asked Dominic.

He nodded. He moved to a sitting position, then looked up at the bluest, brightest sky, far beyond anything he had known before. Dominic was watching from a little way off, obviously not wanting to intrude on these magical moments.

While Thomas was adjusting to a different world, Sarah had already organised that Winnie be part of the circle. The date set was for the coming Sunday. Winnie's daughter, Susie, was to come as well. Sarah had in mind to call her cousin, Alisha, but wasn't sure if Alisha would be strong enough or well enough. She decided to ask her anyway.

"Hi Alisha, how are you feeling?"

"Could be better." Alisha explained how she needed more tests, and she was booked in for that week.

"I'll come with you this time. I should have come before."

"Would you? That would be great!" When Alisha heard about the circle, she sounded even more cheerful. She hadn't had a chance to speak to Thomas, since learning about his spiritual experience and was keen to quiz him. With that arranged, Sarah went off to concentrate on the book Thomas had loaned her. As soon as she settled into her reading chair, she got a call from Rosemary. She had already contacted all the witches in the coven.

"Everyone wants to help, all forty of them. It's amazing!"

Sarah was astonished. "You have forty witches in your group. Good grief, I assumed your coven was just a handful of witches."

"Oh no, we're all over the country from Scotland to Plymouth through to Wales. It's taken hundreds of years to build the coven's network."

"How long?"

"White witches have been around forever. Ordinary people like me and my mother."

"What about the other kind of witch? Ones like Saffron and her sister."

"I don't know how many dark witches there are in the world, but they tend to live in remote places. What they do is questionable. Take Saffron, for example. When I reached out for help yesterday, I threw Saffron's name in the Libellus."

"Libellus?" Sarah didn't understand.

"Sorry, that's when we communicate. She's known to half of them and what came back was, listen to this! It will interest you and your friend's daughter, Susie. Apparently, she worked in a bank in London for ages, then last year, she packed her bags and left. Can you guess who she works for now?"

Sarah knew immediately. "Susie's boss! He worked in a bank! Christ, Rosemary! Are you telling me she works for what's his name... George Smithe?"

"Yes, I think what we're getting involved in is just the tip of the iceberg. You must be careful if you are ever near her. She is a dark and extremely powerful witch."

Sarah almost had a panic attack. "But she attends the yoga classes I run!"

"I had an idea she was in your company, somehow. No worries, she won't have a clue you know about her. Just act as you usually do. I can't imagine you would do anything to get on her bad side."

"That's right. I don't do that, but Thomas does, and he did!"

Rosemary laughed. "I gathered that as well! I like Thomas."

"So do I. Nothing must happen to him."

"I wouldn't worry about that if I were you. He's far too powerful for her, and I have a feeling she knows that."

Sarah sounded exasperated. "How do you know all this?"

"As Thomas is in touch, so are we. Not such a strong connection, but nevertheless, we're informed." she laughed. "You'll need to learn all about witches, especially the dark ones. Both of you must be safe. Thomas is here for a purpose. I'm sure of that. He's the one who we have all been expecting."

Before Sarah could comment, Rosemary said, "Everyone

in the group asked Mum if he was the one who we have all been waiting for. Has he arrived at last? And now, including my mum, that's forty of us – we are all thinking the same."

"I didn't realise you told your group about Thomas?"

"I didn't need to, everyone picked up on it as soon as he finished levitating. It is now history, and that's what we're good at. You must have had an idea that he was different, especially when he levitated. No one can do that. He demonstrated how to defy gravity. How the hell can anyone do that?"

Sarah wasn't sure what to say.

"I think, you've seen other stuff he's done that was extraordinary."

Sarah told her about Thomas's fall off the bike and how it completely healed overnight. Rosemary agreed that it was remarkable and the explanation feasible. "What I know and the rest of us know is, he will need help, it's written in the stars. My mother's grandmother spoke about someone coming and that, my dear, is your Thomas."

"How can that be if he wasn't even born then?"

"Maybe so, but he was on his way. That's it. I don't know anymore."

Sarah considered it all, "I'm more confused now than before you called, Rosemary." Rosemary suggested if she had time, to sit quietly for an hour, sipping a cup of her favourite tea and let everything sink in.

"Okay, call you soon, Rosemary. Oh! One last thing. How do you meet each other if everyone lives so far apart?"

"How it works is, within the forty, there are small groups. These are more localised groups spread around the country. Our group spreads from Surrey to the south coast. We all meet within our group every so often, two, maybe three times a year."

"How many are in your local group?"

"There's seven of us. What I find intriguing..." Rosemary suddenly stopped talking.

Chapter 15

Thomas needed time to adjust. That wasn't surprising as his imagination was so vivid, it was throwing his senses, completely overwhelming him. Dominic decided to join him on the grass, and just sat there peacefully allowing Thomas to cope with the energy and images bombarding him.

Thomas didn't want to look around anymore, but he noticed Dominic wasn't sitting at all, he was hovering. Seeing him like that calmed his mind into a soporific dreamlike state. *I'm loving being here, I don't know why.* He guessed there was a purpose for all this. Somehow his mind, although it had been worked on while he was in his body, needed to be tweaked. He felt oblivious to everything except his inner self. He felt he could stay immersed within himself forever.

Without warning, Dominic popped into his head. *Are you ready to meet other souls?*

Thomas was shaken out of his dream state, realising he had to get on with the task he was here for. He jumped up. "Ready when you are." He recognised a different kind of sound as he spoke. He was now in the realms of 'thought talk', as he referred to it. He was also picking up a gentle humming sound, almost like music. *So soothing.*

Dominic was starting to fade, leaving him to it. He recognised he was using new skills. It wasn't long before he had worked out how to communicate with other souls. Some were obviously on their way up and going through a similar process to himself. Others that were on their way down had a different programme altogether. Thomas couldn't get the same contact with them, and all he knew was that it was a rehabilitation process in the Garden of Souls. Well, that's what he thought he was picking up from souls who were going back.

Not quite, Thomas. It seemed Dominic could just jump into the flowing thoughts that were dominating the Garden. *That's just stage one. There are a few more stages to go through before leaving.*

Thomas was just fine with that. Every second he was there, he was becoming more aware, understanding exactly what Dominic was talking about. He felt as if his intellectual upgrade was now fully functional.

Now, are you ready to meet Jonas Barley and the team selected by a higher power? Dominic's voice flowed through his mind like a river.

Even with his increased abilities, Thomas knew he couldn't come close to understanding what or who the higher power was, so he gave up thinking about that level. Instead, he concentrated on the new voice that was now filling his head.

Welcome, Thomas Pink.

Thomas knew he was in the company of the highest-ranking Shide. It made him feel very humble, and his confidence vanished completely. Reality hit home. This was the most extraordinary place, somewhere beyond imagination. If he had been in his body form, he would have recognised that he wasn't coping, but he wasn't in his body, and somehow, he was hanging on, but only just! Then another sound filled his head. It had an instantaneous effect. Thomas smiled, he was calm and felt comfortable and able to communicate. *Thank you, Jonas Barley.*

You are doing well. It takes a little while to adjust to a higher power, Thomas, Jonas said kindly, *and the best way to do that is by freeing your spirit.*

Thomas was intrigued and felt much more confident. He was ready to learn how to free his spirit. In fact, he was game for anything now.

Right, Thomas, this is how it works. You have been brought here through Dominic and not the conventional way. You weren't called. You were asked to come.

To be with you. And not dead. Still alive. Somehow this idea filled Thomas with deep joy.

Precisely. If you go through the procedure – you'll know, what is said about the end, about death. You will whizz through your life's history. All the ups and downs, all the mistakes and regrets, the compassion used, and anger misused. Every emotion. If you do that, then you'll be as one with all the other souls here. That will be beneficial while you're here, and then when you return, you will have the ability to make contact with souls that have passed and ask for help if you ever get into trouble.

That sounds wonderful, Thomas's enthusiasm had grown beyond measure.

Dominic was thrilled. *I think we have a powerful ally on board.*

Jonas agreed. *Okay, Thomas, be prepared as this experience is going to be emotional.*

No sooner had Jonas uttered those words than Thomas flew into a spiral of spiritual meaning, starting from the very second he had entered the world, right through to this moment in time. He was acknowledging his unfortunate moments, appreciating better times, then looking at the consequences of all his actions. As those dominated Thomas's conscience, an echo pushed its way through the fabric of his life experiences, gently asking "could you have done better?"

Thomas suddenly understood everything that had ever been

required of him. The experience also gave him new meaning and emotional insight. Bewildered, he realised that he had brain fog. Desperately, he tried to rationalise the thoughts rushing in and out of his mind, but this was difficult. He knew the process he had just been through was for souls that had passed and were moving on. But he, himself, was going nowhere, and because of that, the memories had taken their toll. He felt as if he had nothing left inside apart from soul memories. All earthly ones had been stored deep down. Now, he was an old soul so he felt as if he was home, though he knew this feeling would only be temporary.

Are you back with us, Thomas? Jonas asked.

The sudden question startled him. He took a deep breath. *Yes Jonas. Although, I never left. That was unreal!*

Very good. Now, before we go any further, I need to know if you recall all your existing memories. Take a moment, then tell me if you feel your mental understanding has been enhanced.

Thomas embraced his request.

I don't need any help. I know what I have to do, and yes it has worked. All the memories of Thomas Pink are back.

Excellent, that's the first hurdle dealt with. Now, before we move forward, I understand you have a need to tidy up some day-to-day stuff.

Mm. Oh, yes. Thomas then immediately tried the very simple communication system he had set up earlier. He had a pleasant surprise. It worked perfectly and he managed to speak to Sarah. She did most of the talking. He was happy just to listen to her, as she went full on, saying what she had discovered with Rosemary's help, and how she had spoken to Alisha, then best of all, Sunday had been organised. *And how is it going with you?*

Yes, not so bad. I am missing you. A few minutes later, they were saying their goodbyes. Then he checked in with work and there were no problems there. *Now, it is back to business with Dominic and Jonas.*

You are now going to go to an area attached to the rehabilitation section. That's where you'll meet a unique team – your team. These souls are so advanced that they make Dominic and myself look like novices. On this occasion, their purpose is to advance you naturally, so what would take you as an evolving soul thousands of years to achieve, will be attained in three earth days. This takes skill and knowledge. These souls will be assigned to you exclusively, supporting you until the task you have been asked to do on earth is completed.

Dominic joined the conversation. *As you can no doubt imagine, the process is extremely complicated and further than we have ever gone before.*

Thomas was mindful of the other souls who went before him and were unable to achieve what was asked of them.

I know what you're going to say Thomas. Jonas prompted. *What about the others? The ones who struggled and returned prematurely.*

Gosh, you're the same as Dominic! No sooner do I think something... Thomas sensed the two of them smiling.

After your visit here, you'll have the same ability. The others? Yes, we made mistakes. We assumed too much. That will not happen again.

Thomas dared to interrupt. *Am I to assume then that I will be better equipped to deal with the other side?* He sensed another warm smile from Jonas and Dominic.

Yes, replied Jonas.

We won't be losing you, Thomas, said Dominic firmly.

Well, that's comforting. Thomas hesitated and looked around. *Before we proceed, can I explore?*

You can go and do whatever you want. Just around that corner is a gate. Once you go through it, you will see a garden of beauty which is beyond description. Travel as far through it as you wish. Absorb the sights that will tease your imagination, showing you how immature and narrow it is. As you accept that, these wonders, the garden, will be stored within you forever, waiting for you to recall the feelings, whenever you're in need of comfort.

Thomas was sure that he had become part of the Garden of Souls and with confidence growing, announced, *Okay, I'm off to explore.*

Walking around the gardens, he was amazed that he was mingling with other souls. The experience was so great that he yearned to stay. This was absolute peace, and yet he had signed up for a war against a powerful advocate. He chuckled to himself, thinking about the irony of the situation. He was so happy, and he felt the need to experience more. Wanting to stay longer, he had to force himself back towards the area where the advanced souls gathered, ready to transform into some kind of super being.

Ready? he called.

Yes, good, he heard Dominic shout, *I'm about to witness my prodigy being prepared for world changing action.*

Thomas found himself drifting into the area where his super team were waiting for him. He felt a wave of humility smother him. It was almost as if he couldn't breathe and feeling afraid, he closed his eyes. The next thing he heard was Jonas speaking.

That's the first of three sessions over Thomas. It's now time for you to make contact!

Thomas opened his eyes. He didn't have a clue what was what. He was stumbling over his thoughts, dreamy for a moment or two then, bright as a button. *Contact? What contact?* Then it hit him, and he knew as well as Jonas how quickly the time was running on Earth. *Amazing!* He didn't need to be told. That pleased him. His first session was over, and he had learned so much.

Wanting to celebrate, once more, he put his simple communication system into operation and managed to speak to Sarah. Again, she was just as talkative, explaining what she had gleaned from additional books she had borrowed from Alisha.

She had been in contact with Rosemary again and said her expectations of him were growing. He sensed she and Rosemary were hatching a plan of some sort that involved him. It was beginning to be apparent that he would need a special kind of help apart from the souls in his team. The forty witches, Rosemary and Catherine were involved with would be there to support him. *Yes honey, I'm doing well. Everything is going to plan.*

How's your sister?

Sister?

You're doing her house up?

Thomas shuddered; the question made him compound the lie he had told her. Standing in the Garden of Souls made fibbing to Sarah that bit harder. *She's doing okay*. That was a truth so in his mind, this wasn't a fib.

Have you had time to look into the spiritual churches you spoke about? she asked.

Not yet. I've made enquiries and I'm meeting up with people who can give some guidance.

Brilliant. Can't wait to see you.

Me too, honey. Bye.

I'm impressed with the way you've handled your communication issue, Thomas, said Jonas.

So am I.

Jonas laughed. *You're well on your way. A couple more sessions with your team here, then you can put what you have learnt into practice.*

That pleased Thomas but it didn't inspire him to continue with another session as he was far too interested in learning more about the Garden of Souls. Both Jonas and Dominic picked up on that and suggested he do more exploring. With a few pointers from both of them, he set off. Almost immediately, he found himself near a group of learned souls who invited him to join them. He knew he would struggle with their superior knowledge, but he needed to test himself. Managing to understand only small amounts of their thoughts, he gaged his own ability to be very low. It didn't bother him though, because the group gave him comfort, lifting his spirit to heights he had never experienced before, and then reducing their energy allowing him to join in. This gave him a route into each of the souls. Now, he could gather information from their earthly experiences – and beyond. It was mind blowing. These were ancient souls sharing with him all the experiences they had endured.

He only managed to cope with just a few before feeling utterly overwhelmed. He took a very slow deep breath. They immediately understood. It was instantly agreed he could visit them any time. Somehow, this sensitivity allowed him to absorb more thoughts of their experiences, some so intense they mostly passed his imagination by and went somewhere beyond. It was something he needed to check with Dominic or Jonas. He left these ancient souls understanding he needed to build his armoury. Further on, he found others on a level compatible to his own and he was able to use the opportunity to learn as much as he could.

Thomas!

His name echoed through his soul. He was running late. In no time, he was back in the area where his team was waiting to continue his progress to advance his evolution.

Ah, Thomas, there you are, said Jonas. *Have you had your fill?*

Thomas nodded. *For now.*

Excellent. A couple of sessions to go and you'll know how to come here on your own. Dominic will almost be redundant, laughed Jonas.

Dominic was a little put out. *Only almost, Jonas but not completely.*

Thomas was chuffed, realising what a big deal this was turning out to be.

Chapter 15

The next forty-eight hours flew by. Thomas was hungry for knowledge and he contacted as many souls as possible in the time he had. All this, he thought, and communicating with Sarah and with his office. His ability to cope and absorb the teachings had surprised him at first. Now it was becoming second nature. With his confidence brimming, he was feeling comfortable with the challenge being offered to him.

Wandering again, this time, he found himself in an area of absolute beauty. The colours and the light here were astonishing. He positioned himself carefully to absorb all the vibrations generating throughout this truly magical spot. He wanted to be able to store all of it in one of his imaginary boxes, as he did with Sarah's smiles. Just for later. The time passed as Thomas enjoyed the thoughts of nothing except all of this.

He felt a sudden nudge, and Jonas appeared. He wanted to point out a few things Thomas had to learn. *You've wandered far, Thomas. Now, you need to return to the Garden. Unfortunately, soon you are going to do things that will scar your soul, whatever they are, you'll be left feeling sickened.*

I thought, that's why I'm here, so I'm able to deal with ugly stuff.

That's right. That's the real purpose of coming here. And it still is. But your soul will always be yours. That doesn't change. Therefore, the consequences of your future actions, the things you'll do for us will disturb you. That's when your team will step in to work their magic.

Thomas gave it some thought. *I understand. It will be back to the Garden of Souls. How do I return?*

That's easy.

Dominic appeared beside them. He and Jonas led him to a huge obelisk that had names carved into the granite. Jonas stepped closer to the obelisk and with his index finger, he carved the name of THOMAS PINK into it. *All you have to do to return is to focus on this spot and nothing else.*

Thomas was amazed, *Really?*

Dominic stepped forward, *Indeed, Thomas. But before Jonas goes any further and for my peace of mind, you and I are going to put the return to the test.*

That sounds intriguing. Thomas was eager to try. He prepared himself to crash land somewhere. To his joy, he landed perfectly, no jolt or stumble, but this joy was short-lived. Dominic had taken him to a violent site right in the middle of a conflict. There was killing going on right in front of him. The scene turned his stomach. Dominic didn't say a word, but Thomas knew why he had been brought to this spot. He made himself continue to watch the massacre, and strangely, the calming influence he felt in the Garden of Souls kept his mind at ease. He realised that the people dying in front of him were probably going to the place he had just left. In control of his emotions, he focused his mind on the obelisk and in no time he arrived there. But not quite perfectly! He went straight through it and and his head spun.

Pretty good for a start, said Jonas.

Thomas was pleased with himself.

But be warned, if you had been in your body, unfortunately you would have broken a bone or two, not to mention bashing your face up.

Oh.

Let's try it again, shall we?

Okay. Where shall I go?

Back to where you just came from.

Thomas smiled. *How do I do that?*

Have a think about it, Thomas.

He mulled it over. Right, I can think of two ways of doing it.

Go on.

Contact Dominic through the mind process, then travel. The other way is to backtrack through the history I have just created. But I don't know how to do that yet.

Very good, Thomas. Two ways will do although there are three ways of travelling.

Tell me.

You're inquisitive, that is good. The third way is the bird's eye view. Come on, you should get it now, Jonas declared.

I would get it if I knew what I was capable of. Thomas was quiet. He thought for a moment, then came up with the plan. *I'm going to assume I have the ability to encompass the world, then focus on a position or area. Then I'll home in and check if that's the place I need to get to. If it is, I will focus on a point that is set in my memory and then head there. Then I can travel there anytime, is that right, Jonas?*

You'll leave us all behind soon, Thomas. I'm proud of you. Now please go and find Dominic.

Yes, okay, thank you, Jonas.

Ah, you've found your way back then, Dominic stated.

Not exactly as planned. I didn't mean to land so near to the obelisk.

You should be chuffed with yourself! At least you managed to come back.

That's not the difficult bit. It's the manoeuvring, I can't think how that's done.

Well, I'll tell you.

Come on then, Dominic. I want to try it out.

Relax, Thomas, relax. That's the key. Right, here we go. As you relax you can focus on your destination over there and shift your weight to your heels as if you are about to fall backwards.

Immediately, they were travelling!

Doing that acts as a brake!

I remember using my heels when I did that levitation, said Thomas, casting his mind back to that amazing day.

Yes! That's right. Use them now! We're arriving.

Bloody brilliant! Thomas was keen to try it out again. *Don't go anywhere Dominic! I'll be back!* He focused on the obelisk in his head and then he was gone. In an instant, he was back to Jonas in the Garden of Souls. He almost did it, but he missed the obelisk and lost his balance. He ended up rolling across the lawn.

Jonas applauded. *Better but not quite.*

Thomas picked himself up. *Don't go away.* He concentrated for a moment and then landed next to Dominic. It was like he had jumped off a moving bus, his legs took him past Dominic, but he stayed on his feet.

Almost perfect, said Dominic.

Thomas felt pretty good about his attempt to travel smoothly. *Another couple of tries and I'll have this nailed!* he said, as he waved goodbye to Dominic again. This time Thomas landed perfectly in the garden again. *That's better. I have no intentions of breaking any of my bones!*

Good. Well done. Now let's call Dominic here.

I'll do it. Thomas concentrated. Dominic was back in an instant.

Now, before we start on your next ability, do you have any questions? asked Jonas.

Yes, I do. How is it that people can't see Dominic or me when we travel to these different places?

Jonas smiled. *I was wondering when you'd mention that.*

I've thought about it before, but I didn't need to know. But now it's different.

Why is it different?

Travelling with the light is part of my equipment, right? So, what would be the point of using it if when I get there, I'm not actually present? Nobody can see me.

That's simple, Jonas said. *When you return to earth and decide to light travel, your body will go with you. When you travel under Dominic's wing, you don't.*

Thomas frowned. *Where does my body go then?*

Remember when we arrived here? We said you left your earthly self behind. It just gets parked up in a holding area.

Parked up? Thomas struggled with the idea.

Jonas and Dominic laughed. *Don't think earthly. Think spiritually.*

Mm... A body park. Wow, that's awesome!

Dominic smiled. *As long as your soul's safe, you're safe. Now we need to work on your attacking abilities. To learn this won't be so easy.*

Not so easy? What I have just done wasn't easy. So now you expect me to do something that's probably impossible?

Very good, you're showing caution, said Dominic.

Yes, said Jonas, *you'll manage. But...*

Is that a big 'but'?

We shall see, said Jonas. *With Dominic's help, I'll show you what you have to do. Then you decide if it's a big 'but' or not.*

Okay.

What we are about to show you is...

Dominic interrupted. *I think we should let Thomas find out for himself.*

You're right. Let's get on with it, Jonas replied.

Thomas was eager to show what he was capable of. *I'm ready. Come on then, let's go.*

They took him to a quiet place with no other souls around and explained that they wanted him to concentrate on a target.

Thomas cleared his mind. *What do you want me to concentrate on?*

See those poles? See that one on the hill? I want you to take the top off!

Thomas aimed his gaze at the pole and obliterated it. He blew half the hill away too! *Whoa!*

Well, I never! You're generating too much energy. If we let you loose on your earth, you would blow up in a day, laughed Dominic.

Thomas tried again with another pole and then with another and created huge craters in the hills around them. *Perhaps if I understood where the power is coming from, I might be able to control it.*

Jonas agreed. *Okay let's move to a busy spot that will force you to concentrate on a small area.*

Thomas was feeling nervous. Having so much destructive power was such a big responsibility. He had to learn how to control this awesome ability quickly. He didn't want to kill any innocent people.

Chapter 16

Thomas looked around him and he noticed that they were surrounded by souls. *You have to remember that the team has maximised your energy force,* Jonas announced. *We are surprised at how super powerful you have become. You must compensate and show restraint. What you are doing is allowing the enthusiasm running through you to take control.*

Thomas was worried. *Why was I given all this power then?*

For your protection, continued Jonas. *You will meet a lot of unsavoury people on your mission. The name of Thomas Pink will be known within an elite group who have allegiance to the dark side. They will do their utmost to send you back.*

His words disturbed Thomas. *Send me back? You mean kill me, don't you?*

If you want to put it that way, yes. But, if you continue with what you have been doing with us, and keep generating that kind of power, then no one will get anywhere near you.

So why are you bothered about the excessive power I'm generating?

Because Thomas, most situations won't require anything like that level of power. Showing control is important. Bringing attention to yourself isn't a good idea.

Right. So how do I go about overcoming my enthusiasm?

You don't overcome it. You just take control of it. Imagine in your mind getting in front of your power, so in effect it follows you, not the other way round. Get that right and you're in charge.

Thomas sighed. *All this thinking Jonas is hard work.*

Well, that's what's going to keep you safe.

Thomas, surrounded by an incredible number of souls witnessing his progress, listened hard to what he was being told. He was learning. It took him an age to achieve what they were asking of him, but the thinking was paying off. He began to control his power levels.

Now, Thomas Pink, we are going to see if you do have proper control, Jonas announced.

How do you propose doing that?

Dominic will hold an object up in the air, and you have to destroy it while he is holding it.

Really? Thomas frowned. *What will happen if I miss aim? What if I use too much energy?*

It is okay, I would move, replied Dominic.

Thomas thought for a moment. *You can move that fast, can you?*

Faster! A lot faster.

Thomas laughed. *Wow. Okay then. I'm ready when you are.* As Thomas prepared himself, Jonas gave Dominic an object that looked like a square of chocolate.

Thomas looked at it, then he looked at Jonas. *What do you want me to do with that?*

Jonas smiled. *Well, firstly I would like you to pace out approximately fifty metres away from the object. Then concentrate on what Dominic is holding, then destroy it.*

Thomas didn't believe him. He thought Jonas was messing around. He waited for some other instruction. *What do you want me to do? Eat it?*

Jonas shook his head. *Are you going then?*

You're actually serious, aren't you?

Jonas didn't say a word, nor did Dominic.

Okay, I'll pace fifty metres. Then please tell me how I'm supposed to do this. Thomas turned and marched out fifty paces. The effect of the process his team of souls had bestowed upon him was growing. He was developing into an advanced soul, which was stopping him from being rational. As he turned and focussed on Dominic, Jonas spoke. It was as if he was standing right next to him. Thomas realised he could do whatever was being asked of him.

Pull the image of Dominic towards you, Jonas asked.

Doing what he was asked, Thomas amazed himself. He did just that without a second thought. Dominic was now just a metre away, holding that tiny object. Now Thomas could see the brown cube clearly. He watched himself destroy it with perfect control over his powers. As the object vanished from Dominic's hand, the close-up image of Dominic did the same and he was fifty metres away again.

Well done! Jonas was as chuffed as Thomas was. *What you've just learned will be really important. The majority of darksiders will sense your presence from five metres away, but you will have an advantage. Your senses will start to work from twenty-five metres away.*

That's all well and good knowing where the other lot are. But do you want me to destroy them? Or in your words, send them back to the soul maker?

Thomas, said Dominic, *if you know they are there, you will also know how dark they are. That feeling will control your actions. What I would like to suggest, if Jonas agrees, is to take you somewhere on your Earth in real time.*

Meaning I'll be seen?

Jonas nodded. *Yes. Dominic will place you within fifty metres of a dark soul. Then if you will, I want you to walk towards him, get as close as you can and tell Dominic what you feel.*

Okay.

Before we go, why don't you contact Sarah? There's no point in giving her reason to be concerned.

With all the intense training Sarah had slipped from Thomas's mind. He was annoyed with himself for not remembering. Almost immediately he was in touch with her. She was overjoyed to hear his voice. She was missing him. She had just finished a class and she was bubbling with happiness. He asked how she was and asked her how Alisha was doing.

I'm good, but Alisha's not. She has been for the scan and is waiting on the results. He could hear in her voice that Sarah's mood had changed. She needed his reassurance. As if by magic Dominic and Jonas got into his head.

Tell Sarah that you'll deal with it.

Honey, I'm in touch with two healers. When I get back, you and I and the healers will deal with this problem.

Oh, Thomas I needed to hear that.

Don't worry honey. I have to go now. See you soon.

How did you know? Thomas asked Jonas and Dominic.

They smiled. *We'll help you take care of Alisha.*

Dominic tried to explain how life worked for Thomas and the rest of the world. *Life on Earth is intricate, like a jigsaw puzzle with billions of pieces and that's how it should be for you and your lot. But for us there are only thousands of pieces.*

I need time to get my head round that.

You now have the skill to deal with Alisha's health problems, Thomas and lots of other situations that might pop up, added Dominic. *While you're here, it's difficult for you to understand. It's when you return and visit Alisha – that's when all will become apparent. You'll need a little guidance from us to start with, then as your experience grows, we'll become redundant.*

Unless there are exceptional circumstances, Thomas, you'll be your own man, said Jonas. *There's help you can call on if things get a bit sticky. As you know, I am based on your planet, so that's one avenue of help. You can contact me any time. Then there's James Colewater, Jamie, as he prefers to be called. Jamie is from another place; he is not so advanced. He will act as a guardian. You'll meet him as soon as you return to Earth. You will also have help from the children of the Shides.*

Children? Do you mean descendants? asked Thomas, surprised by this concept.

No, they are the blood of advanced souls. Jonas replied.

Is that right? asked Thomas.

The people of earth have stalled on a number of occasions in their progress to reach higher advancement. So, some positive blood had to be injected into your kind to get things moving. All in all, you will have good backup. We can't afford to see you back here prematurely.

That's comforting to hear. I like the idea of being around another fifty years or so. Don't let me make any mistakes!

They both smiled. *You're in good hands. Don't worry.*

I believe you. Now I just want to touch on what we said earlier about Alisha. If I wasn't in this position... I mean, two weeks ago I wouldn't have had a clue. Now well, tell me what I can do to help her?

There are billions of pieces to life's jigsaw, Thomas. Soon, you'll be shown a couple of pieces to put into the correct places.

Thomas sighed. *And that's it?* He looked at the pair of them. No answer. Nothing, not a murmur. *So that's the best I'm going to get. Come on then, Dominic, let's go find the dark soul you want me to destroy.*

In an instant, Dominic took Thomas to a god-forsaken place, full of life, with hundreds of people going to and fro.

Walk in that direction Thomas, Dominic asked, pointing ahead of him.

It didn't take long before Thomas recognised the point of this experience. He felt a sudden repulsion towards someone, a deep unease. *Where are you?* He wasn't sure who might be causing this terrible feeling inside his soul. There were hordes of people in front of him. From out of nowhere, an image appeared, similar to the one earlier when Dominic held up a small object. The urge to destroy this person flashed through his mind. Evil racing through every fibre of his body. He feared that at any moment, this darkness might overcome him. He took in a deep breath and prepared himself to send the evil back to the soul maker.

Good man Thomas, you've got it. This is just a rehearsal. It's not his time. Dominic's voice was calm.

And that calmed Thomas down.

When they returned, Dominic gave Jonas a nod. *He saw him. He's ready.*

Brilliant! If we had actual time here, we would be a little short of it. You'll need to return to your ordinary life soon, Thomas. But I can see you understand that controlling the vibration, controls the state of any object you come into contact with. From total destruction to manipulation, to moving objects around and placing them where you want. Suspending life! You have the ability to do miraculous things.

Thomas wasn't sure he understood all of what Jonas had said.

To understand this, you need to imagine freezing an entity then thawing it out. You can do that by controlling the energy you use.

You mean people when you say entity. Is that right?

Jonas nodded. *If you apply yourself, you'll be able to move anything. Freeze time around them without damaging others.*

Wow, it gets better!

There's more to learn. But I'll let Jamie explain that to you. He likes to be involved from the beginning. You do have a little more time for instruction, but with him.

If time doesn't exist here, how do you know, what's going on down below?

Jonas chuckled. *You're not the only one with a link to Earth,*

In the time left, we can develop the subtleties of vibrational control, suggested Dominic, *I'll show you how, but I'm sure you may need more time. I suggest you practice later when you get back, but before you see Sarah.*

I will. Thomas thought for a moment, *Is that how you healed my face? By speeding up the process?*

That's exactly how I did it, exclaimed Dominic.

And there was no scar because the speed of the repair to my skin never allowed any deterioration? It was like it never happened.

Right again. It's obvious the improvements you're receiving are working. A word of warning though. You must be careful what you say when you're back with your people, Thomas. Remember to keep all you have learned to yourself.

Thomas nodded. *I will.*

Now let's do the finishing touches. What you're learning is how to control the anger that's rooted in your soul.

Thomas worked at getting his pent-up anger under control. He would have preferred more time but that would have extended his programme. They all knew he hadn't one hundred per cent mastered this.

Jonas said gently, *nearly but not quite. Any time you think you need help or comfort, your team of old souls are there for you. Go to them and ask them to help you.*

Thomas decided that it was a good idea and summoned them. Five souls appeared. Their exceptional warmth towards him was something he had never experienced before. He was overwhelmed with a wonderful feeling of joy. His problems would be their problems. He didn't need to ask.

Time to go home, announced Dominic.

Thank you, said Thomas. *Both of you.*

Jonas smiled, *I'm a second away, don't forget.*

Chapter 17

Back in his kitchen, Thomas ran over a few points with Dominic. "When will I meet up with Jamie?"

"I'll contact him. You get your car from the hiding place."

"Okay."

Thomas unplugged the phone he had left on charge, took the keys out of the kitchen drawer, then travelled to the old barn where he had discreetly parked the car. The car's engine was still warm, which puzzled Thomas. *It's almost as if I haven't been anywhere.*

As he pulled onto his own forecourt, Dominic was standing with Jamie. Jamie didn't look anything like the person Thomas had imagined. He was expecting a man with angelic looks. Instead, Jamie was just a normal looking man, with short, cropped hair, dull blue eyes with an olive complexion. Jamie appeared slightly shorter than Dominic, with a much better dress sense.

Jamie held out his hand, "So you're the famous Soul Returner."

Thomas grinned. "I could be. It depends on how good you are at keeping me out of trouble."

Jamie laughed. "Dominic mentioned you need a little practice with your vibrational control?" He turned towards Thomas's car and began to lift it off the ground. Thomas watched in amazement. When the car had reached approximately ten feet, Jamie turned back towards Thomas and Dominic. "Is that the sort of thing you need to practice?"

Dominic just smiled.

"Yep," Thomas said. "That's certainly what I need to polish up on. But I'd rather not practice with my car."

Jamie grinned. "Cautious, eh? I wonder how long that will last."

"Okay, give me your car and I'll practice all day!" Thomas corrected himself. "Oh yes, I know. You don't have cars, do you?"

"I fancy you'll do well, Thomas," he laughed.

"There's no fancy about it, Jamie. Thomas has to do well," advised Dominic. He looked around nervously.

"It's time for action!" said Thomas.

"Well, I've run out of time. If I'm not careful I'll be tracked, but Jamie is capable of finishing the job. Any questions Thomas?"

"How is it that Jamie has different abilities to you?"

Dominic looked at Jamie to explain.

"I come from a lower stage of evolution," said Jamie. "Therefore, I can be engineered to lower the vibrational force. I'm never picked up by darksiders. Dominic's too powerful. No amount of engineering can change that."

Dominic nodded, "It's different with you as well, Thomas. You'll have to use the tricks Jonas showed you to disguise your ability. Remember, one of the golden rules is, if you can't explain it, don't do it."

"I don't remember you telling me that. When did you tell me that?"

Dominic smiled. "Just then."

"Any more little gems you need to tell me?"

"As and when Thomas. As and when."

Thomas screwed his face up and shook his head. "Are you sure you want to keep me alive?"

"That's paramount!" Dominic then glanced over at Jamie. "Any problems or questions, like Jonas, I'm only a second away." He placed his hand on Thomas' shoulder, sending warmth and love directly from the Garden of Souls to him. Then he disappeared. Thomas stood very still for a few moments letting the pleasant feeling soak in.

Jamie jumped into action. "Okay! Let's try your wheelbarrow before you attempt lifting your car."

"That's an idea."

Thomas surveyed the wheelbarrow as Jamie explained the slight difference between destroying an object and controlling one. Jamie's approach was gentle. He spoke Thomas' language, and he found his ideas easier to relate to. Jonas's training method, on the other hand, was super-efficient. That intimidated Thomas but nevertheless, he had taken in all that he had been shown.

Thomas soon got the hang of this challenge. He picked up the wheelbarrow and managed to leave it suspended in the air. Then he turned his attention to his car. Jamie still had that ten feet off the ground. Now full of confidence, Thomas concentrated on the vibrations that were keeping the car suspended. In control of them now, he brought his car down slowly! *Careful, I don't want to damage her.*

Jamie was impressed, but Thomas wasn't interested in praise. He just wanted to learn everything quickly and be able to survive.

Jamie had more information to share that was going to be useful. "There will be times when mistakes are made. Simple things do go wrong. That's when you'll need the Shielings."

"Shielings? Who are they?" asked Thomas.

"They are the children of Shides."

"The Shides? Of course, Jonas mentioned them. He's a Shide himself, isn't he? And I met others in the Garden of Souls."

"That's right. Your lot on Earth are your new soul's children. Dominic's lot call them Shielings. It's the sons of sons. That doesn't mean they're all boys. But there are a good few living amongst you."

"I remember Jonas touching on it. I just didn't fully appreciate their purpose."

"Their purpose is your backup. If all goes wrong, that is."

Thomas frowned. "You mean *when* things go wrong, don't you."

Jamie's face changed slightly.

"I thought that was your job."

"It is. I'm tuned into your being, and I'll know immediately when you're in trouble. It just depends on what's needed. That dictates who flies in to give you a hand."

"Tell me again about the Shielings. It seems to me that you do what they do?"

"Well, if you bear in mind you haven't come into contact with any darksiders yet then what I am about to tell you will be hard for you to understand. You were told about the last returner Joe, weren't you? Unfortunately, Joe slipped up. He was careless. Before I could recognise a problem, he was gone. That's why the Shielings are now in place to help you."

That made Thomas think. "Tell me more."

"Good, you're questioning me. I fancy if anyone can do this job, then it's you. So there is no misunderstanding. I will use the word Devil just so you know who we are dealing with."

"I thought that word was taboo."

"Depends on who you talk to."

"Okay. Tell me about him."

Every bad deed, no matter how small, gives the Devil's department power. As you'll no doubt remember, Jonas mentioned the darksiders."

"Yes."

"Well, the more powerful they are, the faster you will be able to sense their presence."

"Yes, I remember that."

"Well, they're not all-powerful. Predominantly the minions are weak and not much better than the average bloke, but they all contribute to the Dark Power. Are you following?"

"Yep. Go on."

"If a group of them suddenly converged on you, they could combine energy, enough to cloak your vibrational force."

Thomas thought about that. "But you're saying Joe, and probably the others too, vanished off the radar... that was the end of them, right?"

"Correct."

"How many others were like Joe?"

"Two others."

"Did they make mistakes, or were they just careless?"

Jamie was silent.

"Look, we all know they didn't make it, Jamie. Dominic told me that on the first day. I just want to know what I'm up against."

"Mistakes. Carelessness. Or just a sloppy mindset. It's all the same in the end. Dominic also told you how everything was rushed along back then. Things were taken for granted."

"So, the three of them ended up in the Garden of Souls."

Jamie nodded.

"Then why didn't I meet them while I was there? Surely I could have learned from their mistakes?"

Jamie seemed reluctant to open up. "Joe and the other two did return," he said gently. "You couldn't have met them as they and all those that return go to an area to repair or recuperate. Earth can be such a traumatic experience, especially for young souls."

"Well, every bit of help is help." Thomas replied feeling a little anxious.

Jamie nodded and went on, "The more advanced souls have now learnt from previous mistakes and they have handed the responsibility to your team. But this is where it gets complicated."

"So, as well as being advanced a few thousand years, I've also been programmed with all their experiences, haven't I?"

"I think that can be done to certain souls. But you're not one of those. Your soul is virtually untouchable. You just absorb anything useful they could share with you, and then with the effect of the power surge the moment you were born, well, that's just made you into such a powerful soul."

"I don't feel powerful. I feel just ordinary, apart from being able to do the stuff Jonas has taught me. Oh, and you with the car. That's something. I suppose."

"Right now, you're not being challenged, but when the time comes, you will discover exactly who you are."

Thomas was keen to listen, but suddenly he was also keen to contact Sarah and catch up with his work. Feeling overwhelmed, somehow he needed his normal routine back.

Jamie could obviously see what he was feeling. He kept his lesson as short as he could. "You have to be safe. You're not allowed to fail, so when a situation arises, go with your gut instinct. Just do it. Don't question it. Remember, the other lot wants to kill you and will without hesitation."

That hit the spot! Thomas shifted his weight from one foot to another. Real anxiety was creeping in. "I need to try all this out."

"All in good time," said Jamie. "You'll make mistakes, and that's where I come in, and so do the Shielings. Apart from keeping you safe, I'll tidy up any mess you create. Just remember you are part of a powerful team with only one intention and that is to keep you alive."

"So, shall I thank you now, Jamie?"

Jamie smiled. "No, wait till I clean up a mess or two. Now go and see Sarah. I'm off. You know how to contact me."

Thomas thought about what Jamie had said. He felt in a better frame of mind now. He was ready for normal again.

Chapter 17

Thomas checked in with work. Everything had been running smoothly all week. He had the feeling he hadn't been missed! Now he could concentrate on Sarah, but not before he had taken a shower. Thomas looked down at himself and realised how dirty his clothes were and he had no idea why. It then dawned on him the last time he had showered was five days ago. On the day he had left with Dominic. He shuddered as he thought about what he had been through. But then a thought occurred to him that he wasn't in his body, so it was still like Monday morning for him. Even so, he still felt grubby, and a hot shower would be most welcome.

Fifteen minutes later, Thomas was talking to Sarah on the phone. She was concerned about Alisha, who had taken a turn for the worse. Sarah was obviously in need of support.

"I'm on my way over now, honey."

Sarah was waiting outside when Thomas pulled into her drive. When they hugged, Sarah did not want to let go.

"I've missed you, so much."

Hand in hand, they went inside the cottage. "Tea?" she asked.

"Tea! I'm dying for a cup of tea. It's been days since…" He nearly let it slip. He hadn't eaten or had a cup of tea for five days! Now he was desperate. "Yes, please!"

In the kitchen, Sarah told him more about Alisha. "The doctor said she has a tumour, and the scan will confirm this today." Sarah was so sad. A tear slipped down the brave face she was putting on.

This certainly doesn't sound good. He gave her another hug. But she needed more than a hug. What she was looking for was a miracle.

She hung on tight to Thomas. "Did you see anyone when you visited the church?"

He had no choice but to fib.

"Yes, I have learnt a lot considering the amount of time I had."

Sarah looked straight at him. "Will you take me to the hospital a little later? It's in Epping. I know you've just driven back from your sister's but..."

That made him feel uncomfortable. He hadn't driven anywhere really – barely two hundred metres all week, and then only to Sarah's cottage. He realised how the fibs could mount up. "When would you like to go, honey?"

"Whenever. There's no time restriction."

That didn't sound promising. "We'll finish our tea and go then, shall we?"

Sarah nodded, forcing the tiniest smile.

Soon they were on their way to the hospital, which was about thirty minutes away. As he drove, Thomas tried to take Sarah's mind off Alisha. He asked about Catherine and Rosemary.

"You read my mind, Thomas! I was just about to tell you the latest. About an hour before you turned up, I spoke to Rosemary."

Thomas glanced over at Sarah. He hadn't expected that reply.

"It fascinates me listening to what they say." She stopped and looked out of the window.

Thomas assumed she was thinking of Alisha. "Come on, honey. It will be all right."

She stroked his arm, "Rosemary... yes. Rosemary said that one of the witches in the coven – I've forgotten her name, but she's from Blackpool. Anyway, she's heard of Susie's boss George Smithe."

"In Blackpool? But that's miles away. Seems odd. What makes them think it's the same George Smithe?"

"Mm, I thought it was miles away too, but when Rosemary described the man they were talking about, then I knew it had to be him. Jodie, that's her name! Before Jodie moved to Blackpool, she worked for a city bank, and two guesses who ran the department where Jodie worked?"

"You're kidding!"

"Nope! What's more, she reckons he's an evil so and so too."

"But how could she know that? Oh, don't answer that. They're witches, aren't they? So Susie must be right about her boss."

"Looks like it, Thomas. I think all of them are going to have a huddle or something tonight focusing on George Smithe to determine what he is up to.

"What are huddles?"

"I think it's when they all get together, and they will pick up on his power."

"I wonder what will happen if they discover something they don't like!"

"We'll find out tomorrow as Rosemary is calling first thing."

"Good."

They pulled into the hospital gates and parked. The pair of them headed inside. They were allowed to visit Alisha outside normal hours.

As they walked up the stairs to the ward Thomas started to fret. He knew what was expected of him. *What if it all goes wrong? Where is the help? Where is Dominic*? Before he could send a distress signal, a voice filled his mind.

Don't worry Thomas I'm here. You'll be doing the work. I will guide you.

Thomas nodded his head in acknowledgement then realised that was a silly thing to do. Luckily, Sarah was so preoccupied with worry that she hadn't seen it. All the same, Thomas knew he had been clumsy in the way he had communicated. He had to get better at this ... and quickly.

Sarah stopped at the ward door. "Here we are, Thomas. Alisha is in the first bed."

Thomas only just recognised Alisha. She didn't look good. Sarah put her arms around her.

This gave Thomas a moment to contact Dominic. *Please help me Dominic!*

Place your hands on her head then I'll talk you through it, Dominic whispered.

Now Thomas felt more confident.

Sarah turned to him, took his hand, and pulled him closer in.

Alisha had a big smile for him. "Hello Thomas, it's good to see you again. I only wish I was in better form."

He sensed a huge amount of courage coming from her. He let go of Sarah's hand, sat down next to Alisha and took hold of her cold hand.

"I can see you're in the wars, but we are going to work on that."

Alisha smiled.

"Sarah mentioned your mishap in the gym. And then how your face was healed. I had no idea you are connected to the spiritual world!"

"That comes from my mum and dad's influence. Their stories fascinated me when I was a lad. Now all things spiritual really intrigue me."

Alisha was already tiring.

Dominic popped into Thomas's head. *Let's do it.*

Thomas stood up. He adjusted Alisha's pillows so she was upright. "Sarah" he said quietly, "you sit at the end of the bed and concentrate on Alisha's mother."

Sarah obediently moved along. He put his finger to his lips "nice and quiet."

Sarah nodded.

He was ready. He put his hands on Alisha's head and immediately picked up on the position of the tumour. He closed his eyes. He felt as if he was right inside her head. It was a strange sensation. He thought back to Jonas explaining how to focus. Now he understood. In the background, Dominic was encouraging him to raise the vibrations. *Just a little Thomas. That's it. Good. Don't take your eye off the tumour. Can you see it breaking down?*

Thomas was so focused he nodded very slightly, not thinking.

Dominic understood. *Right Thomas, tell me what you see.*

Half of it has broken down. The rest is stubborn.

Think about what you need to do now, Thomas.

I need to raise my vibration more.

Do it!

Thomas was beginning to sweat. His concentration was peaking. He knew it mustn't fade. With great determination he lifted the vibrations further with perfect control. With his mind's eye on the target, he could see the rest of the tumour crumbling away. Seconds later, there was nothing left.

Give it a couple of seconds more Thomas, requested Dominic quietly.

A couple of seconds was about all Thomas could manage. The huge concentration had weakened him, but he knew he had done this tricky job well. He moved his hands gently away from Alisha's head, realising that she was asleep. That was the last thing he remembered. He slumped down onto the floor, feeling completely drained.

In the silence of the hospital room Sarah had closed her eyes. Now she jumped up, startled to see Thomas on the floor. She helped him onto a chair. He seemed okay but so weak. He smiled as she gave him lots of little kisses, "I don't want to pick you up from the floor anymore, sweetheart," she said.

She searched in her pocket and brought out a small bar of chocolate. "Eat this! You're as pale as a ghost."

You do look worse for wear, Dominic said. His words seemed to echo around in Thomas's head. *But you did very well.*

Thanks. It has drained me. I'm exhausted.

Don't worry. Your body will build up the stamina to match your new power. It'll take a little time.

Is this what is going to happen when I am dealing with a darksider? The chances of me surviving do not bode well if it has this effect!

By tomorrow you'll feel better. Then you must come back to the hospital. You need to look and make sure the tumour has gone completely.

And if it hasn't?

If it hasn't? Then call me but the chances of any of the tumour remaining is very unlikely. I'm going now. You have your hands full with Alisha and Sarah.

Thanks Dominic.

Sarah was busy checking on Alisha.

Alisha had woken up and she reached for Sarah's hand, "I feel amazing!"

That wasn't enough. Sarah needed a hug. Then she looked over at Thomas munching on the chocolate bar. "How are you feeling Thomas?"

He chuckled, "I have felt better."

Sarah took his hand, "Thank you so much sweetheart, how do you think it went?"

"I know how it went!" said Alisha. "You don't have to ask Doctor Thomas! I feel brilliant. No pain. No sickie feeling. And my energy has come flooding back."

"Ah! So that's where my energy has gone," Thomas said, smiling. He was relieved that the healing session was over and he began to relax.

Alisha sat up and reached for her dressing gown, "Let's go

to the cafeteria. I have a real fancy for a cup of tea. I'm sure Thomas would enjoy a cup after his efforts."

Sarah couldn't believe her ears or her eyes.

Thomas shook his head. "I don't think that's a good idea. You should rest."

"No!" Alisha was adamant. "I've felt poorly for such a long time, and now I don't. Come on you two! Keep up!"

Sarah looked worried, but Thomas just smiled. There was no choice but to follow Alisha. As they walked along the corridor, Sarah squeezed his hand.

"You're looking better now too."

"That's the chocolate bar you gave me!"

The three of them ordered tea and sat down in the cafeteria. Suddenly two nurses and a consultant rushed in looking for Alisha. "What are you doing out of bed?"

The consultant stared at Alisha. He looked shocked. Alisha was the picture of health. "Something's changed," he said. "What's going on?"

"I feel better," announced Alisha.

The consultant felt her forehead, "I think you should go for another scan," he said very coolly.

Alisha screwed up her nose at the suggestion, but Thomas nodded. "That's a good idea," he said. "I think you should."

"But I don't want to stay in hospital anymore, Thomas."

The consultant frowned "I'll arrange an appointment this afternoon," he said taking out his phone.

"Do I have to go in an ambulance?" whispered Alisha to Thomas.

"No, we'll take you," he offered.

The consultant turned back to them. "I've booked an emergency slot for two hours' time."

"We'll take her," said Thomas.

The consultant nodded, and then he and the nurses walked off.

"I'll be dressed and ready to go in a few minutes," Alisha sounded quite desperate to get out of the place.

"I'll get the car and park outside the front entrance," said Thomas.

Thomas was in good spirits as he made his way along the corridor and out of the exit. The car park was full. He headed towards his car and then spotted a BMW a little way down in the same row as his car with two men fiddling with the car door. One of them had something in his hand. As he got closer, the bigger of the two men, realising that he had been caught in the act, glared at Thomas.

"What are you looking at?" he shouted.

For a second Thomas was confused. He turned to see if they were talking to someone else. There was no one behind him.

The man shook his fist at Thomas and started walking over.

Thomas's confusion suddenly turned to uncontrollable anger. Within a second the BMW blew up. The two men flew into the air. Thomas stared at the devastation and mayhem horrified.

Immediately Jamie's voice came into his head, *Get your car and get out now! I'll check on those low life thieves. Don't say a word. Do nothing! Go!*

Oh, Jamie! Right! Okay. But what happened?

It's a mess. I knew you'd do that! Now move away, I'll deal with it. Get out while you still can!"

Thomas didn't need telling twice. He jumped in his car and pulled away around to the front of the hospital. Sarah and Alisha came out of the entrance just as he drove past the ambulance bay. He pulled over and waved.

They climbed into the car. "What was that loud noise?"

Thomas hesitated. "A car caught fire; I think it exploded."

"We should get our skates on before the fire department turns up or we'll never get out of the gates."

Sarah nodded. "Okay, I'm still in shock. I want to know if what you did for Alisha worked."

Chapter 18

An hour and a half later they were pulling up outside the hospital in London. Thomas looked at his watch. "You have under twenty minutes, Alisha."

"Don't worry Thomas I know where to go."

"Good, I'll park up and join you."

Sarah held back from kissing Thomas. "I keep saying thank you, don't I?"

"Don't be daft," he said pointing towards the entrance. "Look! You had better catch up with Alisha. She's already going inside."

Once Thomas was on his own, feeling foolish, he contacted Jamie. *What happened with the car, Jamie?*

And hello to you Thomas!

Hello, Jamie.

The good news is, you didn't kill anyone, but you certainly damaged both those men! I think they'll be in hospital for a while, and then they'll be arrested for trying to steal the car you blew up.

I don't understand how it happened. The big chap was threatening me for no reason and that really irritated me. Then I didn't seem to be in control.

Your defence mechanism kicked off. I was told it was powerful! But even I'm not sure how it works! All I know is the clever ones at the Garden of Souls did something to you they've never done before.

Oh, I see. So there's no point in asking you then.

I'm not privy to that kind of knowledge. You could contact them. Didn't they give you a directory?"

You're right, they did.

So that's good. I would get on with what you're doing, otherwise Sarah and Alisha will wonder where you are.

Okay, and thanks Jamie.

One last thing,

What's that then?

Do you remember the first time you met Dominic when he came to your house?

That was the second time. The first time was in the gym when he made me fall off the spin bike.

Really?!

He stopped my heart for a moment or two so he could contact me. 'To build the bridge' were his words. I didn't appreciate it at the time. I understand why now.

While they were talking Thomas found a space to park, and now he was walking towards the hospital. *So, what's your one last thing?* Thomas asked.

You allowed Dominic to read your psyche.

That's right.

So, I think it might be a good idea, Jamie said, *if I was privy to that information too, then I'll know how you work. My advice could make life a little safer for you.*

I have no problem with that.

Good. I'll download it immediately.

Thomas stopped at the main door. *I have to go, Jamie.*

Don't forget to contact the old souls. Get your questions answered. See ya, kiddo. And don't forget, you're powerful and those darksiders are going to be toast.

Thomas laughed, *I wish.*

Compared to me you are! See you soon.

Thomas was surprised to see Sarah sitting in the reception area. He thought she would have gone with Alisha. As soon as she noticed him, she jumped up. "Was it difficult to park?"

"Just a little, where's Alisha."

"They took her straight in and asked me to stay here. The scan takes a while."

"Do you want to get a coffee? There's a place just outside."

"No, I want you to stay with me and snuggle up. That's better than a coffee."

Thomas smiled and moved his chair closer. He kissed her and they sat together holding hands. The hour flew by.

When Alisha came out of the scanning room she was beaming. "All done. Let's go home."

"I'll get the car."

"What did they say?" asked Sarah.

"We'll walk to the car. I'm fine now."

Thomas looked at Alisha. "All right. But you know I have to do the same sort of thing as the hospital has done."

She nodded "When do you need to check to see if the tumour has gone?"

"But what did they say?" asked Sarah.

"They are going to call the consultant tomorrow. Stop fussing. I'm better now. I can feel it!"

"Yes, you are right, I want to confirm that, so tomorrow afternoon. Is that good for you?" Thomas asked.

Alisha nodded. "Can we pick up my stuff from the other hospital on the way back?"

"Of course." *It will give me a chance to see first-hand the consequences of my overzealous anger in that car park.*

"I think it would be sensible to have Alisha stay for a couple of nights." suggested Sarah, determined to be careful. "I want to keep an eye on her."

"No! I want to go home!"

"Come on, Alisha, I'm worried about you! What do you think Thomas?"

"Absolutely right. We're not discussing it Alisha, you need to be with us until I give you the all clear."

"Tell us how you did what you did, Thomas?" asked Sarah as they climbed into the car.

Thomas had to be evasive. There was an hour of dodging questions. He kept changing the subject until they reached Epping Hospital.

"You're really avoiding answering, Thomas!" said Sarah, sighing.

As soon as they arrived at the gate and were directed away from the car park, Thomas could see the mayhem he had caused.

A policeman stopped them. "Do you really need to park inside sir?"

"No, we'll park outside. We're only here to pick up some belongings. You girls go in." They climbed out. "What happened?" he asked the policeman.

"A car exploded. We've cleared the area; the bomb squad is here. One good thing, we caught the culprits. They got hit by shrapnel and were in no position to get away." Thomas wished he hadn't asked. "Park just over there as you're here briefly."

It wasn't long before the girls came back out of the hospital gates carrying Alisha's belongings.

"Any problems?" Thomas asked.

"No. The consultant will call as soon as he knows the result. He has spoken to the other hospital. He just took Alisha's temperature and pulse."

"He took some blood again. I hate needles. I'm sure it wasn't necessary."

Thomas smiled. "I've probably got to do the same."

"What?" Alisha thought for a moment but looked worried. "Really? Can you do that too?"

"I'm only kidding, I will just need to place my hand on your head again." Thomas smiled again.

Sarah nudged him. "Come on, let's go home."

An hour later the three of them were sitting in Sarah's lounge sipping tea. Thomas remembered he still hadn't contacted the souls in his team. He needed to understand how the car incident happened.

"Daydreaming?" Sarah seemed to be scrutinising him.

"Just recharging. I'll bring the stuff in from the car. Shan't be a sec." He brushed Sarah's arm as he walked past. She glanced up at him and scrunched up her nose. *She's so pretty*, he thought.

Outside he focused on the old souls. Contact came so fast it almost took his breath away. When he explained what had happened, they already knew. *Your enhancement has gone to the limit*, they whispered. *At the moment your anger levels might be unstable. That is until your soul grasps a certain amount of control.*

How long does that take?

When it happens, you'll know, so tell us and then we'll know. You showed great control when you helped Alisha. Stay safe, they whispered and then disappeared from his mind.

Alisha was sobbing when he came back into the house. "What's wrong?"

Sarah had a smiley sort of look on her face. "I think the past year has caught up with her, and now with what you've done, it's all too much."

Thomas wasn't sure what to say. Alisha's spirit needed lifting. He knelt down beside her. "If I were in your shoes, I'd be the same." She stopped sobbing and looked at him. "I mean they've rejected you up there so now you're stuck down here with us." The tears turned to smiles. Alisha watched him as he got to his feet.

"Thank you," she said, suddenly jumping up and giving him such a hug, she took his breath away.

As much as Alisha wanted to be clear of the tumour, so did Thomas. He needed the problem ended too, and this seemed the perfect moment to check her out. "Sit down Miss! I've just had this feeling. Let's check you out right now."

"What are you saying Thomas?" Sarah sounded nervous.

"Don't worry. It's just for my peace of mind as well as Alisha's. It will allow both of us to move forward. We have a big day ahead. Again! Catherine expects us to be on the ball, especially with the other white witches linking up on Sunday."

Sarah nodded "Right honey."

Alisha sat down. "I don't care! I know I'm all fixed. Come on then, Thomas. How do you do this?"

"Be very quiet and watch me. Then you tell me what I'm doing." He proceeded to place his hands on Alisha's head. With eyes closed, he drew again on the ability the Older Souls had given him. Almost immediately, he found the space that had been occupied by the tumour. It was clear. The vibration that came back was perfect, indicating that things were as they should be.

Dominic popped into his head. *Told you, didn't I?*

Thomas grinned. *Okay, clever clogs, just checking*, he said, speaking inside his head.

Good job Thomas. And make sure you're focused on Sunday too.

I will.

"There's nothing wrong with you, Miss," he announced, giving Alisha a reassuring smile. "Now shall we run over the details for Sunday?"

Alisha beamed. "Told you."

Sarah let a tear escape and roll down her cheek. "Shall we discuss it over dinner?" asked Sarah. "I haven't told Alisha anything about Sunday." Round the dinner table they ran through what had happened so far and the plan for Sunday. Alisha was amazed. She hadn't realised that witches existed. Sarah was quick to point out that they were white witches, and they were completely different from Saffron and her cronies. She went on to tell Alisha about her mother.

Alisha smiled, "My Aunty Victoria."

"Yes, the very same. Catherine thinks my mother was killed. She wants to find out more. That's why we are having the link with her people."

Alisha's smile vanished. "Really?"

"We're not sure," said Thomas quickly, "that's why we're organising this."

Alisha stayed quiet for a moment then looked at Thomas. "What is a link with Catherine's people? What does that mean?"

"Imagine a small circle of people are trying to contact their loved ones who have passed."

"Okay."

"And they all hold hands. The point of holding hands in the circle is to maximise the energy or the vibration we all generate. What Catherine suggests is her people connect mentally."

"How many people are there?"

"I think forty-seven of them are going to take part," replied Thomas.

Alisha looked astonished. For one moment she thought Thomas was joking, but he just sat there looking serious! "Really? Goodness that seems amazing."

"Well, if it works it will be."

"It will work, Thomas," Sarah was adamant. "Catherine explained how they will link up. It will start off at ten o'clock on Sunday morning."

"Sorry," said Alisha, "I didn't mean to sound pessimistic. It just seems pretty incredible."

"I thought the same," said Sarah.

"Am I invited to join you?" asked Alisha.

"Of course you are! The only reason I hadn't asked was because..."

"I know. Hospital. But not now I am okay. So, tell me how it's going to work?"

"Well, this is what Catherine told me. No matter how many sit in the circle, we have to join hands, but it's not a complete circle. You," she said pointing at Thomas, "have to sit at the beginning and me at the other end." Sarah smiled at him. "You know that, don't you?"

He grinned. "I suppose so." He was just sitting there, allowing Sarah to distract him with her explanation.

Alisha wasn't having any of that. "Come on. What else Thomas?"

"Sorry I was just thinking." He could see Alisha was becoming excited. "Right then. Forty-seven witches will link up mentally, leaving both ends open. Catherine will link with Sarah. It has to be Sarah because we'll be talking about her mum. Then a high ender will make contact with me."

"Stop!" Alisha put her hand up. That made them all laugh. "What's a high ender?"

"She will be the next one down in skills and knowledge from Catherine."

"How could you possibly know that honey?" Sarah asked.

"I'm in touch now," announced Thomas.

"Catherine did say you were special. I just didn't realise how special." Sarah rubbed his arm lovingly.

"I'm not a bit surprised at anything Thomas comes out with," said Alisha.

"So, what happens?" asked Sarah.

"On Sunday, I'll send out a signal, and with a bit of luck, we'll have a link between all of us. Oh, once Catherine has linked up with you of course." He looked at her. "Did Catherine talk about a connection word?"

Sarah thought for a moment. "She did say something about connection confirmation, but then she said, not now – let's wait until the weekend. What did she mean?"

"It means you have to give it some thought and create a password, then tell me."

Sarah was miffed. I didn't know that!"

Thomas smiled. "Let's talk it through so we know what we will be trying to do. Come on Alisha, you think about it as well."

"I think we're trying to do something quite incredible. But it's not beyond us," said Sarah. "Just think what we did earlier with Alisha."

Alisha jumped up and gave Thomas a power hug. "You saved my life. So, what we are planning to do on Sunday is a doddle."

Sarah was overjoyed to see Alisha with so much energy. "I'm so glad you're better." She looked at Thomas. "Bad stuff is out there, isn't it?"

He nodded.

"So how will we know who you and Sarah are connecting to?" asked Alisha.

"Precisely. You won't know, unless..." he paused, looking at the pair of them.

"What are you thinking about? Come on."

"You need a word. You know. A sort of password," said Sarah.

"Or a name – that only the circle knows," Alisha suggested. "Is that how it works?"

"And I thought I'd be here for a week! You've got it! We can call Catherine tomorrow and confirm things are in place and settle on the identities we'll use."

"Let's have pudding now! I think we've earned it." Sarah suggested.

The girls went out to the kitchen while Thomas went over

to look at some of the books Catherine had lent Sarah. He had never heard of any of them before. He opened one of them and started to read.

"Cream, honey?" Sarah called.

"Just a tad, please." He walked back to the table to read the book as the girls came back. "Can I take this home?" he asked.

"Of course," said Sarah.

As soon as he had finished the pudding, Thomas left for home, leaving the two cousins to get back to normality. He left it with both of them to come over the following day when they were ready. He hoped it would be later in the day as he had lots to catch up on.

Chapter 19

It was Saturday morning, and Thomas was up early, feeling edgy. He had to do a whole week's work in a day, but right now, he didn't appreciate that his newly acquired abilities might also help with mundane chores. As he switched on the computer, Dominic popped into his head.

Hello, Thomas.

For once in his life he didn't jump. He had finally got used to using this communication tool. *Hi, Dominic. I didn't expect to hear from you. Is there a problem?*

There could be. Something is developing. You probably know that of course?

Things happen. All you lot do is look on. Until now of course, now I'm in the team.

I couldn't have put it better myself.

Go on then, let's have it.

Actually, if you give it some thought, you can tell me.

I was just about to start catching up with work, Dominic.

Don't worry about that. You'll be able to do that in five minutes now. You're faster than the computer you're using! Everything you've done regarding your work is stored in your head as it always was, but now you can retrieve any of it whenever you want to. All of it at once. So, can you give some thought to what's happening? Dominic sounded impatient.

Hang on a minute, Thomas cleared his mind, closed his eyes, and let his mind wander. *Blast! They know I'm here.*

Not you as such. They have been expecting a new source of power, but they haven't a clue who possesses it. Yet!

Are you absolutely one hundred per cent sure of that? I don't want any uncertainty.

Yes, I'm sure. There is no one alive on this planet who knows of you or your abilities. And as a precautionary measure your name has been attached to a... Dominic paused. *I'm trying to find a way to describe what's been done on your behalf.*

Just tell me the consequences! I don't want to know how it was done.

Well, your name cannot be transmitted through spiritual airwaves, so if Catherine wants to discuss you with any of the other witches, your name will not go out. Darksiders can't identify you.

Okay, I'm impressed.

Now, Thomas, all this has come about because of the activity surrounding the other side's disciple, Merston. They know the white witches are on the march. That has suggested to them that the higher power has arrived.

Thomas thought for a moment. While his mind was super-efficient, he still needed to get the basics in his head.

Come on Thomas, you're too slow.

Thomas sighed. *So, somehow they've found out about the interest in Sarah's mother? That involves Merston. They are disturbed by what the witches are up to. The darksiders want him out of the control of Catherine, the witch. That must mean they have a job that only he can do. But hang on. How do they know what we are up to? All we want to know is if he murdered Sarah's mother.* He paused again. *But you could tell me that, couldn't you!"*

You know I can't get involved with that. What I can say is what you already know. When Catherine tried to eliminate

Merston all those years ago, she came up on their radar and has been there ever since.

So that's how they know, Thomas felt miffed.

That's why your name has been tagged.

How can Catherine be so careless?

She may not even be aware of it. For your kind, it was a long time ago. But don't worry, it won't stop you from making a connection, but I would recommend caution.

Meaning?

You must take responsibility for the discipline. Life has become difficult – and more to the point dangerous!

That's all well and good, Dominic, but how do I suddenly take over the control of forty-seven witches? They listen to Catherine. It's going to be rather difficult too if they are monitoring Catherine. Unless... Thomas had a thought. *We need to communicate differently.*

True. It's very simple Thomas. Think.

I've got it! The darksiders have linked to the witch's frequency. Yes?

Exactly.

And as my vibration is much higher, I should be able to lift the circle's vibration to my level. Yes?

That's the way to do it.

All I need you to do then is to sow a seed in Catherine's mind regarding the power source. Change her perception in what she believed from the stories that have been handed down. That way it will be natural for me to take over temporarily!

I can do my bit Thomas, but you will have to visit every single one of the witches in Catherine's coven. You'll have to explain what's been going on and how you, with their help, can change the protocols.

Okay, but that means it won't happen this Sunday.

That's not an issue. After all, this started years ago. Another week won't hurt.

Yep, that's true. You'll have to tell me when you've done your magic on Catherine so I can call and set things in motion.

She'll call you, Dominic said.

Wow, I'll be impressed with that.

Well, stand by to be impressed.

Thomas laughed.

I'll be back in touch. Bye.

Thomas began giving some thought to his visits to the witches. *Could I get them to meet in groups? Ten or so together would be good.* Sarah would suspect something was going on if she found out that he had visited forty-seven witches in such a small time slot.

After all that thinking and planning with Dominic, Thomas decided he needed a cup of tea before trying out what Dominic had suggested to him about working fast. It wasn't long before he was flying through his computer work. This was an added bonus. When the pressure of ordinary work was off, he was able to concentrate on more sinister matters. The next thing he heard was the doorbell ringing constantly. He knew exactly who it would be! Then he heard the old oak door began to creek as it opened, and Sarah shouted out before entering the lounge, closely followed by Alisha.

"Hi, honey!"

The thought of seeing Sarah made him smile. He leapt up from his work and went to give her a hug, but the goodies she had with her got in the way.

"Alisha and I have worked all morning preparing these treats for you, Thomas." She leaned forward over them and gave him a kiss. "Oh, and Catherine has been trying to call you."

Thomas knew why she couldn't get through. It was Dominic occupying his mind. "I must have left the phone in the car," he said.

Sarah reached into the goodies bag. "Try this, Thomas!" She handed him a huge sandwich, "Alisha made the bread this morning."

Alisha smiled. "Hello, Thomas."

"I'll get your phone while you eat," Sarah said, and she headed outside.

Thomas was chuffed. He was being cared for, something he wasn't used to. He did what he was told, sat down, and tucked in. "This is so good. Thanks, Alisha."

"That's nothing. Wait until you see the pudding for tonight!"

Sarah rushed back into the room. "It wasn't there." She looked around. "There it is! On the couch beside you!"

"Catherine said she has called you five times. It must be really important."

"Five times!" Thomas was amazed at how little time it had taken Dominic to give Catherine a different perception. "I don't suppose another five minutes will hurt," he said, wanting to finish his sandwich.

"Just eat quickly. I want to know what Catherine wants," said Sarah, sitting down beside him. With his last mouthful almost gone, she picked up his phone, redialled and handed it to him.

He put the phone to his ear, leaned towards Sarah, and stole a kiss. "Hello, Catherine. Sorry, I left the phone switched off. What's the plan?"

"That's precisely what I was going to ask you!"

He knew he needed to sound a little unsure but convincing. "All those years ago when you were understandably distressed, angry, and looking for revenge. Well..."

"Get straight to the point, Thomas. I'm a big girl."

"Okay, you messed up. What you did to Merston left you vulnerable."

"How?"

He glanced at Sarah and Alisha. They were staring at him. The phone was open. He had to choose his words carefully. "I'm not completely sure but I have a good idea. Merston's lot have been tuned in for the last thirty years."

"No! Surely not?" Catherine sounded horrified.

Now Sarah and Alisha were hanging on every word he uttered. "Jeremy Merston is more important than we thought."

"To whom?" Catherine asked.

Thomas waited. He felt that Catherine should know without him explaining.

"No, don't tell me. That bloody Lucifer! Give me a moment Thomas. I need to think."

"Take your time."

Thomas stood up and began pacing the room.

"I was so upset back then, Thomas," said Catherine. "So angry I wasn't thinking right."

"Catherine, we have a problem now; a thirty-year-old one. But one thing at a time. If you agree, the first thing that must be done is to contact all of your coven by phone. Not in your usual way though and explain why you can't use Jeremy Merston's name over your communication system. His name has been tagged. This is very important – phone only! Otherwise, any communication will be picked up."

"I'll call them all immediately Thomas."

"By phone!" Thomas reminded her again.

"Yes, by phone. How did you find all this out?"

"With a bit of digging and a little help."

Catherine sighed. "Thank goodness you're around."

"And while you're doing that Catherine, do you think you could organise your ladies into geographical groups?" He looked over at Sarah and gave her a reassuring smile.

"You want to see them face to face, don't you?"

"Yes, if that's okay with you."

"Definitely, but it does mean it won't happen tomorrow."

"No, it can't happen tomorrow now. We have to get this absolutely right, otherwise our assailants will crash the circle."

"I can see that. How do you propose to stop them, Thomas?"

"By lifting the frequency used to link up."

"I'm not sure how that happens," Catherine said nervously. "You seem to know what you are doing so I'm not going to ask. I'll get on with the calls. I'll let you know when things are set up."

Sarah and Alisha shouted goodbye and waved as if Catherine was in the room. Thomas knew that the pair of them were unsure about what was going on. He suggested they let the others know about postponing the circle meeting for a week by phone. He emphasised the word phone.

"So, the Devil's been protecting Merston," Sarah sounded deeply hurt and angry.

Thomas nodded. "We're setting this up for you to make contact with your mum. No doubt she'll tell you where Merston's loyalties lie."

"If Sarah gets confirmation, how will we deal with this man?" Alisha asked.

"That's complicated. I need to think about that. One step at a time. This is all new to me. I don't want to be overwhelmed."

"Thomas?"

"Yes, Sarah."

"How do you propose visiting forty-seven witches next week?"

"Well, as you heard me say to Catherine, if she organises her people into geographical groups, I'll only have four places to visit."

"That explains it. Ah, what a divvy I am! I feel bad that you have to cover half the country to sort out my problem."

"It's our problem," said Thomas.

Sarah, chuffed with Thomas's response, gave him a hug. "How far do you have to go?"

Thomas knew Sarah didn't have a clue where places were and was counting on Alisha being the same. "If Catherine does her job properly, I can do it in a couple of days."

"That's quick! I thought it would take longer than that."

He shook his head. "No, I intend on going to the gym next week."

"Okay, I'll call the girls and tell them it's been put back a week. I'll call Susie first. She'll tell Winnie, and Winnie can call the others."

While Sarah was speaking to Susie, Alisha received a text from the hospital confirming the scan was all clear. They asked her to get hold of her friend that had cured her and invite him to attend a meeting. A few of the consultants were amazed at what he had achieved. She showed Thomas the text.

"How did they know I did anything?"

Alisha shrugged. "I don't know."

Both of them looked over at Sarah.

"Hang on a sec Susie," Sarah held out her phone to Thomas, "Susie has dug up some information on her boss. She says she needs to talk to you."

"Okay," he took the phone from Sarah. "How can I help Susie?"

"Thomas! Last night we had a few issues at work and the Minister had to rush off. I'm not sure what it was about. Anyway, as he left, he asked me to pick up a file and go through it, as he didn't have time himself. While I was in his office, the printer started up, so I just happened to glance at what was coming out of it."

"And?" asked Thomas.

"It was just one page, so I grabbed it off the printer and put it on his desk. But there were more documents sitting on his desk. They weren't work papers, so I scrutinized them and because I didn't understand what I was reading, I took copies and brought them home. Smithe is definitely up to something."

"What makes you think that?"

"He's sending money abroad every month to twenty-two different countries."

"Are you sure? He's an MP. Doesn't he have to declare business interests?"

"He does but he hasn't."

"Did you leave the papers on his desk?"

"Of course I did! And I put the single sheet back on the printer. Don't worry. He won't know I've seen them."

"Good. Bring the papers round tomorrow."

"What's your address Thomas?"

"Dancing lane. Just at the edge of the village."

"See you tomorrow then Thomas."

He passed the phone back to Sarah.

"What's got Susie so excited?"

"I'm not too sure," he said. "Something about her boss making lots of payments around the world. She's bringing the papers over tomorrow."

"When are you going to meet the hospital consultants?" asked Alisha, showing the text to Sarah.

Sarah smiled at Thomas. "All clear! But then you knew that anyway, didn't you?"

"I am confident that all is well."

"They want to meet you and hear how you did what you did?" Alisha said.

"But how did they even know?"

"A nurse came in while you were doing your healing." Sarah announced.

"I didn't hear anyone."

"I'm not surprised. You weren't on this planet. I asked the nurse to be quiet and she just nodded and tip-toed out."

Thomas frowned. "Well, I'm not going to meet them. Doctors do not understand about alternative therapies."

Chapter 20

It was Sunday morning and Thomas was up early. Catherine had emailed the address details and as Thomas had hoped, she had grouped the witches into four lots. All he had to do was make contact and arrange times. It dawned on him that when he had travelled through light, he had visualised a spot at a place he already knew and had light travelled successfully. He didn't know these areas, and he was unsure quite how to travel. He didn't have a landmark for any of the four locations. Then an idea popped into his head. If he entered the postcode into the computer then searched for the nearest church, he could print a picture and try to travel to it while Alishia and Sarah were asleep as a practice run. In no time Thomas had printed off a picture of the local church close to the first postcode.

Once outside he looked around making sure he was out of sight of prying eyes and then concentrated hard on the picture. In a second, he was gone. He wasn't quite prepared for his plan to work and he crashed into a huge Yew tree, bounced off it, and ended up on the ground amongst the gravestones. For a minute or two, he was out for the count. He came round in a panic. *Has anyone seen me?*

Thomas checked his watch, and it was only 7 o'clock on a Sunday morning. As luck would have it, no one was wandering around the churchyard. He was safe. *What an idiot I am*, he thought to himself, realising how big a mistake it could have been if anyone had been there. He slowly climbed to his feet, checking to see if he was damaged. He felt alright, but there was blood dripping onto the grass. He felt his face. It wasn't good. He walked over to the church and looked at his reflection in a stained-glass window. Blood was now streaming out of the cut. Not again, he thought. All he had on him to ease the flow was a couple of tissues. *Not substantial enough.* He began to panic. *How on earth am I going to explain this one?* "Come on you idiot, think!" he said out loud.

He began walking around the outside of the church trying to calm himself down. Suddenly, to his amazement, Jamie popped into his head.

What's wrong, Thomas?

How do you know anything is wrong?

I'm tuned into your stress levels. Now what's the problem?

A bloody tree. That's what's wrong!

What? Which tree?

The one that got in my way!

"Oh! That one!" Jamie was beaming as he appeared in front of Thomas. "I thought you had this travelling bit sorted."

"Well I have…ish! I was trying something different. I have to travel around the country next week." He showed him the picture of the church. "I didn't expect it to work instantly and before I knew it, I hit that bloody tree over there. I can't go back like this. Sarah will wonder what I've been doing."

"Well just heal yourself!"

"I don't know how to."

"You have the ability. That was all part of your advancing programme when you were in the Garden of Souls. You probably haven't mastered self-healing yet. It won't take long. In the meantime…"

"What are you going to do?" Thomas was even more anxious.

"I'll do it." Jamie ran his hand across Thomas's face. "All done."

Thomas gingerly touched his face. "Wow! I'm impressed, Jamie. And with you tuning into my stress levels! That's something else! Now I'd better get back. At least I know picture travel works."

"Just don't crash into anything."

"That will never happen again."

"By the way if I were you, I'd wash the blood out of your shirt."

Thomas was horrified as he looked down at the blood on his clothes.

"I like your plan with the picture," said Jamie, and then he was gone.

Thomas focused his mind on a particular spot in Sarah's garden and managed a controlled landing. Much to his surprise Sarah was up and out in the garden. Fortunately, she didn't see him arrive. She did sense that he was there.

"There you are."

"Hiya honey. Did you get a good sleep?"

"Yes. But sorry about the sleeping arrangements. I just wanted to make sure Alisha is okay."

"Don't worry about that. I understand."

"Thank you, honey," she smiled and gave him a kiss. "Goodness! What's that on your shirt?"

He looked down innocently at the blood stain. "I had a nosebleed. I didn't realise it went on my shirt."

"Poor you. I'll rinse your shirt out for you."

"Thank you. Maybe it was because I got up so early," he continued inventively. "I needed to walk and work out the week ahead. I think I have figured how I'm going to get round to everyone. And still go to the gym." He held his nerve. He wasn't fibbing. It was true enough that he'd been working out the week ahead in the suburbs of Manchester. *I've only told a few white lies.*

"So, I will get to see you next week then?"

"Definitely."

She took Thomas's hand, and they walked back to the house. It was early and Alisha was still asleep in bed.

"I'll do breakfast", said Sarah. "Here, give me your shirt."

It wasn't long before Alisha appeared.

"How do you feel?" asked Thomas.

"Fine thanks. Where's your shirt?"

"I had a nosebleed. Sarah is rinsing it out."

Moments later Susie put her head round the door. "Hope I'm not too early?" She looked longingly at the poached eggs, toast, and grilled mushrooms.

"Sit down," said Sarah. "There's plenty."

"Oh, yes please." Susie took the papers out of her shoulder bag and put them on the table. "We'll look at them when we've finished, shall we?"

Thomas leaned over to get the papers.

Sarah stopped him. "Yes, Thomas. We'll wait until we've all finished."

Thomas pulled back. "Yes, Miss."

The papers were laid out on the table.

"These are the copies of the papers from the printer in Smithe's office, right?"

"Yes, Thomas. I think he's got some deal with someone somewhere, "said Susie enthusiastically.

"I don't know about that," said Thomas thoughtfully.

"The ID is obviously someone." He turned the page, and then another. "There must be twenty someone's."

"Actually, there are twenty-two someone's. I've been over the information fifty times trying to make sense of it." Susie replied.

"Twenty-two! Okay," Thomas turned the pages adding up the money columns. "Goodness! He paid seventeen thousand pounds to this particular someone."

"Wow! How much?" asked Sarah.

He passed the paper to Sarah so she could see the figures too.

"How did you add that lot up so fast?"

"How? In my head," The three of them looked at him. "That's what I do all day, figures."

"Add all the money columns," said Susie.

Thomas did it easily. He had always been good at maths, but now he was brilliant and it had only just dawned on him.

"So, how much has Smithe paid out in the past nine months?"

"Four hundred and seventy-three thousand, nine hundred and ninety-nine pounds," said Thomas.

There was dead silence as they all stared at him.

"There's one column I don't understand," he said. "The percentages column. I wonder who gets a percentage of the funds going out?"

"What do you think he's doing Thomas?"

"I'm not sure. Buying something perhaps? It's a lot of money. If he's doing business, he would have to declare it."

"Yes!" Said Susie, "he would!"

"Would it have to do with what he does at work, Susie?" asked Sarah.

"Do you know what he is doing?" asked Alisha.

"I think..." Susie hesitated. "I think he is selling off the ideas that come through our department. That is not right, we should be developing them."

"But then why is he paying money out?" asked Sarah.

"I know! It all seems daft, so I haven't a clue. I'm hoping Thomas can figure it out."

Thomas began to think. "This is going to take some time to unravel. You say he had to rush out unexpectedly?"

Susie nodded.

"So as soon as he had done the payments to all those people, he went out in a rush? Or was it in panic?" suggested Thomas.

"I'm not sure," Susie said slowly.

"What's the difference?" Sarah asked.

Thomas glanced over at her. "In a panic, you make mistakes. In a rush, not so much. I think he left in a panic. That's why he left the papers scattered on his desk. Can you remember what happened the previous month?"

Susie looked at him blankly.

"What I'm asking is, has he ever left as suddenly as he did on Friday?"

Susie nodded, "I can see what you're getting at."

Sarah didn't understand what Thomas was insinuating.

"I'm just thinking there may be a pattern, or routine. If Susie thinks her boss is up to something, then with all that money moving around the world, I'm half inclined to agree with her."

"Up to something?" now Susie was nodding. She seemed more convinced than ever. "This is getting exciting."

Thomas shook his head. "Or frightening, even dangerous perhaps."

"What do you mean?"

"I think this boss of yours means business. It wouldn't be good to cross swords with him. We have to be very careful."

Sarah looked over at Susie, "I think he's referring to you."

Susie frowned. "You sound like my mum."

"This is important, Susie!"

She sighed, "yes, Thomas I am not a fool."

"Do you diarise all his meetings?"

Susie's face lit up. "Brilliant! Why didn't I think of that?"

"Check what he did this time last month. You have to slow down and think a little. There's much more to this."

"I'm on it! But how do we find out who the payments went to?"

"Check the IBAN numbers and account details?"

"But how can we do that, Thomas?" Sarah asked.

"I know someone who can do this for us."

"Who?"

Thomas hesitated. "Oh, just someone I know who works in the city," he lied. "I'll need to take copies and give them to him. You okay with that Susie?"

Susie nodded, "You keep these copies. I don't want them."

"Once we know who's receiving the money, we'll probably be able to work out what's going on."

Susie collected the papers put them in order and placed them on the table. "Oh" she said, suddenly panicked. "Oh, sod it." She went pale.

Thomas looked at her. "What's the matter?"

"I didn't put the papers back on his desk the same way up."

"What do you mean?" asked Alisha.

"They were face up. That's why I noticed them, with all those figures. His work doesn't involve figures. When I put them back, I put them face down."

"Surely he wouldn't remember exactly how he left his desk," said Thomas. "Do the cleaners come in after work?"

"Yes."

"Then the cleaners did it."

"But they're not supposed to touch the desks."

"So what? They did this time. That's if Smithe notices. Don't worry about it."

"All right," said Susie nervously. "I'd better get going now."

"We'll go too, Thomas," said Sarah, "You've got lots of work to do."

"Thanks, honey," he said and gave the three of them a hug.

With little effort, Thomas had already arranged days and times to visit the four groups of witches but he had no intention of taking all week. With the girls gone, he contacted Jonas. It was the first time he had used his communication skill to contact the higher shide since he was at the Garden of Souls.

This is a pleasant surprise, Thomas. I don't suppose this is a 'how-are-you Jonas call'?

Amusing Jonas.

It could be. You are more than welcome to say hello when you like.

How are you Jonas?

Jonas laughed. *Well done, Thomas! How can I help?*

Thomas started to explain. *Normally I wouldn't even think about this but...*

Jonas interrupted. *Go with your gut! You're an advanced human. Ask!*

Well, down to business then. I have twenty-two IBAN numbers. I would like to know who each one is and where they are located.

Do you have the list in front of you?

Yes.

Good. You haven't done this before, but it's one of the little perks of being super-human.

Thomas liked the idea of that. *I'm sure I know what you are going to say.*

You should. You're a gifted man now! Go on. Tell me.

I'm going to focus on this list and transmit it to you. Right? He suddenly realised what that meant. *You're going to store that information in your head, aren't you?*

Of course, and I already have. The fact that Jonas was so matter of fact about it, left Thomas staggered.

Don't get carried away. What you sent to me is trivia! It doesn't need a great deal of thought. If you want to be more sophisticated, then you need to understand what you are transferring. But don't pin your hopes on a miracle cure for some ailment or such from me.

Shame, said Thomas, *I get it. If I want to be super clued up, I've got to be ordinarily clued up before.*

Something like that. But you're doing well. Don't rush.

That was pleasing, at least.

You'll have the information you want by the morning. Is that quick enough?

Super. Thank you, Jonas.

If you need something, just call. Bye Thomas.

With Jonas gone, Thomas concentrated his mind on how to set the circle up with all these witches. Although this was the first time he had tried to do this, he realised timing would be crucial. He needed everyone to tune in at the same moment, and he wasn't sure how to orchestrate that. *I will need to get Catherine involved*, he decided. *After I've paid a visit to all the witches, I will pop down and see her.*

Chapter 21

Early Monday morning, Thomas was getting on with a bit of ordinary work. He called in to check at the office and with everything running smoothly there, he decided to deal with the witches. He drove to his hideaway on the farm, parked up and took out the picture of his first stop from his backpack. *Glasgow. That's a long way. I'm glad I'm not driving*, he thought. He concentrated on the picture. Immediately he was gone. It was an amazing way to travel! He hovered carefully, selecting a landing spot behind the church where he wouldn't be seen and descended gently onto a patch of grass.

I need to find a taxi. He walked towards the high road and rummaged in his backpack for the address book. As he did, he realised he had the address of the Glasgow group in his mind. Soon he was sitting in the taxi on his way to the outskirts of the city. He asked the driver to drop him off just before his destination. He wasn't sure how sophisticated the darksiders were and wondered if he was being tracked.

As he walked along the road, he made mental notes of his surroundings. If he had to come back, he wouldn't need a taxi. "Fifty-eight," he said out loud. A woman with bright red hair was standing on the path.

"Thomas?"

He nodded.

She beckoned him in. "Quickly!"

Once they were inside, the door closed abruptly behind them.

"With all of us here, we may be attracting attention," she whispered.

Thomas followed the woman with the bright red hair into what looked like an early Victorian house. Wallpaper was peeling off the walls, and bare floorboards creaked as they continued down the long dark corridor. Thomas looked towards the ceiling where he could see a collection of webs. *Where are the spiders though?*

"Just a little further Thomas," she said. With that, she stopped abruptly, pulled out a well-worn wand, touched the wall and a doorway appeared. *Woah, this is a witch's house!*

Thomas made his way into the parlour and joined the group. *What a strange place this is.*

"Have you placed a vibe wall around the house?" he asked.

"What do you mean?" The red-haired witch stared at him.

"The protection around the house. Has the power been lifted up?" They all looked at each other. Thomas took that as a no. He smiled at everyone and held his hand up gesturing a gentle wave. "Before we say anything, can you show me the garden please?"

The woman with the red hair gave Thomas an odd look then walked him to the outside door. Not a word passed between them. As he walked down the steps and past a sweet, scented lilac bush in the garden, he felt a weak signal coming from the vibe wall. Instinctively he knew what to do. With a little concentration and effort, he lifted the vibration surrounding the house to a maximum level. Ten seconds later, he was walking back inside. The woman with the red hair was waiting by the door. He smiled at her. "Wonderful lilac. All done now. A spiritual rhino couldn't get through our shield."

"What did you do? How did you do that? Catherine said you were powerful. You really must be the one then?"

Thomas just smiled. "I don't know your name."

"I'm Moira," she said.

One by one the others called their names out. All were from Scotland with an accent to match. With the formalities over and a mug of tea in his hand, he proceeded to tell them why they were needed.

"Catherine believes their old boss Jeremy Merston killed her friend Victoria. We want to find out for sure and why. Catherine tried years ago, but she couldn't complete the task. I want to make it clear what is at stake now."

One of the ladies stood up. "Thomas, is it the Dark Power protecting this man?"

"It's something like that Cicely."

She looked pleased that he had remembered her name. "Is the Dark Power able to get involved with what we propose to do?"

"God's law doesn't allow that," Thomas answered confidently.

There was a hush for a moment. Then a cheer went up.

"So how will it work?" asked Moira.

"Well, as you know from Catherine, the other lot have been monitoring your group because of what she did all those years ago to Merston. But not anymore, I've just seen to that."

"Can I ask a question, please?" asked another one of the witches.

"Of course, you're Katy, aren't you?" prompted Thomas.

Katy nodded. "Catherine said it was Merston's name that the other lot picked up on, which allowed them to eavesdrop."

"Yes, that's right."

Katy paused. "So, is that why you mention his name because you have just created a safe space?"

Thomas smiled. "I've increased the energy level surrounding this house. That's what I was doing outside. Nothing will get back to them now."

Everyone sat back and looked at him admiringly.

Katy shook her head. "Yes, but how did they manage to tap into our group in the first place?"

Thomas knew he needed Catherine on his side. He chose his words carefully. "I would imagine Merston, who was a prized asset back in those days, achieved what he had been asked to do, and allowed himself to drop his guard. That gave Catherine a chance to render him useless! I'm sure that irritated the other lot. So, they tagged his name and waited for it to be mentioned. Catherine might not have put her defences in place quickly enough, so as soon as she communicated with anyone regarding Merston, it would have pinged up in the darksiders headquarters."

"That seems so complicated," Katy looked puzzled.

"Don't worry, Katy," said Moira. "We'll talk about that in depth later. Meanwhile, how can we complete a circle next Sunday? What if they are not around?"

Thomas didn't have to think. He knew exactly what he needed to do. "They will be! So, I'll need you all to take a picture of your home on your phone and send it to me with your postcode. Then I can lift the energy in your vibe wall and that will take away the problem of eavesdropping for good."

They all stared at him.

"But how can you do that?" asked Jessica. "Just from pictures?"

He smiled. "That's a question for another day Jessica." He hadn't had this kind of adulation before. It was unnerving. But now it was Thomas's turn to ask a question.

"There is something I need to know. Tell me, how do you time your remote circle?"

"We choose a radio station we all receive, and when the programme we've selected comes on, we tune into each other."

"We make sure we all have a copy of the Radio Times!" said Katy laughing. "An old-fashioned thing to use, but it works for us."

"Clever!" Thomas was very impressed.

One of the witches raised her hand.

"Yes, Cara?" Thomas remembering her name surprised her and him. Things were happening fast with his development, and he liked being able to recall their names effortlessly.

"I'm Moira's cousin. The dippy one!"

He smiled. "I don't think that."

"I know..." she paused for a moment, "I know how we work the circle when all of us get together. But how will this Sunday work with you and all the other people tied into the circle? What do you think we can achieve?"

He didn't want to sound too dramatic. "It's information we need. I think the best way to go about this is to power up the circle first. We can do that in a couple of ways. Victoria's daughter will sit last but one in the circle, thereby drawing almost all the power to herself. That, linked in with her emotional will, should connect to her mother. I will sit at the other end boosting the energy going out. Then with all your combined power, we will reduce and lower the vibrations coming back from the other side. I can then tweak the energy, so that it is easy for us to understand what the souls are saying. Once we have established a strong connection, I am hoping we will be able to look through a window to where the souls are staying."

The silence and tension in the parlour was almost tangible, until Cara spoke out.

"Do you mean Heaven?" she asked.

Thomas was cautious. "That is up to you to tell me, Cara, when the circle has finished."

He stood up to leave. "Until next week then," he said getting ready to leave.

At the end of Moira's road, he looked at the picture of the church in Manchester and travelled there. He arrived immediately and made sure that it was safe to materialise. No one was around, so he headed for the church gate. The road wasn't busy. *I guess there's no chance of a taxi driving by.* Thomas stopped someone to ask them directions to Three Bit Lane. It wasn't far. He could walk it easily.

Sally's house was not dissimilar to the house he had just left, maybe slightly larger. As he walked down the path, a woman opened the door a little prematurely for his liking. He needed a moment to sense the vibe wall, so he put his hand up as a greeting without saying a word. As he had expected, the vibes were weak in this wall too, so he immediately repeated the process he had used in Scotland. The woman standing in the doorway realised something was going on and stayed silent until he had finished. He walked towards her. "Are you Sally?"

"Yes. I guess you're Thomas. Welcome."

He was shown to the back room, where ten other ladies were drinking tea and coffee.

They smiled when they saw him and asked in unison. "Please tell us what we have to do next Sunday?"

He repeated what he had told the witches in Scotland. He stayed for around forty minutes until he was satisfied they all knew precisely what they had to do and that they were happy to send pictures of their houses for a vibe wall upgrade. Now with the job half done, he headed back home. He couldn't afford for Sarah to see him back so early, so he left his car hidden in the barn.

As Thomas walked, he then thought back on what he had been told by Jonas and the Old Souls who had made the improvements to him about being in close proximity to darksiders. With the possibility looming that he would see Saffron tonight at the gym, he decided to contact Jamie and find out if his suspicions that Saffron was a dark witch were right. Within a moment, Jamie appeared in front of him.

"What can I do for you?"

"Hello, Jamie."

"It's not mega urgent then. You have time for the formalities."

Thomas grinned. "Very good Jamie. Have I interrupted you in some way?"

"Yes, I was sleeping. Now what can I do for you?"

"I didn't think you did that."

"I don't. I was just joking. You've been around Dominic too long."

Thomas sighed. "Remember telling me about coming into contact with the other lot?"

"Yes."

"Then," Thomas paused. "I would know who they were before they knew who I was? Right?"

"Right so far."

"So, if I'm in the same room as a darksider what happens? I can't remember being told how to disguise the fact that I'm a soul returner."

"You were told you would be, but you weren't."

Thomas looked perplexed. "What's the point of that?"

"Initiative Thomas! Initiative! This is probably the biggest challenge you'll face. Searching your mind and asking instead of being told will bring anything you need to know home to you. If you're not careful, your powers will kick off and you will be compromised."

"Right, okay. I can control my powers now. What's the strategy then?"

"It isn't easy. It will take lots of concentration. You'll need to practice."

"How long for?"

"It depends on how you're made, I suppose. The last bloke cracked it in a couple of weeks. He didn't last long."

"What! Two weeks? Nah! It can't take that long. I'm probably going to bump into someone tonight."

"Ah, Thomas. That could be dodgy."

Thomas started to pace up and down. "Could be dodgy? Why didn't you tell me that sooner?"

"You didn't ask."

"Well, I've got just six hours to figure this out, not two weeks. Let's get on with it."

Jamie proceeded to show Thomas the process of lowering his vibrations. Five hours later, he told him he should just get by with the work they had done together.

"It depends on how powerful the darksider is and how much space you put between you and him."

"It might be a 'her'."

"I'll be on standby should you need any help, Thomas."

And with that, Jamie disappeared. Thomas shook his head and wondered how his encounter with Saffron would go later that day. His anxiety was going off the Richter scale.

Chapter 22

Thomas had turned his mobile off early morning. He had arranged to call Sarah when he was done with his witch work. That was now so he called her.

"Thomas sweetheart, where are you?"

"I'm back now."

"Aren't you tired of all that travelling? Is it all good for Sunday? Are you still coming to class tonight?"

"I wouldn't miss it honey and yes, so far, no problems." He avoided commenting on the tired bit. "I still have to see the ladies in Cambridge. Then Bristol. And yes, we're on for Sunday."

"What were the witches like?"

"I think they are all clones of Catherine and Rosemary. They are a breed of their own!"

Sarah laughed out loud. "You are funny."

Thomas showed up at the leisure centre a little early. He noted where Saffron always positioned herself in the class, so he placed his mat and towel at the furthest point from her spot. After some thought, he placed his bottle of water a few meters away from where he hoped Saffron would be working out and then he went back outside to meet up with Sarah. She gave him a big kiss which pleased him.

Mm, "That's nice."

Sarah grinned, "This is a pleasant surprise. You're early."

"Yes, my sweet," he said smiling. "I needed to see you!"

Sarah blushed. "What's the plan for Sunday?"

"I'll run things by you a little later. I have a couple of things to sort out before class."

"What things?"

He thought for a second, realising he had to say something, even if it was a fib. "It's been suggested that when I'm in the hall with Saffron, I should stay as far from her as possible." He hesitated as he thought what next to say. "I'll find out if she is a witch or not. I think she is."

"Did I mention Alisha's gone back home now?"

Sarah had taken in what he had just said about Saffron as if it were quite ordinary. That amazed him.

"Do you want to come round after class?" she asked.

"Yes, please!"

"Off you go then before your witch turns up." A little kiss on her forehead and then he ran down the stairs. As he reached the reception area, he saw Saffron arrive. He ducked into a corner of the cafeteria to avoid her. He had it in mind to walk into the class a minute after it started to avoid bumping into her. Thomas looked at his watch. *Ten minutes to go*. He began to feel really nervous. *What if I can't control the power level? No time for fear.* He ran up the stairs and looked through the door. Everyone was already in place. Thomas took a deep breath. *Nothing to worry about.* He went in, not daring to look in Saffron's direction, he glanced over at Sarah. She smiled. That relaxed him a little. His water was still near the spot he was going to occupy. *All part of the plan,* he thought as he took his place.

The session started with warm-ups for ten minutes. About halfway into the class, Thomas knew there was a moment when everyone did a shoulder stand. In that position, no one could possibly see anyone else. They began the class.

When everyone was on their shoulders, he stood up, not making a sound, and walked in the direction of his water. Now he was quite close to Saffron, and already he could feel a wave of nausea sweeping over him. *Confirmation!* He reached for his water, had a sip, and then casually moved another step towards Saffron to see if she would pick up on his presence.

Saffron wobbled and she struggled to maintain her balance. He moved another step closer. As she fell, he moved like lightning back to his mat. No one had seen him except for Sarah. She mouthed something. *What is she saying?* Now he was back on his mat. Saffron had fallen like a sack of potatoes and was on the floor and groaning. The rest of the class fell too rolling every which way. Thomas kept his head down. Now he had to concentrate on lowering his energy level the way Jamie had shown him. It was surprisingly easy to do. He sat waiting for the class to resume. He saw Saffron talking to her mate Timmidy. He wanted to know what she was saying, so he concentrated on reading her lips, but to his astonishment, he could actually hear what she was saying. This freaked him out. It was so surprising to be able to hear her from so far away that he missed half the conversation. However, he did hear her say, *'I had a sickly feeling come over me. It completely put me off.'* Thomas continued to listen.

"How are you feeling now?" Timmidy sounded concerned.

"I'm fine! The sickly feeling has completely gone. How odd is that?"

"But you still look as white as a ghost!"

Much to Thomas's dismay, Sarah went over to Saffron to check she was okay. While all the commotion was going on, Thomas decided to contact Jamie.

That hasn't taken long. Jamie responded immediately.

What hasn't?

For you to get in touch. Are you out there doing your thing?

Yes, I am on a mission. Now down to business. Is it normal to have exceptional hearing?

You should have exceptional everything.

Why didn't you tell me? It just freaked me out.

You didn't ask.

Not that one again!

With the kerfuffle over, Thomas had to end the conversation. *Must go, thanks for answering me.*

Sarah looked over at Thomas. She knew he was the culprit and had caused the disruption, but she didn't have a clue what was going on. She pulled a funny face at him, which made him feel guilty and he wished he had told her what he was trying to do. He could see that she was upset and this did not sit well with him.

The class got underway again, and Thomas enjoyed the rest of the session. When it was over, he hung back, keeping his distance from Saffron. As the room emptied, Sarah came over to him.

"What happened?" she whispered.

His fears of her being annoyed with him dissipated. Thomas was so pleased with himself. He couldn't help smiling.

"I take it whatever you did, worked, judging from your face."

"Yes, it did, sweetie. I wasn't sure it would, so I'm as surprised as you are."

She tugged his arm, "What did you do?"

He took a deep breath. "When I slipped out just before class, I made contact with the guides. You know, the ones that helped me before."

"I'm beginning to wish I did know them!"

"Wow, you've come round."

"That's because you and your friends managed to cure Alisha."

"My guides, you mean."

"I prefer friends. I've come round because of what you're capable of. It's just amazing. You performed a miracle. Doing that completely turned my thinking upside down! So now you know."

"Okay, can I speak now?"

"You'd better because you're not leaving until you do."

Thomas laughed. Then he concentrated on what he should actually say. "I was told if I could get close enough to Saffron, some kind of energy would pass through me. But I had to be facing her and keep a suitable distance away too."

"How did it go?"

Thomas bit his lip. He was trying not to go into too much detail. Unfortunately, Sarah was having none of that. "Maybe if Saffron was a good soul, then nothing would have happened. I waited for an opportune moment, and then, without being seen, I moved as close as I dared. That's when it happened."

"When what happened?"

"I overwhelmed her. Just being close to her made her feel sick and dizzy. That's what caused her to fall." He could see Sarah was confused with this explanation. "She is evil. I know it now. The guides told me that my pure soul, my very being, is too strong for her."

Sarah looked at him nervously. "Come on then. Let's get out of here. You can shower at my place."

"Are you bothered about Saffron, Thomas?" asked Sarah as she made something to eat.

"No, not at all," he said confidently, "But I had to find out. It's like a jigsaw, figuring out a piece at a time. The next bit of the puzzle is Susie's boss. But he's a different kettle of fish."

"In what way?"

"He's sophisticated. Remember those IBAN numbers I asked a friend to look at? I got the information back late last night."

"The ones from Susie?"

"Yep, I had a quick look and now I have the details of everyone receiving money from George Smithe."

"That was fast. Do you have all the names?"

"Yes, names, where they live, and a payment history from Smithe's account."

"Do you really think we should be doing this? We could get into trouble if we are not careful."

Thomas thought for a moment. "Well, I suppose we could drop it, but if we did, you'd still have Saffron in your class and Susie would probably bug the life out of us when something's wrong. And what about your mother?"

"No, you're right! We must continue. What have you found out?"

"Oh yes," he said enthusiastically. "As we thought, the payments he makes are monthly and all to females. But the best part is," he paused, he could see Sarah was hanging on every word, and she didn't appreciate his hesitation.

"Come on," she said impatiently, "what's the best part?" Then she suddenly clasped her hands together. "You're not going to tell me Saffron is on the list, are you?"

Thomas looked at her, not saying a word,

"She is, isn't she?"

"Yes. Yes, she's on the list."

"What are we going to do?" Sarah sounded panicky.

"Keep this to ourselves for now."

"But isn't she dangerous?"

"I'm not sure, honey. Probably."

Sarah wasn't happy about the idea of a dark witch being in her yoga class.

"Don't worry. Before you knew this and before I had that argument with her, you were oblivious of her being a problem.

Try to get your mind back to that state for the time being until we know what we're dealing with." He gave her a hug. "What classes does she do?"

"I can't think. I'm in a bit of a state."

"Are they the same as I do?" he asked gently.

"I think so."

"Well then, you've nothing to worry about! I can protect you from her."

Sarah gave him a big kiss. "Ooh, I'm glad you're around."

Chapter 23

The following morning Sarah was up early as she had a seven o'clock class. Thomas had an early start too.

"You've got all that driving again! Are poached eggs with toast okay?"

"Yes please, sweetheart."

"When do you think you'll be back?"

"Oh, not too late and it should be an easier day."

He left at the same time as Sarah. The first thing he had to do was drive back home to collect the photos of the churches. Then he proceeded to hide his car in the usual place, checking no-one was around. Taking a deep breath and ready to travel, he looked at the pictures. One church was in Bristol and the other in Cambridge. As before, he had arranged an early meet. Selena's house was on the outskirts of Bristol. Selena was the witch who had organised the gathering. The church he had selected was close to her home. *It shouldn't take me long to walk there.*

He arrived in the shadow of the spire. Down below him, the grass near the wall of the stained-glass windows looked soft. Fortunately, there were no people around. No trees to crash into. He floated down and hurried off to Ashley Lane to meet up with the witches. It took only a few minutes and immediately he went about strengthening the vibration surrounding the house. Out of the corner of his eye, he noticed someone looking out of a ground floor window. He assumed it was Selena, but he couldn't acknowledge that he had seen her as he needed to finish what he was doing. Then he hesitated, as something seemed different. This house didn't feel like the ones he had visited in Glasgow or Manchester. *Something isn't right.* The feeling turned his stomach. He walked out of the garden onto the pavement, but the eerie feeling was still there. He stepped out into the quiet lane. No traffic. No people. Just a horrible feeling in the air. He was not welcome here.

Thomas walked further along the lane. Now he was about thirty metres away from the house. The feeling vanished. He was confused. He wasn't prepared for something like this to happen. He walked back a couple of paces. The feeling returned. Quickly he calculated the perimeter of the band encompassing the house. Whatever this strange feeling was, it had seeped out affecting the surrounding houses. He decided not to do anything to change the energy level until he spoke to the witches in Selena's house. He walked back to Number 4. The garden gate squeaked as he opened it. Ahead of him, the front door was open. He was doing his best not to flee. *Be strong you fool; I can protect myself.*

Cautiously, he walked in. "Selena?"

"We're down here Mr Pink," called a voice.

The narrow hallway was dark and seemed to go on and on.

A skinny little woman appeared from nowhere, startling him. "Thomas! We're all down in the basement. Follow me, please."

He followed her, but as he went further into the house, he felt bad vibes. He was uncomfortable, on edge, and still felt nauseous. Someone, something had a hold on this house. *Catherine didn't mention it. She must have known. Why didn't she tell me?* There were a few questions to be asked.

The basement was cold and dusty. The walls and ceilings were covered in thick webs full of spiders, their many eyes watching and waiting for prey. Thomas shuddered; he did not care for them.

"Let me introduce you to the ladies," said Selena and set about it.

Thomas made a mental note of their names. Despite first appearances, they seemed quite a friendly lot.

"Can I ask you a question, Selena?"

Selena nodded at him and smiled.

He looked hard at her, "you've had trouble with someone in the past here, haven't you? There's a big problem with this house."

Selena took a very deep breath. "Yes, that's right. They said you were good. I can see why," she shook her head sadly. "Such a terrible day."

Thomas brushed that comment aside. He knew he was only good because of Dominic. It was a melancholy thought and to his surprise Dominic answered him.

No, Thomas Pink, you have it wrong. All I have done is give you firepower. It's up to you how efficiently you use your gift.

Thomas was surprised to find he could still be startled by Dominic and in front of twelve witches who were watching his every move, too. To cover up, he had to do a little bit of acting, putting his hand in the air so that it looked as if he was making some kind of spiritual contact. Straight away, there was a hush. That allowed him to focus on Dominic. *Why are you here? I'm in a room full of witches and all eyes are on me!*

You will get used to it, Thomas. My arrival will happen time and time again if I think it will make your job easier. Anyway, you're coping in front of all those ladies doing your hand waving thing, he chuckled. *So, what's the problem?*

Hm… no problem, Dominic, no problem. Can I assume you are going to tell me who Selena has a problem with?

No. You don't need me telling you that. Selena has all the details. The reason I've turned up is because of what she's going to tell you. This is what you're here for.

Then hadn't I better get on with it?

I'm here if you need me.

Thank you, I'll call you when whatever has to be done is done.

Dominic disappeared in an instant allowing Thomas to concentrate on the twelve witches.

They all looked shocked. "What contact were you making? Who was it? It's to do with the house, isn't it?" asked Selena.

Thomas looked at her very seriously. "How long has it been like this?"

"Ten years."

"You've lived like this for ten years?" He was shocked. "Why didn't all of you do something about it?"

"We all got together, but we couldn't undo what was done. The curse is too strong, much too strong."

"What did Catherine say about the curse?" Thomas glanced around the room for an answer. His eye caught a blonde lady who seemed to have a sparkle in her eye and a bit more life than the others. "Sally? Sally, isn't it?"

"Yes," she replied, surprised that she had been picked out.

"Come on then! Tell me."

"Well," she said uncomfortably, "we did tell Catherine straight away when it happened, and we got together to try and put things right. Sally sighed. We worked through the night, but our combined efforts were a complete waste of time. That's when we learned about Jeremy Merston. We were powerless against him, and we assumed we had the same problem."

They all nodded.

Thomas was amazed. "How do you operate with this hanging over your head?"

"We go to Mary's house."

Mary stood up. "Yes, they come to my house."

Thomas looked at her.

"I'm fortunate to have a large house about five miles away, and between us, we have configured the setup, so it's not detrimental to the coven."

"Okay. So you and Selina operate from your house?" he paused and took a deep breath. He could feel how the bad energy was trying to drain him. He looked back at Selena, "and who placed the evil on this house, Selena?"

"I had a run in with the priest when he came to the area ten years ago."

"A priest?! What on earth did you do to allow that to happen?"

"It was me. My fault." Another woman stood up. She was a tall thin woman with long white hair.

The room erupted. All the others disagreed with her. Thomas focused on this woman.

"I'm Carol," she said. Her face had a ruddy complexion, and she looked athletic.

"Do you go running, Carol?"

"Yes. How do you know?"

"You look healthy. Anyway, tell me why you think it's your fault?"

Carol sighed, "Just before the old priest left our local church ten years ago, I had a chat with him at the last fete he'd organised. He was a nice old chap, a proper priest, and he told me about his replacement. He told me that the new priest was coming down from Manchester. I hope he's as good as you, I said, and he suddenly became agitated. That wasn't in his character, so I pressed him on the point. He turned to face me and said quietly. "Watch him! He's bad!"

"Really? What did you say to that?" Thomas frowned.

"I asked him what he meant. He glanced around before he answered. He told me the rumours about the new man were spreading around Manchester like wildfire. Apparently, he had been removed from his parish a year before. The old priest was almost crying when he told me that he had reappeared. And he's coming your way, he said. Be careful. Be very careful. Then too upset to say anymore, he walked off."

"And Carol, you told Selena? That was the awful thing you did."

Carol nodded and was about to cry.

Thomas looked back at Selena. "And then after Carol told you, who did you contact?"

"I called Sally in Manchester. I had to. All the stories you hear I wanted to know the truth. We all wanted to know."

Thomas wondered how a priest could have the power to destroy the good vibes and replace them with evil. *Why would he do that?* "And what did Sally in Manchester say?"

"She said that children began to leave the choir until there weren't enough children left to make it work. Sally's friend had a child in that choir and she told her what she thought had been going on. Shocked by what she heard, Sally put in a complaint."

"And what happened?" he asked.

"Nothing! Well, not quite nothing. A man from the church contacted Sally and came round to her house. Sally's husband is quite fiery. Two minutes after arriving, he threatened the churchman and grabbed him by the collar of his suit and threw him out."

"Then you threatened him, didn't you?"

"Yes, Thomas, we all did. We told him if we hear of anything bad happening in the parish, then we would come for him."

"That must have irritated him enough to throw the dark shadow over the house," Thomas suggested.

"Yes, I guess that is exactly what happened," Selena replied rubbing her arms as if she was feeling icy chills running over her. "He wanted money." After Sally's husband threw the churchman out, Sally did a bit of research and the man that they threw out was named Benjamin Coffee. She found out that he worked in a children's home sponsored by the church on the outskirts of Manchester. Wanting to know more, she went over there to chat with some of the workers. Making sure it wasn't a waste of time, she mixed up a truth potion and sprayed this on her jacket just as she arrived at the home."

Thomas interrupted, "Clever! I've got it, bad stuff, yes?"

"Very," said Sally.

"Well, if there's ever a next time, you take action. You can't make threats. Where does the new priest live? I need to see him."

"Do you really think that's a good idea, Thomas?" asked Carol.

"Good ideas have nothing to do with it, Carol. What's his name?"

"Father Benjamin. He has the use of the house on the church grounds. It's just around the corner."

"I know that church," said Thomas. It was the church he had landed by earlier. "Now, what's his real name because he doesn't sound like a proper priest?"

"I know! Coffee!" exclaimed Carol. "His family name is Coffee."

"Well, I passed that church on my way here. Give me ten minutes or so. When I come back, we can finally get started." The twelve witches crammed into the small basement said nothing, and there was complete silence. *What an odd lot,* Thomas thought as he headed out.

Selena walked him to the door. "You will be careful, won't you."

He smiled and squeezed her arm. Don't worry. "I shan't be long."

Walking slowly to the church gave him a little time to think about what he was going to do. It made him feel rather uncomfortable. *Isn't this what I agreed to do in the beginning? Seek out wrong doers?*

At the church gate, he stopped and looked around. The house was beyond the church. Thirty seconds of psyching himself up prepared him. Then he walked steadily towards the house. As he did, that weird sickly feeling came over him again. It was worse now than when he had approached Saffron in the yoga class. Taking a deep breath he forced himself to concentrate even harder. When he reached the vicarage, there was no one to be seen. An uneven path led up to the front door. The house was ancient and badly in need of repair, but it had a wonderful old oak door. Thomas clenched his fist and banged on it.

From inside, a voice called out, "I'm busy. Come back when I'm in the church!"

Thomas banged on the door again with much more force. "Open the door, Benjamin Coffee."

The door swung open, "What do you want?"

"You, Benjamin Coffee! I want you!"

Immediately the priest reeled back feeling the power Thomas was radiating. Taken by surprise, he stood motionless for a few seconds. "Who are you?" he asked, fearfully.

"Who I am is not important! What is important is that you start discussing any despicable practices you might have carried out."

Horrified, Benjamin Coffee backed away, suddenly realising who he was talking too. "I know who you are! We've all been expecting a replacement. So they found you, did they? Well, I hope you're better than your predecessor! He only lasted a couple of months. It's a shame we didn't get the chance to play with him."

Thomas let him ramble on and took no notice of his words. He had been prepared for a situation like this. Jonas and the higher Souls had prepared him well. It was true. The darksiders were arrogant and far too confident for their own good. Benjamin Coffee took a step forward. "Why don't you come in? I have some excellent communion wine, I would like you to try!"

Don't think just react, Thomas thought. That's what the higher souls had said. He looked at Benjamin Coffee, this man, this so-called priest, who was almost certainly a darksider, and probably very dangerous. Somehow, though, he was staying in control of the situation. He held back, keen to learn something, anything about this dark soul he was suddenly dealing with. It was quite extraordinary that the priest knew of him and his purpose. This was a first and it was intriguing.

"If you think you can return me, think again! I sense that you're not strong enough! Anyway, there are hundreds of us right here in this city," he laughed. "You won't last long. They're probably on to you right now."

Thomas felt ice cold calm. "Do I need to look over my shoulder?" He glanced back over his shoulder. "No one there! I'll tell you what. You tell me where they live and I'll pop round and see them." He could feel the power inside him strengthening.

Benjamin Coffee laughed again, but this time very nervously. "I tell you, there are hundreds of us! Watch out! And that's just the ones I know, so you had better tread carefully before trying anything on me."

Thomas just stood there a few seconds looking the man up and down. He thought about everything he had heard about him, all the wickedness, all the fear and turmoil he had created. "Well, I've taken your advice. I've weighed everything up. Now it's time for you to return."

Benjamin Coffee took a couple of steps back. "You don't have the power for that, you idiot."

Being call an idiot suddenly enraged Thomas, and he growled as he focused on his dark aura and black soul. Immediately Benjamin Coffee was no more. Destroyed like the tumour he had removed from Alisha's brain.

A gentle breeze coming from inside the house picked up the grains of dust that had been Benjamin Coffee and carried them out and away. Thomas stood staring at the empty space, annoyed with himself. He wished he had squeezed more information out of his first returned soul. "I'll have to get a grip on my timing," he said out loud.

Who are you talking to? asked a voice in his head.

Myself, Jamie. Just myself. He started walking back to Selena's house.

I noticed you've just been busy.

How on earth do you know that?

Tuned in. All of us.

Thomas was astonished. *Tuned in? What do you mean? Who's all of us? I'm not tuned in.*

That will come. And you'll meet the others over time. You don't want to get bogged down with that now. You're far too busy.

True. So, if that's all you wanted, I still have more work to do today.

I was making sure you're okay. After all you have just bagged your first darksider.

I'm fine, and yes you're right, I am busy. By now he was outside Selena's house. There was no sick feeling. None at all.

Call if you need help Thomas.

Thanks, Jamie. Bye.

Thomas looked at the house. Now he could create an energy belt here just like he had in Glasgow and Manchester.

He was just finishing when the ladies filed out of the house, smiling brightly. "We felt the darkness disappear ten minutes ago."

Selina appeared next and was in awe of him. "The house. It's back as it was before the priest came all those years ago." She gave him a hug.

Then the others all gathered round him, all keen to know what had happened. "What did you do?" they asked.

"How did you remove the curse?" asked Isabel.

"Yes, how, Thomas?" asked Mary.

"Was it dangerous for you, Mr Thomas?" Asked the older lady Mable, in a fearful voice.

That made him laugh.

"No, it wasn't dangerous. Let's go inside and I'll explain. We're attracting the neighbours' attention out here." As they walked back to the house Thomas glanced up. "Even the birds are back, I can hear them singing."

Selena stopped in her tracks. "Ooh yes!" She stood there listening. Her hands clasped together with joy.

"Come on, Selena. It's over now. Let's go inside. There's a lot to discuss." He was anxious to avoid talking about the incident with Benjamin Coffee, but Selena and the others had lived with the problem for ten years and they deserved to know. "The spirits have dealt with him. He is no more," he said. Thankfully that seemed to satisfy them. Immediately he went on to explain how important it was to have a high level of vibration around each of their houses.

Selena stood up. "Sorry to interrupt, Thomas," she said. "But we've chatted with the others so we're already in the loop. We know what you can do!" All of them opened their bags and produced a photo of their home.

Thomas grinned. "I'm impressed. I wonder if your lot in Cambridge are in the loop as well. It will save me so much time."

"Yes, I think you'll find they are. Your next stop is Heather's house," announced Mable. "She's my niece. And she's an organiser like Selena here."

"Brilliant." Thomas finished raising the vibration around Selina's house. "Selina, you'll be glad to know that you'll all be protected from the darksiders now. Then there'll be no more eavesdropping."

He stayed for more than an hour, drank tea and was fascinated by the stories being told to him. Some tales went back to their great grandmothers. Time was ticking by and he had to see Heather and her coven so decided that he would go.

"It's been a pleasure meeting you all," he said as he left giving each of them a hug.

As he walked away from Selena's house, he took the photos out and flicked through them. With a little time on his hands, he decided to work on each house straight away. It would be safer for them to do this immediately. The demise of the priest could cause a stir. He found a quiet spot and travelled to the first of the eleven houses. Within an hour he had implemented the vibrational level high enough to keep any unwanted energy out. *Now, off to Cambridge*, he thought. *To see Mable's niece. Let's hope the Dark Force doesn't know I'm going there.*

Chapter 24

Amazing! From the outskirts of Bristol, Thomas reached the centre of Cambridge in a moment! Again, the church wasn't too far from The Avenue where Heather lived and where fourteen witches were waiting in her home for him to arrive. He sat quietly for a minute admiring the 15th century church beside him before setting off for his final visit. The ten-minute walk was very pleasurable, he had a deep affection for this city.

When he turned into The Avenue, he saw a group of people outside one of the houses. As he got closer, he realised it was the very house he was heading for. He could see that the people were agitated and he sensed that something bad had happened. When he was almost there the crowd of people noticed him.

"Is that you Thomas?" a woman with dark hair called out to him.

"The very same," He waved and quickened his pace.

"Are you Thomas?" she asked again.

"Yes. Are you Heather?" He held out his hand.

"Yes I am. thank goodness you're here!"

"What's wrong?" He suddenly realised that there was blood trickling down the side of Heather's face. Then he spotted two others on the ground in her front garden with similar injuries.

"What happened?"

"We were all sitting inside waiting for you when suddenly we felt a heavy depression descend upon us. We became aware of a dark spirit."

"This is not good. What happened?"

"Selena contacted us a little while ago and said you were going to see the priest, so we knew there would be trouble."

Thomas was taken aback. He had half expected repercussions, but not this quickly. It said a lot about the network he was up against.

"Anyway, things began to fly around the room. Three of us were hit before we managed to get out. We were taken by surprise and then it was too late to deal with the dark spirit. You understand how we work; we have to be ready to take cover at any given moment."

"I'll deal with whatever is in your house. But first," he paused, "let's look at all your injuries."

"Kate's pretty bad," Heather pointed to Kate lying on the grass.

Thomas went over and knelt down beside her. Blood was coming from Kate's face and seeping through her top too. "I need to touch you," he said.

She nodded.

He rested one hand on her rib cage, and the other one on her face.

Suddenly the blood flow stopped, and the cuts disappeared. She sat up, and then, smiling at Thomas, jumped energetically to her feet. Everyone looked on utterly amazed.

Thomas went over to Margaret. There were glass splinters in her face and blood everywhere. She was sitting down but her injuries were superficial. Again, Thomas placed his hands on the cuts. And as with Kate, she was healed too.

Amazed, Margaret stood up. "Thank you," she said cheerfully.

Now it was Heather's turn and gently, he touched the cut on her face, and it healed instantly. He looked around. "Anyone else?" There was silence. They were all staring at him. He sensed they were more shocked by the way he had healed them than by the way they had been attacked.

Heather's eyes were wide. "After that, what now Thomas?"

"You and the others go for a short walk and I'll deal with the intruder."

They didn't need telling twice!

Thomas called Jamie on his mind phone, as he liked to call it, feeling quite annoyed that he hadn't been warned. He needed to be tuned in and kept informed.

Yes Thomas? You have issues, I can tell. Jamie sounded irritated.

Bloody right I have! Why didn't you tell me about the dark spirit, or entity, or whatever is attacking these Cambridge witches?

It is probably a demon at work, or some ghoul being controlled by a powerful darksider. I can no more see that coming than you can.

That threw Thomas. *What do you mean? You've done all this before, haven't you? Surely you know how darksiders work?*

None of us know how people are going to react to a situation. Not me. Not you. Not Jonas. Not even Dominic. All we can do is be prepared for trouble. A minor point now, although not really relevant, but your predecessors didn't even get this far so that has to count for something!

Thomas put his hand up wanting Jamie to stop, he knew he looked like he was a mad man. *Okay. And I see what you're saying. They must be linked somehow, all knowing the wellbeing of each other – or in this case, their demise?*

It looks that way. But I don't think it applies to their minions. The darksider you sent back was probably one of the higher scumbags. One thing's for sure. You've sent them a strong message.

I've gathered that. Should I be concerned? They know that someone is after them again.

They don't know who you are. And that's how it will stay.

I'd better get on with the job at hand before the ladies come back.

Go in strong, Thomas. I sense that he's an angry one. And take care.

Thomas entered Heather's home. There was glass strewn across the floor, plaster off the walls where furniture had been thrown around. He was amazed that no one else had been injured. Suddenly he felt a surge of dark energy heading towards him. The entity, whatever it was, was invisible. *Terrifying.* Instantly Thomas boosted his own energies into a huge power surge. Instinctively, he knew that it was so powerful it could destroy the house as well as the demon. *Too much. Too much!* In the nick of time, he calmed it a little and then let it go. *Dead Silence. Where is the demon?*

"Thomas," came a whisper from the hall. "Is everything okay? Is it alright to come in?"

He took a deep breath. The air was clear, fresh and he knew that the house was at peace. "Yes come in. It's all over. Just a dreadful mess to clear up."

"We'll sort this out while you do what you have to do outside."

Thomas, now relaxed again, smiled at Heather. "You've all been talking then. That is good to know."

She nodded.

"I assume you all have pictures of your houses?"

"Of course. In an envelope on the mantelpiece. That's if it's still there," she looked towards the fireplace. "Thank goodness, it is!" she sighed with relief and passed the envelope to Thomas.

"I'll take them now then, just in case I forget later," he said, grinning. "Very efficient, you lot. And you understand what I'm about to do?"

A chorus of "yes" burst out.

"I'll get on with it."

As Thomas walked outside, he shuddered. *What if the houses belonging to the other witches are having the same problem? How did the dark source know everyone would be at Heather's place?* He decided not to take any chances and called back to Heather, "I'll need thirty minutes. Will everyone be okay with that?"

"We're not going anywhere."

Thomas powered up the vibrations around Heather's house. Then he called Jamie. *Will you meet me at the top of the road? And in person?* Seconds later Thomas was face to face with Jamie explaining the problem. He gave him half the photos and told him what was required. Jamie looked at the first photo and was gone.

Thomas didn't lag behind. Twenty-five minutes later, they met up at the same place.

"Any problems?"

"One house had a visit. It's wrecked."

Thomas was horrified.

"But my guess is", said Jamie, "these demons are not as sophisticated as you imagine."

Thomas was still concerned how quickly the Dark Force had acted. He was surprised that nobody had been killed.

"I reckon they were going from house to house until they found all of you. The witches were lucky.

"Will you visit the second house? They could have wrecked all of them." Thomas showed Jamie the next picture and waited for him to return. When Jamie appeared again, he could tell by the look on his face that he had bad news. "How bad is it?"

Jamie hesitated. "Really bad."

"This is down to me, isn't it? Sending that scumbag back has had repercussions."

"I suppose so. But don't concern yourself. There are always repercussions. The witches know that better than anyone."

"Whose house, is it?"

"Kate is the name on the back of the photo."

Thomas sighed. "Bloody hell!"

"Why are you so upset?"

"She's the one who had most of the injuries."

"Well, you healed her, didn't you?"

Thomas was still bothered.

"Don't worry. This isn't the first time, and it won't be the last. Jonas has a team of craftsmen ready to deal with this kind of situation, I'll let him know. They'll clear up the mess."

"You're kidding me."

Jamie gave him a look. "Would I do that? Now I think you better tell Kate not to go home tonight. If you show me all the photos, then I will check all the houses and let you know if any need repairing."

Thomas showed Jamie each photo and watched as he absorbed each house into his mind. "Thanks for helping."

"All part of the service!"

Thomas walked back down the hill to Heather's house. As he approached, he felt the energy surrounding it. "Now that's how it should be," he said out loud. Once he was back inside, he was mobbed. Everyone wanted answers, but before he could concentrate on what he was being asked, he had to tell Kate.

"Kate."

"We already know," said Heather. "They wrecked her house too."

"Who told you?"

"Have you forgotten we are all witches? We do have some super powers too! Not on your level though."

He looked at Kate. "It's all to do with what I did in Bristol. I have given the darksiders the hump. But don't worry your house is being taken care of."

Kate wasn't sure what he meant.

"We'll have your house fixed tonight at no cost or the need for insurance claims," he said.

"Really? What's a relief! Thank you, Thomas. I'll stay with my sister until it's fixed. It didn't happen with the other houses, did it?"

"No, I know all is well." *Are the other houses okay Jamie?*

All are fine, kiddo.

That was pure luck, Thomas said feeling relieved. *They all knew already though*, he thought to himself and then smiled.

The witches' curiosity began to grow. "What happened in Bristol, Thomas?" they asked.

"You really want to know?"

"This is new to all of us, so a little enlightenment won't go a miss," said Heather. They all leaned forward in their seats eager to hear what he was going to say.

"The priest in Bristol has gone back. And so has the demon that did the damage here."

"Gone back?" Heather looked shocked.

"To the Soul Maker."

There was total silence. No one said a word.

"Now, shall we get down to why I'm here, Heather?"

"Yes please," she said, nervously.

"Right, there is a lot to say."

Thomas proceeded to tell them the plan for the coming Sunday and the purpose. He gave them a little more insight into the reasons why they were doing it. After he had spoken, they all wanted a turn to speak to spirits in the Garden of Souls.

"Listen," he said earnestly, "instead of us talking about the Garden of Souls, it's really important now for us all to discuss forming the link."

They all nodded.

Now he had to explain how the link system was going to work, with Catherine starting it off at one end, and with him finishing with the receivers at the other end. That meant any of them wanting to receive at one end would have had to come over to Catherine's. That didn't put anyone off, and he agreed to help organise more get-togethers once they had tried it out this coming Sunday. "Now if we are going to be a united team, and I'm going to have your backing, I need to know more about you all."

"Let's make tea," said Heather.

They made him tea and they talked. And when he said goodbye, he had their hugs and gratitude to take with him. Walking away from the house he thought what a big day it had been. He needed some space to calm down and recover. *What a manic day it's been.* Before heading back, he decided to walk around the city. He spent an hour walking through the streets allowing his mind to wander. Cambridge was such a magical place.

Chapter 25

An hour later, Thomas had chilled out and was ready to go home. Then he thought it might be an idea to visit Catherine while things were still fresh in his mind. Seconds later, he was walking down her garden path. He didn't need to ring the bell. The door opened before he reached it.

"I had an idea you were coming, Thomas," said Catherine, smiling. "I hear everything's in place, and you've performed miracles."

Thomas smiled at her. "I wouldn't go that far. We did have some problems along the way, though."

"Come in and sit down," she said. She led the way in and offered him a comfy chair. "Now, about Selena's house. How did you solve that problem? All of us working together couldn't have come close to doing what you did."

"Well..." he said looking her squarely in the eyes. *I need to tell her everything, I know.*

"We thought it was similar to the problem down here with Merston," she added.

Thomas shook his head. "I can see why you thought that, but their Mr Coffee was a powerful entity and was being backed by someone high up on the Dark side. I think Merston isn't as strong, but what you did strengthened his defence, so that has given him the wrong impression. Either way you couldn't have broken through."

Catherine looked thoughtful. "So, what happened with Mr Coffee?"

"He was sent back."

"Why can't we send Merston back?" she asked frowning.

"I know you're really angry with him, but he has clouded your judgement. If I break down the wall surrounding him, then that will send him back immediately. However, we're still not sure if he did what you suspect. And I need to ask him a couple of questions to find out exactly what is going on."

"You're right, Thomas. I've waited long enough to end all this. What's a few more days?"

"We need to consider the fact that the Dark Force may be onto us."

"The demise of Mr Coffee, the sending back of the demon and the fact that you have managed to shut down their link into our network must have got the alarm bells ringing. What do you think they'll do next?"

Thomas didn't have a clue. "We've certainly got their attention. They've shown that by retaliating but they were sloppy. The way they retaliated tells me they don't have a strategy. That could give us an advantage."

"How?"

"They are disorganised, and I don't think they actually realise we're going after Merston. On Sunday, when we visit the Garden of Souls, we can open up what you laid down all those years ago and do what should have been done before he causes us any more grief."

"But you said if you did that, he would go back immediately. I thought you wanted to wait."

"Don't worry, I have a plan."

Catherine hunched her shoulders up with glee and clapped her hands together. "I thought you might. Come on then, tell me."

Thomas paused for a moment. *Should I tell her?*

Catherine looked at him impatiently. "Come on! Tell me."

"Okay, but this is only between you and me."

"Absolutely!"

"On Sunday, oh, by the way, we need to do it from your house."

Catherine nodded eagerly.

"When we activate the circle, the energy levels will be exceptionally high, but I will be able to temper and balance them. As that works, the receivers will have about five minutes to be in contact with the souls they have asked for. After that, contact will fade and at that point, I'll grab your attention. Then if you hold your position, I'll drop the others out of the circle, but they won't know anything about it."

"I'm with you so far."

"Then I will direct all that energy to Merston's place. That should smash the energy ring you placed around him."

"You've found him then?" Catherine asked nervously.

"I did that when I came back from my sister's. He is still close by."

"Why didn't you tell me?"

"Because you would have wanted to go round and try again! Don't look at me like that! You know I'm right."

"Hm, maybe." She thought for a moment. "Will he still have his energy force around him?"

"He will, but it will be so weak, you could break it down in your sleep."

"What now, then?"

He looked at her for a brief second as he thought about what to say next. *How can I explain what needs to happen next?* He chose his words carefully. "You and I will link to the energy that's directed at Merston's house. That will transport us to him."

She stared at him. "You and me? You're joking, surely?"

"No, I'm not, and depending on what we have learnt from Sarah's Mum, we should know what to do, but don't forget we need information out of him too."

"How can we do that?"

"I'm counting on him thinking his lot have left him stranded. After all, he's been no use to them for… what is it? How many years?"

"Thirty."

"Wow, that's a long time."

"It's a good plan, Thomas. But there's a little flaw in it."

"Go on."

"Transporting you and me through space, and us ending up at Merston's house. Well…" She shook her head and frowned at him. "Don't get me wrong. I wouldn't question a thing you managed to do, but if we disappear, I think you'd freak the others out."

"That's why we have to sit the others in the furthest room from the kitchen, and I will tell them not to move for five minutes after losing the connection as it shows respect. That's all the time we will need."

Catherine smiled. "You always have an answer. I'll set the room up for six people, I know Rosemary wants to be a receiver, and you're bringing five with you, aren't you?

"Yes. We've covered everything, I think. Now I just need to ask you a favour."

"I know, you haven't been here. I haven't seen you! No worries, I'll keep quiet, Thomas."

He smiled and gave her a hug. Then he was off and he was relieved to find that his car was safely hidden and hadn't been wrecked. *No sign of being tracked yet.*

Back in his house he rang the office. Everything was in order. Now it was time to call Sarah and report on the day. Thomas smiled as he waited to hear her voice.

"Thought you might have called sooner."

She sounded disappointed. "Sorry, honey. I couldn't contact you any sooner. You wouldn't believe what I've had to do. It's been a hell of a day!"

"I've had a similar day..." she hesitated.

"Go on, sweetness, tell me," he said.

"Well, my lunchtime class was fully booked. I knew that from earlier in the day. Anyway, when I came back for the class, I saw Saffron at reception. Apparently, she wanted to come. That's unusual to start with. But as it was full, Mary on reception couldn't sign her in."

"I bet that went down well!"

"Yes, you're right. She was giving Mary a bit of a hard time. Then as luck would have it, the phone rang, and someone cancelled."

Thomas laughed. "That's her witchy thing working, I bet."

"You might say that Thomas Pink, but when she was in the class, oh what a pain she was! She was really miffed."

"What time was the class?" It suddenly dawned on Thomas that something sinister had gone on if the class was around the same time that Mr Coffee had met his end. *When did I destroy him this morning, ten, ten thirty perhaps?*

"It was the ten o'clock class,"

It sent a nasty cold shiver through his body.

"Are you still there Thomas?"

"Yes," he said, but he was thoughtful. "How did she behave?"

"She was angry to the point of being obnoxious. Something had got to her and whatever it was, she took it out on me."

He hesitated.

"What do you think was wrong with her?"

"Well, it might just be a coincidence, but around that time I had a run in with a nasty piece of work in Bristol."

"Really! Who?"

"A priest."

He heard her catch her breath. "What do you mean a priest?"

"That's just the guise he used. He did have a church, he was installed as the priest, I mean, but he was really bad." Thomas knew he had to be careful. He didn't want to say too much at this stage, particularly over the phone. He wasn't sure how Sarah would react. He described to her what happened at Selena's house, leaving out the gritty bits and avoided mentioning exactly what had happened to Mr Coffee.

He could tell Sarah was shocked, especially him connecting Saffron's behaviour with the goings on in Bristol. "That means they must be linked somehow?"

Thomas gave a sigh. "It's looking that way."

"Oh, Thomas, this is scaring me." she said nervously.

"Don't be scared, honey. I can take care of you."

"I know you can. But aren't you outnumbered? There's Susie's boss and the man he had that meeting with at the seminar. There's the lady from Rachel List's class, Saffron and her sister, and it's anyone's guess how many more! Oh, and I forgot all the people Susie's boss is paying. There are so many of them, Thomas."

"But you've forgotten our team, Catherine, Rosemary and all the others! And from Sunday, we'll probably have even more. Plus, with what I have just done strengthening the coven, it means the other lot can't listen in anymore."

"You're just saying that to comfort me."

"No, I wouldn't do that. You know I wouldn't do that."

"I guess not. But tell me, what will change on Sunday?"

"On Sunday, you and the others will make contact. You with your mum and whoever the other white witches decide to use. As contact is made, there will be an understanding between you and your mum – and whoever she brings along."

"Thomas," Sarah interrupted, "I need to be looking at you. I need to see you while you explain. Can you come round?

"Off course I can. Do you mean right away?"

"Please. We can discuss everything over an early dinner. I'll make something while you drive round."

"I'm on my way."

As he drove, he thought about the last few hours. *What a day! Mr Coffee, that arrogant scumbag, winding him up. Then a demon being sent to damage anyone who got in the way!* What bothered him most of all was the speed at which the demon had been summoned. The two incidents had opened his eyes and the enormity of the task ahead was a lot to take in.

As Thomas drove over to Sarah's, he found himself thinking about all that had gone on. *Who could be so organised and be able to send something evil so fast? Susie's boss? He is the prime suspect. Could he be involved? Mm...*Thomas thought, tightening his hands on the steering wheel. *I bet he is. And what about Saffron's behaviour. Why did she turn up unannounced without booking that class? That was unusual. Is she involved somehow with Susie's boss?* He was sure that she was. He thought about what Sarah had said. *Maybe it's true. Perhaps there are too many of them.* "But two less now!" he shouted out defiantly.

As he pulled into Sarah's drive, it dawned on him that he should have contacted Susie somehow to find out if there had been any adverse reaction from her boss.

Sarah appeared at the door. "You didn't waste any time."

"Well, you sounded uneasy, so I left immediately."

She flung her arms around him then kissed him. "That's understating it. I'm a bit more than uneasy."

"Nothing will happen. I'll make sure of that. I had a thought as I came into your drive."

She eased out of the hug and looked at him. "A good thought, I hope? Come on, let's go inside. You can tell me while I dish up dinner."

"So, what were you thinking?" asked Sarah as they ate.

"Well, it's to do with what you said earlier about how many we're up against." He gave her an encouraging smile. "We should keep a log on who we suspect of being on the other side.

That way, we'll have a better idea of what we're up against. What do you think?"

"I like that. It's a sensible plan. Actually, I don't like it, but you know what I mean."

"And another thought."

"What's that then?"

"I have this nagging feeling that Susie's boss is involved somehow."

Sarah nodded. "I wouldn't be surprised, what with Saffron playing up today."

"Exactly. So, my thought was, you could call Susie when we finish eating and ask how things are going with him."

"Yes, it's early. She'll still be at work."

"You could casually ask if her boss had been agitated today."

"But what if she asks why I want to know?"

"Just say I'm working on something, and you're not sure what. Be a little vague. She mustn't find out anything yet."

Sarah put down her fork and pushed her plate away. "If this wasn't so scary, it would be exciting."

Thomas frowned. "Look, I'll do the dishes while you make the call. I'm sure you'll be on the phone for a while!" As he began gathering up the plates, Sarah came over and gave him another kiss. The softness of her lips made him tingle all over as usual. He looked directly into her wonderful blue eyes, struggling to get his words out. "You have the most wonderful lips ever! I don't think you realise quite what they do to me."

Sarah's face lit up with her beautiful smile. "And what about the rest of me?"

He thought for a moment. "There aren't the words to describe the rest of you."

Her eyes glistened with tears. "I love you, Thomas Pink."

Thomas nodded unable to reply. *I love you too and I will tell you that one day.* "You are my everything," he replied.

Sarah picked up her phone, put it on speaker so Thomas could hear too, and dialed. "Hello Susie, it's Sarah."

"Sarah! Goodness! Is anything wrong?"

"Nothing's wrong. I've put you on speaker so Thomas can hear you."

"You've never called me at work before! This must be important."

"It's just that Thomas asked me to give you a buzz, something about your boss Mr, whatshisname?"

"George Smithe."

"Yes, George Smithe, did he act a little strangely today?"

"What? This morning!" Then Susie almost whispered down the line. "How the hell did Thomas know that?"

"I gather from your reaction that he did. Around 10am?"

"He certainly did!"

Suddenly the line went quiet. They heard a voice in the background, but it was hard to make out what was being said. "Yes, Mr Smithe." A few seconds passed in silence. Then Susie whispered. "He's gone. Where was I? Oh yes! He was having a snack at his desk when his mobile went. He spoke, and then he jumped up and rushed out of his office and didn't say a word to anyone. He had two meetings scheduled for the afternoon, but I know he didn't turn up for the first one because I had a call asking for him."

"Thanks, Susie."

"What's happening? Is it to do with the list?"

"Hang on a sec. I'll ask Thomas." She put her hand over the phone. "Can I say why you are interested? Was it something to do with the list she gave you?"

Thomas nodded. "Yes, say that."

"Susie? Yes, it's something like that. He's still working on it. Can he call you later when he is sure of the facts?"

"Okay. Is he going to class tonight?"

"Yes, I'm sure he is, but if you talk to him about it there, be very discreet."

"Don't worry. I'll wait until the class has finished and everyone has gone."

"See you tonight then, Susie."

Sarah looked at Thomas. "I think you're on to something with George Smithe. You heard her, she'll make a beeline for you after class. What will you tell her?"

"I may have to fib a bit."

"Why don't you sit in the garden for a while and relax? You could do with it. That's where I go when I have a problem. And I want to catch up on a book Catherine gave me."

"Good idea, sweetie."

No sooner had Thomas sat down in a garden chair than Dominic popped into his head.

Recharging Thomas?

And hello to you, Dominic! Yes! I've had a busy day.

You've had a good day, Thomas.

Surely that's not a compliment, is it, Dominic?

As I said, you've had a good day. But you could have had a better day.

So, how would you have dealt with the day?

Dominic laughed. Actually laughed! *You're learning my ways. I'm impressed. Maybe I would have gone for the demon with a bit more care.*

Why's that?

You couldn't have known his power, and although he would be unable to send you back, he could have made a dent in your energy source. That would have meant a trip to the Garden of Souls.

I'm not so sure. Do you think the other lot would waste a powerful demon on a bunch of white witches when a lessor one would do?

Dominic seemed surprised by Thomas's logic. *You understood that, did you?*

That, and I sensed immediately that the demon they sent me was weak. I made sure I was more than covered. I have no intention of returning early! And what has the Garden of Souls got to do with it?

You sensed the demon's power? I'm impressed. But if you are seriously damaged, and by that, I mean your energy source, then the only way of healing is back to the Garden.

I wasn't told that.

Some things are better not to know. But the demon you dealt with has pushed your intuition to a new level. Did you know that?

No.

You're evolving and improving all the time at an accelerated rate.

Say the outcome hadn't turned out that way?

Then, we're always here. You're important to us. You did well, Thomas. I am proud of you.

Thank you. Now I do need to ask, have I set the witch circle up correctly?

You certainly have. It's very powerful. Just concentrate carefully on controlling the energy. This way the receivers, as you call them, will get a wonderful surprise. I must tell you you've had an incredible number of souls watching you set this up.

Thomas smiled. *And were they impressed?*

Impressed is not the word. You blew their minds.

That made Thomas feel brilliant, then humble. *Thank you.*

I'll leave you to chill out. Stay focused. Things are going to warm up, pretty soon so be prepared.

Okay, Dominic. Bye.

"How are you feeling, honey?"

Sarah's greeting startled him. He was miles away. "You're right. The garden works wonders. I'm feeling great now. When do we have to leave?"

"In about ten minutes. Have you had any thoughts on what you are going to say to Susie?"

"I think so. I'll be vague. Too much information might put her in danger."

"Sounds good. Make sure Saffron is not around when you're chatting too."

"Sure. I'll stick with you until the hall is clear. I've just had a thought. Do you think Saffron knows Susie is George Smithe's personal assistant?"

He had to think. "Saffron didn't see us in Sudbury. That would have been the time for her to figure it out, so I wouldn't have thought so."

All the same, Sarah looked concerned. "If it came out, it could be dangerous for her, couldn't it?"

"You're right. We'll need to choose our moment carefully to talk to her. Come on. Let's go."

At the leisure centre, they saw Susie was early and she was sitting in the cafeteria alone.

"I'll set the class up while you explain to Susie what we have in mind," whispered Sarah.

Thomas kissed her on the cheek and went over to Susie. "Hiya!"

Susie greeted him and was her usual bubbly self. He smiled. He liked her pleasant gung-ho attitude. As soon as he sat down, she was on at him, wanting more information. He looked around quickly, checking who was nearby. He put his finger to his lips.

"Who are we looking for?" she whispered.

"Saffron."

"But she's not here," she whispered.

"We don't need to whisper then."

"You're confusing me, Thomas."

He laughed. "I'm just trying to be safe, Susie. That's all."

"Ah."

"Sarah thought it would be a good idea if we wait until class is finished, then we can chat about what's been going on, and discuss Sunday."

"Is it on for Sunday, then?"

Thomas checked the room again. "No Saffron. All has been arranged, but with one slight change. We have to go to Guildford to get the best results."

"I don't care where we have to go. I can't wait."

Thomas glanced at the clock above the door. "We better get a move on, or we'll be late for Sarah's class." He knew he had to keep his distance from Saffron, or she would recognise him as an enemy. When he and Susie reached the yoga hall, he peered through the glass door.

"Didn't I tell you Saffron's not coming tonight?" Susie announced.

Thomas turned. "No, you didn't. You just said she wasn't here."

"Sorry. She cancelled while I was queuing."

"Good." Thomas breathed a sigh of relief as he pushed the door open. He could relax and enjoy his workout. *I wonder why Saffron cancelled. Something is not right.*

Chapter 26

After the class, Susie joined Thomas in collecting mats and bands and stacking them. It was down to business as soon as the others had gone.

"Do you think your boss knows that you go to the same class as Saffron?" Sarah asked Susie.

"I doubt it. I've never spoken about my social life to him before." She looked at Thomas. "Why did you ask me that?"

"It's pretty obvious some kind of deal is going on between your boss and Saffron," he said. "And there are others involved. What we don't want is for any of them to link you to me."

"But why would they do that?"

"If on Sunday everything works as well as I think it will then I will be in possession of information that, if used, could seriously derail your boss. Just like today, he was unnerved for some reason."

"But Thomas, how on earth did you know he was unnerved?"

Now he would have to fib. "I was in contact with the other side earlier today and I was told to be careful. One of theirs had a mishap and this caused a shock wave."

"But what's that got to do with us or even my boss?"

"The witches I've been in touch with gave out the information that caused the mishap. That's why Sarah phoned you."

"A mishap?"

"That's what they called it."

"Maybe a mishap means someone is now out of the picture. So, Sarah rang me because you needed to know the reaction, if any, from Smithe? And he did react. Maybe that means there must be a team of them? Not just the scumbag I work with?"

"There! I think you have it."

"So, what now?"

"What you mustn't do is dig around in his office. I think he'll be on red alert. Let's just see what happens on Sunday when all of you make contact."

"What are you expecting to happen, Thomas?"

"I'm hoping we'll receive information about the list you copied from his desk."

"I thought you had worked that out."

"I..."

"Shh!" Sarah interrupted him. "Another class is coming in. Let's carry on with this conversation downstairs over a coffee."

When they reached the canteen, Susie looked around her to make sure nobody could hear. Thomas knew that she was eager to ask lots of questions.

"How will we learn what we need to know through a circle?" asked Susie as she and Thomas sat at a table. Sarah went to get the drinks.

"Two reasons. First, this is probably the most powerful circle ever assembled."

"And the second?"

"I'm going to ask questions."

Sarah arrived at the table with drinks and a little sweet something to nibble on. "Are you getting there?" she asked.

Susie looked worried. "I know how important this is for you, Thomas. And for all the other people involved now. I can't believe all this is because I moaned about George Smithe the day I met you. And now everything has got so complicated. I am sure I'm going to mess it up on Sunday."

"Don't be daft. You won't. It's very simple. And when we arrive,

I'll go through the details with you. You just concentrate on someone who has passed, and you will be able to communicate with them. You'll see as soon as it's rolling and then you'll relax. You'll get an insight into the other world. And don't forget, I'll be in the room next door."

Susie cheered up. "Okay, don't worry about me. I'll keep my head down until you say otherwise."

"That's right!" said Sarah.

"Where shall we meet then?" Susie asked. "Shall I drive?"

"What about my house like last time?" suggested Sarah. "Then Thomas can drive us down to Guildford, so you'll have time to think about what you are going to ask."

"What time do you want us, Thomas?" Susie asked.

"It starts at ten, so maybe seven if that is not too early for you? It won't take us three hours but we have to make sure everything is in place, so I want to be early. You remember we talked about how it would work. And remember I said how it's critical to stay in place for at least five minutes after the session?"

Sarah and Susie nodded.

"Susie, have you checked with Caroline and your mum to make sure they're coming?" asked Thomas.

"You'd have a fight on your hands if they were kept away."

Thomas smiled.

"Why do we have to wait five minutes after the session before moving?" asked Sarah.

Thomas had to think fast. He put his hand on her shoulder. "Two reasons. You will have called on spirits who are risking a lot to be with you. It's just showing them some respect."

"What's the second reason?"

"You'll be so emotionally drained that you'll be only too happy to sit a while longer and recover."

"How do you know all this?" asked Susie.

He shrugged his shoulders, "I guess it's to do with my mum and dad. They used to tell me lots when I was young," he sighed.

It reminded him how much he missed them. He swallowed the rest of his coffee and then looked at Susie. "Could you explain to your mum and Caroline what we've just said? It's taken a lot of effort to put this together. Nothing must go wrong."

"Yes, of course Thomas," Susie replied finishing her coffee.

"So, we're done. Let's go, don't forget to be careful at work."

Susie nodded, "I will," she said as she went off to her car.

"Are you staying tonight, Thomas?" Sarah smiled at him.

"Yes, please. But will you drive? I feel drained."

"I can tell. You need a good night's sleep. Are you sure you're doing the right thing? I don't want you getting poorly."

"It's just that things are a bit hectic at the moment. I need to adjust. But don't worry. I can do it."

"Okay, honey."

Sarah hugged him before they got into the car. As they drove along, he gazed out of the car window. Sunday was looming. Everything was moving fast now, and not being in complete control was new to him. This was a job where if mistakes were made, then the consequences could be deadly. *I don't want anyone to get hurt or I will never forgive myself.*

He was nearly asleep when they arrived home. The day had taken its toll.

"Why don't you have a warm bath with oils while I make us something to eat?" Sarah suggested.

"That sounds perfect, honey."

The following morning Thomas woke feeling refreshed. The bath and Sarah's sweet care had worked wonders. She was already up and busy cooking.

"Breakfast in fifteen minutes," she called to him.

"I won't be long; I just need to shower."

He showered and dressed in record time. Over poached eggs, the pair of them chatted away. Then Sarah mentioned Alisha and how the senior surgeon had contacted her again.

"What did he want?"

"Can't you guess?"

"How I did it, I suppose."

"I know you said you didn't want to see anyone, but Alisha didn't quite say it that way to the Registrar." She looked at him sweetly, appealing to his softer side.

"What would you like me to do?"

She leaned across the table and squeezed his hand. "Go with Alisha and meet with the surgeon."

He hesitated for a second and then pulled a face. "Okay."

"Can I come?"

"Sure. When are we going?"

"I'll call Alisha. I think she has the surgeon's work timetable."

"Gosh! He's keen."

Sarah leaned towards him. "Considering what you did, I can see why?"

He sighed. "Let's get it over with."

Sarah grabbed her phone and called Alisha. They chatted briefly then Sarah looked at Thomas.

"Any time?"

He nodded.

When she put her phone down. "Alisha says thank you. She can't wait to see you and give you a big hug."

He smiled. "When are we going, sweetness?"

"We are meeting him midday tomorrow. There's a two-hour break between my classes."

"Are we leaving from yours then?"

"Yep," Sarah glanced up at the clock. "Oh no!" She jumped to her feet. "Look at the time! I'm running late."

Thomas stood up, "Don't worry you go. I'll clear away. See you tonight."

Sarah grabbed up her things, gave him a kiss. "Love you!" she called.

"Me too, you."

Chapter 27

Ten minutes later, Thomas was out of the door himself. There was his company work to do, then he had a fancy to visit Columbia again. He knew Columbia was the place that would test his abilities to the full – a dangerous place. The thought of going there sent shivers down his spine. There was one small problem that was bothering him. He remembered when Dominic had taken him to Columbia, they had been behind time. They had also travelled as spirits, invisible to the naked eye. He didn't know how to deal with that, no matter how hard he applied his mind. He needed to get a handle on being visible in dangerous places. He contacted Jamie.

You called Master Thomas? echoed Jamie. He sounded as if he was chuckling.

I did, clever clogs.

Jamie appeared right in front of him with a big smile on his face. "How can I help?"

"Where have you just come from? What were you doing?"

Jamie grinned. "You always ask that. I was just checking on things."

"You always say that. What sort of things?"

"You're asking for specifics."

Thomas nodded. "Yep."

"Curiosity, is it?"

"Definitely not. Educational! I'm part of the team."

Jamie smiled again.

"In that case, I'll tell you. Somewhere in the world, a team of research scientists are working on a project that will ease a major ailment afflicting humanity. They're close, but they're faffing around, missing the obvious. My job today is to nudge them in the right direction."

Thomas was astonished. "I understood that we had to get on with life by ourselves."

"Mostly, yeah. But in certain areas, you're not moving fast enough,"

"But, so what? Does it matter?"

"Your 'so what' suggests discontentment. That can fuel the Dark Force. That gives them more power. And that makes it necessary for you to be here. Now, do you feel that was educational?"

"What does it feel like to know everything, Jamie?"

"If only Thomas! Now how can I help you? Why did you call?"

"I want to travel behind time. How do I do it?"

"That's an easy one! Remember when you sorted out the communication phone in your head, just before you entered the Garden of Souls? So you could contact Sarah while you were there."

Thomas nodded.

"Well, it's no different from that. All you do is place a timepiece in your mind with the correct date and time, then when you decide to travel, you can set the time back by up to a week. It's that simple!"

Thomas laughed. "Well, it seems so! But I'm curious now. Why can't I travel further back in time?"

"That's because time travel can damage the mind. It won't bend beyond a week. To travel back further, you have to go down another route."

"And that is?"

"History. If it happened, then it's history, and we can follow that. When you're ready, I'll show you."

Thomas felt excited. This idea opened all sorts of possibilities.

"What do you have in mind, Thomas?"

"I thought of travelling back to some of the places Dominic showed me."

"Why would you want to go back to those dreadful places?"

"Homework. I want to see what I'm going to face later."

"Well, these past few days you've had a taste of what's to come."

"If you had told me what I would be doing now a couple of weeks ago, I would have freaked out. As it is, I'm okay with this so far. It's the next couple of weeks that are bothering me."

"The key to it is not to think about it. React when you have to, just as you've done this week."

"Sure, nerves get in the way! I must remember that."

"That's it! Now, why don't I show you how to travel back through a history line instead of you going back to South America?"

"That sounds miles better."

"Good," Jamie began to explain. "If you touch any object and establish it in your mind, then think back in time, you will travel to the time and place of its origin."

Thomas hardly dared to believe what he had just heard. "You're kidding."

"I thought you'd like that."

"Can we try?"

"And, there's something else you might like."

"What's that?"

"When we get to the origin, you can, if you want, control the return to suit you."

Thomas wasn't quite sure he knew what that meant. "Does that mean coming back ten years at a time, or fifty years, or on any time scale? Is that what you mean?"

"You've got it."

"How awesome is that!"

"Are you ready to try?"

"Oh yes!"

"What do you have that's old?"

Thomas knew immediately. "This house."

"Yes, of course! And the oldest part?"

"We're standing in it."

Jamie looked at the old wooden beams. "One of those will do. Right! Put one hand on the beam and the other on the wall."

"Why are we doing both?"

"To focus on the house, we don't want to go back to when the beam was a tree."

"Oh. No, course not."

"Ready?"

"Yep. We're going to be invisible, aren't we?"

"Of course, we don't want to give anyone a heart attack, do we?"

They both placed one of their hands on the beam and the other one on the wall.

"Concentrate. On three, count back in your mind three, two... one." At that precise moment, Jamie brushed Thomas' hand to make sure they both ended up at the same place. And they did at the beginning of the life of the house!

They were standing in the same room touching the same wooden beam and the very same wall, but now there were people around them, very grubby and weather-beaten people. They were all working hard, preparing vegetables, washing them in an old wooden bucket. One was sweeping the floor, and another was setting a fire in a simple grate. Thomas stared at them. Life was obviously hard. He looked around. This was one of only three rooms. That must mean they were way back in the fifteenth century. He was so fascinated that he couldn't utter a word. Jamie wandered off, leaving him to enjoy the experience. The house was so different. He could hardly recognise the layout. The smell of the house, however, was just the same and that made him smile.

He stepped outside the door to look at the garden. There was no garden, just crops, everywhere. He turned to look up at the house and saw it as it had been in the beginning. *Smaller. Much smaller.* It had been extended repeatedly over the centuries, to become a substantial size house fit for modern living. He stood there fascinated, drawn in by everything he could see. He would have stayed for ever if Jamie hadn't come to stand beside him.

"Back we go? It is not good to stay too long," he said.

A second later, they were back. Thomas collapsed into the nearest chair, needing to sit down. He was feeling emotionally drained, he couldn't speak.

"That's what I expected, Thomas. Time travel is difficult to handle, but it will get easier as you continue to do it. I'll need to accompany you the next couple of times until your emotions toughen up. Then you can travel on your own. When we get to that point, I'll show you how to visit your family history."

Thomas's eyes widened as he stared at Jamie. "Is that what I think it means?"

"Yeah, but you'll need to be a whole lot stronger before we try that on you!"

Thomas just sat there, open-mouthed. "Why wasn't I told this before?"

"It has to be earned."

"It's hard to imagine travelling back through the family."

"In the meantime…"

"I know, there's a big job ahead. You don't have to worry. I'm focused."

"Good. If that's all, I'll go now. I need to nudge a scientist or two." He smiled and disappeared.

Thomas stayed in the chair, mulling over the events of the last couple of hours. He hadn't been to Columbia, but he knew how to get there now. Meanwhile, there was the problem of Smithe. He sat thinking and began fitting the pieces together. What was baffling him were the payments going out every month around the world. He had half a mind to pay a visit to one of Mr Smithe's benefactors, but as quickly as the idea came in, it left his thoughts. Then he thought of nosing around Suzie's boss's office. *No, that would be far too dangerous.*

His mobile rang.

"Thomas."

I was just thinking about her! "Hi, Susie. Anything wrong?"

"Maybe and maybe not. I can't be sure. I have an update."

She sounded a bit dizzy. He smiled to himself. She was up in the air as usual. "What have you got? We need everything we can get on this scumbag."

"He's just left the office. He's on his way to meet Saffron right now."

"How do you know?"

"I've just heard him say meet me at the usual restaurant in an hour."

"How do you know it's Saffron he's meeting?"

"Because he mentioned her name."

"I don't suppose you know where the restaurant is, do you?"

"I could go through his petty cash receipts?"

"No, don't do that."

"It's not risky. It's part of what I have to do. The only problem is that he eats out most days, so I might not be able to tell which restaurant."

"Okay. But be careful. Did he leave immediately after he said one hour?"

"Yes."

"Then it won't be a local restaurant. More like one in Camden, or Marylebone, or even Paddington. That should narrow it down."

"You should have been a policeman."

"Sometimes I think I am!"

"I'll call you back."

Thomas looked at the time and made a note. If he could get the right restaurant, he could go back on today, tomorrow! Then he could listen in on their conversation. He was quite chuffed with himself, considering he had only just learnt how to do that not an hour earlier from Jamie.

The mobile went again. Susie was calling. "I think I have it. Como's in Camden, and he has used a different card from the office one. It must be his personal card. That means it is not Government business."

"How many receipts have you found?"

"Six, and they are all for two people."

"Sounds promising." Thomas knew exactly what was coming next from Susie.

"Thomas, how are you going to find anything out unless you're a fly on the wall? You'll be seen."

He couldn't tell her how he was going to listen in. *Oh well, another fib I guess.* "You forget I have men working all over London. I can organise one of them to wait outside the restaurant to confirm if it is Saffron or not. That will be good enough for now."

"Okay. The phone is ringing, I have to go. Let me know how you get on, Thomas."

Should I go to Camden and listen into their conversation? How close can I get to them without being seen?

Chapter 28

With a little time on his hands Thomas made the decision to take the trip to Camden. He knew exactly where the restaurant was, so he noted how long it had been since Smithe had left his office. *Thirty minutes to go*. He decided that he would leave in twenty minutes. He knew how to hold back from appearing for a few moments just in case they arrived at the same time as he did. *No. Maybe this isn't a good idea. I'll go right away. It will be safer. Mm, the street will be full of people. I'll have to be really careful not to be noticed when I arrive out of nowhere. Maybe this isn't such a good idea either.* He was in a quandary. He thought for a second. *Land on a roof behind time so I am invisible?*

Moments later, he landed on some red slates. Not wanting to slip off the roof, he moved to the edge and looked around. He saw an empty shop with a passage to the entrance. *That'll do*, he thought. *It will give me cover*. Now down on the street in the passage he came out of behind time. He had to be especially careful now he was visible. Saffron would be around somewhere. He assumed she was already in London when she had talked to Smithe.

He peered out from the passageway. There were not many people around to notice him, so he stepped out into the street to find number 37 Como's, the restaurant Smithe and Saffron were meeting at. Cautiously, he moved along the busy pavement, using the shadow of the buildings for cover and looking nervously at every face he could see. *Oh no!* He spotted Saffron on the other side of the street. There she was, right outside Como's. He changed direction and ducked into the nearest shop to watch without being noticed.

"Can I help you sir?"

He looked around. To his horror, the shop he was now standing in was a lady's lingerie shop. He had to think fast. "I'm just waiting for my wife; I think I'm a little early."

"That's fine. Call if you need any help."

Thomas mingled amongst the rails of underwear, pretending to be interested. He glanced out through the display window across to the restaurant, hoping Smithe would hurry along. A fancy car pulled up almost outside the restaurant. Smithe stepped out of it, and then it whizzed off. Smithe made his way towards Saffron. After a brief exchange of words, they walked into Como's.

That was good enough. Thomas looked across to the shop counter and managed to catch the assistant's eye.

She smiled. "Seen anything you like?"

He shook his head. "My wife needs to choose. I think I'll go look for her. She must be lost." Safely outside, he turned away from the restaurant and discreetly made for a quiet side street to use to travel back home. *If I walk into the restaurant then they are sure to see me.*

Seconds later, he was checking the clock in his own kitchen. He would have just enough time to speak to Susie before meeting Sarah for lunch. Reaching for his mobile, he sent an inconsequential text with just his initials, as Susie wasn't allowed personal calls at work. He was hoping for a quick response before leaving. It worked. The phone rang as he was making his way to the car.

"Any luck Thomas?"

"Yes, you were right. They did meet. The chap I used described them to me over the phone."

"Are you sure?"

"Definitely."

"What do you think they're up to?"

"I haven't a clue. Something unpleasant, no doubt. We'll keep working on it, but I'm sure it has something to do with the payments you uncovered."

"Have you found out any more about that?"

"That's next on my list. And don't forget, Susie. Keep this to yourself. No one and I mean no one, can know what we are doing. Not even your mum."

"You worry too much," she said brightly. "I know. Not a word. Bye."

Thomas felt quite bemused by her attitude. She seemed completely unfazed by it all.

When he arrived at the leisure centre, Sarah was finishing her last class of the morning. He had hoped to do a short workout before meeting her, but he had run out of time. It usually bothered Sarah when he missed training sessions, but after telling her about his morning she was fine.

"Okay, I'll let you off just this once," she said, laughing and leaning across the table to kiss him. "Do you think this should be logged in the journal?" she said.

"What? You kissing me?"

"No dafty. Saffron and Smithe meeting. It might come in handy if we enter the times and dates. We may eventually see a pattern emerge."

"If you think so, I'll sort it out when I get home."

With lunch over, they arranged to stay at Thomas's house for the night. The old house fascinated Sarah, especially at night when the creaks and groans seemed to be exaggerated. Thomas thought about how today he had seen it as it was hundreds of years ago. He couldn't tell Sarah about that.

She turned up early as usual and straight away asked to hear some of the old stories about the spirits that occupied the house when he had first moved in.

Thomas smiled. "You want to hear about them again?"

"I like you telling me stories. The scary ones around the house with the lights out and you with the torch on."

Thomas made his way to the cupboard to find the torch. Then headed directly to the fuse board with Sarah close behind him, giggling nervously. With his finger on the On Off switch, he turned to look at her. "Ready?" he asked in his best spooky voice.

"Yep."

He threw the switch, and immediately, the pair of them were in darkness.

By the weak light of the torch, they fumbled along slowly, making their way to the hall. Then together they began to clamber up the narrow creaky stairs. Now Sarah's nerves started to take hold. On the first-floor landing, she began to giggle nervously.

"Shush," Thomas whispered. "You'll frighten them."

That made things worse. Sarah's giggle was now constant.

Thomas switched the torch off and, in an eerie voice, said, "What was that?"

Sarah let out a little scream and grabbed his arm. "What?"

"Come on! Noisy Jim is waiting for us. You go first."

"Me?" With wobbly legs, Sarah climbed the second flight of stairs ahead of him. This stairway was much steeper, with no banister, and the stairs creaked even louder. Holding the torch level was difficult. The beam bounced on and off the walls catching cobwebs that were home to the biggest spiders. It freaked Sarah out even more.

"Nearly there," he whispered. "Shall I call out to noisy Jim?"

Sarah clutched Thomas's arm. "Go on, call out to him. But quietly. Just in case."

Thomas couldn't help but laugh.

"Go on!"

"Noisy Jim, are you there?" he whispered.

There was no reply.

"He must be asleep,"

Sarah giggled nervously again. They climbed up to the top of the stairs. They were about to rush bravely into the bedroom when Sarah's phone rang. The sound startled the pair of them. They both stumbled and fell into the room. The torch rolled away across the floor into the darkness. The phone continued to ring.

"Back to reality!" laughed Thomas.

"Hello?" Sarah was still giggling. "Yes, Susie. I'm at Thomas's house and it's story time. We're ghost hunting! Yes, okay." She felt for Thomas's hand and passed the phone over to him. "She wants to speak to you."

"Hi, Susie."

"Sorry for interrupting your game."

"Game! It's not a game. It's the finest ghost hunt in the county. Now, what's wrong?"

"Oh yes, silly me. I had to work late tonight. I've only just left. Smithe came back to the office late, and I'm sure he didn't know I was still there. Anyway, I overheard a call he made to someone called Tony. That's the same name Caroline and I overheard when we were listening in on the conversation in Sudbury. I'm sure it is."

"Yes, I remember that name." He sat in the dark watching Sarah find the torch, and then she crept away downstairs with it.

"Well, Smithe left soon after that, so I checked on the last call. All calls are logged here, so it was easy. The area code was 01787. That's Sudbury."

"But what was he saying to Tony in Sudbury?"

"I took it down in shorthand, word for word. I'll read it to you. Listen. 'Tony, it's happening again, but this time it's powerful. The priest has gone. A top-ranking soldier has gone too. Our ear into the witch's coven has been closed down.'" Then there was a pause before she continued. "'Tony, we need a searcher immediately!' Then I think they made arrangements to meet tomorrow. There! That's it, Thomas. What do you think?"

"Are you sure it was 'searcher' he said?"

"Definitely. And I am sure they made arrangements to meet tomorrow."

Thomas was concerned. "You be very careful, Susie," he said. "You're sailing close to the wind. If he found out you were listening in, who knows what he would do? Be very careful."

"I will, but I didn't plan this one."

The lights came on and lit up the old staircase he was sitting on. Sarah was coming up the stairs, "I know you didn't, Susie. I'll call you tomorrow after Sarah and I have talked it through. I'll talk to you soon. Bye."

Sarah stared at him. She looked worried. "What's wrong, honey?"

"Susie's boss is definitely in the thick of it, and what Susie has just said confirms it. Come on, let's go downstairs and enter what she said into your journal. Things are going to get tricky."

Chapter 29

The following morning Thomas was up earlier than usual. He hadn't slept well. He had been mulling over what Susie had told him, and he had a good idea now what was going to happen. He was going to be hunted down by a darksider's searcher. His only advantage was that at least he knew it. He could prepare.

While Sarah was still asleep, he took the opportunity to contact Jamie on a mind level, explaining what had happened and the conversation Susie had overheard. *Should I be concerned?*

When he answered, Jamie sounded as if he was concentrating hard. *This is unusual. Your predecessor didn't get these issues. You are breaking new ground. Smithe, do you think he's high ranking?*

Yes, he's given us that impression.

Then yes, we should be concerned. He could command a top searcher.

How does a searcher work? How will I recognise or find him?

I've got a good idea how the searcher could trace you. This is what I think will happen. The searcher will go to the last place he thinks you caused damage.

But that's Heather's place in Cambridge!

You will have to go there and wait for him and then, you'll be able to dispose of him. I promise you that you'll know when he's coming, and he won't expect you to be there.

But that might compromise Susie. She's the only one who could know about the searcher.

That's plan A. Now let's see the other options. The energy you have placed around the houses belonging to the witches is more than adequate to keep a searcher at a distance. Theoretically, Heather will be safe. Let me have a think about Susie.

What if Heather leaves the protection of the house when he shows up?

That's a good point, Thomas. There's only one thing for it.

What's that?

Every witch will have to have an individual energy force around them.

How the heck do I do that?

Well, as this wasn't foreseen, you weren't given the ability to do this. Unfortunately, I'm the same, I can't do it either. You'll have to make contact with your team of Old Souls and tell them what you need. And when you've done that, you'll need help from the head of witches. Catherine, isn't it?

Yes.

You'll need her to create a tab spell and send it to Heather's house. She'll understand what's to be done.

Thomas was amazed how Jamie had come up with a solution in a matter of minutes. *At least there is a solution.*

The spell will allow you to track anyone that has been charmed. Then you can see if the searcher is following them, and you can strike whenever and send the searcher back really quickly, so Susie's involvement isn't exposed.

I'm on it now. Thomas declared, feeling grateful that there was a way to protect Susie and the witches from harm.

Call me if you need help.

Thanks, Jamie.

Thomas wasted no time contacting his team in the Garden of Souls. He explained what was needed.

I'll come to you, Thomas. Choose somewhere safe, one of the Old Souls called.

He chose to meet at his old barn and seconds later, he felt a presence. He was in front of one of the Highest Souls. He glowed. The aura around him was so intense, it took Thomas's breath away. He just stood there, in silence, soaking up the purity the old soul was radiating.

"Thomas! No time to waste then." The Old Soul cupped his hands on the top of Thomas's head. Thomas's mind went completely blank.

"All done, Thomas."

"Really? Are you sure you have done what you needed to do? You only had your hands on my head for a second."

"It didn't take me long. You can now safeguard the witches. You have little time, so I'll leave now. You're doing a good job."

Then he was gone, and the barn was just as it was.

Heather! Thomas thought. *First of all, I must make her secure.*

Back at the house, he checked the time. *Sarah must still be in bed. If she is, maybe Heather is too.*

"Morning, Thomas! You're up bright and early."

He swung round. "Oh, you're up! I couldn't sleep, sweetie. Do you mind if I go for a stroll for ten minutes or so? I need to think."

"You go ahead. I'll be in the bathroom longer than that!" She gave him a kiss. "Off you go."

All Thomas had to worry about now was if Heather would be up. Not wanting to waste time, he decided to speak to Catherine first. She was an early bird. As she answered the call, he travelled to her house.

"What's wrong, Thomas?"

"I'm outside!"

Catherine opened the door. "How did you do that?"

Thomas ignored the question.

"Oh yes, I forgot. Nothing to do with me. Come in. What's the problem?"

"I think we've upset Susie's boss."

"I think you've upset more than just him."

Thomas nodded. "Probably. Anyway, they're sending a searcher, and I think he's heading for Cambridge."

"Heather's house!" Catherine was panicking. "I'll call her."

"She's safe while she stays inside. What I need you to do is call her in a calm manner. Tell her not to go outside. Not even in the garden. Not until I get there. Then you need to create a tab spell."

"How do you know about the tab spell?"

"I have a friend, Jamie."

"And what else does he know?"

Thomas shrugged. "Loads of things. Now can you do it?"

"Of course, I can. I'm a witch."

"Quickly?"

"I can do it quickly and with my eyes shut!"

"Let's get on with it then. Make the call to Heather. All the others will need to be put in the picture as well. I have to do that right now."

"How on earth are you going to do that?" Thomas waved the question away.

Catherine grinned. "Oh yes, nothing to do with me! This is doggy stuff, Thomas, but it is exciting. Much better than the humdrum stuff I'm used to."

Thomas nodded. "Yes, but it's dangerous. And the searcher's power is something I don't know about, so we can't take any chances."

"And Sunday?"

"Sunday is all set. That should be the catalyst to put an end to the evil that's growing. Nothing must stop circle from taking place."

Catherine nodded and picked up her phone "Heather? Small problem! Thomas will be with you in..." Catherine glanced at Thomas. He held up two fingers. "A couple of minutes. Tell everyone he'll be around." She turned back to him. "I'll call the others now. Then I'll do the tab spell."

"How long will it take for the spell to work?" He was on edge now. He suspected that the searcher was already on his way.

"About thirty minutes. After that, Moira in Glasgow. I'll ask her to contact the others while you concentrate on Manchester. Then I'll ask Sally to contact the others and so on."

"I'll be faster than you can contact them, but it has to be a team job."

"I'm very impressed with what you can do. Thomas, why do you look so down?"

"Well, just think, if Susie hadn't worked late, we wouldn't have known."

"It's luck, Thomas."

"But we can't get by on luck."

"Witches believe in luck. It's a powerful ingredient created from previous actions. And you'll have loads more coming your way, I just know it."

Only five minutes had passed since he had left Sarah. He reckoned he had another fifteen minutes to make the other forty-one witches safe. He went to Heather's house first. His work there took him moments to heighten the vibrations around her. "Don't worry. You will be safe now, Heather." He told her. "I'm off to Margaret's, let me know if you sense any bad energy nearby."

Seventeen minutes later, the job was done. As he walked into his house and up the stairs, he couldn't help feeling pleased with himself. Thomas bumped into Sarah coming out of the bathroom.

"Are you feeling any better, darling?"

"Mm, lots. Let's have a quick breakfast?"

She nodded. "Then I'll be off to work."

"What time is the hospital appointment with Alisha's consultant?" he asked.

"Ten o'clock, and please don't be late, Thomas. Pick up Alisha first, then me."

"Okay, honey."

Once Sarah had left for work, he was desperate to contact Catherine to check on the spell. She hadn't wasted any time and had already placed the tab spell at the church house where the priest had met his end. She had also covered Heather's home too, protecting it from all evil.

Thomas was impatient to know how the spell worked, so he travelled to Guildford while he was still speaking. "I'm outside. Open the door, please!"

"You've done it again!" Catherine said, staring at him.

"Yes, I know! Don't ask. I am sorry. I wish I could tell you more."

He followed her along the dimly lit corridor and down half a dozen dark steps. All he could see was a glint of light breaking through a crack in the door ahead of them. Catherine reached into her pocket and withdrew a ring of keys. The keys were an odd shape, and the door didn't seem to have a keyhole. *How are we going to get in?*

"Do you know that you're the first uninitiated person to enter this room?"

"Fascinating! But how are we going to enter?"

She huffed grandly and turned away from him. Facing the door, she broke into a full mantra that he didn't understand. As she jangled and fiddled with them, the keys separated from the ring and left her hand, attaching themselves to different parts of the door.

"Whoa! Now that's magic!"

Catherine looked at him. "Of course it is, Thomas," she said smugly. She turned back to the door again and waved her arms around in circles. The door suddenly unlocked itself and began to open slowly and silently. Catherine beckoned to him. "Come into my spell room!" He followed her in and looked around as he entered. "I am privileged, Catherine, but I do need to see for myself how the spell will work. I'm up against a thing that's been sent to hunt me down."

Catherine nodded. "And it's our duty to keep you safe. Now come and look at these." She guided him to a cluttered corner of the room. There was a pile of parchments on the workbench. Thomas assumed they were spells.

"May I look through them?"

"Yes but look at this one first." She held up a parchment. "This is the tab spell, an ancient recipe handed down through our family over centuries. But it's a secret."

Thomas laughed. "I don't suppose I'd understand it anyway."

As if it were all part of a plan, Rosemary joined them, "What wouldn't you understand?"

"This!" Catherine waved the spell parchment in the air.

Rosemary smiled. "You're right, Thomas. Unless you can read Latin?"

He shook his head, happy to be ill-informed on this occasion. After all, this was their job and not his.

"No doubt you've figured out. This is mother's favourite spell!"

Thomas grinned. "So, am I allowed to ask how it works?!"

"It attaches itself to an evil intention."

Thomas stared at her. "How?"

"The origins of this spell go back over a thousand years. Maybe more. Our ancestors weren't the ones who created it. An old Druid did. Old word has it the village was under constant threat, and the village people came to our family knowing what we practised and asked for help. We worked on different solutions, but none were powerful enough, so my family paid the old Druid a visit. Because our family had taken care of him over the years, he was keen to help. It was said his powers were so strong that his kind had banned him from practising, so he left his clan for a life on his own."

Thomas stared at Catherine with a look of disbelief.

She pointed to a pile of documents, "All these have been handed down through the centuries." She offered him another parchment.

"What's this?"

"Have a read, Thomas, but be careful how you handle it."

"This one isn't written in Latin," said Rosemary.

He glanced at the writing. '*On this day in the year nine seventy, Anno Domini.*'

His mind began to spin over at an incredible rate. He wished he could borrow this, so he would be able to go back in time and see precisely how this and the tab spell were created. *Not today, I'll save that for another day.* He continued reading, now absolutely convinced Catherine was a first-class witch. When he had finished reading, he shook his head amazed. "These are so impressive, Catherine."

Rosemary nodded. "And the old Druid helped the village stay safe by placing his tab spell around the outer perimeter, allowing plenty of time for the villagers to prepare if they were threatened by evil intention. And believe me, there was plenty to be afraid of back then."

"How can we use the spell now?"

"What mother and I have done is, we've put a little kick in the spell. We are not sure of the searcher's energy. This spell is exceptionally powerful."

"And still undetectable?"

Catherine raised her eyebrows, and Thomas realised he had

made a mistake questioning her ability. "It's as delicate as a summer breeze! When it's attached to the searcher, he'll be completely oblivious." She smiled. "So, what would you like to know? Perhaps when will we know if it's attached?"

He nodded. "Well, that is one of the questions."

Catherine reached for another old parchment and placed it on the table. It unfolded by itself.

"How did you do that?"

"Again," Catherine raised her eyebrows, and looked at him hard, "Do I ask you how you do your job?"

"Yes."

"And do you give me an answer?"

He smirked and shook his head. "No!"

Catherine seemed to be enjoying herself. For the short time she had known him, he had done amazing things that were beyond belief. Now, this was her moment.

"So, tell me how you track him?" Thomas asked.

She pointed back to the old parchment. "Take a look."

"It's a map!"

"It's much more than a map, Thomas," said Rosemary. "The map is linked to the spell."

"I think I might need lessons in this witchy stuff."

Rosemary laughed. "While we wait for the searcher, shall we have tea?"

Back upstairs, in the kitchen, the morning light was streaming through the windows. Thomas started to unwind and relax. "Sorry if I woke you, ringing so early this morning, Rosemary."

"You didn't. I'm always up before Mother, and she told me all about the problem."

"Ah."

"The tab spell is amazing. You'll see. The searcher won't get far," declared Rosemary.

"Yes, but shouldn't we be watching the map on the parchment?" asked Thomas.

Rosemary glanced across at her mother and then suddenly smiled at him.

"While you sip your tea, keep your ears tuned in."

"Ears?"

At that exact moment, there was a screeching sound in the distance.

"There, that's what I'm talking about. Can you hear that?"

"Wow! What a noise! I think the neighbours at the end of the street can hear it."

"Come on, Thomas!" said Catherine excitedly, jumping to her feet. "The searcher has been picked up."

The three of them hurried down into the spell room, eager to be the first to see the spell working. The map, as Thomas had called it, was lit up and was showing the area the searcher was in. Cambridge! *Heather's house!*

"Shall we call her?"

"No, Thomas, let the spell run its course. The searcher should be leaving soon enough. He's picked up on you now. He'll track your movements."

Thomas became anxious when he heard that. "That means the searcher could track me to my home?"

"It doesn't work that way," Catherine assured him. "There's a six-hour window. Then, your history is gone. All the searcher has is the soul's scent. That will enable him to create a mapping system, but that takes quite a while. He'll need at least a dozen signals to initiate his system. Before that can happen, you will send him back. And permanently."

"Well, you two are bloody clever. How on earth do you know all that?"

"We're witches, Thomas! That's how."

Thomas gulped the rest of his tea down and concentrated on the parchment. It wasn't long before he noticed the searcher was on the move. "Look, he's heading south. On his way to London, maybe? Meeting up with Smithe, Susie's boss, I shouldn't wonder."

"What's your plan?" Rosemary asked.

"I was thinking of following him until he's far enough away from Heather and then suspend him in time. Perhaps park him up somewhere for a day and then deal with him after I have got his measure. But it must be before Sunday."

Catherine nodded. "Good idea. Keeping him suspended with a life force won't arouse any concern." She placed her hands over the map, and mumbled words of some description. Immediately the map changed and focussed on the searcher and his exact whereabouts.

"Oh my!" Thomas shook his head in disbelief.

Rosemary laughed.

Catherine picked up her pad and wrote a description of the vehicle the searcher was in and handed it to Thomas. "Go get him!" she said with true venom in her voice.

Thomas looked carefully at the parchment. To him it was just a map, despite what they said. "I know that place."

The other two looked at where he was pointing.

"It's a very busy area. How do you propose doing this?"

"Well..." He started to bite the inside of his cheek. He needed a moment to think. Then he knew. "Right! I've got it. Yes, that'll work!" he glanced at the map again.

"What will work?" asked Rosemary.

"He won't tell you," said Catherine.

But Rosemary looked put out. Thomas just made a gesture with his hands. "It's not my..."

Rosemary anticipated what he was going to say. "Yes, Mother did tell me how it is! There are some things we can't tell each other!"

Thomas studied the map again. He knew he had to be precise with the timing. He waited for a couple of moments. Then he turned and ran out of the spell room, up the stairs and along the dark corridor.

"Let us know how you get on!" he heard Catherine call.

A second later, he was hovering above the car, using the trick Jamie had shown him after he had crashed into the tree on the church grounds. Now all he had to do was wait for a break in the traffic. It didn't take long for the road to clear.

Instantly, he appeared one hundred metres in front of the car, making it swerve off the road. The car rolled and came to a grinding halt with its wheels spinning in the air. He went straight in for the kill, suspending the searcher in time. He hauled him out and tossed him aside. The shocked look on the searcher's face caught Thomas by surprise, as well as the size of him. *He's huge! Dominic didn't mention this!* Thomas took a moment and took note of what he was up against. The searcher was wearing a suit, collar and tie, as if he was a city gent. But the look in his eyes told Thomas everything.

Raising the vibrations around the car he instantly destroyed it. It disintegrated into miniscule fragments. He brushed them all aside and quickly buried them. He checked the road and verge surfaces carefully. *No one must see there has been any accident here at all.* With the crash scene tidy, he gathered up the powerless searcher. He knew exactly where he could hide him. He could use the place where he kept his own car and hide him in the barn. Nobody will find him there. *Should I send him back now? No, I need to make sure I am strong enough. Soon I will know.*

Chapter 30

Once home and inside the barn, Thomas looked around. He chose a particularly precarious spot high up in the roof beams, somewhere nobody would look. He placed the searcher there carefully. Now he needed to contact Catherine to get confirmation that what he had done had worked.

"Is he still on the map?" Thomas asked her.

"Parchment, Thomas! I'm going down now."

"And?"

After a minute or two, he could hear her in the spell room. There was a sharp intake of breath. "He's vanished!"

"Good, it worked."

"Am I allowed to ask how?"

"Your spell works with the intricacies of history, right? A millisecond behind time?"

"Yes."

"What I did was scramble my historic trail, giving the effect that beyond that moment, the car crash I set up never happened."

"I'm so impressed with you, Thomas. The spell is as old as the hills, and you figured it out in thirty minutes."

"No. All I did was work out the principle. I could never create it."

He heard a scuffle. "Thomas! It's Rosemary. Do you have everything under control?"

"Yes, Rosemary. Yes, it's taken care of. We just need to keep our ears to the ground, though. It won't be long before the other lot figure out what we've done."

"Don't worry. We're all on alert. Just deal with that scumbag tomorrow, please!"

Time! Thomas checked his watch. He was running a little late. He had to leave now to collect Alisha if he wanted to avoid upsetting Sarah.

With a few minutes to spare, he pulled into the drive of Alisha's home. He was impressed with the design of the garden at the front of the house. The shrubs were an array of colours creating a wave of beauty. It was the first time he had ever noticed her garden. While he was sitting there thinking about the flowers, Alisha appeared.

"Bang on time, Thomas," she said, sliding into the car.

"I've been given my orders."

She gave him a gentle kiss on the cheek. "Thank you for coming."

"That's okay. Now, what do you want me to say to this doctor?"

She grinned. "Sarah has told me about you. Say something believable. And in a pleasant kind of way."

"I can manage that!" he laughed. "Now let's pick Sarah up."

Within an hour, the three of them were walking from the car park to the hospital entrance. As they got closer, Thomas noticed a young child sobbing and clinging onto what must be her mother, as there was a striking resemblance. The mother was tearful too. Thomas couldn't bear to walk past. "Everything all right?" he whispered to her.

The mother stared at him, tears streaming down her face. "I just have to tell somebody. Somebody. They said there's no hope. My husband. It's just a matter of time, they said."

Thomas looked down at the little girl. "I'm so sorry." He placed his hand on her shoulder for a second and felt her distress. But what else could he say or do? He went to the others.

"What's wrong, Thomas?"

"That poor little child's father has a very short time to live."

They all walked on in subdued silence towards the reception area. There, they were directed to a small conference room. The surgeon was waiting for them. He greeted them and explained that he would be joined by others who were interested in Thomas's skill too, and if that would be okay, half asking, half assuming that he wouldn't mind.

Thomas nodded begrudgingly. The next moment Dominic popped into his head, *I know you're busy, but I need a word,*

Thomas sighed. "Excuse me," he said to the surgeon. "I'm just going to get some water."

"I'm so sorry. I should have thought of that." The surgeon stood up and went out the door. "I'll fetch a few bottles."

As soon as he left the room, Thomas headed for the door himself.

"Where are you going?" asked Sarah.

"I have someone coming through, honey. Sorry, not good timing. I won't be long."

Sarah nodded. "Don't be sorry. You've got a couple of minutes."

Thomas went out into the corridor. *Dominic? What is it?*

That little child. You have to save her father.

Really? After his busy morning, Thomas wasn't feeling in the best of form, and now this was being thrust upon him. *How? I don't even know what's wrong with him!*

I do. It's his heart. It's always been dodgy, but he never knew.

Thomas remained silent.

Believe it or not, you'll need him in the future.

Then why is he dying?

I've told you before, life is always changing. Mistakes are always happening. You don't have much time. Go to his room. I'll guide you. It will take two of you, though.

Thomas looked back. The surgeon was holding the door open, and behind him were two more men.

I must go, Dominic, the surgeon's back.

As Thomas went back into the room, Sarah caught his eye. "Was everything okay?" He gave a sign that said both yes and no. She looked mystified.

The surgeon smiled. "Here you are. Water!" He put the bottles on the table and went to close the door.

Thomas seized the opportunity to lean over the table and whisper to Sarah. "Five minutes and you'll need the loo!"

She raised her thumb discreetly.

The surgeon and his colleagues sat opposite them. "These are the two specialists I told you about. Gentlemen, this is Mr Pink."

While the idea of talking to these men didn't sit easily with him, Thomas was still willing to listen to what they had to say. As the surgeon began to go through Alisha's medical history with them, there was a knock on the door, and a student nurse entered carrying a large brown envelope.

"Mr Arbutt, sir." She handed it to the surgeon.

"Ah, the CT scans. Thank you." He looked across at Thomas. "Please excuse us for a minute or two while my colleagues examine the history of Alisha's tumour."

That was the signal for Sarah to express her wish to use the loo. "Excuse me too," said Sarah. "Where is the toilet?"

Thomas jumped up. "I'll show you," he said. "Back in a sec, Alisha."

As soon as they were outside the door, he whispered. "We need to find that child's Dad. Remember the little girl in the car park?"

"Why?"

"I'll explain in a minute."

They hurried down the corridor to the reception, when Sarah suddenly stopped as she spotted a store cupboard. She whizzed in and grabbed a white coat. "We might need this." She didn't put the coat on, but just rolled it up.

"Stay behind me," she whispered. As they approached the reception desk, she handed the coat to Thomas. "You stay here, trust me."

He waited, watching her talk to the woman behind the counter. Moments later, she walked back towards him and beckoned to him to follow her. Along a corridor, at room A1 she stopped and indicated to him to stay back. Thomas didn't have a clue what was going on, but he knew he could trust her.

She knocked on the door and entered. A moment or two later, the mother appeared at the doorway entrance, with Sarah talking to her. Sarah pointed down along the corridor. The mother nodded, then went off following Sarah's directions. Now Thomas could move in.

"You won't need the coat."

He abandoned it on the chair.

The little girl was sitting by her father's bed. She stared at them both.

With the door closed, he called Dominic. *What now?*

Put the child's mind at ease and then ask her to start talking to her father. When she does, get Sarah to put some weight on the man's shoulders, keeping him down.

Thomas leaned across towards the child. "Hello, I'm Thomas. This is your daddy, isn't it? You told me about him in the car park, remember? Daddy's sick, isn't he?"

The girl nodded and looked like she might cry again.

"I want to try and help him. Sarah is here too. She's going to put her hands on your daddy's shoulders."

Sarah did as Thomas had asked.

"Now, can you talk to your daddy? Tell him something nice?"

The little girl patted her father's hand. "Daddy, I saw a picture of a bear, and he was smiling at me."

Now, said Dominic, *you put one hand on his shoulder, and the other over his heart.*

Thomas followed his instructions.

That's right. Now concentrate on me. And listen very carefully, Thomas. The energy I'll be sending could be overwhelming. You must focus on me. Nothing else! Nothing! Ready?

I'm ready.

Now.

The sudden surge of energy gave the child's father a huge jolt, so strong it almost put Thomas and Sarah on the floor. He started to perspire, and his legs began to shake under him. The girl looked horrified, but he and Sarah stayed in position.

Done! he heard Dominic say.

Thomas fell to his knees. The little girl jumped up and ran over to hug him as if she knew everything was going to be okay. "Daddy's better now," he whispered to her. He got unsteadily to his feet and, for a moment, had to take Sarah's hand to stay upright.

Sarah gave the little girl a kiss on the forehead and opened the door. The mother was coming back along the corridor. She turned back to the child. "Daddy will be alright now. And Mummy's coming back. Bye-bye, darling."

"What just happened?" Sarah asked, as they hurried away along the corridor.

"I'll tell you later. I'm not even sure myself. Come on! We'd better get a move on. Alisha will think we've deserted her."

When they walked into the meeting room, Thomas apologised. "Sorry, we went the wrong way. But I'm sure you needed time to discuss the CT scans?"

"We think there was a problem with the scanner," said one of the specialists.

"It's the only answer," said the other one.

Thomas was bemused. "So, there was nothing wrong with Alisha?"

Alisha nodded. "So, I didn't have a tumour!"

Thomas ran his finger along the edge of the table. "What was wrong with her then?"

"Who knows? We're only doctors, not psychics."

Sarah caught her breath sharply. Alisha looked away. They had a good idea what was coming next.

Thomas was incensed. "Doctors? I wouldn't go that far!" he said, "You're not capable of communicating with people, let alone healing them."

"Are we done?" asked Alisha's consultant, collecting up the papers.

"Definitely!" said Thomas.

"Well, thank you, Mr Pink."

Sarah and Alisha left the room. Thomas paused at the door and looked back at the three men. "I would normally thank people for their time. Not on this occasion. You've just stolen mine." He turned and walked out. As he came along the corridor, he saw Sarah beckoning to him.

"Quickly, you must see this! Look!"

"What's going on?"

Sarah gasped. "Look, do you see who is checking out of the hospital, Thomas."

It was the man he had just healed. "I'm not sure that's a good idea." He was about to go over to him when Dominic popped into his head again.

It's best not to talk to him. Don't worry. He's healthy. Just weak. Let him go home.

Thomas stepped back and watched as three nurses tried to dissuade the man from leaving, while his little daughter held on tightly to his hand and his tearful wife clutched a small suitcase.

"Please, please, Mr Bradwell. At least wait for your surgeon."

Refusing to stay, Mr Bradwell and his family began to make their way towards the exit. The nurses desperately tried to force them back. "Mr Arbutt won't be long."

Thomas recognised the surgeon's name. It was the same arrogant man he had just been speaking to. He nudged Sarah. "Shall we stay a while?"

She made a face but nodded. Alisha didn't understand what was going on.

"Why do you want to stay?" she asked.

"Come and sit down," said Sarah. "I'll tell you all about it."

They all sat in a corner of the reception area. Thomas was curious to see what Mr Arbutt would make of his patient's miraculous recovery. It wasn't long before the surgeon turned up. The senior nurse was quick to explain the turn of events.

"But why on earth is he out of bed? When I saw him earlier," Mr Arbutt said, "he had only hours to live."

"Well, we have all examined him. And another consultant has seen him. He's certainly in the best of health now!" said a senior nurse.

Mr Arbutt was utterly confused and was muttering to himself. "How could I have made such a mistake?"

"What do you want me to do?" the senior nurse asked.

"Mr Bradwell should stay for more tests."

"Why do I need tests?" asked Mr Bradwell, turning sharply. "I'm not sick anymore." Suddenly, his little girl looked over and saw Thomas. "Look, Daddy!" she said, pointing. "There's Thomas and Sarah. They are the ones that helped you."

Mr Arbutt swung around.

Thomas gave him a little wave. Then he smiled at the child and stood up.

"He has that look in his eye!" said Sarah, anxious to leave. "Come on, Alisha. He's going to have another go at the surgeon I don't want to be around when he does."

"Good, let's go," said Alisha. "He's such an arrogant man."

Just at that moment, one of the hospital cleaners came through carrying mops and buckets. Thomas pointed to him. "May I suggest a career change – Mr – err Arbutt, isn't it?"

Mr Arbutt stared at him in anger.

Sarah cringed and was thankful that Mr Arbutt didn't respond. Alisha smiled.

Mr Bradwell came back to shake Thomas's hand. "Thanks, mate. Thank you so much."

Mr Arbutt stared at them all then backed away. The nurses looked down their noses at him as he retreated down the corridor.

The senior nurse turned to say goodbye to the Bradwell family. "Good luck, and keep safe, Mr Bradwell."

Thomas, Sarah and Alisha followed the Bradwells out of the building. Once outside, Mrs Bradwell took the opportunity to interrogate Thomas. She was full of questions. The strain she had been under the past few months was showing, and she cried a lot. After a few minutes of chatting with Thomas and watching her daughter talking happily to her husband, the anxiety gave way to relief. Thomas explained what he had done, but he did leave Dominic out of the conversation.

Sitting altogether on the hospital grounds with the child sitting happily on her father's knee, made Thomas feel on top of the world. They chatted a while longer, getting to know each other. Thomas was interested to discover what James Bradwell did for a living. Apparently, he was a software designer and ran an IT department for a top German bank. Thomas was impressed, but he wasn't at all sure why Dominic had suggested James Bradwell might be of help to him in the future. Nevertheless, names and contact numbers were exchanged, and arrangements made to meet up in a couple of weeks.

Walking back towards the car, Alisha started the questioning again, trying her best to understand Thomas's ability. She was amazed that he had been able to save a complete stranger when he had so much going on in his life trying to stop evil. "It's completely beyond me," she said hugging him.

This started Sarah off. "Yes, Thomas. You have to tell us more!"

"I'm working to instructions from a higher power," he replied, desperately wanting to tell them everything. *I just can't, I promised.*

"What higher power?" Sarah sounded very determined.

"What can I say? I really haven't a clue what's going on."

"What do you mean, Thomas?" asked Alisha. "You're the one doing it. How can you say that? You're talking twaddle."

Thomas stopped in his tracks.

Sarah faced him accusingly. "That Mr Bradwell had hours to live! No matter what you think of his surgeon, he's worked in medicine for years. He must know what he's doing. But then you show up, Thomas, and bring his patient back, virtually from the dead!"

This was all so awkward. He didn't know how to respond. *What can I tell them?* "Well," he said tentatively, "I don't know what you want to hear."

"Something more substantial, Thomas." said Sarah.

A thought flashed in his mind. "Okay." He glanced at Alisha. "Who would you like to contact on Sunday?"

Sarah glared at him. "You're trying to change the subject, Mister."

Thomas laughed. "I'm not. Tell me, Alisha!"

Alisha began fidgeting. "I don't want to go down this route."

Sarah sighed. "Go on, tell him. Otherwise, this will take all day."

"My mum?"

"And what are you going to ask?"

Alisha looked at Sarah.

Sarah shook her head. "He's trying to distract us."

Thomas smiled broadly. He fancied he was getting on top of the situation.

"I want to know..." Alisha hesitated.

"Tell me?"

"I want to know what happened to my dad!" She stared at Thomas. "You're not going to tell me you know, are you?"

"Oh no. Only your mum would know that. But after she tells you on Sunday, ask her how I did what I did."

Alisha stared at him, speechless.

"Then you can tell Sarah."

Sarah shook her head. "No. I'll find out for myself on Sunday. From my mum. That's if it works, Thomas."

"It will work!" He knew it would. He had gone to great lengths to set the circle up for Sunday, he wasn't going to listen to any negative nonsense.

"I don't mean it won't work," said Sarah quickly, realising that she had offended him. "What I meant was, what happens if we don't get intelligible answers? After all, it's not like making a phone call."

"With forty-three witches controlling the biggest circle in history, you will not fail to understand, no matter who you make contact with. And it's better than a phone call, I promise! I'll be controlling the vibrations coming in, and it will be just as we're talking now. Crystal clear!" They both looked at him in awe. "Maybe the first question you should ask your mother, Sarah, is what caused the radiation leak?"

"You are right," said Sarah. "The thought of that scumbag Merston being linked to my mother's death makes me so angry."

"Yes," he replied, putting his hand on Sarah's shoulder. "Are you satisfied now?"

"You've just about wiggled out of all our questions, Thomas Pink!" laughed Sarah, as she grabbed his arm and started walking towards the car again. "Then there's Alisha herself."

"And that question is?"

"In my pending file, Mr Pink!" said Alisha.

Thursday finished with the three of them at Sarah's discussing over dinner exactly what they were going to ask on Sunday. The girls spoke of their mothers, both of whom had died at an early age. Thomas couldn't understand where both fathers were, but he had no doubt he would soon find out.

Chapter 31

The following morning, he left Sarah's before the sun was up. She had an early class, while he was anxious to check on the searcher stored high up in the rafters of the old barn. He was doing his best to be cautious as recent events had shown him how fragile life can be. Now, he appreciated being alive more than he had ever done before. To be absolutely sure, before going out to the barn, he contacted Catherine on his mind phone and asked if she could see the searcher through the spell on the ancient parchment.

Give me a moment, Thomas. I must go to the spell room.

While he waited, he thought how extraordinary it was that his mind phone could connect to any ordinary phone. As if to illustrate this, Rosemary picked up on the phone line too.

Are you dealing with the problem today, Thomas?

Hi Rosemary, yes. I'm planning to take our friend to Ireland.

When?

As soon as your mother gives me the okay. I need my movements checked. I must be sure no one's tracking me.

Hang on. Mother's coming. She has her thumb up. The searcher is not registering.

Are we meant to be tracking you? he heard Catherine ask.

Yes Mum, Thomas asked if we will.

Ask him to call now on our mobile.

Thomas did and keeping the phone to his ear, he then made his way into the barn and he looked up at the beams. "I'm linking in with the searcher now. Anything showing Rosemary?"

"No. nothing. Whatever you did yesterday is holding well."

"We're going back to the spot in Cambridge now, just to be absolutely certain," said Catherine.

He asked a second later, "anything?"

"No, nothing!"

"Great. Are you ready to go on a little Celtic trip?"

"We're ready."

He pulled a picture of the beach in Southern Ireland out of his pocket. A moment later, they were there. Just before he let them appear, he checked it was safe. There was no one around. *Good.* He unravelled the bind holding the searcher and waited for Rosemary to panic.

It was immediate, Rosemary sounded scared. "Thomas, I can see you! No! I mean the searcher. He does not look happy!"

Urgently, Thomas increased the vibration. For two seconds, he watched how the body cells divided into minute bubbles, becoming smaller and smaller, until they descended down like grains of sand and sank deep into the beach. Thomas sighed with relief.

"What are you doing?" asked Rosemary. "Where's he gone now?"

"All done," He watched as white foam from the water's edge spread out and splashed over where the searcher had been.

His mission completed, Thomas transported everyone home. "Knock, knock, Rosemary. I'm outside."

"Outside? Our house?" She opened the door in amazement. "When are you going to show me how you do that?"

"Didn't you see my broomstick," he replied cheekily.

Catherine was standing behind Rosemary, laughing. "I've heard that one before, Thomas."

"So, what did you do?" asked Rosemary.

"I sent him back," said Thomas.

"This won't be the end of the searchers. There will be others." said Catherine.

"We've found another spell," said Rosemary. "This one goes back centuries as well. It will stay open as long as required."

Catherine nodded. "Yes. It's a broader spell and not as subtle, but it will pick up on a new evil that can put you at risk."

As usual, Thomas was grateful for their help and left them feeling in high spirits.

Back at home, he had time on his hands, so he decided to check on one of the twenty-two addresses Jonas had given him against the bank IBAN. He chose the highest paid witch. She lived and banked in San Paulo, Brazil. It wasn't hard to find the address and a picture of the bank on his computer, using the mapping system on the internet. He could even find the house she lived in. The safest thing to do would be to travel behind time and be invisible. Even though it was only six in the morning over there, he certainly wasn't going to take any unnecessary risks and get caught snooping.

The bank looked like any other foreign bank. As it was so very early in the morning, it wasn't open. He passed through the wooden door and had a good look around. Nothing untoward. Satisfied, he swapped the pictures in his hand. Now he was looking at the house where the person receiving the money lived. Seconds later, he was walking around the outside of it. As with the bank, he wasn't sure what he was looking for. Nothing stood out. The house was reddish in colour and had clearly been neglected. He found himself in a dusty back yard and could find nothing unusual there. Thomas studied the information he had brought with him. *Is this the correct address? Yes.* So *why is someone with so much money coming in each month staying in a place like this?*

Suddenly he realised he had travelled behind time. He couldn't pick up any bad vibrations because he was just a shadow of himself. To be in real time, he would have to re-establish himself into the present moment. *No problem.* Now he stood in front of the bank again, this time as himself. There was a little more street life now with people coming into the city, delivery drivers, road cleaners, shop shutters opening. *Noise.* He checked the time. *Almost seven.* An hour had flown by. He needed to get back to that house.

Ten minutes later, he was walking down the unmade road towards the red house. An array of ramshackle buildings that were used as homes caught his eye as he walked. The house he was looking for was up-market compared to these. He walked on and spotted the maroon, reddish coloured house again. As he got closer, he began to feel poorly. A feeling of nausea swept over him, and he began to perspire. He stepped back, not wanting to get any closer.

Bloody hell! This is a seriously bad witch! He thought to himself. He turned and walked quickly back the way he had come. He didn't like the symptoms he got when he was close to such dark evil. He stopped and gave himself a talking to. *You've got to toughen up. You can't walk away like that!*

Thomas began to pace up and down as he thought things through. The account numbers on the list given to him by Susie definitely belonged to darksiders. Her boss, Smithe was one too, it seemed. *But why? And how?* He decided to stay, but as a shadow again. He stepped back a second in time. This would allow him to nose around the house looking for clues. Before he could enter, he heard a door slam around the back of the house and he caught a glimpse of a slim woman with jet black hair heading for a beaten-up Volkswagen. As he got closer, she climbed into the car, he guessed that she was no more than thirty and very attractive. That threw him. *A pretty dark witch! How can that be?* Then he thought about Saffron. She was easy on the eye as well, all be it from the waist up, and she was a dark witch too. *They may be beautiful on the outside but inside they are rotten.*

The car pulled away. He followed close behind. The journey took around thirty minutes along small, unmade dusty roads. *No wonder her car is bashed up, these roads are a nightmare.* When she was a few miles out of town, she pulled over to sit a while. As a shadow, Thomas was able to stand just feet away from the car, waiting to find out her next move. He was just wondering why she had stopped when she picked up her phone and speed-dialled someone. He didn't know what she said but whatever it was, she had obviously got the answer she wanted. She grabbed the keys from the ignition and jumped out of the car. From the boot she took out an old black case. It reminded Thomas of a doctor's bag. *Perhaps she's a doctor. Maybe there are other people living in her house who are witches.* There was only one way to find out for sure, and that was to appear in real time. The problem with that was he would be exposed and being near her made him feel really sick. She was walking away from the car. He decided to stay in the shadows and follow her.

She walked for a few moments back towards several dilapidated and apparently unoccupied buildings with bars at the windows. As they walked past, he didn't notice anyone. As they approached the next building, again with bars at the windows, he realised that it was a compound of sorts. *Maybe it's a prison.* There were bars at all the windows and secure wooden gates at the entrance. She stopped at the gates and said something into the intercom. It sounded like she was saying the word 'Kamilah'. *Is that her name?* Immediately a smaller door within the gates opened. A soldier was standing there. *Or is it a policeman?* Thomas couldn't be sure. Whatever he was, the man was armed, and he looked as if he had only just got out of bed. *How scruffy and unshaven he is.*

"Kamilah!" He said and stepped aside to allow her in. Thomas followed.

Obviously, Kamilah knows this place.

She made her way to a small office block. Thomas had a quick look around. It was definitely a prison. *At least one hundred cells, I reckon.* He decided that once he knew why Kamilah was here, he would check the place out.

As she approached the office block, another soldier or guard greeted her by name, as she did with him. Thomas didn't catch his name, but he got the distinct impression this was the man in charge.

After a short exchange of words, the two of them went on to a smaller building, separate from the others. The two guards there moved aside. The warden unlocked the door. Thomas didn't wait. He slipped past them. Inside he saw medical supplies, a secure bed and purpose-built interrogation chairs. Straps were attached on the arms and the legs of each chair. *This place is definitely a prison.* From this room, there was a small passage leading to other rooms and Kamilah and the warden continued down it. Thomas went ahead of them. He could hear groans coming from somewhere.

Without warning, Kamilah walked through him. *How extraordinary!* It made him shudder. He hadn't experienced that before! Now he was following her from the passage into a darkened room. There she placed her bag on a table that was close to a prisoner strapped into a chair. The man in charge came in and handed Kamilah a grubby file full of papers and left.

Kamilah unpacked her bag and placed six small bottles filled with different coloured liquids on the table. Thomas peered at them. None were labelled. Then she opened the file and began to flick through until she found the document she was looking for.

Thomas stood behind her to see what she was reading. It was written in Portuguese and knowing he wouldn't understand it, but his ability to memorise heightened now, he read all he could see with the plan to translate it later.

Kamilah certainly didn't seem to be in any hurry. The prisoner sat there, not saying a word. Suddenly she tossed the file onto the table. "Andres, you are a catch! Twenty-three killed by your hand," she said in her native tongue.

Thomas was amazed. He could understand what she was saying. He needed to confirm that he wasn't dreaming. *Jamie!*

What can I do for you?

I just understood everything.

I don't understand.

She's talking in Portuguese, and I understood her!

It's simple. Relax! Every language is stored in your database. When you need to, you pull up the knowledge from within.

Wow! Thanks, bye! Thomas didn't want to miss any of the conversation.

It fascinated him the way she had placed the bottles out on the table. It showed him that she had such a tidy mind. *Or maybe there's a procedure she likes to follow.* He memorised the coloured bottles and the order she had placed them in. If he couldn't figure out what she was up to, then perhaps Catherine and Rosemary might. He peeked into the bag. It was empty. *What's she waiting for?*

It was as if she heard him. She stood up and selected a bottle, unscrewed the top and drank the contents. That took him by surprise as he had imagined that she was about to force them down the throat of the prisoner. Then she picked another one and unscrewed the top. This time she walked in a circle around Andres, pouring the contents of the bottle on the floor. Andres stared at her as she made her way to the other room. Thomas followed her until he reached the doorway. He was keeping an eye on Andres as well. Kamilah sat down and fiddled with her phone.

Meanwhile back in the other room, a blueish vapour began to rise from the concoction that had been poured on the floor. Andres looked agitated. The room he was in was filling with blue mist. *What is Kamilah doing?* Thomas went closer and looked over her shoulder. She was playing a game*! I don't believe it! She's one chilled-out witch!*

Andres had started shouting and was in a rage, calling her vile names. Then there was dead silence. Kamilah stopped playing her game. She put her phone down and went back into the other room. She shook Andres. He was limp and didn't respond. Satisfied that he was out of it, now she positioned the table in front of him. Thomas watched her and was mystified. It seemed time was vital now as she mixed different concoctions together into a clear glass container with a hinged lid. She lined that up in front of him with the lid open. Then she went to her bag and opened what appeared to be a secret compartment. Thomas was surprised. He hadn't noticed that. Inside was another little bottle filled with a clear liquid, but smaller than the others. She took out what looked like a syringe but without the needle.

Quickly she syphoned some of the liquid from the bottle into it and moved back towards Andres. She grabbed his hair and pulled his head back. His jaw dropped open. Without hesitation, she emptied the contents in his throat. A moment later, Andres began to shake. Kamilah moved away from him and pressed herself to the wall. Thomas moved back too. As he watched, the man's shaking gathered pace until he was in a permanent state of seizure.

Aghast, Thomas watched as a stream of light flowed out of Andre's mouth and into Kamilah's glass container on the table. After a few moments, Kamilah walked cautiously back towards the table. It was as if she expected something else to happen, but nothing did. She pulled the lid down on the jar and made it secure. Thomas stared at her. *What a powerful witch she is. But why does she want the essence of this man's soul?* He was sure that this is what Kamilah had extracted from him. *I must remember every detail of all this and speak to Catherine and Rosemary.*

Kamilah packed her bottles and the glass jar carefully into her bag then moved the table back to check on her victim.

He was just coming round. "What happened?"

"You fell asleep," she said and left.

Thomas followed her as she strolled over to the small office. To Thomas's surprise, the man thanked her for treating the prisoner.

Treating him. Is that what she did? I don't think so! Frustrated and running out of time, he decided to leave San Paulo and make his way back to Guildford, wondering if Catherine would understand what spell Kamilah had performed and for what purpose.

Rosemary opened the door "Thomas! What's wrong?"

"You won't believe what I've just seen!"

They headed for the spell room where Catherine was working. She listened carefully, until she stopped him. "That's complicated, Thomas. Rosemary, note down every word while I ask the questions."

Thomas's ability to remember every detail was impressive, but Catherine kept on asking him questions.

"Are you sure you've told me exactly what happened? Exactly?"

Thomas nodded.

"Then she's mixed spells. This witch you've found, Thomas, she's exceptionally dangerous."

Thomas frowned, "will she be a problem?"

"You're with us. Don't be silly." She made her way to a large metal cabinet. "Say your half of the spell key, Rosemary? I have a good idea, but I need to check on something."

Thomas heard Rosemary mumble something but didn't have a clue what it was. Catherine finished the chant off, and magically, one of the cabinet draws rattled and opened.

Thomas quickly moved out of the way. He hadn't noticed the cabinet before. "Must be important stuff in there," he said.

Catherine turned and smiled at him, then mumbled another few words, and the cabinet disappeared for a moment, then appeared just as quickly.

"Precious, Thomas! Precious stuff!" said Rosemary. "Mother has spells in there going back forever."

Now Thomas was even keener to have a look inside.

Catherine fumbled with the files inside. "Oh dear, I'm getting old, Thomas. My fingers are stiff."

"Nonsense," said Thomas. "Come here. Give me your hands."

Catherine watched as Thomas held both her hands and concentrated for just a moment on her stiff fingers.

"My hands are getting hot, Thomas. How do you do this? My hands are hot!"

He released her. "Hot, and good as new. You'll have no trouble getting out your files now."

Catherine wiggled her fingers, astonished. "Nothing wrong. Nothing!" Her fingers were flexible again. Her eyes filled up with tears. "Thomas!"

Thomas smiled. "Are we going to stand around all day?"

"Come on, Mother." Rosemary gave her a hug.

Catherine began to rummage in the cabinet drawer with no trouble at all, but then she stopped and began to fiddle with her hands. She was so impressed with what had just happened she had forgotten the spells she had in mind.

Smiling at her mother, Rosemary peered into the cabinet and grabbed a bundle of files. "These are the oldest parchments. It has to be amongst this lot."

"How old are they?" Thomas was curious.

"Maybe a thousand years or more."

"Really? How do you keep them in such good condition?"

"Just a simple spell. It stops them deteriorating."

"I could do with a spell like that on me," said Thomas.

Rosemary smiled. "Yes, it's a pity it doesn't work on us! Anyway, I bet you won't need it, you will probably live forever just as you are." She placed the whole bundle on the table and took them out of the files, then gently separated the parchments. She looked at each one, then placed the spell face down, carefully keeping them all in order.

"Do you know what you're looking for, dear?" Catherine asked.

"Ah, you are back with us now, Mother!" she said laughing. "Yes, I know. As you mentioned, that witch is really clever. She must have combined three spells. But how she has managed to do what she did is beyond me."

"Can you see anything there? What spells do you think she's used?" asked Catherine.

"One of them has to be the containing spell."

Thomas noticed that Catherine was back in complete control again. "When you saw the witch extract that poor man's soul, where were you, Thomas?"

"In a prison cell in Brazil."

They both looked at him shaking their head.

"She might have mixed an exorcist configuration spell, too," suggested Rosemary, still searching. "That's why she had all those bottles. But I'm struggling. There has to be a spell to find the route to the soul."

Catherine smiled. "You're nearly there. I think!" She looked at Thomas with a quizzical look on her face.

"Don't ask me. I haven't a clue." Thomas replied.

"I do. In fact, I have more than a clue. Where did you say she lives?"

"San Paulo."

"South America. That should tell you, Rosemary."

Rosemary still looked baffled.

"The Incas!"

"Ahh! Why didn't I think of that?"

Thomas stared at them both. "Is one of you going to tell me then?"

"The ingredients for the spell only grow in South America," said Catherine.

"The ancient Incas used them as a cleanser for evil souls."

"And if that witch can do it, then we can too," declared Rosemary.

"But why would she be doing that to prisoners?" asked Thomas.

"I think it has a lot to do with Susie's boss," said Catherine. "There's definitely something going on."

"I think you're right," Thomas agreed. "What will happen to the prisoner?"

"What was the condition of the prisoner after the witch had done the extraction?" asked Catherine as Thomas was leaving.

"Quiet! Very quiet."

"There is little that can be done for him. A body won't survive long without a soul." Catherine said sadly.

Chapter 32

Back home, Thomas decided not to train or do anything. Completely exhausted, he collapsed into a chair and ran through the events of the day in his mind as he usually did. He had done everything he could to cover his back. In no time at all, he was asleep. An hour later he woke, startled by his phone ringing.

"Are you okay, Thomas? I was expecting you to come over."

"I fell asleep. Sorry, honey. I've had such a crazy day."

"I'll bring a quiche over and we can talk about it."

At the table, they made plans for the following day. They decided that they would pop round to see Alisha, do a little shopping and then end up at Sarah's. The starting point for everyone was at Sarah's. Sunday was the big day, and it was almost upon them.

When Sunday came, Thomas noticed that everyone seemed tense. Before they left for Guildford, Thomas ran through the procedure again, making sure that Sarah, Alisha and others understood the plan and to reassure them. He wanted to ram home the importance of waiting five minutes after the session was over. He stretched the truth a little, saying it was an essential courtesy to the other world, as he had said before. "Have you all got pencil and paper to record what you see and hear?" he asked. Sarah smiled weakly and held up a notepad and pen.

Two hours later, Rosemary greeted them at the door. Thomas introduced each one.

"The yoga seminar! I remember most of you."

Then when they were all inside and settled, Catherine explained her role in the circle and reminded them what a big moment it was. "For us all! We have a little over thirty minutes to wait. Tea or coffee, anyone?"

Soon the right positions were taken up with some guidance from Catherine. It was now eight minutes to go, and excitement was building.

"I've given some thought to Mr Merston, Catherine," Thomas whispered to her. "I think we should keep him alive. Five minutes won't be nearly long enough to extract the information we need. We're almost sure he's responsible for Victoria's death, but there's much more we need to ask him."

"What will you do with him then?" she whispered.

"The same as I did with the searcher. I'll need a place to store him for a bit."

"Christ Thomas! We have five minutes to go now, and you're changing the plan!" Catherine exclaimed.

"Five minutes won't be enough with him," Thomas whispered.

Catherine thought quickly. "I know a place! The old tyre factory on the Guildford Road."

"I'm not sure where that is."

"You drove by it when you came here this morning. The factory is just by the traffic lights. On the right coming in my direction." Thomas nodded. "Now we have just three minutes, Thomas."

"Well, what are you waiting for?"

Catherine smiled and sat down in her place.

Thomas turned the radio up so all could hear and raised his voice, reminding them all again. "Don't forget everyone about waiting five minutes," he announced, "but right now when the time comes over the radio, you focus! You focus on whoever you have chosen to speak to." He glanced at his watch. "One minute to go." He turned the volume up higher.

Sarah began to shake. Alisha squeezed her hand. "It's only your mother, so don't worry."

Rosemary looked across at them with a reassuring smile.

Catherine looked over at Thomas. "I hope this is the end of the saga. It's been thirty years and I need this issue resolved."

"Ssh," said Thomas, with butterflies in his stomach.

Nine o'clock struck.

Immediately Thomas could feel power sweeping round the country, from here in Guildford to Glasgow, down to Manchester, on to Bristol and Cambridge and full circle back to him. The energy jolted him physically. It was so much more than he had expected. It needed to be held at a lower level before communication could start. He knew that. He was shaking. He needed to dig deep. The circle was complete, but the connection was erratic. He recognised his breathing was much too fast. He had to slow it down if this was going to be successful.

"Deep breathing Thomas! Come on." He could hear himself talking out loud. After a few seconds, his breathing started to feel easier. He relaxed just a little. Now he heard voices in his head. Someone had made contact already. Before long, his head was bursting with conversation. It was hard not to be emotional. Uncontrolled thoughts started to flash through his mind. He clenched his fists, upping his game and did his best to stay in control. He knew now how much he would need all his power immediately after the session to break through the energy source protecting Merston.

In a thatched cottage in Suffolk, George Smithe met with his counterpart, Tony Barnstable.

"Your message sounded urgent, George."

"The searcher has vanished! Do you know how serious this is?" George spat.

"Nonsense! Searchers don't vanish. They find people who have."

"Well, this one has vanished. Contact whoever is controlling him, Tony. I want this searcher back on the bloody job. Too much time has been wasted."

"He was assigned to you the day you asked me. I don't understand, what's happened?"

"On Thursday evening, I sent him to Cambridge to pick up the trail from where we lost the demon. Then the searcher made his way south. I presumed he had figured out what had happened. Now he has vanished into thin air."

Barnstable shook his head, not sure what to make of the information he had just been given. "He couldn't have just disappeared. We're talking about Janus. This is a top searcher. You can't just lose him."

"Worse! Thirty-six hours later, he made a brief appearance in Southern Ireland and then vanished."

"How long is brief, George?"

"Ten seconds. Now his energy source isn't showing anywhere."

"There has to be some explanation." Barnstable paused for a moment. "When did we lose the connection in the witch's coven?"

"At the beginning of the week."

"And what was the demon doing when he was destroyed?"

"Checking on the lost connection."

"You mean throwing his weight around?"

"Well, that's what demons do."

"Not anymore, George. We must all be more subtle and tread carefully. Maybe the witches have found a powerful ally? We'll have to deal with the problem. But not right now. We have a much more pressing issue to deal with."

"Right. We will need a little help." George said staring hard at Barnstable.

"What's happened now?"

"Same problem."

Barnstable went to the window and stared out. "How far behind are we?"

Smithe took a deep breath. "I'm guessing a few months."

"Damn! It's getting worse," Barnstable tutted.

"I know. There are a few issues. First is storage. The dark element seeps away after a while."

"And what's the next problem?"

"Recruitment. At the last seminar, we managed to recruit only one. I was hoping for five or six. Then there's the power. It still drops as we collect. That's a ten per cent loss, and there's nothing we can do about it." Smithe was annoyed.

Barnstable turned back to him. "Well, that's not quite true. We could lift the energy this end."

"That's dangerous. We could wreck the system. Then what? Unless you know how to organise an upgrade. We've been through this fifty times, and we can't make it work."

"We can now," said Barnstable.

Smithe let out a big sigh. "How? How can we do that without compromising the operation?"

"I've found an engineering company in Germany."

"And just what did you say? How did you explain to them without them suspecting anything?"

"Don't worry. I was light on the truth."

"If their engineers get an inkling of what we are doing then…"

"I said, don't worry."

"I don't have time for mistakes, Tony. Come outside. I need some air. And you can tell me how you're going to persuade me to agree."

Chapter 33

Ten minutes into the spiritual contact session, Thomas prepared to ease off the energy control he had on the circle. This would allow contact to die gradually and free him for the most important question. He had to ask if Jeremy Merston had deliberately exposed Sarah's mother to radiation. He sat down next to Catherine. He didn't have to ask. She was sobbing.

"All those years."

"Are you okay? We have to go."

"She spoke to me! I still miss her, Thomas."

He put a comforting hand on her shoulder. "We have under five minutes to break the power source protecting Merston," he whispered.

Catherine looked at him tearfully.

"We need to leave."

Catherine nodded and stood up. She grabbed a small potion bag from the table, and they were gone.

It was far from guaranteed that Merston would be where Thomas was expecting him to be, but oddly he could feel a new sensation helping him. Now he was being guided by Sarah's mother with her knowledge of ancient spiritual law. He closed his eyes, trusting her influence and came to realise that spiritual law was a sophisticated guiding system which was used for soul redemption. When he opened his eyes, he and Catherine were in Oldham.

"There he is! The b******!" hissed Catherine.

The vibrations from Thomas hit Merston immediately, and he fell to the ground. Out came a small glass phial from Catherine's potion bag. In an instant, she had thrown the contents all over Merston.

Brushing himself down, he snarled, "What have you done?"

She swung round. "You must tell me how you got me here, Thomas. It's just incredible how you found him!"

"Tell me what was in the phial?" Merston demanded, his eyes rolling.

"Truth potion! I want answers!" Catherine replied looking at Thomas to assist her.

Thomas raised the vibration over Merston but not too much. "He's unconscious, and we now have under four minutes. That's not enough time to go into any detail."

"There's only one question I need to ask. And that's why."

"We can't stay here in the middle of town," Thomas said, looking at the busy street.

"Give me ten seconds then take him to the tyre factory, Thomas."

He nodded and brought Merston back from his state.

Immediately Catherine went for him. "Remember me, you b******?" Her fist was shaking in his face. "Tell me, why did you do it?"

Merston was screaming out in pain.

"What's wrong with him?" Thomas asked.

"The spell's taking hold, and he's trying to resist."

"Isn't it a truth spell?"

"Yes, but with a kick."

Thomas grabbed Merston by the scruff of the neck. "You're running out of time! Tell her!"

Merston was doubled up with the pain. "I was ordered to," he whispered.

Catherine went for him as if she would murder him. Thomas pulled him free and went straight to the tyre factory. Thomas parked him high up in the roof beams of the factory. Merston balanced there, frozen in time and unable to move. He was unconscious, his eyes had glazed over.

Thomas whizzed back down to Catherine. "Come on! Time is of the essence!"

Caroline and Rosemary were heading for the kitchen, Rosemary knew what the whole idea for the gathering had been, of course, but Caroline didn't. She was spaced out from being in the circle and absolutely amazed by being able to talk directly to her grandparents.

"That was brilliant. It was so real. I actually spoke to them!" She paused for a moment, looking tearful.

Rosemary gave her a hug. "Come on, let's make tea."

Thomas looked around the room. *Where is Sarah?* She hadn't moved from her seat. The expression on her face said it all. He sat down next to her, putting his hand over hers. Comforting someone wasn't his strong point, but he decided to try. "Honey?"

She raised her hand. "I'm not ready to talk yet."

Indeed no one in the room seemed to want to discuss their experience. The silence in the room was only disturbed by the rattling of cups. Caroline was still struggling to stop herself from crying as she put the tray on the table. Thomas noticed the saucers had more tea in them than the cups. If he had known the effect on everyone, he might have chosen another route to get to Merston.

Caroline sat down, apologising for the mess in the tray, but he saw how she drank some tea before anyone else to calm her nerves. She was still shaking. Thomas was sure that something she had been told had disturbed her.

Thomas was beginning to realise that the spiritual connection had caused some harm. Everyone looked fazed. He looked over to Alisha. Of all people, she should be looking happy. *She looks quite calm.* All the same, he decided he wasn't wanted here at the moment and quietly left the room.

Out in the hallway, he heard Jamie's voice.

Thomas? I need a moment or two.

Jamie. It's a bit awkward at the minute.

I can imagine, said Jamie, *but this is important, you need to find some space on your own.*

Thomas slipped out of the back door. *Okay.*

You did well, better than I thought you would...

But? There's a 'but' isn't there?

You were caught on CCTV in the old tyre factory.

Thomas winced. He thought back. *Sod it! It was when I came back down from the roof after stowing Merston, wasn't it? Will they spot him when security turns up?*

Maybe not.

So there is a chance they will see him then?

Maybe not.

Just to be sure, I'll go back and check, sighed Thomas.

Catherine was standing at the back door. "What's wrong?"

"We were spotted at the tyre factory on a security camera."

"How could we have been? Who told you?" Catherine looked puzzled.

Thomas was in no mood to explain. He wasn't sure what to say anyway. "I'll pop back just to check on Merston. I won't be long." He brushed past her into the house and was gone.

Merston was out of sight. Thomas contacted Jamie. *No problem here. What should I do next?*

You need to wipe the image off the security system.

Is it on-site?

No, it's based in Bagshot. I'll send you an image of the place in your mind.

The picture appeared immediately. *That's cool, Jamie. I didn't know you could do that.*

Thomas hovered for a moment when he arrived in Bagshot. He wasn't at all sure what he needed to do and took a moment to think. Time was short, and inside the computer room of the security company, there was no one around. Without hesitation, he powered himself up and like a bull in a china shop, he blew the computer to bits. *Well, that wouldn't work anymore, and the tape will be fried!*

Jamie popped into his head, and he was laughing. *Yes, very restrained. Now get out of there!*

Back in Guildford, Thomas casually walked up Catherine's front path.

Sarah opened the front door. "Where have you been, Thomas?"

"Walking. I needed to clear my head. There has been so much going on and things got a bit heavy in there. You okay?"

"Yes, honey. I'm sorry if I was off with you upstairs. It's just..." Her eyes filled with tears, and she started to sob.

Thomas pulled her close. "Let's leave it for a day or two. We can talk about it later."

"Thomas, he killed my mother. He stole her from me. That won't ever sit well with me, no matter how long I give it." She was shaking.

Along the hall over Sarah's shoulder, he caught sight of Catherine. He gave her a discreet nod so she would know he had taken care of the Merston problem.

"Don't worry honey, I won't let him hurt anyone ever again."

Chapter 34

Smithe was standing on the veranda looking over the garden. "What do you think of my garden? I have a new gardener."

Barnstable glanced around. "Yes, yes, George! Let's get on."

"So, the German company?" asked Smithe.

"The top man suggests we use them."

Smithe swung round. "The top man?" He was now concentrating fully.

"No, no, not him. I mean Glasseye."

"I am not sure. I will only agree to that on one condition."

"And what's that?"

"We do the upgrade in stages. Every step, Tony. At every level, we run a test."

"Well of course, George, of course."

"Do you appreciate what that means?"

Barnstable smiled. "Not really. That's your job."

"No, George! It's our job! What it means is that someone, and not just anyone, has to be at the sending site in Brazil. South Africa?"

"Who do you suggest we send?"

"Let's work on one thing at a time. Let's get the engineering company and see what they say."

In Catherine's kitchen, there was more tea, and this time with biscuits. Thomas sat back and let them discuss their experiences. He was eager to find out what they had discovered.

"According to my mum," said Rosemary, "My great, great grandmother was an incredible witch. And now I've met her! She has created hundreds of spells that are still used today. And she told me something really exciting." She pulled a strange face. "What you do dear, she said to me – what you do, you take a lemon and lime, and my name Hanna Clisoll written down in reverse on a small piece of paper. Llosilc Annah." Rosemary spelt it out in a funny voice. "When you have those, dear, go to your mother's spell chest and find the tab spell."

Rosemary's impression of the crackly old witchy voice was making everyone laugh. She went on in the same odd way. "Lie it face down on a flat surface first. Then you must cut the lemon and lime in half. Exactly. It's very important the way you do this. Put one-half of the lemon and one-half of the lime together and place them in your mother's spell chest. That is precisely where the tab spell came from. Now take the other two citrus halves and place them together in your hand. Now you squeeze so the juices mix. That must be done for a minute. Then take them apart, and with just the lemon, hold it above the spell parchment, making sure you cover the whole area. Now toss the half lemon over your head. That's finished with."

The whole room was silent. Everyone was hanging onto every word now. Rosemary was whispering, too, adding to the drama.

"Next, take the lime and place it on the tab spell parchment. Start pushing it around, making sure you cover every inch. As you're doing that, place the paper with my name on it on the parchment, and move that around with the lime." Rosemary hesitated.

"Has anyone written this down?" asked Catherine. They all shook their heads. She turned back to Rosemary. "What's next?"

Rosemary looked blank and shrugged her shoulders. "Nothing."

Everyone gasped!

"But what was it for?" asked Caroline.

"And why would your great granny create a spell and go to such lengths to hide it?" asked Winnie.

Rosemary frowned, "I have no idea."

"Probably not needed at that time?" suggested Catherine.

"And now it is," Thomas said. "Only one thing for it, Rosemary."

"What's that, Thomas?"

"Get a lemon and a lime and carry out her instructions."

"Yes!" came a chorus of voices.

"But not right now," said Rosemary. "I need to write the spell down, think about it and make sure I'm in control."

"My turn!" said Susie. "I had all these dark shadows coming towards me, and I wanted to run away."

Thomas understood that, but her mother didn't. Winnie looked worried. She put her arm round her.

"I don't want to talk about mine," said Alisha.

"Nor do I," said Sarah.

"I quite liked mine," said Winnie.

Thomas moved across to sit next to Caroline, the daredevil girl who, back on the yoga weekend, had gone off with Susie to spy. She was shaking.

"Are you okay?" he asked.

"Mm, I'm still a bit shocked. I saw my cousin Peter. He had an accident a couple of years ago." A tear rolled down her cheek.

"You don't have to tell us," said Catherine.

Caroline shook her head. "No, I must talk about it; otherwise, it will gnaw away at me. It was very strange. He took me to the most wonderful places. And into dazzling light with an abundance of colour." She looked over at Catherine. "It was breathtaking."

Catherine nodded. "How wonderful."

"Then, just as he left me, he said...." There was a pause.

"What did he say?" Thomas asked softly.

"He said 'I hope you don't see these things again for a very long time. Don't come back early as I have'. Then he disappeared."

Thomas nodded. "I think he was showing you paradise," he said comfortingly.

Caroline burst into tears.

"It's been a traumatic day for all of us," said Sarah.

Thomas looked around the room, feeling a little guilty that he thought being in paradise was amazing. Most of the others had not had such a good experience. Catherine had wanted to murder Merston. Susie, although she seemed tough, was nervous, enough to worry her mother, Winnie and Sarah didn't want to talk about their experiences. Nor did Alisha. Caroline was crying and shaking her head. Rosemary was the only one, it seemed, who was still up for anything.

When they were back at Sarah's, to give her space, Thomas worked in the garden chopping the weeds out with the hoe while Sarah stayed inside. He was relieved when she called to him through the window and sensed that she wanted to talk.

"Tea and scones?"

"I'll just put the hoe away." *Here we go*, he thought to himself.

Inside she sat down at the table and began pouring the tea. Then she looked up at him. "It was like a picture show in my head. She showed me so much that I became confused."

"Your mum?"

"Yes. She kept mentioning the Shieling. What did she mean, Thomas?"

"I've never heard of that word before," he frowned, unsure what to tell her. "What context did she use it in?" He bit into his scone.

"She said 'you are a Shieling, my daughter. You must use your birth right to protect yourself'."

Thomas almost choked on his scone. *She's a Shieling? My Sarah?* He knew exactly what she was talking about. Jonas and Dominic had explained what a Shieling was while he was in the Garden of Souls. *But how on earth can I explain what they are to her?* Fortunately, Sarah continued to talk.

"Then, she said, 'my daughter, what you're entering into is very dangerous. The man I worked with was instrumental in my death, but it goes much deeper than that. Be careful and stay close to the one who's been chosen'. Then at the end, she said, 'be happy'."

Thomas sat there, concerned by what he had heard. "You don't know what she means, do you?"

For the second time that day, tears rolled down her face.

"Come on, honey," he said, "it's time for a hug."

She clung to him. "You're meant to be the expert, Thomas."

"I'll find out."

"What about Merston? What happened to him?"

Now he really had to be light on the truth. "He's trapped in a spell from Catherine."

"Can we talk to him?"

"Do you really want to talk to the man who was instrumental in your mother's death?"

Sarah took a moment. "Is Catherine going to finish off what she started years ago?"

"Definitely! But now, with what your mother said, maybe someone really does need to question him."

Sarah looked up at him hopefully. "That's got to be you, Thomas."

"Well, I think I'll need Catherine's help. She has a knack for finding the truth."

"She's a witch, that's why."

Thomas nodded.

"How do you know where he'd be?"

"I was given spiritual information."

Sarah looked miffed. "You didn't say anything."

"There was no point. We couldn't have dealt with him."

"Yes, but..."

He smiled, "But now we can. With the power we generated this morning, we've broken through the energy created when Catherine did her thing years ago."

"When she attacked him?"

"Yes. And now he's bound to one place. He can't escape."

"When do you plan on seeing him?"

Before Sarah could say anymore, he interrupted. "Tomorrow's not a good idea."

"How did you know I was going to say that? Okay, not tomorrow."

"Tomorrow is too soon. We need everything to calm down." He wiped the tears from her eyes with his thumbs and then wrapped his arms around her again not wanting to let go. "Everything is going to be ok," he whispered.

Chapter 35

When Thomas arrived at Catherine's at 7 am, he was met with some excitement. Rosemary was chuffed with herself. "I have figured out my great, great grandmother's secret spell! And it has a purpose."

"Tea, Thomas?" suggested Catherine.

"Of course."

"Toast?"

"Mm, yes please."

"Rosemary's also had some success with your dark witch from Brazil!"

Rosemary presented him with a parchment. "It's the tab spell, the one written in Latin. And here's another one I've discovered on the other side."

"What's this one called? I can't read this one either."

Rosemary laughed. "It's in French."

"Oh right," he said smiling. "I was never much good with French."

Catherine jumped in. "It's as good as the tab spell, Thomas. Maybe even better!"

That grabbed his attention. "Tell me then! What does it do? What's its purpose?"

"Do you remember asking me about the truth spell I used on Merston?"

"The one with the kick in it?"

"Yes. This is a protection spell similar to the high vibration protection you gave all of us. And this definitely has a kick!" She hesitated. "In fact, it's amazing."

Thomas looked at her and then at Rosemary. "And?"

Catherine smiled. "Patience, Thomas! We're enjoying this! Rosemary?"

"The spell has the ability to give back what your attacker is trying to give you!"

Thomas sat very still.

Rosemary looked at him. "Thinking are we, Thomas?"

"So," said Thomas, carefully, "are you saying, if an assailant attacks you or me with, say a knife with the intent to kill, he would kill himself instead."

"Yes. And it goes further. If your assailant has done harm before, then that will also harm him."

"How can you know that?"

"It's written down."

"Written where?"

"As with all spells it's within the body of the written instruction."

"Can we test it?"

Rosemary shrugged her shoulders.

Catherine looked at him. "Easy! We'll use it on Merston."

Thomas was disappointed with himself. *Why hadn't I thought of that?* "But first we ask a question or two!"

"That's if he knows anything relevant. He's been out of action for a very long time."

Thomas nodded. "You've cracked the other spell as well?"

"I have. It wasn't difficult, but..."

Thomas sighed. "There's always a 'but'."

"This is a big but. Why is this Brazilian witch capturing evil from a dark spirit and storing it in a jar? I think you'll have to go back there again and find out."

Thomas didn't fancy that idea. He thought about the money the witch was being paid. "It has to do with Susie's boss. It's got to be for him."

"You're only guessing."

"Yes, I know Catherine, but if you two witches don't know what she wants it for, I doubt that a witch would have use for that stuff."

"Stuff?"

"You know what I mean. Magic and things."

Catherine glanced angrily at him and then over at Rosemary. Rosemary just smiled.

"We need to ask why she's receiving so much money every month from Smithe," suggested Thomas.

"I suggest you ask Merston," said Rosemary. "Go on, both of you, go and deal with the scumbag."

Thomas looked at Catherine. "Shall we go pay him a little visit, Catherine? I am sure he can't wait to see us again!"

Catherine nodded and the next second the pair of them were up in the rafters of the tyre factory looking at Jeremy Merston's contorted face.

"How long does that truth concoction of yours last?"

"Months, Thomas."

"Okay. What if I bring him down and suspend him just above ground level? I will bring him round, then I'll step back, and you dig a little?"

Catherine couldn't wait. Once he was down and awake, she was eager to interrogate him.

"Be very careful," said Thomas. "Questions only, remember? I'll have a look around to make sure we're safe." For the first few moments, all he could hear were screams coming from Merston. If anyone was around, then they would hear. Then Merston settled down.

"Thomas," Catherine called.

He hurried back. "Why is he on the floor?" he asked.

Catherine sighed. “He’s messing around.”

“Yes, but why is he on the floor?”

Catherine seemed reluctant to elaborate.

“Come on, Catherine!”

“I’m angry. I have no patience for this person.”

“You were with him for two minutes. Now he’s on the floor.”

“I’m sorry.”

“Don’t you appreciate the importance of this?”

Catherine screwed her face up. “He gave me the impression he didn’t care. He was so cocky I zapped up the spell.”

“Oh No!”

“Just a little, Thomas, I promise.”

“Did the extra spell put him on the floor?”

“No...He’s lying on the floor because I punched him.”

“How do you expect to get any information out of him if you punch him? You step back and I’ll deal with him now. We don’t want to freak him out anymore. We want him to talk!”

Catherine reluctantly stepped away.

Thomas crouched down and placed his hand over Merston’s face. He came round instantly; Thomas dragged him to his feet. “Why did you kill Victoria?” he asked aggressively.

Merston stared at him. “How has the bind been broken? Where has my protection gone?”

“You don’t need to know that.”

“But you do!” Merston said. “If the witch who placed the bind,” he looked over at Catherine, “and that’s her. If she has cancelled it, that will send a warning out and my people will come looking for me.”

“Thirty years later? How can you be so sure?”

Merston rubbed his neck nervously. “They would. I know they would. Don’t ask anything.”

“You want her to sort you out again, then?”

“It’s not her who worries me.”

"Who then?"

"You! You're the new one, aren't you?"

Thomas just looked at him. "Maybe. So you should be very careful then."

"I was under the control of a sector."

"Which one?"

Merston glanced away.

Thomas raised his voice. "I'll ask the questions. You give the answers. I make the rules. Is that clear?"

Merston nodded.

"Which sector?"

"133."

"Why was Victoria killed?"

Merston stayed silent.

"Answer!"

"She found a way of suppressing the addiction in addicts."

Catherine gave a scream, Thomas stepped in front of her. "All in good time," he said to her. He placed his hand on her shoulder, and in a nano-second, she had been moved to a different part of the tyre factory. "Stay there until you calm down."

"Thomas, don't leave me here," she called.

"I will bring you back when you have calmed down. Now be quiet! Let me get on." Merston stared at Thomas. "You're going to kill me, aren't you?"

"Mr Merston, I don't kill. I just send people back. It's the soul maker's decision what happens from there."

Merston looked utterly terrified. "If you don't kill me, they will. That would be the end. No soul maker. Just the end."

"So, what choice have you got?"

"For the past thirty years, I have done nothing to compromise my soul.

"But you had no choice. The deed was done."

"Maybe, I have the same right to redemption as anyone.

The longer I'm around and resisting temptation, the better chance I have."

That threw Thomas.

"The question I need to ask is, who untied the bind?"

Thomas glanced over at Catherine at the other end of the tyre factory, then turned back to Merston. "Me. I organised it."

Fear had been showing on Merston's face, but when he heard that, the fear began to slip away.

"All that means is your lot are none the wiser," said Thomas.

"Almost true, but I still have the same rights as anyone. Because you are who you are, and with me showing remorse, surely, I have another chance? My lot, as you refer to them, know nothing, and from this moment, they are not my lot anymore."

"So, I suggest you start talking right now!"

"What do you want to know?"

"I'm not going to ask – you're going to tell me. I want every tiny detail. And if I think you're holding back on anything – anything, then don't complain when I..."

Merston raised his hand. "This is my only chance. I have no intention of giving you any reason to dispose of me."

This wasn't exactly what Thomas had expected to hear. On the one hand, he had Catherine who was at the other end of the tyre factory wanting to tear Merston to bits, though she had calmed down. Then there was Sarah, who was in two minds about what should be done with this man. He knew he needed to do something big to numb the feeling being shared here now by the two of them. *But what?* The only thing he had going for him was the information Merston could give him.

Then an idea came to him. If he could flush out the darksider who gave Merston the order to kill Victoria, then that might be good enough to satisfy them. In an instant, he was beside Catherine, stretching the truth and trying to convince her that it was not a good idea to destroy Merston.

"All these years I have suffered and you're asking me to wait?" she cried.

"Come on, Catherine. You're a rational person. Wouldn't it be better to flush out the darksider that is responsible?"

"And what about Sarah?"

"I'll deal with Sarah. Now come back with me and listen."

Huffing, Catherine followed Thomas.

"Right, Merston! Begin!"

Merston started from the first day he had an encounter with a darksider, the one who eventually ended up running sector 133. Both Thomas and Catherine were shocked at the number of people who were involved.

"And how many sectors are there?" Catherine asked.

"Twenty. Maybe twenty-five."

Thomas did the sums. "So that's three hundred per sector? Catherine, that's thousands of darksiders!"

She pulled him to one side. "Perhaps I could live with the idea of Merston being an asset but if you think I am going to be nice to him, then you have another thing coming," she whispered.

Thomas smiled. The plan was taking shape. Now all he had to do was win Sarah over. But there was one more question.

"Where are we going to keep Merston?" asked Catherine? "We can't leave him here."

"You can tie him to his house."

"Of course, I have the perfect spell,"

"How will I get provisions?" asked Merston overhearing their plan. "I get hungry!"

"Online shopping!" said Catherine.

Thomas pulled Catherine to the side so Merston couldn't hear them. "How long will it take you to place the spell?" asked Thomas.

"Two minutes."

"Do you have everything you need?"

"Yes."

Thomas put his hands on Catherine and Merston's shoulders and the next moment, they were outside Merston's house, on the other side of Guildford.

"Go inside," said Thomas. "But remember – if you put one foot wrong then I will send you back and..."

Merston nodded and walked up the steps to his front door.

Immediately after the door closed, Catherine cast the spell. A strange purple light flashed across the house.

"The toad is secure. Home now!" she said triumphantly.

Chapter 36

Rosemary welcomed them with open arms. After Thomas started to explain what happened, he suggested putting a bind in with the tie spell. "We don't want darksiders getting in."

"I can, but is there any need? Nothing has changed as far as they are concerned," said Rosemary.

"Is it the same spell you used when we dealt with the searcher?" asked Thomas.

"You mean the warning spell alerting us when additional darksiders enter?"

"Yes."

"Are you saying there might be a new darksider? If so, I'll have to modify the spell. That calls for a nice cup of tea." Rosemary headed towards the kitchen.

"No, not a new one". Thomas calls out, as she walked away. Thomas glanced at Catherine. "There is one already here and I am quite sure that they will come looking for Merston."

"This is a dangerous game we're playing. We could lose your informant," Catherine said looking worried.

"Five minutes ago, you wanted to tear him to pieces! Now you're concerned about him."

"Don't be awkward, Thomas. Anyway, I've come round to

your way of thinking. I'll modify the spell. Keeping Merston alive means we could wipe out all the scum. Now tell me precisely what you have in mind?"

He hesitated. *Should I tell her?* He didn't have to worry as Catherine knew exactly what he was thinking.

"So, you want to mask Merston's life force. That will send a message to the Section, won't it? They will no doubt send an aggressive darksider."

"Yes, a soldier."

"So, he'll be sent to see what's going on. And you'll be waiting for him!" said Catherine. "And then you'll do what you do. Then what?"

"Simple. You put the same truth spell on him as you did Merston. And he will have no option but to tell us how to locate the top darksider. Once I have that information, you can change Merston's life force back. Timing is imperative. We'll only have a few minutes."

"Then change Merston's life force back sooner. When the soldier shows up, we won't wait."

"Yes, you're right! Good thinking. We can create some confusion. Hopefully, that will stop them from looking any further."

"Then we'll have two darksiders to deal with! The soldier and the one who runs the section. What happens to him?" asked Catherine.

"The boss? I'll wait a couple of weeks and then send him back to the Soul Maker."

"I'll need another spell from you to wipe the amount of time we've had with the soldier from his memory. Or he has an accident. I will need to work out the finer details and then I will let you know."

Catherine smiled. "I can arrange the memory spell. That's easy. But we have to be exact with the time."

"Yes, I'll use the stopwatch on my phone. The time is critical! We want the soldier to walk away just confused."

Catherine looked sideways at him. "You think you're clever, Thomas, don't you?"

"You're the clever one, Catherine," he laughed.

Just then, Rosemary walked into the spell room with the tea. "What happened?" Thomas let Catherine explain.

Rosemary stared at them. "He's still alive? I've lived with the damage he did to you for the past thirty years! Please tell me you're joking."

"Yes, dear, he is alive but listen..."

When it was all explained to her, and what had been provisionally decided, she understood.

"Thank you, Rosemary," Thomas said.

"Let's get the spell going," suggested Catherine.

Thomas waited. He needed that in place before altering Merston's energy force. An hour passed and he was becoming impatient. He began pacing up and down in the spell room.

Rosemary stopped what she was doing and went out to the kitchen. She came back with some more tea. "Here, sit down and drink this. Another five minutes Thomas and we're done."

He took the mug. "Thanks. Will we need to go back to Merston's house to set the spell?"

"No, we can cast it from here."

Catherine turned around from the workbench and smiled. "It's done, Thomas. I'm finished! Now you can do your bit."

He was up like a shot. "I'll be back in five minutes. I need to mask his life force." He hurried out of the door and was gone.

Back at Merston's house, he took a deep breath and called on all his resources to enable him to create an energy wall so powerful it would block the life force coming from Merston. That should do it. *Now let's see how long the section takes to pick up on it.*

In less than five minutes he was back at Catherine's. She described to him exactly what she had done, and Rosemary showed him how the spell had been linked to him. He wouldn't have to wait for either of them to inform him of darksider activity.

"Wow, that's impressive! I wonder how long it will take them to notice." Immediately he had mentioned the darksiders, an alarm sounded in the spell room and in his head at the very same moment.

"There's your answer Thomas, eight minutes!" Rosemary said gleefully.

"I'm off!" he said. "I'll be back for you shortly, Catherine. Is everything ready?"

She nodded. "Yes. Now go but be careful."

Instantly he was back at Merston's house.

The spell was set to trigger the alarm when evil was fifty metres away from the spell source, so it would be easy to spot the darksider before Merston had any idea what was going on. His eyes narrowed as he watched the darksider walk towards the house. He looked quite normal, apart from his height. *Well over 6ft!* He was wearing a light-coloured trench coat, down beyond his knees. His rough looking face was heavily set. He walked slowly towards the house whilst looking around, as if he was expecting trouble.

Thomas was between him and the target, Merston. With his phone ready he set the stop watch. The darksider was now twenty metres away and already Thomas was feeling a wave of nausea washing over him. *He must be a powerful soldier.* He waited. *Closer, a little closer. Now!* He smothered the darksider with energy force. Then he turned and removed the force controlling Merston's house. All that took just moments. Now all that remained, was to keep the darksider somewhere safe while Catherine did her part of the job.

In another moment, back at the old tyre factory and well out of sight, Thomas was placing the darksider into a subdued frame of mind. *Now to get Catherine.* They were back in seconds, and she was splashing her truth concoction over him. Immediately the darksider began revealing all his secrets. Catherine made notes where the section was based, how many members, their projects, plans, and the unlimited funds they could call upon. What he didn't know was who was in absolute control.

Although he didn't know who the top man was, Thomas knew who managed the section in his sights, and had names of some of the others, and he was satisfied. But there was still the tricky bit to do. The timer on the phone was showing four and a half minutes. He had to get the darksider back to exactly where he had been so Catherine could perform the second spell to erase the four and a half minutes, plus a few safety seconds. Thomas looked at her. She nodded, and he whisked the three of them back to the street, hoping no one was around. Their plan all worked with military precision. He pulled Catherine back. The spell had disorientated the darksider.

Thomas spun around and watched in horror as out of nowhere, three lads on motorbikes appeared. Riding at a pace. They went straight into the darksider, leaving him sprawled across the pavement, then sped off shouting abuse back at their victim.

Catherine jumped high in the air, shocked at what she had just witnessed. Seconds later, when they had returned to her house, she was still shocked. "What happened?"

Thomas started to laugh.

"Why are you laughing?"

"Sorry, Catherine. I forgot to tell you that I was organising those lads to add more confusion. But at least now, the stunt we've just pulled off can't go wrong."

"What did you organise, Thomas?" asked Rosemary.

Catherine told her.

Rosemary thought he had done well, but Catherine didn't comment.

"Now I need to go straight back to make sure it's all worked, and the darksider hasn't continued on to the house."

"Better get on then," said Catherine.

As Thomas left, preoccupied with Merston and the darksider, Rosemary called after him. "We need to talk about your witch in Brazil!"

"I shan't be long."

Immediately he was back at the scene, and he was just in time to see a passerby giving the darksider a hand up.

"Are you alright?" he heard the man ask.

"Thank you, I'm fine." He did sound quite shaken, but then to Thomas's horror, he turned and continued to make his way toward Merston's house.

Quickly Thomas slipped across the road. Now he was behind the darksider, intending to take action. *One zap, and perhaps the same Irish beach might be the place to take him.*

A phone rang and the darksider stopped. He reached inside his jacket for it and took the call. A moment later, he turned around. Now he was walking away from Merston's house, back towards Thomas. *Five metres. Four metres and closing.* Thomas moved to the edge of the pavement, keeping his head down, looking at the road, carefully controlling his energy force. He could hear the darksider muttering. "False alarm! They should get their act together!" As he passed by, Thomas felt a wave of deep dark evil turning his stomach. He wanted to throw up.

As they drew further apart, relief swept over Thomas. The evil influence subsided. He crossed the road again, looking back, giving himself a chance to check the situation. It was all clear now. The darksider had obviously been told it was a false alarm. After all, Merston's life force was back again and now the darksider had gone. Dealing with the soldier had been nerve-racking! *Now all I have to do is explain this to Sarah.*

Back at Catherine's house a second later, Rosemary had another problem to present to him.

"First, listen to this," he said and explained what had happened.

"So, the plan is working so far," she said smiling.

Thomas held up crossed fingers.

Rosemary nodded. "After you hear what I have to say, I think you'll need another plan. Thomas, you'll need to sit for this."

He screwed up his face and obediently sat down.

Rosemary pointed to the pile of old manuscripts. "I've been reading some old ones, and I have a good idea what your witch is up to."

Thomas just stared at Rosemary. "I'm not going to like this, am I?"

"No, not a lot."

He let out a sigh. "Go on then, tell me."

"Your witch – by the way, what's her name? I can't keep calling her your witch."

"I'm not sure. They seem to call her Kamilah, but that might not be her real name. She is number twenty on Smithe's payment list."

"Okay, then let's call her Miss Twenty! She has worked out how to store dark matter from evil souls, and the only reason I can see why she would need to do that is..." Rosemary hesitated.

Thomas frowned. "Tell me."

"She is going to introduce it to another soul."

"And what will that do?"

"The only reason for that is to create a super evil being."

"Why would she want to do that?"

"Because she's being paid to do it, I guess! What you should be asking is why Smithe wants her to do that!"

Thomas thought about the payment list. He was confused. "Well you've called her Miss Twenty, but so many others are on that list. I can't figure this out." He looked over at Catherine.

"Don't look at me, Thomas! I haven't a clue."

"I think you should go back to Brazil and do a bit of spying," said Rosemary. "I can make up a list of what to look for in Miss Twenty's spell room. Then it might be an idea to visit another witch on that list you have."

"To see if they are doing the same?"

"Yes, exactly."

"I think you're right. I will. I'll sort that out as soon as you give me a list. Don't forget I'm not a witch, so do it in English please!" Thomas said smiling.

Rosemary laughed and led him to the spell room. She pointed to shelves of ingredient bottles. "These are the kinds of potions she'll have if she's doing what we think she's doing. And there should be a temperature-controlled storage facility too. The dark matter needs to be kept cool to control the evil."

"Would that mean it could be difficult to move?"

Rosemary hesitated, unsure by what he meant.

"Could she send it by plane?"

"Oh no. That would be impossible. It's much too volatile for that."

"Right! I'm going to get to the bottom of this now! Stand by the phone, and I'll call you from Brazil!"

A moment later, the air was hot and dusty, and he was looking inside the dark witch's house. Nobody was at home. He whizzed around on the ground floor. *Nothing*. The first floor was void of anything witchy and had very few cupboards to check. *Nothing*. He had a quick look in the roof space. *Nothing*. Back downstairs, he looked for a basement. *None. Where else?* Suddenly he remembered the car had been parked round the back somewhere, so he went outside.

The car was parked next to a building that looked like a garage but twice the size. Inside, there was space for the car, then a wall beyond that. Thomas moved forward and then stopped dead in his tracks, he could sense the witch. *Is she on the other side of the wall?* His shadow stepped through into another room. *Absolutely amazing!* He found himself in a mini laboratory, the witch was busy working, distilling something. *A juicer, perhaps?* He got a little closer and noticed that whatever liquid ran from one outlet, something else was coming out of the other outlet. *What is that liquid?* The concoction oozing out of the last outlet was being fed through a hose into what appeared to be a power socket, only much larger.

He needed to make a closer inspection. There were vials and glass containers on every shelf, just as Rosemary had predicted. He could see that he was definitely rubbing shoulders with one of the dark witches. He made a mental note of exactly what was there to tell Rosemary. But her idea that there should be a cold storage unit was wrong. He couldn't see anything like that.

The still had finished and switched itself off. Now closer in, he could look at the metal box, the part that looked like a power socket and he realised that it was much more sophisticated than he had first thought. He could see it must have a one-way valve because when the witch removed the hose leading from the still into this metal box, nothing escaped. *What is going on here?*

There was a cap sitting on top of the box and Thomas watched as the witch reached for that and screwed it tight into the inlet where the hose had been attached. Kamilah picked up the box, walked across the laboratory and opened a concealed door. Thomas hadn't spotted that. He peered into a tiny room and was astonished again. Now he was looking at an IT room with super electronic computer wizardry within. *Are these computers*? The witch placed her container box on the strange computer and plugged in leads to connect the box to it. Then she opened a drawer below, reached in and brought out what looked like a copper bracelet with two lightweight leads attached. Thomas watched on, fascinated as she placed the bracelet around the wrist of her right hand. As she did it, he noticed marks on her arms. *Burn marks?* Suddenly he remembered Saffron had similar marks on her neck, but he was still none the wiser about what was going on.

The witch plugged the bracelet leads into the computer too, and sat down on a small stool. The computer was on, and the box was coming to life. She leaned in and threw another switch. The power surge dimmed the lights, and she let out a sudden screech and words Thomas didn't understand. She quickly pulled the bracelet from her wrist and dropped it. *Is it burning her?* Thomas had no idea what he was witnessing. *I've seen enough!*

Moments later he was knocking on Catherine's door.

Rosemary opened it. "That didn't take long! How did you do?"

"Can we go to the spell room? I need to point out what she had?"

"Are you alright?"

He nodded and as they walked, Rosemary turned and gave him a worried look.

Catherine appeared at the end of the hall. "Come on then, Thomas. Let's see if we can work out what your Miss Twenty is up to."

In the spell room, Thomas cast his eye over all their containers "Here, this stuff," he announced pointing. "She had this. Only she had it in huge jars. And this..." He went along the shelf, pointing out what else he had seen. Then he explained what she had done.

Neither of them could think what she had been doing.

"Leave this with us," said Catherine. "Rosemary will do a bit of research. She's good at that."

"One last thing before I go."

"What?" Catherine asked.

"Sarah is sure to ask about Merston. It will look to her as if it were your decision not to send him back. Are you alright with that? She is going to go mad when she hears."

"Yes I am. Don't worry."

Chapter 37

Thomas arrived home mid-morning. He assumed Sarah would be taking a class. He wasn't sure whether to meet her there or wait until she called. At that very moment, the phone rang.

"Hi, Honey. Are things okay?"

"Mm, yeah."

"I've given some thought to Merston." She seemed upbeat, which was a pleasant surprise.

"What's that, honey?"

"I've decided I have no right to decide his fate. I trust you'll do what's appropriate."

Thomas thought for a moment. *Should I mention anything?* "Okay," he said hesitantly.

"I want to talk to my mum again. Can I?" Sarah announced, taking Thomas by surprise.

"Well, yes." *Maybe this is an opportunity to keep Sarah in the dark a little.* "I'll have to ask how to do it. Is this going to lead somewhere?"

"Yes, Thomas, it is! It's going to lead to I want to know."

He giggled. "Okay, I'll work on it."

"Thanks honey. See you tonight."

"You will! You definitely will." He put the phone down. He

had a lot on his mind, and he knew she wouldn't give up on her quest. He had to find a way for her soul to mingle with her mother's. *Jamie!* That was the answer. He focussed.

Within moments Jamie answered. *What's up?*

Thomas explained and Jamie didn't do his usual and come up with a working solution. Instead, he suggested Thomas contact the main Shide, Jonas Barley.

This is a big deal, Thomas. Only Jonas can deal with this.

That wasn't what Thomas wanted to hear, but it seemed he had no choice. A moment later, Jonas was in his head. For the second time he explained what he wanted. Jonas listened without interruption. When he'd finished, Jonas suggested they meet up later at his city office.

As you haven't been before, I'll meet you outside Mansion House Station. Does that suit you, Thomas?

Yes. Thank you, Jonas. When?

I have a meeting shortly, but I'll be free in an hour. I'll contact you then.

Thomas went back to Jamie. *Jonas is the only one who can sort it out for you. It's a very sophisticated request, and he is the only soul that can make it happen.*

Before I go, tell me, what do you have in mind for Merston? Jamie asked.

Nothing gets by you! Thomas chuckled.

I'm your watchful eye looking out for you. I have to know.

That's comforting, Jamie! So, he's tied into his house and can't go anywhere. But there's a small fly in the ointment.

What's that?

He's showing remorse. Or so he says but he could be faking it to save his soul.

You have to take that as gospel! You can't be the judge. And don't forget he was under Catherine's truth spell.

That's true. But the job I'm doing for you lot has made me judgemental. I have no intention of taking chances. I can't send him back, but I'm going to use him to flush out as many of his sector as I can. I'm going to start in a week or two. No, a little longer. Maybe four weeks. Then I'll attack section 133. That will keep whoever's pulling the strings on edge.

Be careful. Rumour has it that these sections have enormous numbers of people.

I gathered that from talking to Merston.

Good. Did he tell you how they could reduce your energy level?

Thomas pulled a face. *I should have known that,* Thomas thought. *Maybe that's where you come in, Jamie.*

Go on.

You'll be with me!

Jamie laughed. *You do remember I'm not allowed to get involved or help in your activities.*

How could I forget? But you're here to protect me should I go gung-ho into a bunch of darksiders, aren't you?

You wouldn't do that, would you?

Yes, I would!

In that case, great. Some action at last! What's the plan?

Jamie's words took him by surprise, and he was glad to have an ally. Thomas hadn't made a plan, and to keep Jamie on board, he had to think fast. *Well, I know where the main man is and his top cronies too. But what I don't know is names and what they look like.* He weighed up what he remembered. *When I had my enhancement, I was bombarded with information. It didn't mean much to me at the time. But now... How do I organise a Searcher?*

Jamie grinned. *Your brain is working overtime. That's another little job for Jonas. He'll tell you. Sounds like you have a plan. Don't forget, if you have any issues give me a shout. I'll be ready when you're ready. Bye kiddo!*

It was less than an hour later when Jonas contacted Thomas. *Are you ready?*

As soon as Jonas asked, Thomas was standing outside the Mansion House Station. Thomas smiled. *Well that was good timing.*

"You've mastered travelling," Jonas said shaking his hand.

Thomas nodded. "An argument with a tree taught me to focus."

"The one in the church grounds, if I recall." Jonas knew everything. He looked around, checking that it was safe to leave the street. "I'll take you to the basement office. It's secure."

A moment later, Thomas was being shown around. He immediately noticed the lack of windows and doors.

"As you can see, only our people get in."

"Yes, I can see that." He sat down with Jonas and began to explain the problem. "I'm sorry for intruding on your time. I didn't think this would involve you."

"That's not a problem, Thomas. Normally it wouldn't, but the circumstances surrounding Sarah and her mother are unique. There is one thing though, if Sarah pushes for more contact, it will ignite history that she may not be prepared for."

Thomas instinctively knew he shouldn't ask about the history surrounding Sarah and her mother.

"And Thomas," Jonas continued, "you will be pulled in. You must be careful and stay absolutely focused."

Thomas leaned forward, hoping Jonas might elaborate.

"What you are working on at the moment, Thomas, is within your capabilities," Jonas paused. "But..."

Thomas smiled. "There's always a 'but'."

"It's only a little 'but'. And Merston giving his contribution has helped."

"What's the 'but'?"

"Levi Smallcast. He's the 'but."

"So, he's the main man, then?"

"Yes. He's in Merston's bunch. Evil as they come, and with that comes power. One to one, you're more than his match. But one to one may not happen. That's when you could run into trouble. So, remember, concentrate and do not get distracted."

"You mean Sarah."

"Yes. And what comes with her."

"I'm not sure I have a lot of choice," Thomas said, "Pandora's Box has been opened."

Jonas gave Thomas an understanding smile. "I agree. Just be very careful. You have great ability now. Use it and put Sarah's distraction in another box, to be opened only when it's safe to do so."

"Don't worry. I'm on it."

"Now, down to business, Thomas. I'll open a channel directly to the soul that is Sarah's mother. All you have to do is tap into the activity you created on Sunday that has just passed."

Thomas nodded slowly, biting his lip and thinking hard while Jonas explained.

"Don't be concerned. It's simple. Concentrate on that day, and you'll get a picture in your mind, just like a television screen. Concentrate on Sarah and get inside her mind, as you know you are capable of doing. When that's done, you'll be in the thoughts going to her mother. Then contact through history is yours. You'll have the ability to allow Sarah's soul to mingle with her mother's. You will be the instrument."

Thomas sat quietly for a moment. "Is there a time restraint or limit?"

"No, it will be set forever. It's history."

"When do you think I could do this?"

"It's set already. I've just opened the channel."

"Wow! That was quick."

"Just be aware of the consequences before you act."

"Of course. Should I try to explain to Sarah that she may not like what she gets?"

"I don't think any amount of persuasion will work."

"Why?"

"Her mother's soul is calling out to her. Since the contact on Sunday, a bridge has been formed, and Victoria will not give up."

"Why."

"Because the love of mother and daughter is the most powerful emotion there is. She knows about you and your destiny and the dangers you, and now her daughter too, will face. She will go to any lengths to protect Sarah from unnatural danger."

"What about me?"

"You have us."

Thomas pulled his coat closer. "This isn't simple, is it?" He needed to know more. "Exactly how does this history travel work? It's baffling me."

"If you consider how far you've come in the past month, you've done exceptionally well. But your fast track through evolution is all well and good, but what it can't do is re-set your rationale. That's where the frustration develops."

"So, how do I overcome that?"

"You ask."

"Okay. How does history travel work?"

Jonas thought for a moment. "Do you remember one of your early days of school, when you were very young?"

Thomas nodded.

"That's memory, and that's the path you travel down. Memory is history if you think about it. And it makes sense."

Thomas puffed his cheeks out. "I suppose so."

"What else do you have on your mind?"

"I need a little help to deal with Levi Smallcast and his soldiers. I know where to find them now, but I don't know who's who. And as you have mentioned, he's powerful. I would find it helpful to know his movements and hopefully those of the others too. My plan is to hit the top and work down, one at a time. Then maybe panic the rest of them and send them scurrying."

"Sounds like a good plan. I gather you want the services of a searcher, then?"

"Yes, but not any searcher. I do have a name in my head – Magli Qualm. I don't know who he is, but I've assumed my team of old souls armed me with his name?"

"I'm impressed. Yes, you're right. Your team of old souls would have done that. Even I am amazed at what can be done. So Magli it is. Is now a good time?"

"I didn't expect you to say that."

Jonas smiled. "Let's get it done."

Magli instantly appeared! Thomas almost jumped out of his skin. Jonas greeted Magli warmly who then introduced him to Thomas, who was quite shaken by the suddenness of the searcher's arrival. Magli was very strange. He was nothing like anyone Thomas had ever seen before. An overgrown leprechaun came to mind.

Then Magli spoke. "Don't concern yourself about my appearance. This is my natural state and…" Magli transformed himself. Now he was completely different, almost normal looking.

"Christ! How did you do that?" asked Thomas.

"Evolution, Mr Thomas. It's just evolution."

"I'm impressed."

"So, you should be Mr Thomas. So, you should be," said Magli.

Thomas laughed and turned to Jonas. "How many years forward do I have to go to be able to do that?"

"About a hundred thousand. Give or take."

"Ah, I'll stick with what I've got then! Shall I explain the situation to Magli?"

"Yes."

Thomas told Magli about Merston and the plan he had in mind. "It will take time, of course."

"Why wait? What is your time scale, Mr Thomas? It will take me only a day to locate the top ten. Then you can pick them off. I could advise you when they are vulnerable."

Thomas looked at Jonas.

"With Magli looking out for you, why not, Thomas?"

He took a deep breath. "I'll be ready when you call Magli."

Jonas smiled. "Now you've been here, Thomas, you can do away with the Mansion House Station meet. Just turn up here if you're unsure at any time."

"Thank you, Jonas. And thank you, Magli, it has been a pleasure."

Chapter 38

A little later, Thomas arrived at Sarah's yoga class and was in time for a hug before the rest of the class turned up. With Saffron expected, he lowered his vibration right down to an undetectable level and sat in the corner waiting. Sarah, unaware of that complication, began to organise the class as they arrived.

Just as the class was about to start, Saffron rushed in, in such a hurry she almost tripped over the pile of mats by the door. She quickly acknowledged Sarah and made her way to her usual place, the spot she had made her own.

"Right, everyone. Shall we begin?"

Thomas stood up, ready to start stretching. Casually he glanced over to check Saffron's body language. He noticed the stress on her face and the tension in her shoulders. *What is going on with her? Has she talked to George Smithe? When Magli and I start attacking Section 133, how long will it take for Saffron to find out?*

"Are you with us, Thomas?" called Sarah.

He glanced around. Everybody had turned their heads to the left. With a little grin on his face, he joined in.

When the class finished Thomas helped Sarah collect the mats to clear the hall. She picked up the last mat and placed it on the pile. "Are you coming over later, honey?"

"Yes, please," he said, really pleased that she had asked. "I'll follow you back. And we can discuss what we were speaking about this morning."

Sarah's eyes widened with a look of nervous excitement. "Ooh, yes. And we'll have something to eat."

Over dinner, the two of them decided they would try – 'try', as Thomas put it, to contact Sarah's mum at the weekend. Sarah was thrilled, but Thomas was apprehensive. *I just hope and pray that nothing bad happens. I don't want my Sarah hurt.*

Two days had passed. Now Magli was suddenly in Thomas's head.

Mr Thomas, are you there?

Thomas chuckled. Magli had such a polite way about him. *Yes, Magli, I'm here.*

I've made some progress, Mr Thomas. Two and three on the hit list have been mapped. They have been arrogantly swanning around as if nothing can touch them. That makes them an easy target. But the top man, he's another matter. He's either clever or nervous. I think he knows you're around, Mr Thomas.

Tell me more.

He has two powerful companions – two darksiders who are always with him. They protect him and the space around him. I can't see past them.

Maybe we need to separate them – somehow. Thomas hesitated. *And in the sector – how many do they have?*

Lots.

Are you talking hundreds?

Yes, Mr Thomas. There aren't that many with enough power to bother you unless they team up and that would be only twentyish. The rest are uninitiated and don't pose any threat.

So, they are normal humans?

Not quite. Do you want time to think about it?

Are you sure, that's it? I've thought about it.

That was quick. There is nothing more to report. What's your plan?

I need to contact my friend, Catherine.

The witch?

Yes. She has a spell that can control whoever she wants. What about using that to isolate the two benchmen? Then I could move Mr Levi Smallcast out of contact as well.

Magli remained silent.

Then we'll use the same spell that was placed over Merston's colleague. Thomas began to explain how he had controlled the soldier that was sent to investigate Merston's life force.

Magli sighed. *It won't be as easy as that, Mr Thomas. The soldier you dealt with was powerful, yes. But these three combined have super powers. I don't know how your witch Catherine will be able to get close enough to perform her spell.*

These two benchmen, are they in your top twenty? Thomas asked.

No.

No? How's that?

Because they are just a power source, Mr Thomas. A temporary power, though.

Where does their temporary power come from?

It's complicated. I sense Levi Smallcast has been prolific in doing dark deeds for his masters. That gives him privileges. One of those is extra protection if he chooses. Extra protection includes insight, which could cause a problem.

That's a warning system, isn't it.

Yes, and it probably has a range of fifty metres. Unless your witch can dispense her spell from fifty metres away, your plan won't work.

Is Levi Smallcast untouchable then?

Magli wasn't sure.

I'll contact Catherine and see what she can come up with.

You check with Catherine. Mr Thomas, and I'll check out who this Mr Smallcast communicates with. It might actually be worth the effort to keep him around.

Thomas agreed. *I'll contact you within twenty-four hours.*

Back at Catherine's house, Thomas sat down to explain the problem. Rosemary wanted to know why with their help, he couldn't deal with the three of them in one go. Her question meant he had to go into greater detail, which was exhausting, and he did it with some reluctance. He was relieved when they finally understood the problem.

"Can your spell be delivered from a distance?" he asked.

"No!" They both said firmly.

"Such a sophisticated and powerful spell has to be delivered up close," said Catherine.

Thomas sighed. "Plan B then."

"And what's that, Thomas?"

"I haven't a clue," Thomas growled. "I'll have to think. I will just need you to be prepared."

"We'll work on what's possible today, Thomas," said Catherine, "and I'll call you when we're done. Okay?"

Rosemary jumped up. "Thomas, are you with us?"

Catherine was staring at him. "What's wrong?"

"I'm getting a buzzing in my head again." Thomas clutched his forehead. "It's been on and off for a couple of hours now. I can't shift it. My concentration is suffering. It must be to do with Sunday. It probably overloaded my brain. That's if my brain's still there."

Catherine looked closely into his eyes. "I'll make a potion for you," she said. "Your mind is going too fast, Thomas. You need to stop and relax."

Rosemary agreed, "I'll do the potion. Two minutes, Thomas. That's all it'll take."

"Then what?"

"Then you'll know what's causing the problem. Now just sit there and relax if you can."

Thomas did as he was told. His mind was now spinning. Two minutes later, Rosemary presented him with a glass containing the most obnoxious smelling substance ever. As she handed the glass to him, he looked at her in amazement. "What's in here?"

She stared at him, astonished he was even asking.

"There must be something dead in the glass. It smells awful."

Rosemary laughed. "Just drink it and stop whinging."

He obeyed, confident that she knew what she was doing. After all, she was a witch. The potion worked almost immediately. The buzzing stopped. He sat back and made himself comfy and was about to doze off when suddenly a voice came into his head. It was crystal clear. *Jamie? No, not him. Magli? Not Magli, either.* Then it dawned on him. The voice was female. He sat bolt upright in the chair, concentrating on the voice.

Thomas? It's Victoria, Sarah's mother.

"What is it, Thomas?" asked Rosemary.

"Ssh," whispered Catherine.

Victoria spoke again. *A bridge has been made that allows me to contact you, thank goodness. You must know I have an interest in your movements and the work you have been asked to do.*

Thomas stayed very quiet.

Think of me as one of your helpers. Take your time, Thomas. I understand this wasn't what you were expecting after sipping the concoction Catherine thought of and Rosemary prepared for you. Catherine certainly hasn't lost her touch.

No, I mean yes. Thomas could hear his own voice inside his head again, just as if he were talking to Jamie or Jonas. *This is because of Sarah, isn't it?*

That's the easy analogy and maybe the answer for you at the moment. But it's way above that. Sarah needs to be kept safe. That means I need to keep you safe.

Thomas was beginning to relax and settle into the conversation. *I'm all for that! I assume you're not sure about my approach in dealing with Section 133.*

Perhaps you need to be more subtle. The plan is okay, all bar one ingredient.

What do you have in mind?

A young shieling.

That's the second time I've heard that word. Thomas hesitated. *You mentioned that to Sarah. What does it mean?*

This is not the right time to explain Thomas.

When will it be the right time?

You have a task ahead of you. Let's concentrate on what's to be done. When are you thinking of starting?

With your help, as soon as I can.

You have to arrange the time and place with Magli then, but make sure you have the spell organised. Contact me on the day. Then I'll explain how a shieling will help you.

As suddenly as she came, she was gone.

"So that was the buzzing in my head." Thomas said to himself, realising now he was speaking out loud. He could feel himself shaking.

"What was it?" Rosemary sounded excited.

"She's gone now."

"Come on, Thomas, what just went on?"

Catherine put her hand on Rosemary's shoulder. "Give him a moment," she said quietly.

Thomas took that moment to catch his breath. He was in two minds about whether he should mention it had been Victoria he had been speaking with. *No, I won't mention any name.* "A spirit wanted to make contact." He hesitated and then standing up very straight and tall, he turned towards Catherine. "All that buzzing in my head, driving me mad. It was Victoria!"

Catherine turned white. Her eyes welled up with tears. Rosemary put her arm around her mum. For a moment or two, the only sound that could be heard was a clock ticking. Then Catherine wiped the tears from her cheeks.

"What did Victoria want?" she asked quietly. "Why did she contact you?"

"And how?" asked Rosemary.

"She said she wanted to help, as you are doing. She said that you will have a way of delivering the spell at close quarters. She also mentioned you haven't lost your touch with the potion I just drank, Catherine."

That lifted Catherine's spirits.

Rosemary stared at him. "She spoke to you? She knows what we're doing?"

He nodded. "But I'm not sure at the moment how all this is going to work."

Catherine stood up calmly. "I suppose we'd better get on with your spell then."

Rosemary gathered up the empty potion glass. "It'll take six hours to prepare and another four hours to settle."

Catherine and Rosemary had work to do so Thomas left. Now Victoria was involved in orchestrating the downfall of section 133, his plan had changed. He needed to connect with Magli. He was home alone, so he focused on him.

Mr Thomas! Can I assume you have it worked out?

With a little help, yes.

I will transfer Mr Levi Smallcast's movements. You will have whatever you need. Clear your mind, please. Ready?

A second later, Thomas had as much information on Mr Levi Smallcast as Magli had. *Now I can see an obvious spot to tackle him.*

Where will that be, Mr Thomas?

When he is leaving his mother's house.

Yes, no doubt you've noticed he's on his own for a minute

when he leaves his mother's house and contacts his minders. Did you notice anything else?

Yes. His mother's house is a permanent fortress. The man is certainly organised. This isn't going to be easy.

You are right on both counts, Mr Thomas, but as long as you're as disciplined as he is, then you will have no issues. If I might suggest, you should hit number two and number three straight after. They are easy targets now, but that could change after the demise of Mr Levi Smallcast.

Thomas had thought of holding Smallcast and trying to gain information, but now with Magli suggesting immediate action, he was having second thoughts.

He's an important man in the organisation, Mr Thomas. They won't like anyone taking out one of their favourite players. It won't be safe trying to hold him.

You're so right, Magli. I'll send him back immediately. That goes for his minders and the other two up the chain as well. Then I'll back off.

I will leave it with you then, Mr Thomas. Call when you need me.

I will. Thanks, Magli.

Thomas's confidence was growing. Now he felt brave enough to call on Victoria to explain how he proposed to deal with Levi Smallcast and to mention the time and place.

Immediately, Victoria popped into his head. *I'll arrange a meeting point a few minutes away from the house where Levi Smallcast's mother lives. The shieling will meet you there, you will pass the spell over, so it can be delivered at close range.*

How will I know who the shieling is?

She'll know you, Thomas. Have you told Catherine and Rosemary that instead of them, a shieling will deliver the spell?

That's a point. I will do that now.

They won't need such a sophisticated spell now. Tell Catherine. And then she was gone.

Seconds later, he was back at Catherine's. "A little change of plan, Catherine. Sorry about this."

"Okay, what do we need to do?"

When he explained what he had learnt, Catherine understood what had to be done.

"It won't take as long now. See you tomorrow, Thomas. Before you go, what are you going to do about the witch in Brazil?"

"I don't know yet. Let's deal with Levi Smallcast first, then see."

Chapter 39

It was late in the afternoon when Thomas arrived at the leisure centre. He headed for the exercise hall. Sarah was preparing for her next class as he walked in.

She greeted him with a huge smile "Thomas! I wasn't expecting you."

He gave her a hug and a kiss. "I'm not here for the class honey."

"I've got fifteen minutes or so before the class starts." They stood together over by the window. "Do you know Saffron came to the early morning class?" she said. "She's never done that before."

"I didn't know that, she's probably stressed if she's in cahoots with Susie's boss."

"Maybe. But she mentioned going away for a few days."

"Going away? Strange, I would never have imagined witches going on holiday. Where's she going? Witchtable? Or maybe Sandwitch?"

Sarah grinned. "Very good! I don't think she had a choice the way she was moaning."

"Why? What was she saying?"

A couple of pupils walked in preventing Sarah from replying, and behind them, more followed, ready for the class.

Sarah gave him a quick kiss. "Stay at mine tonight and I will tell you there?"

Thomas nodded.

"She said something about South America," she whispered.

"South America?" he exclaimed as he walked towards the exit. *This is not good. Not good at all!*

The following morning, they both left at the same time, Sarah headed off to the leisure centre while Thomas returned home. He needed to prepare for the confrontation with Levi Smallcast and Section 133. He had decided not to tell Sarah about her mother contacting him and offering him assistance. He wasn't sure how Sarah would react. As soon as he arrived home, Catherine called to tell him the spell was ready.

"Do you have any more information on how it's going to be delivered?" she asked.

"No. I'm waiting for Victoria to let me know. No, that's not right. I've got to contact her and arrange to meet up with a shieling. Don't ask me. I don't know who that is yet."

Catherine sounded really excited. "This is gripping news! Do let me know, won't you?"

"About the shieling?"

"Yes, yes. When are you coming over?"

"I'm outside."

She laughed. "I don't think I'll ever get used to your travel arrangements!"

Thomas smiled broadly as Catherine opened the door.

Rosemary called from inside. "It's all done, Thomas. Let me show you."

On the work bench was a small, sealed glass vial filled with clear liquid. Next to that was a simple wooden box with what looked like cotton wool packed inside.

Rosemary picked up the vial and placed it in the box. "Remember, Thomas. This is important. The lid has to be unscrewed, then the liquid is thrown over the target." She closed the wooden box and handed it to him.

"Be careful," said Catherine.

"What would happen if it went on anyone else? Say someone passing by."

"Nothing. This is based on just darksider evil and is harmless to anyone else."

"How can I ever thank you both?"

"It's the other way round. I should be thanking you for putting Victoria's soul at peace."

He thought about that. "Maybe she doesn't want to be at peace. I have a fancy she wants to go to war."

Catherine looked at him. "That would be our Victoria."

Back at home, he concentrated on Victoria. Seconds later, she was in his head.

You've wasted no time, Thomas. Now all I need to know is the time and place.

He suggested four o'clock in the afternoon that day. *Levi Smallcast visits his mother in Badshot Lea. It's Lower Weybourn Lane. The two minders always wait outside. I'll be at the top of the road holding a small wooden box. Inside is a glass vial. The lid has to be unscrewed and the contents have to be thrown over both of the minders.*

Then just hand the vial to the shieling. Let her do that. Don't worry. They won't pick up on it. The shieling is an innocent.

Right.

So then, what are you going to do after that? Victoria asked.

As soon as the shieling has done her part, I'll move down the lane. When the mother's front door opens, I'll make my move and send Mr Levi Smallcast back. Then I'll do the same with the minders. After that, I need to return to Guildford, where another two section members can be sent back before they get to hear about Smallcast. That should disrupt the others. Hopefully, I will be able to pick off a few more during the next few weeks. But what about the shieling?

I'll take care of it.

Thomas had four hours before he needed to liaise with Victoria's shieling. He decided to pop into the leisure centre and see if Sarah had more news about Saffron's trip to South America. He decided not to take his car. Driving was such a drag now since he had the ability to light travel. Moments later, he arrived at the edge of the car park. It was quiet and no one was around, so he made his way over to the entrance. He checked his watch. Realising Sarah would still be in her class, he decided to wait in the cafeteria.

Winnie and her daughter were there having coffee. Susie beckoned him over.

"Hi, Thomas! Are you waiting for Sarah?"

"Yes but I'm a little early."

"Do you want a coffee?" asked Winnie, pushing her chair back.

"Thanks, Winnie."

Winnie went over to the counter.

"What's happening at your office? Anything?" Thomas asked Susie.

She nodded. "I almost called you the other day. Smithe had a big argument over the phone. I'm sure it was with Saffron."

"I thought they were best buddies."

"They are, but he wanted her to do something that really pissed her off."

"What?"

"Travel somewhere. I heard her shout that he was sending her halfway around the world! Obviously, she didn't like the idea, but he seemed to persuade her somehow."

"Do you know where she's going?"

"I think she's going to Brazil."

"Brazil? Do you know when?"

"Today. Why?"

"No reason. I just don't like being in the same class with her."

A mug of coffee landed on the table in front of him. "Here you go, Thomas. One coffee!"

"Thanks, Winnie. That's so kind of you." He took a sip.

"There's Sarah," said Susie.

Sarah made a beeline for Thomas and gave him a kiss. *I don't need to ask Sarah anything now, Susie has told me all I need to know about Saffron.* There was no need for more questions. "Hi, honey!" he said. "I thought I'd pop in and say hello."

"Are you staying?"

"Unfortunately, not. I've much to do."

Thomas drank his coffee while the others chatted. When Sarah went to set up her next class, he left too. Out in the car park he looked to see if anyone was around before disappearing. As soon as he arrived home, he checked the flights to Brazil. There were three flights. *Which would she be on?* At her house, there was no sign of her. He checked what time he had left. There were only two more hours before meeting up with the shieling. But he would need a clear mind to do what he had to do later, and this was bothering him. *I needed to find out which flight she is on, so I have no option but to travel behind time and go to the airport.*

In the busy terminal, he scanned the information board and found the desk number for San Paulo. The travelling time was approximately twelve hours, so he felt he had more than enough time to get there and back before Saffron met up with witch number twenty. As he approached the boarding desk, he caught a glimpse of Saffron in the crowd. *What luck! And all down to Susie.* Saffron was about to check-in. He looked at the information board again. This flight was leaving in two hours. That gave him fourteen hours before he had to concern himself with meeting up with Saffron and the witch in Brazil. Now he could safely leave all this for the moment and concentrate on Levi Smallcast.

It was time to meet up with the shieling. Thomas looked at the wooden box and wondered why the lid was screwed down. *No point taking the box.* He took out the vial and visualised Lower Weybourn lane. He began a cautious walk in the direction of number twelve. About fifty metres from the house, he could see the two henchmen. He turned and started to walk back when he heard someone calling his name.

"Thomas?"

Just a wisp of a child, maybe seven or eight years of age, opened the gate of a house near him. She had angelic features, the whitest of hair, with a wonderful aura glowing around her.

"Hello," she said smiling.

He stared at her, startled. "Hello," he said cautiously.

"Have you brought it?"

Thomas frowned and glanced around. There was no one else here.

"My name is Alaska. Have you brought it?"

"Are you... Are you the shieling?"

"Well, of course."

Thomas hesitated for a moment, bemused. Then he dug into his pocket and held out the vial.

Alaska smiled at him. "Are you prepared for this?"

Thomas blinked and then nodded.

"Then wake up, Thomas! It's happening and you need to get over me being a child."

With the vial in her hand, Alaska skipped off down the road towards the two henchmen as if what she was about to do was just by the by.

Thomas crossed the road and walked in the same direction. He didn't take his eyes off the child. With every skip, she drew closer and closer to danger. His stomach began to churn. She was only a few metres away now. She stopped and took the top off the vial and then carried on. One of the henchmen glanced at her briefly but paid no attention. Now she was just a step or two away. She stopped again. Thomas's heart sank. He watched as she approached the henchmen. She was talking to them as she moved in closer. Then to Thomas's utter amazement, the henchmen bent down, allowing her to throw the liquid spell right over them both. They froze to the spot!

That was Thomas's cue. *I must not make any mistakes.* He moved fast, passing them on the other side of the road. Further along, he crossed over and walked back. Levi Smallcast would emerge from the house any second now. He looked at his watch. *It is time to rid this world of evil.*

The front door opened, and Levi Smallcast walked out of the house towards his protectors. Thomas frantically looked around for Alaska. She was nowhere to be seen. There was no time to check she was safe. He only had seconds to finish what he had started. He moved swiftly towards his target, Smallcast turned. For a moment, he didn't react. Then he glanced towards his men. Turning back to face Thomas and glaring at him, he released a tremendous surge of evil power. Right at that moment, Thomas caught a brief glimpse of Alaska, then refocused on Smallcast and only just avoided being sent back himself. He just managed to deflect the power away in time. The surge of energy travelled on, hitting an old oak tree and splitting it in two with a deafening crack. Now finally focused and completely wound up, Thomas drew on his energy source, and directed it at Levi Smallcast. His victim was no more. Then he turned his attention to the henchmen and sent them both back as well.

The front door of the house opened.

Alaska screamed. "Look out!"

Over his shoulder, he sensed more danger. He dived to the ground. Too late. He felt excruciating pain in his right lower leg. He had been hit! But surely only the mother should be in the house?

Alaska was screaming. "Attack, Thomas, attack."

Still lying on the ground, he summoned every ounce of power he had in his soul, pushed himself to his feet and released it. But now he was out in the open, in full view of anyone. This was going to be a life or death battle. His energy surge shook the ground and all that might have been in the house were gone. *Silence. Complete silence.* He couldn't sense any more danger, but did he need to do more?

"Come on, Thomas! You must go!" cried Alaska.

"Christ! Where's the house gone?"

"Come on!" Alaska cried. "You destroyed it. We need to cover our tracks."

Thomas stared at her. The tree is split in two. The house was demolished. "How do we fix it, unless you can pull lighting from the sky?"

"That's exactly what I had in mind," she said, taking his hand and pulling him clear.

Suddenly a bolt of lightning hit the spot where the house had been. Thomas almost fell to the ground in shock. "How on earth did you do that?"

"I'm a shieling! If you're going to deal with the other two darksiders, I think you must go now."

"Hang on! What was the other power coming from the house?"

"I don't know. You need to work that one out for yourself," she said, squeezing his hand and then Alaska was gone.

Still in pain, Thomas began to heal himself, but this time the process was extremely slow, and was slowing him down. Feeling the pain ease a little, he rushed to Guildford. As soon as he located numbers three and four, he sent them back. He watched them disintegrate in milliseconds into tiny particles, feeling quite relieved that they were gone. He knew Magli had been right. They were definitely part of section 133. Now two more darksiders were gone and Thomas was feeling relieved that everything, had gone to plan. *Not bad for a day's work. I wonder who will come out of the woodwork next.*

As soon as Thomas returned home, Jamie was in his head, but he sensed that Jamie was tense. He was in no mood to take any criticism from anyone. Not even Jamie. His leg was still painful, and he was miffed. He had come very close to being sent back himself.

Jamie was concentrating on the positives and avoided talking about Thomas's near-death experience. *That was some show you put on in Lower Weybourn Lane.*

I had a little help from a shieling called Alaska.

A shieling! You're developing, kiddo. So, what happened to your plan to go gung-ho into a bunch of darksiders then?

That's for another day! Anyway, I think I've caused a bit of a stir. Somebody opened the door of the house. I'm sure it wasn't his mother.

His mother? Jamie sounded astonished. *Were you expecting to see his mother?*

Yes, well, no. Not literally. But she's supposed to live there, and he was visiting her as usual. I am sure that wasn't his mother! It was something else. A super powerful something else. If it hadn't been for the shieling warning me, I wouldn't be here. As it is, I just had my leg dealt with, and now I'm struggling to heal it.

Mm, I now know exactly what you met. It was a Casanal.

A what?

It's a dark entity. They are so powerful and the vibration seeping from them can be disguised. There's no way of telling who they are until you confront them. I'm surprised the entity showed himself. That is most unusual. Tell me exactly what happened.

Thomas went through the details from the time he gave the vial to Alaska to the moment he hobbled out of the gate.

You're really blessed, Thomas! A Casanal is an incredibly powerful entity. You're right, and if you hadn't had your Shieling with you... well, I am sorry to say this but you wouldn't be here.

That didn't do much for Thomas's mood. Now he wanted to know what had happened to the Casanal.

I'm not sure, Jamie hesitated. *You say you dived to the ground avoiding his attack.*

That was more luck than judgement.

The only thing I can come up with is when this Smallcast went for you, he knew he couldn't draw on his benchmen's power. The Casanal was his only option. He drew on his power. How you deflected it was a miracle. Maybe it's the amulet you're wearing around your neck.

Thomas ran his fingers over it, remembering how he'd been given it in the Garden of Souls and feeling pleased it might have helped him. He thanked them.

But the best bit is... Jamie sounded almost in awe of what he was saying. *The best bit is when the front door opened and the Casanal went for you, it didn't appreciate that Levi Smallcast had drawn on some of its power. And it didn't have enough time to build up its reserve!*

How can I avoid this problem in the future?

Having patience might work!

Thomas sighed. He knew he had rushed into things. Patience wasn't a strength of his. But he decided that was about to change. He had to make the effort. *What would a Casanal be doing in a house in Badshot Lea?*

As far as I'm aware, Casanal are a direct link to you know where?

No! Do you mean? He…?

Ssh! Ssh, we don't say it ever!

Dumbfounded, Thomas put his hand over his mouth and felt awkward.

Jamie was now whispering. *They supply a conduit from one to the other, down there to up here. It's a source to replenish top darksiders with power when evil deeds sap their energy. The one consolation is they can't leave where they are based.*

Thomas nodded and kept silent.

You just did amazingly well, but when you were telling me about it, you sounded fed up.

I've been lucky. If I hadn't been, I'd be dead now. I didn't expect that to happen.

Jamie laughed. *Maybe, the whole point of you having the amulet is for situations like today. Remember your witchy friend explained how luck works? Take care Thomas and don't worry, you are in good hands. See you soon, kiddo.*

Thomas sat awhile and ran through the events of the day and what Jamie had told him. He realised he should have been far more diligent, especially concerning the energy protecting the house. *Why on earth would Levi's mother need all that power surrounding the house? It certainly wasn't for her son's benefit – he had his own henchmen. I need to be more vigilant.* He realised it had been a big mistake not to investigate what he was up against before taking the darksider on. Luckily, Sarah's mother had protected him through the shieling and he was thankful for her help. He could hear her voice in his head.

I know this isn't a good time to speak to you, Thomas, but…

Victoria! No, no! It's fine. I was just thinking about you. I'm just really annoyed with myself.

Then think on this. A bright young scientist, full of ideas, who knew how to protect herself, allowed her life to be taken in her workplace, doing what she knew, what she had trained for. We all make mistakes, Thomas. You got away with yours. I didn't.

Thomas lowered his head, what Victoria just told him had put things into clear perspective and reinforced his decision to work with Dominic and the team.

Thank you, Victoria.

Can I ask what your next move is?

I have to go to Brazil and listen in on a conversation between two dark witches. It's to do with what's going on in Sudbury.

That sounds intriguing. What's going on in Sudbury?

I don't know, yet!

Something sinister no doubt! Stay sharp, Thomas. Trust nothing. Not even your instincts. I know Dominic told you otherwise, but you're not ready yet. Just look at the facts. And be careful. Sarah mustn't lose you.

She won't.

Bye, Thomas, dear.

Bye, Victoria.

Acknowledgements

My thanks to the following who have helped me with my debut novel.

Felicity Fair Thompson for years of help.

Natasha Murray for all her good suggestions.

Helen Weston who proofread this book.

Aimee Hinton who put in a lot of effort.

And last but not least: Maria Ward for the illustration on the book cover.

About the Author

John Weston is a business man who has spent his entire life building companies.

He was inspired, at a later stage in his life whilst going through his third divorce, to start writing fiction on a ferry to the Isle of Wight listening to a group of excitable school children sitting close by.

John is a family man, he is father to five children and six grandchildren.